the
PHARAOH'S
BUILDERS

Book One of the Pharaoh's Land Series

the PHARAOH'S BUILDERS

Book One of the Pharaoh's Land Series

HEATHER PERRYWINKLE SMITH

Happy Publishing

THE PHARAOH'S BUILDERS

Cover and Interior Design by Roseanna White Designs

Published by Happy Publishing, www.HappyPublishing.net

First Edition

ISBN: 978-0-9896332-7-7

With gratitude for Gary M. Douglas and Dr. Dain Heer
Access Consciousness® founder and co-creator, respectively

For their ceaseless invitation and inspiration
to embody the oneness and infinite being I truly be.

Prologue

Spinning in the infinite space of the cosmos and embraced by the insistent pull of its sun, Earth is a radiant gem of green and blue. Embodying the infinite colors of creatures, flora and fauna; the possibilities of oneness abound in a cacophony of exuberant living. The earth sings in joyous abandon with the creation of itself. The natural rhythms and cycles of living and dying all contributing to something greater, sustaining itself by its ever expanding more. The very molecules dance and play with a dynamic presence of being and the quiet "yes" of desire that creates a future where everything thrives.

The living of all things is a raucous celebration that spreads across the surface of the entire planet, and pulses through it; all except with those who walk upon two legs.

The majority of the two-legged beings here make themselves blind and deaf to the beauty and rhythms that hum and buzz through all things. They fight and rage, they despair and complain. They feel alone in the world and at the same time do everything to make themselves separate from the natural oneness. They cleave tightly to proving they are right in their choices for control, for smallness and the "taking" energies they function from. The world they create is one where a mother would kill her own daughter to take her inheritance of royal succession. It is a world where a father would beat his son to make him capable of dominance by sheer brute force. It is a place where people's idea of success is how much they can claim dominion over more people and land than anyone else. It is a world where magic is used to keep people under control by its awe. Where anyone might be bought and sold, slave to the will of a master they did not choose. The struggles and often petty, wonton ugliness of everyday life is common for many. They consider it normal life.

And yet there are a few who sense the celebration of the endless symphony of living and profuse abundance that is all around them. It calls to them and infuses their life with a beauty not recognized by most. They would have a world that lives in communion with the sense for following the feather touch of possibilities for a greater future calling to come into existence. Playing with the natural desires of joyful and prolific living embodied in all creatures and plants, along with the very body of the earth itself, they request of the molecules and it becomes so. They dream of a future where people reach for the oneness and know they are embraced in the reaching. These few would strive for a generative future of kindness, caring and dynamic creativity that contributes to the oneness and joy of living for all. These rarefied people are known as Builders.

Ten thousand years ago in Egypt, before there were gods, there was Pharaoh.

The rule of the Pharaoh is absolute. There is no justice system, no religion, no large military force, and no power to question or challenge the actions of the Pharaoh. The current Pharaoh-Ra is lord of the realm, administering his will upon all the people of Pharaoh's Land. He only has those who carry out his command, those known as "Keepers of the House of Pharaoh."

The Keepers do his bidding. Most lack in imagination and are happy to live off the abundance of their Pharaoh, taking what they are given or allowed. Rarely seeking to improve upon the realm of life they administer to, they take, they consume, they maintain the status quo. They do not question the family lineage that has ruled Pharaoh's Land for a thousand generations.

Pharaoh's Land is vast, stretching over a month's journey by camel or horse in any direction from the palace city of El-Gizah. Following from there is a natural barrier of desert in all directions. There are always some traders who know the way through the desert. From time to time there are a few naive or brazen enough to attempt conquering Pharaoh's Land. Those that try are usually found as bones in the sand, or captured and turned into slaves themselves. There are no known peoples of great number or ability to overcome the might of the Pharaoh.

Rich in natural resource of every kind, the Pharaoh enjoys a splendor and power not seen before. Pharaoh-Ra has taken the known world to a new level of prosperity and possibility.

9

Unlike Pharaohs before him, he diligently works to bring into his life those who embrace the oneness and strives to create a different world for those lives he commands.

He has commissioned a great monument for the future. A future of promise and possibility, a future built on the oneness; an enormous pyramid.

It is those few who would create a greater future; a future that embodies the oneness who rule all of Pharaoh's Land. Though they are surrounded by those who would kill them to take their place and the seat of Pharaoh, for now it is a time for building.

Chapter 1

It is day's end and all have left the deep and gouging quarry, save for one man.

Standing on the very edge of the precipice, the Pharaoh's Land spreads as far as his eyes can see. The long shadows of day's end as the sun sinks into the horizon cools the blaze of discontent filling Bilal's being. His heart aches with the smallness of his life. As he reaches out into the glory of colors washing over the land stretched out before him, he takes in a deep breath. A thread of lightness seeps into his world with the intake of air.

Gazing upon the expanse before him ushers a great relaxation deep in his body. The hot wind blows up the face of the rocks and flows across his body invigorating the sense of relaxation. The heat of the wind seeps into him softening the hardness, the bracing against the harshness that eats at him.

Unclenching his fists, he sighs again, letting go, expanding. As he drops his barriers to the ugliness of his life, he allows in the beauty before him. The wind becomes a caress of his body. Like gentle and nurturing feathers gliding across his bare chest...his neck...his cheeks; until the caress of the wind becomes a caress of his very being, nurturing, healing.

The sense of expansion continues within him now, within as well as outward. It is as though the wind is blowing right through him, cleansing the space between the molecules. He takes another deep breath, reaching farther into the space of air and sky and heat and silence of the land before him. Another breath and he allows his senses to sink deep into the rock under his feet, down and down into the richness of mineral.

It is only in these rare moments of respite, when the other laborers and enforcers have left, that he has the slightest sense of being. That choice itself becomes real. One step forward and he can plunge to his death. One more breath and he knows another possibility hints at existing. It comes with the wind, the heat, the spaciousness that overcomes his senses when he is alone, standing on the edge - where his choice makes a difference...to him. It is these moments he knows he has the will to continue living. He will find something greater. He will be something greater.

Bilal steps back from the edge with a new sense of possibility, and heads into the waning light of day and into the darkness of his everyday life.

Stepping out from behind the mountainous pile of rubble hiding her from his view, she wonders; *"could he be the oneness so rare in the untrained?"* He is different, not just his imposing stature. Not just his light skin and blonde hair, or that he is a foreigner in bloodline. It is his presence, his being. He stands out even if he did not look different.

She had seen him once before standing on the ledge, alone. She could sense the struggle, the internal conflict. It was one choice, would he jump or would he stay living on? She knew he would not jump, he did not. It was the tug and tingle of the oneness that told her this. She would watch him transform, embracing and inviting the oneness, invoking it, becoming it. He had no idea how strong it was in him.

She watched him walk back to the pillars marking The Pathway. She watched the familiar blurring and ripple of air as he passed through the space between the stone pillars; the Pharaoh's gift to the people. Two pillars set like a doorway that allow the people to travel in the blink of an eye anywhere marked with pillars in the Pharaoh's land. Think of the marker at the location you wish to go to and you are transported in a blink to that location. If the space between the pillars is clear it is open for travel. If there is a blur and ripple in the air of the space between the pillars, then someone is about to come through at your location. It is the custom to stand to the right so people don't run into each other coming into or out of The Pathway.

With the quarry cleared of people, Angyet could start her task. She walks to the towering stone let loose off the cliff earlier today. A base stone. It is massive, five-men high and twenty long. Work was progressing with the construction of the pyramid. It was built up to the third level of the massive base, it would rise a little more quickly when this level was complete. Never before had such a monument been attempted.

Angyet's hand gently runs across the surface of the stone, sensing the chisel marks the laborers left behind. The brute muscle so many considered the only possibility left a vibration of intensity like a thin cloud on the stones surface. No matter, it would contribute to her work like fuel for a fire. All energies contribute when functioning from the infinite awareness that is truly available. *"Simple fools,"* she thought to herself. *"If only they could know the truth in front of them."*

Angyet is a Builder. *The Builder* to be exact. Be it physical actualization or something untouchable - she is one of the few with the capacity and awareness to bring into existence that which is requested. She creates, simply by request and the capacity for being the oneness. It is she who makes the choice to be communion with both the molecules and the space between the molecules. Appearing as magic to those without the eyes to see; it is both natural to her and a capacity she developed over years of practice.

To be a Builder brings her the greatest joy. Though she is surrounded by those who would use her powers against the people of Pharaoh's Land to control and have dominion over all if they could. For at this time it is only she who has powers so great she can alter reality itself. She knows this and trusts other people's knowledge of the extent of this only to a small few; the Pharaoh, his daughter, and Naruub.

As *the* Builder of Pharaoh's Land, she is considered one of the Pharaoh's greatest assets. Rare and prized, Angyet enjoys a freedom few possess. To have the favor of the Pharaoh is an enviable position for most. She carries it well. No one would suspect the truth of the razor's edge she walks to keep the House of Pharaoh intact and with a future they all could live with.

Standing alone in the failing light of the quarry, she continues to run her hands across the surface of the stone before her. As she moves that familiar thrum begins to turn on, in her body and being. The sensation intensifies. It is the vibration of the very molecules themselves singing. Now she will begin.

She deepens her breath, the relaxation increasing the intensity of the energies running through her body. She reaches out with her body and being, calling upon the oneness to fill her, flow through her and pour out from her. Like a soft breeze whispering possibility, inviting, invoking movement... the molecules begin to pulse and hum as they are caressed by the oneness. Her hands tickle as the energy increases. It is like a swarm of bees sensed, but not seen or heard. A humming, buzzing vibration emanates out of her hands into the stone, into the space between the molecules of the stone itself. The chisel marks on the stone, sharp and gouging begin to quiver and the edges melt. The ripple of change radiates out in waves, like rough water suddenly calming to utter smoothness, the reverse of dropping a pebble in water. What was only moments ago a rough sea is now a lake of glass that is the surface of the massive stone. The rough hewn rock is now a rectangle piece of precision; perfectly straight, perfectly square on every edge, to the exact proportions required.

It is hard to imagine a woman so fine of feature and

appearing so tiny beside this mountain of stone could so easily and quickly alter the very stone itself – in only moments, ten tons of stone had been transformed into precision more exact than the eye can see. Even the underside was a smooth perfection.

With a twinkle of satisfaction, Angyet steps back, taking in the transformation before her. Not with her eyes as the sun has set and the moon has not yet risen, rather she sees with her senses the living body of stone. She never tires of the thrill and potency of being the oneness; the simplicity of request that is the true nature of reality. The willingness of something as solid and real as stone to be as changeable as the wind... it is a reality few are willing to have. With such capacity she appears as a God. None would guess it is as simple a capacity as breathing itself.

The Pharaoh likes her to work at night, adding to the great mystery of the powers of the Pharaoh. When the laborers arrive in the morning to behold ten tons of stone changed from the rough hewn rock they left at the end of the day to an object of perfect smoothness and angle, they tremble in awe. It keeps them in place. And even if they see it as it occurs, they still don't believe it is possible. The pain in their muscles and aching body that cut the very stone from the cliff screams in retaliation to the very idea of it. They rub their eyes in disbelief and convince themselves they did not witness what they just witnessed. They prefer their lack of comprehension to the awareness of the impossible becoming possible.

The task at hand complete, Angyet walks away with a new purpose. She is always invigorated from inviting the oneness.

When the vitality of the oneness is pulsing through her, she is alive as few dare to be. One of her greatest pleasures is to explore all the other possibilities for expression of the oneness available to those who know. There is one person she can always play with: Naruub.

The Pathway ripples and Angyet steps from between the pillars marking The Pathway and heads toward Naruub's dwelling.

She enters unannounced, yet he is waiting. The room is swimming in sensorial pleasures. Every surface is covered with something soft, sensual and beautiful. Naruub stands amongst the luxury, another object of beauty impossible to take her eyes from.

As Angyet's toes sink into the plush floor tapestry the soft spongy sensation sends a wave of energy through her body. Never before has Angyet met someone capable of receiving the intensity of the oneness, let alone expanding and increasing it, until Naruub.

With a deep sigh of the satisfaction to come she whispers with a smile; "let the games begin." A soft deep laugh is her only reply.

As a night of pleasure begins, elsewhere only more pain and suffering will be inflicted.

Chapter 2

As Bilal steps from between the pillars of The Pathway towards home, renewed with a sense of well being and possibility, he wonders at that odd other sensation: the tug. He has noticed it only a few times before. Strangely enough, he felt it when he stood at the precipice before, and one other time at the markets of House of Pharaoh. That sense of being watched, but not the usual sensation of danger or need to hide or shrink away. Rather this sensation has a warmth, an embrace like the blessed wind; yet somehow with direction or intent pulling at him. *"Whatever could it be?"* he muses.

The Laborer Realm is where the over fifty thousand slaves of the quarries and manual laborers are kept, along with another one-hundred and fifty-thousand slaves who service the households of the Keepers, when they do not live with their Keeper. It is a city of shambles and squalor unto itself;

where flesh is bought and sold, and death hangs in the air as a putrid perfume of hopelessness. This is what Bilal has known as home.

This place of sweat and tears is divided into sections by slave master. Abar Iberak lords over the largest area, owning almost one-third of the work force. This amounts to roughly forty-five thousand people at any one time, give or take the daily death and insurgence of fresh bodies acquired in one way or another. At least twenty other slave masters squabble and fight for the purchase of their slave's muscle by the Pharaoh. The pyramid Pharaoh-Ra is constructing is the largest undertaking of any Pharaoh before him and the riches to be made are plentiful.

Abar Iberak is a ruthless merchant of flesh. Shrewd in his dealings, he counts bodies in coinage and skill or physical beauty as leverage for greater gain. The only thing that really gives him pleasure is gaining the upper hand in all he does. He covets anything that gives him increase in money, control over others and status.

His most prized possessions are Drekkar, Emilia and their son Bilal. These three rare beauties have added substantially to all areas of importance to Master Iberak. From the farthest reaches of conquest and capture of slaves, none look like the three of them. No one had ever seen hair the color of wheat and blue eyes like the sky, before them. No other slaves are as handsome or exotic. No other slaves have the physical prowess and stature. No other slaves work as hard to contribute to his gain.

Though his property, over the years, Drekkar had become his confidant and trusted comrade in the building of his little empire of flesh and toil. Best yet, Drekkar drives his own son harder and more relentlessly than he himself would have. A quality Abar could not have dreamed up himself, yet has relished as he watched it unfold over the course of Bilal's life.

Through the shamble of what one might call streets of the Laborer Realm, and on the far side, is Bilal's family home. Though born a slave, he enjoys a bit of amenity. His parents were from the north, born free and of a vastly different land and people he knew almost nothing of. His parents would not speak of it but quite rarely, and did not share but scanty detail.

This was painfully obvious in the daily reminder of how he did not fit in.

Both of his parents were tall and more massive in stature than anyone around, and his height was greater still. His father was a hulk of a man, large shoulders, hands that made most adults look like a child, literally as strong as a camel. He was a giant among men here and yet Bilal made him look not quite so large. At the age of eighteen now, he was an impressive young man. Their master made sure everyone knew it. Because they could physically outdo anyone they gained in privilege and respect amongst the other slaves and Freeman laborers alike. And there were other reasons...

Over the years, Master Abar Iberak had used them to bolster both his wealth and reputation as someone who will get his way. Wielding his family as weapon, tactic or enticement, he had been often harsh and at the same time generous. At least what he considered generous, as a slaver. They were not worked to death. They had food, shelter of their own, respect or fear amongst others. The respect and fear was of the most value to Master Iberak.

Their home, though not more than a shack with a dirt floor, was theirs. They did not have to share it with the other slaves Master Iberak owned. Slightly away from the dinge of the Laborer Realm, they enjoyed a little more quiet, a little less dust and rancor of bodies. But it was his mother who truly made it home.

Emilia was standing in the door watching her son approach, emerging from the dark into the light of their humble home. *"When had he turned into a man?"* she marveled. Her shoulders straightened a little with pride. Even with such hardness, his entire life a slave, he has a grace about him, she thought. His true heritage has not been squelched, though he knows nothing of it. He would be considered very handsome in her home land. Here he was outright exotic, a true standout.

She opens her arms to him, that familiar warm embrace that is the only true peace and gentleness Bilal had ever known. "Mother," he says softly. "Come, there is dinner," she says. "Tell me of your day. How does the pyramid progress?"

They enter speaking softly. "Another foundation stone is freed off the cliff today. I wielded the final blow to let it loose." Bilal says with a sense of some pride.

"Aw, that is wonderful, son. You know Iberak will be bragging tonight!" Emilia ushers her son in and to the table with food she has prepared for him. They continue to speak of the day in hushed tones and the closeness of mother and son.

Some time passes and the early night is beginning to hush, when Bilal's father stumbles into the door way. He has obviously been drinking. In far too loud a voice for the quiet of the day ended, Drekkar barks, "Ah my son. Another fine accomplishment today." He waves his hand in a grandiose gesture and look of disdain. "Is that all you have got? Making your father look bad?"

"Not tonight father," Bilal sighs. He knows what is coming. His father steps to the table where they sit. Slamming down the mug he had in hand, and at the same time he is swinging to punch Bilal in the side of the face. Bilal leans back from the fist so it glances him only lightly as he stands knocking over the bench he sat upon. With one swift and mighty crushing blow he catches his father under the chin; lights out. His father crashes to the floor like a limp rag. Quiet overtakes the room again.

"Sorry mother." Bilal walks out into the night.

Away from the buildings and the insanity of his father Bilal walks out into the darkness to regain his composure. He heads out into the desert sands and quiet.

Bilal's mind races. "*Why can't his father leave be? Never a moment's peace. Never true appreciation. Never an acknowledgement. Why can his father never be truly happy with him, for him?*" He does not understand. The better he does, the more his father taunts, the more the violence. It has been a life of violence. His father so often curses his mighty size, his strength. Always pushing to the limits of endurance; his father is relentless. When he does not batter his body, he beats at his mind, his being. Always his father is demanding more of him. To what end? They are slaves. No future, no possibility. He shakes his head. He has no tears left in him, just the determination he will not be destroyed by what he cannot comprehend and has struggled so hard to survive.

When he was younger he thought he could please his father. At twelve years of age Bilal was larger than most men of Pharaoh's Land. Both his father and Master Iberak looked at him like a cash camel, a money-maker in fists and muscle. They would put him in the rink to fight for wager. When he lost, his father beat him more, until the day came that he never lost a fight.

It did not take long. He had skill, he was observant and very agile, regardless of his size. He made it into a game of how quickly he could knock the other man out. Word spread quickly, soon he was fighting at ridiculously unfair odds and yet he always found a way and won. He started to like it for awhile; the crowd, the cheering and frenzy. A moment of recognition in a thankless life...until it was taken to the next level; death matches.

He had reached fifteen and was undefeated for the last year when they placed him in his first death match. It was nearly more than he could bear. Physically he was unmatched no matter whom he faced. It was the wanton ugliness of it all, the sheer brutality; it took a toll on his very being. He liked nothing about it. That his own hands and skill were used by his father and slave master to bloody ends ate at him. That he had no choice about it ate at him even more.

To build was one thing. Swinging sledge hammer to stone, the crafting of monuments; even the simplicity of a well-split stone was glorious to him. That he was proud of, he did not care the lowly status and appearance of menial labor. Or, even that he was a slave with no choice in the matter. He got to see what his hands created. He would gladly work to death in the sweltering heat of the rock pits and quarries. Fighting, on the other hand, was the antithesis of him.

He could not help but be good at it. His father and Master Iberak made sure of it. Father would find a few words of encouragement or beat it into him. Iberak would reward with women and drink, hot baths and new clothing. Or, finer cloth and trinkets for his mother.

He hated them for it. He hated himself almost as much.

As the cooling of the night enveloped him he began to relax again, his mind quieting. There it was, the blessed thrum of the earth seeping into him. He stopped where he was, the buildings all out of sight, and lay upon the ground. Reaching out across the desert dunes with his senses and feeling the sand in his hands he makes a concerted effort to let it all go. Surrendering to the silence of the night, the softness of the sand against his body, he could breathe again. Another deep breath and the ugliness he knew as his father drained out again, washing away into the oneness. The endless night sky brilliant with a million stars increased the thrum; it's nurturing embrace returning him to himself.

Chapter 3

It is a new day.

Bilal's muscles ripple with strain as the sledge hammer comes down, breaking another impossibly large slab of stone from the wall of the pit. He is given a wide birth as he accomplishes more than most men his age or size. He is young to wield such a large hammer with so much skill. Larger than all his age, or much older than he for that matter; he has used it to his advantage considering what he was born into. It is rare to ascend when born a slave.

He had started before sunrise. He liked getting to the quarry before the cadre of slaves, enforcers, masters and Freemen; before the sweat and pain of impossible tasks. They are the Laborers. Cutting massive solid granite pieces that are the foundation of the pyramid, death is a daily occurrence. Be it overworked, under fed, too weak from sickness or broken spirit, accident or defiance; several would die today. And the building would carry on. The command of the Pharaoh and thousands of bodies straining to bring it into existence would make it so.

Bilal was taking a moment in the shade with a piece of bread and cheese as he had already been at work for a few hours. He heard footsteps next to him but did not look up. There were only a few men who walk directly to him and he would know those footsteps anywhere.

His father's hand comes down hard striking him across the face. He is large; it doesn't hurt him physically anymore. Even in a rage, his father is no longer strong enough to inflict true pain. It is the intent that crushes him. "*Why? He wasn't doing anything, just sitting here eating. Ah well, there was last night. Except his father had started it, whatever 'it' was. There was never a clear reason. What did he do wrong?*" He searches his memory for the offense given that would invoke such rage. He could find none, which just adds to the degradation of being that he struggles to cope with. His face hides the internal turmoil, not that his father would notice anyway. No words exchanged, he stands up and walks out into the day, back to work at the great pit.

Bilal takes his frustration and confusion out on the stone at his feet. He is the strongest laborer and has the most accurate swing of any man. His prowess is respected by all the other workers. Even the guards, ready to whip the belligerent or laggards, do not touch him. No one can deny his ability, all but his father.

Drekkar is not of Pharaoh's Land. He was young when

his journey began, too young at barely thirteen. He was not supposed to go. He had followed the men for a week before he was discovered. The leader was impressed with his gumption, more than he was irritated with his lack of obedience. Since he was the third son of the House of Von Kesslar the man allowed him to stay as long as he carried his own weight and made himself useful. The man leading this expedition sent word back to the Von Kesslar family so they would know where their son had gone. Since they never heard word back, and no one came looking for the boy, he was allowed to continue on.

This was a journey with no surety of return. They were headed south, farther than any ballads sang about, south of the snow's ability to reach. Or at least that was the only legend they had heard of, that such a place existed. They would find out. If there were people or only vacant lands, they would know what lay beyond their world to the far south.

Bilal knew nothing of his father's lands to the far distant north, he had been born along the way. He came into this world soon after his parents had been captured and put into slavery. Pharaoh's Land was his home and all he knew, although his height, his face, is hair, and his eyes all add up to the undeniable reminder that he is different. Somehow that difference pained his father who seemed bent on beating it out of him. As though beating him could erase the invisible wrongness that marked him in his father's eyes.

Bilal yearned to know of a different kind of life, everything about the world he lived in felt wrong. Like a fly pestering him in the back of his mind, always there was a nagging sense that surely something greater must be possible. "*This can't be all there is to life,"* he would think to himself. He silently searched for a spark, a lightness of being, and indication of the impossible becoming possible. He had seen it a few times in his life, fleeting moments that spark of more; which only invigorated his sense of hope.

"Maybe today, maybe today..."

Chapter 4

It is now late in the day and the Laborers rush about in a flurry of activity. The news had spread like a wave through the crowd. "The Pharaoh is here, The Pharaoh is here." As quickly as the uproar came, a hush descended and all heads turned as the procession poured through the pillars of The Pathway.

A party of at least twenty accompanied the Pharaoh to the quarry this day. The Pharaoh liked to see the progress of construction himself. Speaking with the foremen and reminding the laborers what they work so hard for...the great honor of it all, be they slave or Freeman. The laborers were mostly slaves; captured in skirmishes on the edges of Pharaoh's Land or bought by those who trade in flesh and then hire out the muscle.

A slave never knew how long they may or may not live, so most dared stop what they were doing to sneak a look at the

Pharaoh. Others kept moving, though more quietly now. Close to fifty thousand hushed workers is a marvel to behold in itself. It spoke to the highlight of this moment in their miserable lives; a spark of beauty and purpose that would lift them up.

Amongst the crowd of the procession a little girl runs between the men and few women with them. She is pointing here and there, checking out every person, every pile and project of construction. Pharaoh had brought his daughter today. Ra-Milania is a precocious five-year-old whose hand-servant could not keep up with her. Bolting sporadically in every direction like an angry bee, she is now exploring a mountainous rock pile, but no one is paying attention. Even the hand-servant is caught up in the gaping cuts into the cliffs and massive structure of pyramid in the far distant background, now almost one quarter built.

Bilal stood with his father a little away from the rest of the crowd. At a small rickety wooden table and work cart, they had been speaking with their master Iberak and the foreman, discussing fissure lines and the progress of the next block of foundation. The two other men had just left Bilal and his father Drekkar to move closer to where the Pharaoh walked, trying to catch his attention in hopes of a few direct words.

Though everyone is enthralled with watching the Pharaoh, Bilal is watching the girl. He faintly smiles at her glee and mayhem. Her abandon is a joy to behold.

It had been three years since Bilal had seen the Pharaoh's daughter Ra-Milania. Last time he had laid eyes upon her she was in the arms of a man-servant being carried through the markets of the House of Pharaoh. It was a moment he has never forgotten, fleeting as it was.

It was a rare day that Master Iberak had brought him along to the meandering hustle and bustle of the great markets of the House of Pharaoh. This market was filled with the industry that decorated, furnished and made extravagant the Keepers of The House of Pharaoh and the royal family itself. It was only at this market one might happen upon the royal family. Today was such a day.

Bilal stood a few feet back from Master Iberak, staying out of the way, while also remaining close enough at hand that he would not keep his master waiting, even for a moment. An odd sensation began to tug at his chest, not unpleasant, yet unlike anything he had known. It was then the forward guards came clearing the walkway filled with people "Make way for the House of Pharaoh!" Everyone stood aside in silence and waited for who might approach, eager to be able to say they had seen someone from the royal family that day.

It was the spouse of Pharaoh, Ra-Maharet with her little daughter carried in the arms of a man-servant close behind. Other women were with her, perusing the fabrics and tapestry in this section of the market. Bilal stood still and silent, having never been this close to the royal family. He was excited but dare not show it. As they approached, Ra-Maharet stopped directly across the walkway from him. With that, the man-servant carting little Ra-Milania turned, and the wide-eyed two-year-old looked up directly into the eyes of Bilal. Breaking into the biggest grin, she reached out her arms to him. Bilal's heart swelled and a grin began to spread across his lips. That tugging sensation was exploding into a spacious joy filling his chest. Wow, no one had ever looked at him like that before! He perceived an embrace of his entire being in the longest most wonderful seconds of his then fifteen years of life.

Just as quickly one of the women, thinking the out reached arms were meant for her, took the toddler from the man's arms, and with that the party moved on.

This moment of interaction was a spark of light in the darkness of his life. It would sustain him in the intensely darker days that were about to come.

Now here, three years later was that beautiful spark again, wandering toward him.

She had been meandering closer, exploring the nooks and crannies of the rocks beside Bilal. The sound of crumbling so familiar to Bilal grabbed his attention. No one else is reacting, no one hears the deep undertone. This has all the sounds of a big one...Without hesitation he moves. In what seems a singular motion he grabs the girl by the arms spinning around and shoving her into his father's hands, then embracing them both in a protective hug. In the same instant somehow they are all several feet from where they were, as a huge pile of boulders come crashing down. A terrible splintering sound fills the air as the table and hauling cart that had been near where they were previously standing was in pieces under the rubble. A cloud of dust billows out covering the three of them and settling. All three of them would have been crushed. Impossibly they stand, untouched inches from death.

"Did I really just do that?" thinks Bilal. Like confirmation, a small short giggle escapes the little girl; "Hehehe."

The shouting that came with the mini land slide had called

everyone's attention. The Pharaoh was already moving towards them, waving dust from his face and shouting his daughter's name "Ra-Milania!"

Drekkar's face had such a look of surprise it was a wonder he had not fallen down. He was holding the child to him, protecting. His eyes widened as it registered that the Pharaoh was coming straight to him. He looks at the girl, looks at the Pharaoh and drops to his knee. Head bowed he holds the child out at arm's length.

Unmoving and hardly able to breathe he closes his eyes dreading what may come next. He feels the child being taken from his hands. "Little Mila! Oh, child! Are you harmed?" Covered in dust only on one half of her from being hugged to the strange large man, she blinks wide-eyed and smiling ear-to-ear but dare not speak. Pharaoh embraces her seeing she is unharmed, and he peers at the man knelt before him.

Pharaoh looks down at Drekkar with a slight smile; "Stand."

Drekkar hesitates, keeping his sweat drenched dusty head bowed.

"Stand man. What is your name? Speak."

Drekkar stands, trembling and stammering he says; "I am Drekkar, Drekkar Von Kesslar Lord Pharaoh."

"*Why did he just say his family name?*" He had not spoken it since he left the place of his homeland long ago and far away.

"Are you a slave or Freeman Drekkar Von Kesslar?"

"I am a slave of Master Iberak Lord Pharaoh."

33

"Ah yes, of course, Iberak. You are not of this land, how did you come to be here?" asks Pharaoh.

"I and my wife were captured many years ago and brought here. This is my son, Bilal." He reaches out grabbing at Bilal's arm, being sure to keep his eyes averted from looking at the Pharaoh, though it is not easy as he is almost a head taller. Bilal was also on one knee looking like a stone statue for the dust that covered him. He stands now with his father, head bowed.

"For your act of bravery that saved my daughter; from this day forward you and your family are free. You will be given insignia letting all know the House of Pharaoh is your keeper. Thank you for saving my daughter's life. It will not be forgotten in the House of Pharaoh." With that the Pharaoh turns and walks away, speaking softly to his daughter who is still clinging to his neck.

As Pharaoh-Ra heads towards the pillars of The Pathway he raises his hand to summon Master Iberak to him. Pharaoh-Ra pretended not to know who the two wheat haired sky blue eyed men were; but everyone knew of them, even the Pharaoh. It was going to take great compensation to appease Master Iberak for what the Pharaoh had just taken from him. The Pharaoh was prepared for this moment.

Master Iberak walked to the Pharaoh red faced and fists clenched, ready to explode. He dare not speak for fear of what he might say that he could not take back. It took everything he had not to lose it completely. Pharaoh walked quickly becoming surrounded by his guards and keepers and speaking intently with Master Iberak. They step between the pillars without hesitation.

The crowd parts as whispers spread like waves through the onlookers.

Drekkar stands, mouth open and blinking dumbly. *"What just happened? Did the Pharaoh say 'free?' Could it truly be?"*

"Father! Father, did you hear? We are free!!! Father!" Exclaims Bilal, he hugs his father at which his father again drops to his knees. Embracing his son, silent tears run down his face...freedom. Nineteen years a slave and in the blink of an eye, he is free, sweet freedom once again. And not just him, but his entire family!

Bilal had never seen his father cry before. With a gentleness he did not know his father possessed Drekkar Von Kesslar reached up and wiped the tears from Bilal's cheek; that he had not noticed until that moment. When they both could stand again, only slightly recovered from the shock of this life altering moment Drekkar speaks. "Son, let us go home to your mother."

They pass from between the pillars of The Pathway towards home elated. Both are smiling, which has never occurred before; the two of them together smiling, happy. Just a few strides and Drekkar touches Bilal's arm. "Wait son. There is something I must say before we take another step." He takes a deep breath and looks his son in the eyes. "Son. I have hardened my heart to you all these years. You must now know it was not without cause. Every blow has been to harden you, that no amount of pain would stop you. I have been tireless in training you for one day to come. The day to win our freedom by brute force if need be, then to reclaim what is rightfully ours, well yours. I have been preparing you son. You are a Von Kesslar!"

"That is supposed to mean something to me?" Bilal exclaims bewildered and incredulous.

"Von Kesslar is my family name, your family name. It is a name of a land so far away, no one here has ever heard of it. In that land, you are of royalty son. Von Kesslar is one of the ruling families of the north, the greatest of families throughout all our history of the north!" exclaims Drekkar.

Bilal is dumbfounded, this is beyond what he can take in. "What?" he stammers.

Looking him in the eyes again with both hands on Bilal's shoulders Drekkar says "Son, I will never strike you again. I am proud of you son. You have exceeded my greatest hopes of the man you would become. You may never thank me or be grateful, but know I have done it all for your future, for the inheritance of your rightful legacy." Now it is Bilal's turn to cry again, he embraces his father, the weight of years of incomprehensible torture and pain cracking open and beginning to drain from his being.

Amongst tears of joy and release Drekkar whispers; "Come, there is so much to tell and your mother is much better at this than me."

Bilal and this mystery of a man he has known as "father" continue with quick strides home.

The tug at Emilia's chest was stronger today, something had happened. She stood at the door in anticipation. She sees her men approaching, something is different; not only are they both smiling, they each have an arm over the other's shoulder. This is something she has never seen before. She rushes forth and they run to her, scooping her up and exclaiming in unison "We are free! We are free! Em, we have been given our freedom today!"

Tears burst forth all over again as Bilal and Drekkar stumble over each other recounting the events that had just transpired. The three of them move into their shack of a home; tear streaked, laughing, hugging and happier than any of them dare dream could be.

No more withholding, Bilal's parents would tell all they had held dear and never spoken of with their one and only son.

Chapter 5

The three of them are huddled around a bowl of fire, like conspirators they are whispering. "Now Ra! We must bring him now. Please, please, pretty please!" little Ra-Milania blinks at her father, pleading with her cuteness. The Pharaoh cracks a smile, "He is not ready little one." He looks to Angyet, "What do you say?"

"Ready or not, I say we start. We thought we'd have more time but they are moving more quickly than anticipated. They are getting bold," replies Angyet. "Yes!" blurts Ra-Milania. She hops down from the seat and says, "Bedtime." Without further good nights she rushes into the darkness and off to bed.

The Pharaoh and Angyet chuckle both at once. Such a joy, how could either of them resist her plea? Not that it took convincing, ready or not, they both knew it was time.

Angyet speaks quietly, "I'll go once they have been moved and settle in a little."

"Yes, let us begin in earnest," says Pharaoh.

Pharaoh rises, taking Angyet's hand gently and presses it to him lips. "Thank you Angyet. With you here I know all will be well. You give me peaceful rest, knowing you watch over us." The Pharaoh too moves into the darkness disappearing to his private chambers.

Angyet leans back into the chair looking into the light of the oil fire bowl on the table before her. The slight heat of the light fills her. With a relaxation of body and expansion of spaciousness she reaches out into the great oneness. *"What next?"* she ponders.

It is her pleasure to serve Pharaoh-Ra. Few know the truth of the man who, from the first moment of their meeting, was a friend. Together they were crafting an unlikely future, a future beyond what most consider possible.

Pharaoh-Ra is not like other Pharaohs before him. For him what is most desirable is that each person no matter their background or station be the greatness they are capable of being. He encourages creativity and ingenuity. He likes people who are willing to take charge of what they know and take that knowing and applying it to the betterment of all.

He strives to empower people to know that they know and recognizes there are many who prefer to make what they consider not possible as more real than the adventure of exploring what might become possible. There are many who are happy to be told what to do and think they have no choice. But, then there are a few who are different.

There are those who strive to develop their capacities of embodying the oneness and empower all those they interact with to become all they can be as Angyet and Pharaoh-Ra do.

To move objects without physical touch as the Movers do is the least of the capacity of a Builder. The Builders are more rare and small in number yet far outdo the capacity of The Movers. The public difference is that no Builder makes a display of it, nor do they hide it; they embrace it as a way of being in the world regardless of who does or does not notice. It is the joy of being these capacities and awareness that is most valuable to a Builder. That joy combined with how her capacities can contribute to increasing the oneness thrills Angyet to no end.

With this awareness and the guidance of the previous Builder Hamadi, and the trust of Pharaoh-Ra, Angyet has become a leader in the creation of the future of all of Pharaoh's Land. Quietly and without fanfare Angyet has been diligently working to undo the forces that would destroy the possibilities for oneness to become the predominant energy of Pharaoh's Land.

Those with the eyes to see get the gift of these capacities and the generosity of possibility that can be created, they experience gratitude for having a Builder in their midst. The Pharaoh-Ra has such gratitude for his Builder Angyet. Friend, confidant and hope for his daughter's future he rests in her capable hands.

Tomorrow will begin a new chapter of possibility, oddly enough in the hands of three slaves.

Chapter 6

The Von Kesslar family sat together at their humble table, tears of joy at their new found freedom continuing to flow. Drekkar and Emilia Von Kesslar would finally put words to all they held most dear and kept hidden within. Their son Bilal would now know everything. Their homeland, their people, their heritage; the secret hopes they had for their son. Like a damn now broken, they would spill forth their life before their son had been born and of the circumstances of his birth. How they had come to be slaves, how they had current plans for escape.

Drekkar began "This turn of events has changed everything. I had not said anything yet Bilal, but your mother and I had been planning escape for the three of us. Because you have done so well in your death matches and the construction of the pyramid is going well, in one more moon Master Iberak had been planning on taking the three of us north with him. He would not deny how much easier it is to have us with him, so things go smoothly for him by bringing us along."

Master Iberak was going to purchase more slaves as his stocks have depleted more than he likes. "As you know, several have died in accidents in construction in the last few weeks."

He also recently sold some of his beauties to the households of Keepers who prefer servants that are easy on the eyes. He needed new women for his brothels. It was a rare event that all of them would be together, and in the north no less. They would not miss this opportunity.

"Once north we were planning to kill master Iberak and anyone who might get in our way. From there we would head north by any means available, we would go home," explained Drekkar. "We have been hoarding away anything that might assist us along the way that we can easily carry with us. Your mother and I are getting older and you are old enough now, this was our chance. Can you believe it? Now we can just walk out of this miserable life, we can go home!"

Bilal had sat silently listening, reeling with the revelations his parents laid out. He had no idea his parents felt this way about returning to their homeland. Because they never spoke of it, he had thought them ashamed, or resigned to the life they now had. He hadn't dreamed they had such ambition for leaving. Though his life had not been pleasant by any stretch of the imagination, Pharaoh's Land was all he had ever known, it was home to him.

As Freemen, they had a huge variety of possibilities open to them. They had skill, they had a reputation known by many and could use this to their advantage to create a new life here. They were free to do anything. It was a lot to take in and more choice than they were used to.

Emilia and Drekkar Von Kesslar spoke through the night with their son Bilal, pouring their hearts out, making amends of their withholding and so much unspoken all these eighteen years of his life.

These were not the only secrets in Pharaoh's Land. There walked among the people a few with exceptional capacities and magical ability in their communion with the oneness of the planet and all the molecules of creation. They only reveal themselves by the calling of the tug that tells them this is the time, this is the place, this is the person. They are called Builders, and the one that had been called to Pharaoh's Land was a great hope for actualizing the future this Pharaoh yearned for.

Chapter 7

The Freemen filter through every level of society and station. From working side by side the slaves in the quarries all the way to position in the House of Pharaoh. Their life is what they make of it. Bound to none and by none, they create themselves. Using their beauty, wit or skill and circumstance to seize the possibilities that present themselves; falling or ascending according to their own making.

Pharaoh's daughter Ra-Milania has shown indications of the capacities of the oneness since her first cycle of the sun. In the short five years of her life this capacity has grown and grown more dynamically than most comprehend.

With the grace of the oneness, the Pharaoh has been lucky enough to have an advanced Builder in the woman Angyet. She is also someone to guide Pharaoh's daughter and assist her in development as a Builder in her own right. Not for hundreds of generations had there been a Builder who was also Pharaoh. A Freeman from the west, it remains a bit of a mystery to most how Angyet came to Pharaoh's Land. It would appear by chance the Pharaoh discovered her. He was in the public gardens milling about with the society that visits. A place to informally meet and converse with artisans, merchants, his Keepers and visiting people from all across the land.

He stood speaking with Keepers of the water-works, they were updating him about the irrigation systems of the crop lands. As usual, all eyes were on him, as everyone strained to overhear his conversation and wait for their moment to speak with the Pharaoh. He noticed her standing alone and away from most others. There was nothing overtly spectacular about her outward appearance save maybe her jet black hair that was long and unusually straight. Yet the Pharaoh couldn't help watch her, he found himself drawn to her and curious. He noticed tiny braids at her temple that she had pulled back into a small knot at the back of her head which kept her hair from falling into her face. She appeared friendly to those strolling by and was unassuming in demeanor. He noticed how observant she was of all her surroundings. She seemed to be taking it all in, yet she had not looked towards the Pharaoh, at least that he had noticed. This in itself was unusual especially with someone obviously new to the Pharaoh's gardens.

Those he spoke with did not notice his lack of attention as he watched her. Suddenly she was spinning to her left reaching out and grabbing the air as though to take hold of something. Though she did not hold it physically, floating in the air at another arm's length from her, and writhing as though caught in hand was a black moccasin. With one step toward the suspended asp, her other hand came around swiftly removing the head in the single slash of a small blade. The body of the now headless asp dropped to the ground, along with the removed head. It was only then she looked around to see if anyone noticed; no one had, except the Pharaoh. He had seen it all. They locked eyes, both rather surprised. It was as if it was only the two of them there, truly no one else had noticed a thing.

The Pharaoh suddenly reaches up, summoning; "Garden keepers, come!" He steps between the men he was listening to and heads straight to her. Seeing the Pharaoh approaching she drops to one knee, head bowed. All heads now turn in curiosity as the Pharaoh addresses this woman no one has seen before. "Please, rise. What is your name? What brings you to my gardens?"

She rises, speaking softly and looking at him directly; "Lord Pharaoh, I am known as Angyet. It is the tug Lord Pharaoh that brings me here. It is only these last few moments that reveal for what reason." She looks him in the eyes as few dare, searching if he registers the meaning in her words. She notices his eyes widen at the same time his body subtly relaxes.

He hears the garden keepers arrive behind him. Speaking to them he says; "Looks like you missed this today, please remove the snake this woman has so kindly spared us. Bury the head properly and take the body to the kitchens, make sure Rimmel gets its skin."

With that he reaches out his hand to the stranger he has been pleading with the universe somehow be delivered to him; "We shall have the snake for our meal later, to honor its sacrifice. Come Angyet, let us speak. There is much to speak of."

The onlookers whisper, "Who is this strange woman the Pharaoh himself allows to touch him? Whatever could this mean?" No one dares approach as the Pharaoh is obviously not to be interrupted when so engaged.

Angyet and the Pharaoh walk the garden for many hours, deep in conversation. Mostly in hushed tones and sometimes breaking into laughter, they speak as what looks to be old dear friends.

Without formality, Angyet spills forth of her journey to the House of Pharaoh; of how the tug of the oneness led her there that day. She knew not where it was taking her, but as any true Builder she followed the tug, knowing it would expand the possibilities for a greater future; not just for her, for everyone.

It was only in the few moments of communion with the asp that many of the pieces of fleeting awareness came together. The snake asked its life be taken, it no longer wished to live. With that it revealed the dangers hidden in the House of Pharaoh by a barrage of images and senses it shared with Angyet. Upon completion of the communication she chopped off its head, with gratitude and thanks; honoring the asps request to end its life. With oneness all is knowable, all contributes to more awareness. The animals, the plants, objects, the elements - all things speak and contribute.

"Thank you for heeding the call of the tug Angyet. My Builder grows old and is nearing death. I have been requesting for a long time the oneness deliver the strength and security of a new Builder." The Pharaoh's relief is written across his face and in the sincerity of his voice.

"My daughter is of utmost concern, she is young, just past two cycles of the sun now. Since nearly first born she has shown extensive indication of capacities of the oneness. With my lifelong friend Hamadi, who is the current Builder, growing very old, I have feared he would not be here to guide her, to contribute to her development. But, now you are here and a new door has opened."

"It is not only the aging of my current Builder that is of concern; it is the mother of my daughter as well. She has grown distant, no longer willing to share a bed with me. At first I thought it was a phase having just born her first, but it has continued. She seems to have no desire to further the family lineage which I find most odd and alarming as time goes on."

Eventually moving in doors, they speak continuously far into the night. Easily revealing the depths of their being, their challenges, their aspirations; this is the gift of those who are as the oneness. There are no secrets. The trust in self and the awareness of what is true makes it easy to know what one's choices will create. It makes it easy to know the truth before you, be it spoken or unspoken. With no barriers to anything or anyone it is easy to find intimacy with those whom others would call strangers.

That was two years ago and the friendship and camaraderie that was sparked then will now expand to include more people with the rising of tomorrow's sun.

Chapter 8

It was in the quiet just before dawn was breaking across the Laborer Realm, there came the sound of footsteps walking with purpose. The Von Kesslar family having been up all night and still sitting around their small table and speaking in hushed tones heard the sound of footsteps approaching. Unfamiliar footsteps, they stopped speaking and Emilia pushed aside the ragged curtain that was their doorway. She returned to the table, sitting and waiting for the person that approached. A man in excellent clothing arrived at the doorway, rather hesitantly looks at the three of them saying without certainty; "Von Kesslar family?"

Drekkar replies first. "Yes." All of them instantly stand, seeing this is someone from the House of Pharaoh, though they have no idea who he is.

A look of relief comes over the face of this man, obviously unfamiliar with the Laborer Realm. The three of them had never noticed him in the Laborer's Realm before. Without introduction or invitation the man clears his throat entering the house and begins; "In the name of the almighty Pharaoh-Ra, you are declared Freemen." He then hands them each a small papyrus scroll, tied with a leather string. "These are your papers declaring you Freemen. Keep these as proof, that none may deny your new status. Keeper of Records also has record of your past ownership by Master Abar Iberak, and your new status as Freeman as declared by Pharaoh-Ra himself. Each in name; Drekkar Von Kesslar, Emilia Von Kesslar, Bilal Von Kesslar."

They are speechless, but manage a nod as a scroll is handed to them each in turn. The man next pulls out from some hidden pocket three small bags of fine fabric. From one he removes a large pendant of gold with a long chain, also of gold. They all three gasp at the shining beauty of this object they can see even in this dim light of pre-sun rise and candles. "This is your insignia. Present it for all you require." He can see from the blank looks on their face they have no idea what he is talking about. He explains; "House of Pharaoh is now your Keeper. Present this insignia when you purchase any goods or service and the House of Pharaoh will pay for it. It is for furnishing your home, food, drink, clothing, finery and adornment. Anything you need and desire for the comfort of your living is yours by asking and showing the merchant this insignia."

"Oh," they all exclaim at once.

"Here, let me show you." He holds the pendant in his hand

revealing a gold circle almost the size of his palm with the sun held up by a scarab, a water lily and egret that is the symbol of the Pharaoh-Ra carved in low relief. He flips it over showing a pin and hook on the back and how the chain can be removed. "You can wear it as a necklace or a broach, as you desire." He steps forward placing it around the neck of Emilia. It hangs low, down to her belly. Then removing the others he places them on Bilal and Drekkar each.

This is beyond their comprehension. They have never touched anything of gold, or of such beauty. This was theirs? They each are tentative in touching them, though all are now standing taller with wide-eyed pride.

The man continues with yet more good news. "Pharaoh-Ra has given you a new home in the Artisan Realm. You will be moved there today." Looking around the shack and shamble of their small hut, he comments; "It should be easy, I see there is not much to be moved."

Amongst gasps of awe, the three of them come together hugging with yet more tears. Bilal exclaims; "Can this really be happening?"

Emilia looks to the messenger; "Is this true? Can this really be? All of this for us?"

Drekkar whispers; "Bless the Pharaoh-Ra, may he live forever."

With a small smile the messenger replies quietly; "Yes. This is true. It is all true. You have saved the life of the Pharaoh-to-be. Ra-Milania is alive because of you. The thanks of the Pharaoh shall have no bounds. Would you be able to bring everything you would like to come with you right now? If you can carry all you would like to have with you now, you will not have to come back to this place."

The three of them look around the room and contemplate for only a few seconds. Emilia replies first. "I am sure we can gather our things in just a few minutes. We will do so now." They move quickly about and in ten minutes they are all ready, each with a small bundle slung over their shoulder or across the chest with a single strap bag.

"Come, I will now take you to your new home." Impressed with their swift decisive action, Rimmel steps out the door, leading the way.

The Von Kesslars follow out the door into the rising sun of their new life. The three of them hand in hand, they follow close behind the messenger from the House of Pharaoh.

Chapter 9

Master Abar Iberak is livid. He sits motionless and silent in a room strewn with busted furniture and dead, broken bodies that lay awkwardly about. In his rage of such loss in one day he has killed eleven of his slaves. He sits on one of the stools in his tavern, now empty of people and life. Alone and surrounded only by bloody, dead bodies and filth, he is unable to move for the loss of all that is so valuable to him and what to do next.

The darkness that has descended on him is a stark contrast to the new found freedom being discovered by those he just lost.

Chapter 10

Bilal, his mother Emilia, and father Drekkar step forth from the pillars of The Pathway with the messenger of the House of Pharaoh. They have emerged at the crest of the hill in the middle of the great causeway outside the palace. To their right is the great House of Pharaoh, to their left and straight ahead spreading down the hill all the way to the water's edge is the Artisan Realm. Located next to the palace for ease of delivery of all the goods of finery, beauty and luxury the Artisan Realm is a mix of houses in all sizes and shapes for the variety of function and service provided. The third street down the hill runs directly into the huge double door entrance beneath the palace.

Emilia lightly touches the arm of the messenger asking; "What is your name, kind man?"

With a slight bow of the head he replies; "I am called

Rimmel. It is my pleasure to meet you Emilia Von Kesslar."

"I don't recall ever seeing you before, not that we travel in the same circles;" Emilia laughs shyly at the brashness of her own joke.

"It is not often I leave the palace grounds, or go beyond the markets of the House of Pharaoh for I am Keeper of His Royal Person," replies Rimmel.

"What exactly is that?" asks Emilia.

"I am the body servant to the Pharaoh my dear. I dress him, groom him and make sure he is presented properly," Rimmel says both humbly and with a smile of pride for the honor of having such position.

They all look wide-eyed at Rimmel. Emilia manages another question; "Whatever are you doing fetching us from the Laborers Realm? I don't understand."

"Yours is a special circumstance that requires delicate handling. It is not my place to explain. What I can say is that it is in the interest of the Pharaoh that you are moved both discretely and quickly. Besides, the home you are going to was my father's. Please follow me." With that he turns and heads down the hill, turning left at the second cross street they come to. Five houses down he stops in front of large arched double doors with a pottery planter on either side, each containing a small shrubbery trimmed to perfection.

"Here we are." Rimmel takes a key from his pocket and hands it to Drekkar.

The doors themselves are a piece of art. Made of wood, the middle of each side is decorated with intricate inlay of a bundle of flowers cascading down. Inlay design of interlaced vine, leaves and flowers edge the borders of each door.

"Please enter," say Rimmel.

Drekkar places the key in the lock of the door and it easily turns. He opens the door and peeks inside. With an excited in-breath he pushes the two doors open, "Look!" he exclaims.

The doors open wide. Emilia, Bilal and Drekkar step inside. Rimmel follows with a smile on his face. It is a small courtyard with a fountain in the middle. Cozy, but large enough to be a mini-garden with small fruit trees on the left side against the house.

"This was your father's house?" asks Bilal.

"Yes. My father was a master artisan specializing in decorative inlay for furniture. He loved flowers. You will find many details of flowers here throughout the house. To the right was his workshop. To the left is storage and small servant quarters. Straight ahead is the main living area, come, let me show you." Rimmel strolls across the courtyard opening another double door into the main living area.

Here was a spacious open room for entertaining and lounging, on the other side three sets of double doors were already open to another veranda with low railing and the most amazing view of the Artisan Realm flowing down to the river's edge and down the valley. It took their breath away.

Drekkar exclaims "We get to live here? But where is your father Rimmel? Where is your family?"

"Yes, really, you get to live here. My father passed on a few years ago and this place has been mostly empty. It is a shame for it to be unused. I am happy for you to be here. This was the home where I grew up, however I no longer live here with the position I hold. I live in the palace and have no other family."

Emilia says "We don't know how to thank you enough. We are honored and will care for this home well. Please show us more!"

Says Rimmel; "Here to the right is a bedroom and private quarters and connects through to the workshop. To the left is another bedroom, dining area. There is also a downstairs area, you can access it here to the left, or outside from the veranda." He walks to the left just around the wall and down the stairs. They reach the bottom.

"There is the kitchen with cellar storage, private rooms and one more bedroom. Straight through here, the last bedroom has its own patio." He continues walking through and onto the patio. It was like a secret garden with a stairway back up to the main veranda.

They head back upstairs to the main bedroom. He goes to the dressing area and shows a pile of clothing on the dressing table. "I have brought these clothes for the three of you. It is not likely much will fit well, but please try it out. I will be happy to have clothing made for you, you can pick out your own fabrics at the market and I will have them made to fit properly. The Pharaoh wishes you to make yourself at home. Please, do not be shy about asking for what you require and desire. Remember, you need only show your insignia to the merchant and it will be taken care of by the House of Pharaoh."

Bilal, Emilia and Drekkar then look down at their worn, drab rags with the brilliance of the insignia hanging around their necks and laugh both in embarrassment and the humor of the dramatic juxtaposition of the gold insignia and the raggedness of their clothing. Rimmel's lack of judgment has made it easier to take in the reality that all of this is actually happening. Moving forward with this mind-bending change of reality is beginning to sink in, with the ease of his kindness.

The three of them thank Rimmel profusely.

Gracefully receiving the thanks and gratitude of the Von Kesslar family, Rimmel then excuses himself with the simple words; "I will check in on you tomorrow, please do explore, make this your home, for now it truly is yours." With that he lets himself out.

The warmth of this welcoming and the beauty of this new home opened Drekkar and Emilia's hearts more deeply that night as they revealed to their son more details of their homeland and the truth of their hidden past before their life as slaves to Master Iberak.

Chapter 11

It had been seven days since the Von Kessler's had moved into their new home; the gift of the Pharaoh. They really could hardly believe it. The house was modest for those of the Artisan Realm but more extravagant than Bilal had ever been in for any length of time, let alone call home. And the view was incredible.

After moving Bilal, Emilia and Drekkar had been left to their own devices; free to roam the city as they will, able to purchase anything. They were all still in shock about it and rather shy to test it out. Could they really have anything just for the asking?

They had purchased a few of the basic things for everyday living, fabric for making new clothes and more food than they had ever had at one time. Everything was decadence beyond what they ever had before. Even the most modest of items in the Pharaoh's Market was better quality than the markets of the Laborer Realm and products that Master Iberak would allow.

Rimmel had visited every day as he said he would. He continued to put them at ease, make them at home and educate them about life at the palace and what was possible as someone who's Keeper was the House of Pharaoh.

This was a whole new world. Even the idea of not having to go to the quarry and labor all day was a stunner, let alone the reality of it. In addition, to have the luxury of each other's company and be enjoying it was truly an unimaginable turn of events. The three of them were spending the days and into the night talking, sharing and revealing so much of what each of them had kept hidden.

It was Bilal who was doing much of the listening. His parents had an entire lifetime before he was born. They spoke of a world he had never known existed. So far from this land was the life they spoke of it seemed as a dream to Bilal. A world in which he is royalty was as opposite as it could be from the life he had known.

And that the hardship he had endured was training him for this life in the North? This was still hard to hear that his father had a reason for what he did and that it was to prepare him for this life he had never heard about before. He was not sure this was a place he would ever like to go to.

Drekkar spoke of the land of his birth. Drekkar explained that his family is one of the three royal houses of the north. For five hundred and sixty annual cycles of the sun, no other families have had a king on the throne other than these three

Houses. The Von Kesslar family, the Bonderfaust family and the Strudwick family. The Von Kesslar's had held the throne most often. Though Drekkar was thirteen when he left home the family history was drilled into him since birth.

Succession is not given in the North, it is taken. Whomever ascends the throne must challenge the current king and kill him in a show of public combat. The winner cuts off the head of the defeated to maintain their throne or to take the place of the current king.

Now it was beginning to make some sense why his father had always pushed him so hard; brutal training for taking the throne by force in a barbaric custom of succession. As the third son, not much was expected of Drekkar, and that was confirmed when no one came to fetch him when they discovered he had left with the expedition party that had no promise of return. Bilal on the other hand was the first born son of a Von Kesslar, which meant he had the right to challenge for the throne.

Drekkar spoke proudly of his family and heritage, for him it was a greatness to strive for. He honored his family name by preparing Bilal to ascend the throne.

From Bilal's perspective his father was even less different than he supposed of their slave Master Iberak. Both believe in taking what they could by force. They had the point of view that overtaking by brute force was the glory of a man. Though Bilal had seen this in action his entire life and himself been subject to it, it really did not make any sense to him.

For what reason would you not first ask of someone? He had always found people to be more cooperative and willing when asked. This had always been obvious to him. Force was rarely required, though often delivered in the world he had grown up in. Getting clarity about his father's underlying points of view started to shed light on what Bilal had never been able to grasp before. In the world his father came from to be the most dominant force was the paramount perspective of his entire existence. It explained so much about his father's actions. It did not make it okay in his own mind, however it gave him some ease in finally seeing what was true for his father. This also was revealing for what reason, though his mother was never violent with him, she also did not ever try to stop Drekkar or protect Bilal from him. Learning the why of it did not give as much relief as he had hoped it would.

Drekkar still had not explained much of how he had gotten here to Pharaoh's Land. How he ever left his homeland in the first place. So far he spoke of meeting Emilia and their love and devotion and of the joy of him, their one and only son. Of course it had only been a few days of freedom and there was much to tell.

For the first time in Bilal's life the three of them together were actually enjoying each other's company, be they talking or not. What a miracle to have laughter and friendly conversation in their house. None of them had returned to the shack of their old home or the Laborer Realm at all, the past eighteen years could practically be forgotten in the new-found ease and happiness of their everyday living. For the first time they all actively spoke of creating their future.

As they all relaxed into their new surroundings, Bilal was surprised to find that nagging sense of desiring more lingered.

Though this new life was glorious, this did not satisfy the sense of greater possibilities that niggled at him. *"Surely there must be more than this? What would it take to grasp what whispers and tugs at him? Was the Pharaoh's granting of freedom all that is possible, or is there more?"* He wondered.

Chapter 12

Angyet arrived at the door of the new home of the Von Kesslar family. She pauses for a moment before knocking. She was buzzing with excitement in anticipation of what was about to come to fruition; the beginning of a truly new possibility for everyone was whispering to come into existence. Never before has there been the possibility of so many Builders coming together. It would appear the universe was conspiring to bring a multitude of Builders to this land, at this time. Of course there was a long ways to go. Bilal had no idea of his capacity, he had no training, he did not know of the gift he is. There were many choices to be made, many steps to take.

The next step was to knock on the door of the Von Kesslar's that she now stood before.

It has been another informative evening with Bilal's parents. They have finished a light and leisurely meal and Bilal was rising to clear the table when he gets a tugging sensation in his chest. He recognizes it at once. He had only felt it a few times before, when he saw Ra-Milania for the first time in the market, and twice alone at the quarry when he stood on the cliffs edge.

The next moment comes a knock at the door. Since Bilal is already risen, he says, "I'll get that," and heads to the door. With only just having been granted freedom they had no servants or slaves of their own, and truthfully the thought of having any did not occur to them.

Bilal goes to the door opening it. He drops to one knee at once recognizing the Builder Angyet. He is so surprised he blurts, "What are you doing here? I mean, welcome, please come in." He dare not rise, though managed to move a bit to the side so she may enter.

"Bilal, please rise, and thank you. May I speak with you here alone for a moment?"

Rising Bilal replies. "Of course." He is wondering how she knows his name and is now even more surprised and curious.

"I have come to summon you to have audience with the Pharaoh tomorrow. He would like you to come alone, without your parents. Will you please come?" She asks.

"Yes. I would not refuse. I don't understand why you ask if I will. It is my duty and my honor," replies Bilal now even more perplexed.

Ignoring his comment, Angyet continues. "Did you notice a tug at your chest a moment ago?"

"Yes. How did you know that?"

"It is the oneness Bilal, telling you that those who are oneness are near." Without missing a beat, she continues, "In the morning a messenger will come to escort you to the Pharaoh. Good night Bilal." With that Angyet touches him lightly on the arm and a wave of energies pass through him like warm jasmine scented air caressing every molecule of his body. He melts on the inside taking in one short orgasmic breath as Angyet steps past him and out the door into the night.

"Did she just say what I think she said? How does she know about that tugging sensation?...And that touch! Wow." Bilal is dazed and feeling wonderful, bursting with a sense of joyful possibility and peaceful contentment all at once. That was the most unusual conversation he had ever had. *"What is the oneness?"* he wondered. He had heard a little, mostly that it was the mystical powers of the Pharaoh and the royal family. That it was what made them rulers and undefeated for a thousand annual cycles of the sun.

He floated back into the dining area to give his parents yet more good news.

"Who was that Bilal?" asks Emilia.

"I have been summoned to the palace for audience with the Pharaoh. A messenger will come in the morning to deliver me," replies Bilal.

"Whatever could it be about?" wonders Emilia out loud.

"I have no idea, they did not say, just to be ready first thing in the morning," says Bilal as he sighs with satisfaction.

Chapter 13

The morning has come with the rising sun. Bilal has already been awake for hours but remained in bed in anticipation of the day ahead. He gets up with the sun and makes a pot of the spice tea him and his parents had just discovered in the House of Pharaoh's marketplace a few days earlier.

Going out on the veranda with the cup of tea warming his hands, he watches the colors of the sky transform from deep purple blue of night to red, vibrant pink and orange. Letting the coolness of the air wake him up, he sips the flavorful tea. He takes the moment to feel the warmth as it moves down his throat and into his chest and belly then radiate outward and into his limbs. He closes his eyes savoring the complexity of flavors and the warmth spreading through his body. Expanding his senses he notices the sounds of the morning birds chirping and singing to the rising sun. He plays with how far away he can hear their singing, seeing if he can identify the type of bird by its song. Opening his eyes again, he takes in the landscape of the view before him. The brightening of the morning sky is like the expansive lightness spreading through his entire reality day by day with each new change. He breathes deep, stretching his senses out to meet the new sun.

He hears the softness of his mother's footsteps approaching. She also has a cup of the delicious tea in hand, as she approaches she says with a sigh, "Glorious isn't it?"

Bilal takes his mom around the waist and hugs her to him. She rests her head on his large muscular shoulder. "Who would ever think we would become so lucky?" he replies.

"Are you excited about seeing the Pharaoh today?" she asks.

He laughs, "I have been awake for hours in anticipation."

"That is wonderful son, I am so happy for you. You truly deserve this, you have endured so much. The world is opening to you Bilal, and I could not be happier about it!" She gives him a squeeze again and pulls away. "I'm going to bring your father a cup of this amazing tea. What a wonderful way to start the day!"

Going to the kitchen with his mother, Bilal puts together a bite to eat. He hopes he will not have to wait much longer for the messenger to arrive. As he eats he hears laughter from his parent's room and it puts a smile on his face. It has been such a rare thing in his life to hear that sound. He sits back in satisfaction of what has transpired in such a short time.

Finally he hears the anticipated knock at the door. He jumps up and heads to it, with the growing sound of laughter coming from his parent's room. In just a few strides he is across the courtyard and opening the door. The messenger lifts his head with a jerk and a look of surprise as he is in the middle of adjusting his shirt. Apparently Bilal has opened the door far quicker than the messenger anticipated. The man drops his hands, standing up straight and clearing his throat greets him; "Good day. Are you Bilal Von Kesslar?"

"Good day, yes I am," replies Bilal with an ear-to-ear grin so unlikely and unexpected from a man having spent most of his life as a slave.

"Please follow me." With a nod of the head he turns to leave. They head up the hill to the pillars and marker at the crest of the hill where he and his parents had first come to the Artisan Realm. The messenger stops just before the pillars, turning and looking at Bilal expectantly.

Bilal touches the shoulder of the guard summoning him to the House of Pharaoh. When traveling to an unknown location through The Pathway, one must be touching another who knows the marker at the intended location. Once there he could see the marker to know the place and get there again on his own. He did not know exactly the cause for the summons, but the generosity of the Pharaoh had yet to know bounds with his family. The Von Kesslars had been introduced to an unknown world of ease, pleasure and abundance. Everything was being provided for, they need only ask.

As they stepped through the pillars Bilal caught his breath. The room he entered was stunning. He could not have imagined pillars of The Pathway would enter a room, and that a room could be so large as to make the pillars look truly like a small door. Marble floor stretched out before him with subtle patterns of inlay. Pillars far to each side created a procession leading the eye to the open end of the building, into what looked to be a lush garden. The ceiling arched high with colors, patterns and images he had never seen before. Somehow it was bright way up there, he could not comprehend how. So much beauty!

He was born and raised close to the palace, yet Bilal had never been inside. So controlled was his life by Master Iberak, he had rarely been outside the Laborers Realm. His life centered around the quarry and construction area of the Temple of Ra situated next to the Sphinx, and up to now the construction grounds of the new pyramid. His entire life had almost no interaction with the Keeper's Realm, Pharaoh's Market or sprawling palace grounds.

The guard seemed not to notice the breath taking grandeur. He gestured to Bilal to follow him, they headed in the direction of the open end and across to the left. Trying not to gape with mouth open he followed. As they approached the last few columns there were large double doors to the left. They looked to be metal and as they walked closer, he could see shapes of animals, people and foliage bulging from the metal. Such fine work, Bilal wondered how such a thing would be created. The only metal he had seen before made straps for door hinge, blades for axe, or hammer heads, chains and shackles; items for slavery, labor and simple utilitarian use.

As they came through the doors he sees Pharaoh and his daughter Ra-Milania sitting, they look like they have been expecting him. He drops to one knee instantly, head bowed he speaks clearly; "Lord Pharaoh." He can't imagine for what reason he would be called here.

"Please, Bilal, rise. Meet my daughter."

Little Ra-Milania sits beside him, as usual with an ear-to-ear grin. It seems the only expression he has ever seen on this little girl. She sat silent though radiant and apparently just about to burst with excitement.

"This is Ra-Milania, whose life you have saved." Bilal looks up surprised. Rising to his feet he blurts "How did you know?"

"I know almost everything dear boy. I would like you to know much more. Do you have any idea why I have called you here? Please be direct, there is no need to be shy here Bilal." He speaks sincerely.

Bilal replies hesitantly; "I would have no idea my Pharaoh. I cannot imagine what you would want with me."

Pharaoh speaks; "I have a proposal for you. As you are now a Freeman, it is truly your choice to say yes or no. My daughter is in need of a personal guardian. I know your upbringing, I know you have the skills for it. I ask that you look after my daughter providing security of her well being. Her safety and her very life would be in your hands."

"You would be required to be at her door upon her awaking, and the last to be with her when she goes to sleep. You would accompany her in all things, no place would be barred to you. Your family would maintain their new home and in addition you would have a room both next to my daughter's and in the guard's quarters."

"I do not ask this lightly. Would you consider this? I will give you the day to come forward with your choice, Bilal Von Kesslar."

Hearing these words Bilal is bursting with excitement. That sense of tugging is so strong it is as though his heart might jump out of his chest. There was something magical and wonderful with every interaction he had had with Ra-Milania and the idea of protecting this child day in and day out thrilled him. His world was exploding energetically, it was as though his molecules were beginning to clang together with the joy bubbling up inside.

Kneeling upon one knee once again Bilal solemnly looks Pharaoh in the eyes, replying; "I have your reply Lord Pharaoh. I do not require time to dwell upon this. It would be my deepest honor and true pleasure to serve. I can think of no greater use of my life, humbly I accept."

"Wonderful Bilal!" Pharaoh-Ra sits up on the edge of his seat, grinning widely.

Unable to contain herself any longer little Ra-Milania jumps up onto the chair, throwing her arms wide she shouts. "Beeeelol!"

And with that flings herself into the air at him exclaiming, "Catch me!" as she lands with a thud against his chest. He grabs her before she drops, a look of shock on his face. She wraps her arms around his neck. "Hi."

Looking down at her beaming grin he bursts out laughing. "Hi there."

"I knew you would catch me. Stand up." A little awkwardly

he stands, holding her to him as she continues to cling to his neck like a little monkey.

"As you can see my daughter is quite excited about you! It was also her request for you that solidified this choice." A little cryptically he comments; "I'm sure she will tell you all about it. As you can see she is not shy. Little Mila, why don't you show your new guardian around."

"Yes! Great idea father. I will give him the grand tour." She says lifting her chin to look more regal, though she still clings to Bilal's neck. She looks to Bilal and says, still smiling broadly and now batting eyelashes; "Put me on your shoulder and I will show you everything!"

Pharaoh continues; "I will like to speak with you again tomorrow. Please come back after your morning meal and meet me here. There is much to discuss and it will take some time. Now Mila, please continue, he is all yours."

Bilal gingerly sets Mila on his right shoulder and she exclaims; "Wow, this is WAY up high. Is this what it always looks like for you Bilal?" Before he can reply as he is still reeling with these new and dramatic turn of events, she continues; "Come, let us to the gardens." She points towards the door with one hand, and with the other turns his head with her hand to point the way.

Bilal looks back to the Pharaoh for confirmation. Pharaoh gestures out the door; "Please proceed. You are now hers. Please know your questions, concerns and anything of importance are welcome, day or night; I am at your disposal with regard to my daughter. Go now little one, show Bilal around."

With that the giant of a man who is Bilal, personal guardian to the Pharaoh-to-be, turns and walks out the door; Ra-Milania perched on his shoulder. One arm resting around his neck the other pointing here and there. The Pharaoh smiles as he overhears his daughter welcome Bilal into her world.

"I knew you would say yes Bilal! I am so happy you are here. We are going to be the best of friends. You'll see…there, over there are the public gardens, that is where we are headed now. This is the public hall for all the large gatherings. Over there is the library…"

The Pharaoh's daughter is at home secure in her knowing of that which will give her a greater future now that Bilal is part of her life.

Chapter 14

Though small in body and young in age, the daughter of Pharaoh, Ra-Milania is bright and sharply aware of both her situation and the people surrounding her. The oneness has made her knowing exceedingly acute and she is dynamically capable in ways almost no one can image of a five-year-old, or a person at any age for that matter. With Bilal now by her side, and also far more capable than he yet knows, Pharaoh-Ra's daughter is supremely happy.

She described every building, every person they came across, she knew them all; she never missed a thing. It delighted and boggled Bilal's senses. Perched on his shoulder like a little bird singing, they stroll the grounds outside. She asked him to stop at the wall overlooking the river as it wraps around the south east side of the House of Pharaoh. "Please set me down here on the wall" says Ra-Milania. It is the perfect height so he can be standing and she can look him in the eyes. She speaks with all sincerity now; "You can ask me anything Bilal. Whatever you do not know about, whatever you do not understand, please ask. I will never withhold anything from you. We must have no secrets. I will tell you anything. And please call me Mila. When we are alone or with father, or Angyet there is no need to be formal."

"I understand, Mila. You have been very thorough, and I will not be shy with you," he replies also with utmost sincerity.

"Good." She says with the nod of her head. It is startling, her way of speaking as an adult, being such a small child. Bilal finds it endearing and somehow puts him at ease. He can be himself with this little girl. No barriers, no need to secret his inner world or what is true for him. This day is a gift he could never have dreamed of in many lifetimes.

"Help me down would you Bilal?" Bilal takes her tiny waist and lifts her, light as a feather he gently sets her on the ground. "Now," she continues, "Let me tell you of some of the rules and customs as my personal guardian." She begins to walk on towards the Artisan Realm situated below the great House of Pharaoh and sprawling down to the river's edge. She walks with hands clasped behind her, a master of her realm, that of the Pharaoh-to-be. Bilal walks beside her, surprised he need not take as small of steps as he would imagine.

"Little bee," he muses with a small smile listening to his new friend and guide.

"You have authority and right of way above all others, besides father and mother. You are equal in rank to my parent's personal guards but in regards to me, you outrank them. With me you can go anywhere I go. If not with me, no one really has authority to stop you but they may not like it and try to. Don't let them, ever. It is the growing secrecy in Pharaoh's Land that is one of the greatest concerns we have."

"You are the only person, besides mother and father, with unlimited access to my personal living chambers. You may enter unannounced. The others may only come and go at my request. You will have a room next to mine, and as father said, a room with the guards as well."

"In addition to the insignia you were already given, you will be given the insignia of the Keeper of the House of Pharaoh that are only for those who guard the family. You will be outfitted with the proper attire, but really you'll get to pick what you would like to wear. Rimmel will help you with that."

She stops and looks at Bilal. "I am so glad you are here. I have been waiting for you." With that she jumps up in excitement, "Can I ride on your shoulder again? Please, please, pretty please?"

He laughs, "It would be my pleasure Ra-Milania, I mean Mila." He gently takes hold of her and places her on his shoulder again. They continue on the easy downward slope of the walkway towards the Artisan Realm. She tells him about the barges that bring food from the crop lands and how they sometimes take them up the river to look at the quarries and the building of the pyramid from the view of the water.

As they reach the corner that turns under the palace there are pillars and a marker. "We'll go to my rooms now Bilal, I'm hungry. Enter The Pathway here." Bilal steps between the pillars of The Pathway with Mila still perched on his shoulder and steps out into an exquisite room. Bilal lowers Mila to the floor and with a grand sweeping gesture of the arm as she walks to the large balcony she says; "And these are my rooms. My rooms face the rising sun as my time as Pharaoh will be dawning soon enough. And, it has the most amazing views, look!" She runs back to Bilal grabbing his hand and pulling him to the balcony to see.

He thought his view was great, this was truly breathtaking. Like being on top of the world, the balcony wraps around almost two thirds of the room. "Here, you can see the pyramid over there and a little of the Laborers Real, and the Artisan Realm below, all the crop lands over here, then the river as far as the eyes can see, that is the roof of the palace public great room, there is the tree tops of the garden and the rooftops of Keepers Realm. Okay, I'm done. Let's eat, shall we?" Mila turns towards where they had come and yells loudly; "Piloma!"

An immediate reply comes "Yes, I am here."

Bilal looks to see a woman in her forties, short and round with a kind face. "Yes my dear what would you like?" Piloma knows the voice of hunger when she hears it.

"Piloma, this is Bilal. He is my new guardian. Bilal this is Piloma, my hand servant." As the mini adult only a five-year-old that is the Pharaoh-to-be can pull off Mila says; "Please make Bilal comfortable and give him anything he requires or requests. And I'm starving. Would you bring enough to feed us both? All of my favorites please. Thank you." With that she climbs onto the day bed arranged to be in the shade and overlooking the view and plops down with a sigh.

Piloma bows her head and hurries out the door.

Bilal gets a puzzled look on his face. Looking back into the room they had just entered by means of The Pathway he realizes that there is no marker and there are no pillars. "Mila, can I ask you something?"

"Yes Bilal, anything," replies Mila with a yawn.

"How did we get in here? There are no pillars, no marker?"

"Ah, very observant. I was wondering when you would notice. This is my first secret to share with you, come sit here." She motions to the daybed next to her.

He sits a little awkwardly next to the tiny girl. "Come on Bilal, make yourself comfortable, really. Put your feet up, like me." Mila demonstrates by stretching her little legs out and crossing her feet at the ankle as she leans back against the back rest.

He smiles a little sheepishly but obeys. Turning so he is completely on the daybed, leaning back he stretches out his feet, crossing his ankles as Mila demonstrated. He actually fits, without his feet hanging off the end. He takes a breath and relaxes just a little, looking sideways down at this little wonder of a girl who had been blowing his mind all day.

"Like this?"

"Yes, very good Bilal. Wonderful! Aahhhhhhh, isn't this nice. So, you were asking something?"

"Oh yes." He had actually forgotten already until Mila asked. "Um, how did we get in here? There are no pillars, no marker. How do I know where to enter, or how to enter here? Besides walking in I mean," Bilal looks with a wrinkle in his brow.

Mila sits up pulling her legs under her and leaning forward

with wide eyes of enthusiasm and begins.

"Okay, so you know how Ra has placed pillars and markers all over the Land of Pharaoh so people can move from place to place in the blink of an eye. And you have been taught that you must know the marker at the location you are going to in order to get there. And that the pillars and markers are like a door in the middle of the road, or someplace obvious."

She says with exaggeration; "Well, there is a whole other network of hidden pillars and markers that only a few people know about. Look at the wall here, see those four half columns on the wall that look like decoration. Notice how two columns on the left are a little closer together? Those are actually pillars of The Pathway. And the marker is anything in this room that you can see from when you first enter through the pillars."

She covers her mouth giggling, thrilled with the revelation of this secret. "Come on, let me show you! We'll do it quick, before Piloma gets back."

With that she hops off the daybed and walks to the pillars hidden in plain sight as the architecture of the wall. She holds out her hand to Bilal who is now standing beside her. Taking her hand, they step forward. What looked to be solid wall was the familiar space as between the pillars he has known. In a blink they were stepping into the lounge room he had first met them in that morning. They were in the corner to the right of the door, hidden from most of the room. Mila giggles. "Back we go," and she turns around and steps back into the wall that is space and into her room.

Jumping onto the daybed again, she continues in a whisper; "We have them everywhere really, but well hidden. I'll show you." she looks with a conspirator's sideways smile. "Not very many people know about them and we would like to keep it that way. Even Piloma who has been with me my whole life does not know about very many and we don't allow most people to use them if they do know. Let's play a game. Let's see if you can find them! Oh, I hope Piloma comes back soon with food! I'm sssssstttaaaaarving."

Bilal sits again on the side of the daybed, looking at Mila. "Thank you Mila, it has been a wonderful day. I am happy to be your guardian. I am very honored that you would consider me for such a position. Can I ask you something?"

Mila replies with a large smile; "Yes."

"Why me?"

"You saved me Bilal! No one noticed the rocks falling, but you did and you didn't hesitate," replies Mila. With that she gets up and hugs him around his neck. He hugs her back, not sure what else to say, he is moved beyond words. No one has ever been grateful for what he did for them like this. He has only known people to beat him for not doing enough, fear him, lust after him, want something from him, or for what he can do for them. Gratitude for him being him was something totally new and foreign.

She starts to speak again but stops with the sounds of footsteps approaching. Sitting down again she expectantly looks at the door. It is Piloma returning with food.

"Ah, yes! Food;" says Mila with enthusiasm as she sees Piloma enter the room with a large platter of food and drink. Piloma sets it on the small table next to the daybed. Under the table is a shelf with more small trays for them to eat off of on their laps as they lounge.

"Have as much as you like Bilal. Piloma, I will expect you to be helpful to Bilal in all that he asks of you. Please make him comfortable and at home. He will be keeping me safe now."

"Of course Ra-Milania," replies Piloma with a nod. "Anything else, dear?"

"No, we are good. You can leave now," Mila says as she pops a grape in her mouth and works on loading up her sitting tray with delectable bites of meats, cheese, bread and fruits. After both Bilal and Mila are sitting back munching on their meals, Bilal continues; "Sooooo, secret pillars, huh? They are everywhere? I will try and point them out to you as you continue showing me around, how about that?"

"Yes, excellent!" exclaims Mila between mouth full and the next bite. "I will show you more tomorrow after you meet with father."

"Wonderful Mila. Thank you and thank you for today. It has been one of the most amazing days of my life, I very much enjoyed your company and it is my honor to serve and protect you now," Bilal says with utmost sincerity and reiterating his gratitude.

Mila and Bilal continued to chat for the next hour about her life at the palace. What it was like their and the protocols for how to conduct himself as her guardian, at least as seen by a very bright five year old.

It is difficult not to cry with the warmth and kindness this little girl and her father, the Pharaoh has shown him today. He is surprised to not be embarrassed by that and he lets the tears fall freely when they come. A new world was opening up beyond what he ever imagined possible. It washed over him like a warm embrace of being he had always hoped for but lacked to find in everyday life, at least until now.

This time spent with little Mila whispered of those possibilities he had known must exist, that he could not yet comprehend how or what they might be, but that they did. Today was a confirmation of those whispers of what he knew to be true that no one, until now ever spoke of.

He wondered, would his parents understand any of this? He was not sure he yet had the courage to ask and find out. The oneness certainly was never a topic of discussion in his home before.

Chapter 15

Bilal had spent the entire day with Mila and now was headed home. He had stepped from the pillars of little Mila's room and out onto the causeway at the top of the hill of the Artisan Realm.

He looked out at the view of the houses and river below and with a deep satisfying sigh thinks to himself; *"Whatever might tomorrow bring?"* with that tears do come to his eyes with the gratitude of just how lucky he had become over these last few days.

He walked the streets of the Artisan Realm until the sun went down, taking some time by himself to soak it all in, such extraordinary change in a very short time. It was such a magical thing to be around someone so happy, so genuine and forthright. Both the Pharaoh and his daughter gave him that sense of well being as when he stood on the cliffs alone...he couldn't explain it, he just knew he could be himself when he was with them. No pretense or guarding was required. It was what he had been seeking his entire life. The thought of leaving this behind, when he was just finding it was unbearable.

He wondered what his parents might say about today's turn of events. He was not sure how they would take his acceptance of the Pharaoh's offer. They had been speaking so much of going north. The uncertainty and violence of the culture his parents described and how to reclaim their place was not appealing to him in any way, even if it did hold the possibility of making him king.

Arriving home and opening the door, the sounds of jovial conversation spilled out into the courtyard welcoming him. Rimmel was with his parents out on the veranda enjoying food together.

"Ah son, there you are! Come, we could not wait to eat, but you have made it in time before it is all gone. Rimmel has just been telling your mother and I of some of the antics of little Ra-Milania."

"Such a darling girl." Rimmel sighs with a smile. "She has brought such joy to the House of Pharaoh. And what a wit, the things she says! Oh, just wonderful."

"Funny you should mention her, it just so happens I have spent the day with her myself!" says Bilal in some anticipation. "Mother, father, you will not believe what happened today! As you know, Pharaoh-Ra summoned me to him this morning. Well, he has asked if I would become the personal guardian of Ra-Milania, can you believe it?"

"Oh son, such an honor" says Emilia breathless.

"What did you say?" asks Drekkar, a shadow crossing his face.

"I said 'yes' of course. How could I refuse the request of the Pharaoh, he has been so generous with us? Ra-Milania was there when Pharaoh asked me, she was so happy I said yes, she literally jumped on me with hugs! I spent the day with her as she gave me a tour of the palace and instructed me on my position with her. I never met a child who could speak as an adult. She impressed me very much. I know we have been making plans," Bilal continues a little cryptically. "I would be so honored and pleased to hold such a position, I hope you are not upset with me." Bilal was very glad Rimmel was there at the moment. He could see the darkness behind his father's eyes though he had a smile on his face.

"How could we be upset, you are a man, free to choose as you will. It is an incredible honor," says Drekkar softening a little.

"Congratulations Bilal, a well deserved honor. I am sure you will carry it out well," says Rimmel with a satisfied warmth to his voice. He seems not so surprised and genuinely happy for Bilal. "And I am sure I will be seeing much more of you then. You must be outfitted properly and that is my department! Wonderful, wonderful Bilal. With that I will take my leave for the night, and certainly see you again soon. Thank you all for a lovely evening, and for making my childhood house a home once again. I am most pleased." With that, Rimmel gets up and as usual shows himself to the door.

As the door closes behind Rimmel, Bilal sits tensely, anticipating his father's upset. Before his father speaks he says, "Father I know you and mother have been speaking of going home, but this is my home. The land you speak of, the family and tradition is foreign to me. Here as a Freeman and now as guardian to the Pharaoh-to-be, I can make something of myself. I can do something that is meaningful to me and now it is my choice to make. For the first time in my life, my life is my own and I will not forsake that for anyone. Not even you. I hope you will honor my choice."

Drekkar speaks first, "I do not blame you son. It is more than any of us could have hoped just a few weeks ago. You have suffered much and I have been a large part of that. But your family, your heritage; you are royalty yourself, you need not serve."

"You don't understand, this is different, so very different. I serve, but not as a servant. I am there of my own free will, I am respected in a way I never knew was possible and I can contribute to creating a greater future." Tears fill Bilal's eyes and spill over. "Mother, father, my choice matters to her, to Ra-Milania, even to the Pharaoh himself. This is what I choose, will you honor me with your support?"

Both Emilia and Drekkar stand and go to their son embracing him, they both say how proud they are. He is a man now, a Freeman at that, he can choose what he will and they will support him. It is more than Bilal dare hope. His parents had never spoken with him this way, he had never know them to have such allowance. It was very unexpected and the tears fell more easily with relief and gratitude.

The unexpected opening with his parents and how they honored his choice expanded the sense of something greater on the brink of showing up. How much more would tomorrow glimpse that sense of magic trickling into his life?

Chapter 16

B ilal awoke early again with excitement for the adventure of a new day. *"What else is possible today?"* he wondered. His life had become an adventure, each day more wonderful and amazing than the previous. The Pharaoh had asked him to return so they could speak more. His heart raced with joyful anticipation. He would walk the grounds this morning as it was still early for meeting the Pharaoh.

He headed out to the lower entrance of the palace, just a few streets down and over from his new home. He walked the river side of the palace watching the rising sun, thinking of Ra-Milania in her rooms far above. This was the beginning of a completely new and different life for him. He was a Freeman now. He could choose anything, do anything, be anything. To have the invitation of the Pharaoh and his daughter was way beyond anything he would have imagined or dreamed of just a few weeks ago. His heart swelled with gratitude for all the turn of events of these previous days. He continued to wonder how he had become so lucky after such a hellacious upbringing.

He was strolling the palace gardens staying close to the entrance ready to go in now, but as the sun had only just risen above the horizon, he thought he was still too early. He let the movement relax him as he walked, taking in the elegance of the gardens. In his eighteen years as a slave he had never been at the palace or seen man made beauty such as this. Only glimpsing the palace from afar, it was much grander than he ever imagined. Seeing it up close, he soaked in the beauty of it all.

He only really knew the ugliness of the Laborer Realm. The little beauty he found there was in the satisfaction of splitting rock that was impossible for others to accomplish, or the view from the rocks edge, his dear friend and love Lili. His life up to now had only moments and glimpses of beauty in a sea of misery, pain, death and ugliness. This world he was being introduced to was a sea of beauty in which he had yet to find anything ugly. He was not naïve enough to think it did not exist here, for there were people here and with people was always the potential for cruelty and ugliness. Nonetheless, to be surrounded by such beauty gave him a sense of possibility he had not known before. It gave him hope that something greater truly is possible, beyond that which he had been aware of up to now.

With that expansive sense of possibility filling him as the beauty that filled his eyes everywhere he looked, he headed for the palace entrance. Passing through the impossibly large doors, he took a deep breath again stunned by the architecture of the great hall. Climbing the few steps to the lounge he had met Pharaoh-Ra in the day before he looks wide-eyed, seeing the Pharaoh sitting there waiting. The Pharaoh is looking at him with a faint smile, though he does not speak. Bilal enters the room quickly, stopping three feet away from the Pharaoh and dropping to one knee he says, "Greetings Pharaoh-Ra. I hope I have not kept you waiting."

Raising his hand palm up Pharaoh replies, "Good day Bilal. Thank you for asking, I have only just arrived. Please come sit here by me, there is much to discuss."

Rising Bilal sees a small table laden with food next to Pharaoh, and another chair placed at an angle so they both may see people approaching from up the stairs and also easily look at one another while speaking. Bilal notices the strategic placement with some admiration as he takes a seat.

Bilal's mind tells him he should somehow be more uncomfortable being this close to the Pharaoh-Ra. It was not that many days ago he was covered in the dust and sweat of the quarry, as a slave who could easily never see the Pharaoh but from a distance at best. That he could be here sitting next to him about to converse was beyond imagination, yet he was relaxed. Being in the presence of the Pharaoh he found put him at ease. This was something he could not easily wrap his head around, yet it made him smile on the inside.

"I trust my daughter has been a suitable tour guide?"

"She most certainly has Lord Pharaoh. She was quite thorough and most agreeable company. I know she is young, but I admit it is some of the most interesting conversation I have ever had. I have never known someone to have so much to say!" remarks Bilal with a smile.

Pharaoh-Ra laughs, "Yes, my daughter does not lack in conversation, nor opinion. You should find her most direct in her request of you, as you will find me Bilal. I would like to explain more why I have asked you to become my daughter's personal guardian and educate you about your position, responsibility and what it is I am truly requesting of you. Please be direct and honest in your replies and this will go well for us both."

"I don't understand it, but somehow both the directness of you and your daughter puts me at ease. I feel like I can be myself around you, unlike most people with whom I must guard myself. Why is this?" Asks Bilal a little shyly.

"I put no barriers up to you Bilal, nor does my daughter. You are likely to find there are a few others that give you this same sense of ease. Trust that sense of ease, for the energies of a person you are aware of never lie." Pharaoh-Ra leans to take a piece of fruit and before he eats it he continues, "Besides, I am Pharaoh, I can always have you killed as easily and I can spare you. I have no need to defend, all choice is mine." With that he eats the fruit awaiting Bilal's response with a spark of glee in his eyes and a faint smile.

Bilal is so surprised by this and the truth of it, he laughs a short laugh. "Ha! This is true but I get that this is not really the reason to have 'no barriers' as you put it."

"Very observant Bilal. You are correct. I choose to have no barriers to you because it gives me more awareness of all the energies you are, and of everyone around. It gives me infinite choice in all situations to have no barriers. It is a secret of being aware that few know, or ever discover. Having no defenses of being makes you the most powerful person in the room, not the weakest. Remember this."

"Yes Lord Pharaoh, I will. May I ask you about Ra-Milania?"

"Yes," says Pharaoh-Ra.

"Is it really appropriate for me to be with her every moment of the day? When she arises and when she goes to sleep? When she eats, bathes, and dresses? You truly wish me by her side, without anything being inappropriate? It is a little hard to comprehend you would trust me so completely with the Pharaoh-to-be. I mean, we have only just met."

"I must confess, though it did appear to be an accident that got you here Bilal, it was by design," says Pharaoh-Ra.

"We have been watching you for some time and ceased the moment to take you from the Laborer's Realm and the life you knew. We need your help Bilal. You are different, and I am not talking about the color of your eyes or hair, extraordinary as those are. You are not like most other people, you have qualities I seek to be surrounded by."

Pharaoh goes on, "Have you ever wondered how people could be so ugly to one another? Have you ever thought there must be something greater for how people could be with one another? A way of being that is like a warm embrace, inviting you to everything that is great about you and the other person, both?" Pharaoh pauses to see how Bilal replies.

"Why yes. Every day this is something I have yearned for,

dreamed about and wonder how I can go on for lack of finding it. When the ugliness of people is the most crushing I have gone to the cliffs edge at the quarry and stand contemplating if I shall jump. It is always the beauty of the land before me, the elements of the wind, the light, the heat and the quiet peacefulness of the earth that brings me back from that edge. Somehow I am renewed when I reach out and touch that beauty," says Bilal earnestly.

"Ah yes, I know of what you speak very well. It is the oneness. Have you heard of the oneness? The oneness is that breath of possibility whispering through every molecule. It is that warm embrace of being that the earth gives you when you reach out and connect with it and allow the beauty and presence of it to touch you the being. This connection with the earth is also possible with people when they are willing. Your awareness of this connection is only the beginning of what I speak of. I have asked you here to begin your education, should you choose it."

Bilal is smiling and his head is reeling, he is not sure why and he does not really get exactly what the Pharaoh is talking about; and yet somehow he knows it is everything he has known to be true and never heard spoken of before. He blurts; "What do you mean not an accident? The rocks fell on purpose? What is a molecule? That connection with the earth can be had with people? And there is more? Forgive me Lord Pharaoh, I speak out of turn." Realizing he got carried away in enthusiasm, he bows his head waiting for reprimand.

Pharaoh laughs, to Bilal's surprise there is no reprimand for speaking so. "Ah, you caught that about the rocks falling.

It was Mila who made those rocks come down. She has that much trust in the oneness, in herself and in you Bilal. She knew you would save her, and she may have helped a little."

"What? Really? I mean how?" He looks incredulously at the Pharaoh and at the same time a smile is quickly spreading across his face. There is such lightness in these words.

"That may take a bit to explain, but I will try and it will likely answer the rest of your questions as well. Would you like anything to eat? Please help yourself to anything here." Pharaoh waves his hand over the table of food and drink. Bilal now notices the cup that was set for him, already filled with drink and takes a sip. His eyes close as the most wonderful rich and fruity alcohol envelops his taste buds.

"Thank you Lord Pharaoh," says Bilal with a sigh. He has no idea what this drink is but he likes it very much.

Pharaoh-Ra begins.

"A molecule is the smallest element of physical creation. It is what makes up your body, these clothes, the food, this palace, everything. It is also what makes up the elements of water, the earth, air, fire and stone for example. What gives you that sense of connection and ability to sense the spaciousness you get with that connection is the oneness. You as a being are the oneness. You are the energy, the space and the oneness that makes that connection possible. You can choose to have that connection and function from it, or you can choose to refuse that connection. The more you refuse the possibility of that connection, the less you are aware of and capable of."

"The elements of the oneness are energy, space and consciousness. Every molecule in creation has an energy of its own, a space of being of its own and a consciousness of its own. Everything has an energetic element to it and the energy never lies. Energy does not ever diminish either, it can be changed however and you can request of it. Space is that sense you get when you are on the cliffs edge, when you are expanded, open, invigorated and your being is peaceful. Consciousness is the ruling element; your choices and request direct and invite the possibility for actualizing that which you request. The consciousness of every molecule responds to your request when you are being the oneness. Energy and space are the avenues through which your request is both made and delivered. Does that clarify things for you Bilal?"

Bilal notices somehow the Pharaoh spoke with more than just words, like he was being that which he was speaking about giving Bilal an experience of it. He was enthralled. "I am surprised to say yes, it does. How did you do that? It was like you were being what you were talking about and I was experiencing it."

"Again, very observant Bilal. You were experiencing it and you noticed, that is one of the things that makes you different. I am being the oneness when I speak of these things. When a person speaks congruently with what they are being it is very obvious. It takes someone who also speaks congruently with what they are being to notice this."

"So do you mean to say Mila requested of the rocks to come down?"

"Yes."

"And she knew I would grab her and somehow remove her from being crushed?" Bilal says questioning.

"Yes. She did not know how you would accomplish this, only that you would. What else did you notice about that moment?" inquires Pharaoh-Ra.

"Well, that I moved Mila, my father and myself an impossible distance that did not match my footsteps. How is that possible?" asks Bilal in wonderment.

"That is the power of the oneness and your request of it. It is never a question of 'how,' it is that you can. Would you be interested in training with such things? It is both Mila and my hope that you would join us in the exploration of increasing all of our capacities as the oneness."

Pharaoh is impressed with this young man before him. Brighter than most people he has met who are many years older, with far more extensive an education. *"He is very observant, he doesn't miss a thing,"* thinks the Pharaoh with delight.

"Really? You would train me in such things? That is why you brought me here? Wonderful, I would be deeply honored Lord Pharaoh. Yes, I would say yes. I do say yes." Bilal can hardly believe this could be his life. He is not quite sure what he is saying yes to, only that it is without reservation everything he knows he has been seeking and asking for but never had the words to express.

"Protection of my daughter is also truly required Bilal. And you have both the awareness and fighting skills to provide the kind of protection Mila may need one day." Pharaoh says a little cryptically. "I know it may seem unlikely but you are the kind of friend and companion we have all been asking for. And I don't know about you, but this isn't the kind of conversation

I usually have with someone I just met, or those whom I have known for many years for that matter."

Now it is Bilal's turn to laugh. "Well, since I have been at the palace it is the only kind of conversation I have had! Thank you, thank you Lord Pharaoh. My heart sings to know what you request, require and desire of me. I will do my best to fulfill it. This reminds me, the only other person I have ever heard speak as you do is The Builder Angyet. Will she be involved in training me?" The warmth of his heart increases to that tugging sensation he has had only a few times before.

As if on cue, Angyet steps out from the hidden Pathway pillars behind Bilal. Pharaoh sees her and welcomes her.

"As a matter of fact, yes she will be intimately involved and she is here right on time. Good day Angyet, you are looking radiant."

Bilal turns around wide-eyed to see Angyet approaching, he realizes she must have come from the hidden pillars Mila showed him the day before. She smiles at him and approaches Pharaoh kissing his hand. To touch Pharaoh is an indication of status few possess.

"Good day Lord Pharaoh. Bilal, it is wonderful to see you again." When she speaks all those sensations of her gentle touch return, embracing and expanding him; this time without physical touch.

"Angyet, good day. Thank you, very nice to see you as well," Bilal replies with a bit of a flush to his cheeks. His mind tells him he would like to be uncomfortable but once again he only melts into the nurturing relaxation of being without pretense or defense that he is learning comes with being in the presence of those who function as the oneness. He sits back as Angyet pulls up a chair conveniently close by to join them.

Chapter 17

"I was just discussing some of the fundamentals of the oneness with Bilal. He is quite astute. You have been very accurate in your recommendation of him Angyet," comments Pharaoh-Ra casually.

"You recommended me Angyet? I am so very grateful. But we have never met, how could you know me to suggest such a position? I don't understand." Bilal is a little bemused and curious what she will say.

"When a person has a deep connection with the oneness the knowing that is available goes far beyond the common interactions that people define as both knowing someone and connection. I do not have to meet you to know you more than you know yourself. I consider this a precious gift, an honor to know the depths of your being and the beauty of who you are as a person that functioning as oneness reveals."

Bilal would like to be embarrassed, yet finds it comforting the revelation of Angyet's exploration of him.

"Do you recall my question the night before last about the tug? That sense of connection and pull at your chest?"

"Yes, as a matter of fact I felt it again just before you entered the room," replies Bilal a little surprised with acknowledging his awareness of it.

"And are there other times you have noticed that sensation?" inquires Angyet.

"Yes, when I was alone on the cliffs edge at the quarry, each time before I have seen Mila which was when she was only a babe and when she came to the quarry," replies Bilal still confused.

"What if you were not alone there on the cliffs edge? The oneness was there embracing you Bilal. As you reach out into the spaciousness of that beautiful view and connect with the heat, the air, the light, the presence of the earth itself; were you not embraced? Did you not have the sense of returning to you, washed clean of the ugliness of the violent denial of being you have been surrounded by slaving in the quarries and fighting in death matches? Did it not undo and cleans you of your abhorrence of what Master Iberak and your father demand of you? Connection with the oneness always returns you to you dear Bilal."

Tears fall from Bilal's eyes unchecked. He is broken open and grateful for it. That she knows this about him is like coming home to a home he never knew existed. As Angyet speaks she evokes all she is describing in words, reaching into the depths of Bilal's world with a gentle presence that holds no judgment or wrongness. He melts into her embrace of being.

Angyet continues, "That tug at the cliffs edge was my presence...I was there observing you, seeing what you might choose. That you have the courage to take all the pain and suffering you see in the world and experience yourself on a day to day basis and yet choose to reach for connection with the beauty of this planet and find the space of beauty within you tells all of us who embrace the oneness everything we need to know about you. You have far more courage than you know Bilal. You have far more strength of character than most people are able to recognize. We are the ones who are honored to have you among us."

"That you know exactly of what we speak Bilal is why I trust you with my daughter and her very life. You are home now Bilal. As much as we are offering you, you gift us likewise with your presence," Pharaoh-Ra says softly.

Angyet hands Bilal a napkin to wipe his eyes. He has no words at the moment, his tears say it all. He looks Pharaoh-Ra and Angyet in the eyes both in turn; the gratitude radiating out in thanks of this unexpected acknowledgement and recognition.

Having a few minutes of silence, taking in the moment with each other Angyet speaks again, "This connection we speak of is only the beginning Bilal. You are naturally adept at connecting with the oneness. What we are offering is to educate you with what else is possible because of that connection. We will never tell you what to choose or what to do with that connection, we are only interested in you developing your unique capacities with it. Pharaoh-Ra, Mila and myself play with this connection, we practice and explore what we are capable of with it each day. There are a few others that you will be introduced to as well. We are inviting you to join in this practice of a way of being and functioning in the world, as oneness."

Pharaoh-Ra continues, "There is a lot more going on here than can be seen by the eyes. We could use your assistance. There is much more to tell. But first let us eat, the day is still young."

"I don't really know what to say. I am honored and grateful beyond words. You have seen the depths of me and put to words what is truly in my heart that I never could speak of, let alone find someone who might understand. That you find what is true to the core of me as valuable is so much more than I dare hope for. All I can say is yes, I will be here with you and for you." Bilal leans back in his chair taking in the moment and these two beautiful people sitting before him.

"Wonderful Bilal! Thank you," says Pharaoh-Ra.

The three of them help themselves to the food and drink before them, enjoying each other's presence and new found camaraderie.

"I have to ask, what is this drink? I have never tasted anything so wonderful," says Bilal taking another sip.

"It is a special blend of fruits prepared over several years for each batch, my personal brewer has created it. He won't give the secret of it even to me, but he calls it 'Nefertari', as it is the most beautiful flavor!" replies Pharaoh-Ra, taking a sip himself.

Bilal looks around and notices how quiet it is. "How is it so quiet, where is everyone?"

"I have asked for privacy. Believe me this is not normal to have it so quiet especially early in the morning as the palace prepares for the day. What we speak of is not for common knowledge and I do not wish to be overheard. We will move to my private chambers, but first let us eat then walk the gardens a bit. I wish to show you around myself some and tell you about the palace."

The three of them enjoy their meal together in silence and the satisfaction of their new found and blossoming friendship.

In this burst of expanded oneness blossoming in the palace, those with the dark heart of conspiracy walking in the shadows are becoming a little more pale in its wake.

Chapter 18

Ra-Maharet sat indignantly looking at the man before her. Jahi is an initiate and the head Mover's hand servant. "Why are you here and not Eka-ar?" asks Ra-Maharet with irritation.

"I am sorry your majesty, he is running late and he had sent me to tell you he cannot get here in time. He would ask you do not wait but rather give him until tomorrow," says Jahi apologetically.

"Tell him it better be good news and worth the wait. Do not make me wait again." With that she gets up and leaves.

Jahi follows behind bowing his head up and down.

"Yes, yes I will tell him."

She steps into the pillars of The Pathway at the entrance of the Temple of the Movers and out into the hallway next to her rooms. She has asked Pharaoh to place pillars of The Pathway within her rooms, but he says that now that the Builder Hamadi is dead he does not know how to do it. The secrets were not passed on. She thinks he is lying but she cannot prove it and cannot call him on it. She is greatly annoyed with the lack of control and not getting her way.

No new pillars had been built in many years, since before she was wife of Pharaoh. She knew Pharaoh had pillars within his rooms, and she knew of two hidden pillars in the public rooms on the lower floors. There must be more, but she had not been able to discover them yet. Clenching her fist she was determined she would. Six years as wife-of-Pharaoh and she continued to find things Pharaoh has kept from her. She tells herself it does not matter, she has the Movers on her side. This is far greater than any secrets the Pharaoh thinks he has. Only briefly she doubts her request to have her own chambers separate from Pharaoh. It had been a few years now and she wondered if it did not give her as much advantage as she supposed. She lifts her chin a bit, convincing herself she was right and banishing the thoughts of doubt.

The Movers have the singular capacity of moving objects without physically touching them. They have become a cult of sorts over the decades. Growing in numbers they have gained seekers, initiates looking to be trained. To keep it elite and difficult to attain they have developed complex form and structure into ritual and hidden teachings. They create their mystic and intrigue with elaborate public display of their capacity. Elevating themselves with the combination of public display and secrecy; they slowly have gained power and influence. Even the ear of Pharaoh-Ra's spouse Ra-Maharet.

Dressed in saffron robe and acting with great ceremony, the Movers are the ones to transport the huge stones from the quarry to the construction site of the pyramid. Foundation stones, each the size of a small house are levitated a few inches from the ground. Standing three to each side and one in front and back the incomprehensibly large stones smoothly float as though on water with each step of the Movers. They are also the ones to move the stones into place; all without physical touch of the stone.

Eka-ar, Keeper of The Movers is swiftly becoming one of the most influential men in all of Pharaoh's Land. He and his Movers are an impressive power inviting awe, even worship amongst the people. Eka-ar has secretly placed his loyalty with Ra-Maharet, betting on both his own position and her ambitiously grand vision to alter the course of all of Pharaoh's Land.

The guards open the doors for Ra-Maharet to enter her rooms and she looks with satisfaction at the splendor of her chambers and the view of the gardens and Keeper's Realm spreading out from her balcony. From the balcony and far to her right is a full view of construction of the pyramid. As the pyramid rises from the desert floor so does the power and prestige of the Pharaoh. Ra-Maharet revels in the progress of its construction and all it means to her and her future.

Chapter 19

Seeing they are all finished eating Pharaoh rises and says, "Angyet, will you please gather Mila to my rooms and met us there? Come Bilal, let us walk."

As they move down the stairs Pharaoh looks to his right nodding to a man who stands twenty paces away, he looks as though he had been waiting. He scurries off to the far end of the great hall opening the doors and people stream in. The guards at the garden end of the hall stand at attention while the Pharaoh-Ra and Bilal pass by and out. There is a small crowd waiting at the bottom of the steps here as well. They look excited upon sight of the Pharaoh and begin to move forward to speak with him if they may. Seeing Pharaoh-Ra is accompanied they pause assessing if they may approach or not. The crowd slumps seeing the Pharaoh engaged with Bilal. The crowd whispers among themselves. Most have heard of this man, grand in stature and striking appearance with hair the color of wheat to his waist and eyes the color of the bright blue sky. They all step aside, clearing a path and allowing them to pass.

The Pharaoh himself has been describing the layout of the palace and where things are. He asks Bilal, "Has Mila told you about the hidden pillars?"

"Yes, she has. She would like me to have it a game that I may guess where they are. She would like to see if I can find them on my own," replies Bilal.

"Well maybe we will play a bit of a trick with my daughter. There are several I would like you to know of and not wait to guess where they might be. When I say you have full access for protection of my daughter, I mean it. I would like you to be able to do this well. Your task is large enough and you will have work to do. It is my desire to give you full advantage with everything that is at your disposal.

"My personal guards you shall be introduced to and I would like them to make you familiar with the palace grounds in person. There are some things even they do not know, that you must. I would request you lend your fighting expertise and skills to their training. In addition I would ask that you put in extra time and effort with my daughter's guards. She has asked to be able to select her own and has already begun the process. I'm sure she will tell you all about it."

"As for Angyet, she is The Builder as you know. This means much more than just being in charge of the construction of the pyramid. A Builder's true purpose and talent is in their capacities functioning as oneness. A Builder is someone who is an architect of reality, able to create a future based upon the request of the molecules and having connection with all things. She shares my vision of creating a future far greater than that which is the currently apparent direction of things. I will wait until we are all together with my daughter before I say more. This is just to say, you are being invited to a much bigger purpose and target than protection of my daughter, though that will be a vital part of it all. Is this agreeable so far Bilal?" asks Pharaoh.

"Yes Lord Pharaoh," replies Bilal simply.

"Please never be shy about asking questions or sharing your concerns or hesitations with anything that is presented to you. You are invited to be part of my life, my world and the creation of the future of all of Pharaoh's Land. It is very important that you are choosing of your own free will and in full awareness of what you are being asked to take part in." Pharaoh-Ra has stopped walking to face Bilal. He touches his arm lightly and looking him in the eyes continues, "I have nothing to hide from you Bilal, you are free to ask anything. I do not say this lightly or to be polite."

"I understand Lord Pharaoh, I will not hold back. All that you have spoken of shows me that what I hoped only in my heart of hearts is truly possible. To know that the oneness I have glimpsed can be so much more than a moment of reprieve from the ugliness and smallness of life is like a burden lifted from my very being. That I personally could play a part in the creation of living beyond that smallness is greater than I dare dream before. I think I might not ever sleep again I am so excited to learn more!" Bilal replies with enthusiasm.

With a twinkle in his eyes Pharaoh replies, "Well then, let us delay no more. Shall we meet with Ra-Milania and Angyet?" He does not wait for reply but turns the corner around the pool of the garden and to a huge pillar of the garden walkway. He walks around the side that is away from the line of site from every direction. "Touch my shoulder Bilal, there is a set of pillars here." He looks ahead at the pillar in front of them noticing two lines carved as grooves marking The Pathway. It looks like part of the carving that decorates the great pillars. Touching Pharaoh's shoulder they step forth and out into the private chambers of Pharaoh-Ra.

Mila and Angyet are sitting close to each other talking quietly and intently with one another. Without hearing a sound, but sensing the energy, they both turn and look as Bilal and the Pharaoh enter the room.

"Bilal!" says Mila as she jumps up and runs to him, arms out stretched. She jumps up into his arms with a big hug.

Pharaoh-Ra looks with feigned displeasure, "What about me?"

Giggling Mila wriggles her way out of Bilal's arms to be let to the floor and just as enthusiastically says, "Ra!" and jumps into her father's arms kissing him all over the face. Holding her in his arms he walks to the seats arranged for all of them and sets down Mila. She stands on the couch next to him as he takes a seat, his arm still around her small waist. She leans on her father with her arm around his neck, the usual ear-to-ear grin on her face as she looks at Bilal and Angyet seated before them.

Mila can't contain herself, she blurts out, "What did you

talk about so far?" She would like to say so much more but manages to stop herself by biting her lip while she looks back and forth between her father and Angyet.

Pharaoh-Ra speaks first looking at Bilal, while speaking to Mila saying, "We have introduced the basics of the oneness and how it works, but not in terms of what might be possible in how to apply it or ways to practice increasing his capacities. I have told him of your guards, but have left it to you to explain what you are doing and what you would like his help with. You will have to leave time for him to work with my guards as well little Mila," he says with a wink to his daughter. "I have waited for all of us to be together before sharing our greater vision for the future and about those who oppose us in our endeavors."

"Okay" says Mila, satisfied she has not missed anything she wanted to be part of.

Chapter 20

A ngyet speaks next, "Do you have any questions so far, Bilal?"

"Connecting with the beauty of the earth and what you are telling me is the capacity for connecting with the oneness; I always looked to as a way to feel better. To know that I could go on living through what I faced each day. Are you saying it is the connection with the oneness that made it so Mila could pull down the rocks at the quarry, and so that I could move us all out of the way in what looked to be an impossible situation? Can you explain more, it is still so unbelievable even though I have seen it with my own eyes and participated!" asks Bilal.

"Yes," replies Angyet. "As Ra has said the oneness allows us to request of it. It does not matter how this is possible, the important part is to know that it *is* possible. The oneness is always looking to support and create more oneness, so any choice that contributes to that will be brought to fruition most quickly and dynamically. All three of us have desired to make it possible for you to come here to the palace and though it is in Pharaoh's power to take you from Master Iberak and your family that path would not have been the best choice for a number of reasons. When you follow the awareness the connection with oneness imparts, everything always turns out greater than we can imagine on our own."

"Both Master Iberak and your father have been very invested in both using you and molding your future for their gain, there is very little that was possible for breaking that grip and the future they were aiming for. All of us prefer an outcome that is both greater for all involved and that people either don't fight, or have no ability to stop. We did not plan the events, we followed the energies of the oneness allowing it to lead us to the possibilities we all were asking for."

"For example, Mila knew to accompany her father to the quarry that day and use her age to appear to be out of control as any inquisitive five year old wandering about giving her hand servant trouble would appear to be. Seeing your position next to the mountain of rocks with only you and your father close at hand was the ideal situation to create something that would give reason for taking you from your life as a slave in the quarries. Saving Mila's life would create such a reason. It was not pre-planned, it was unfolding and obvious to those with the awareness to follow the energy and recognize the opening presenting itself."

"Mila pulling down the rocks allowed you to step into capacities you did not know you had and save Mila's life at the same time. This in turn gave a publicly justifiable reason for the Pharaoh to be able to take you from Master Iberak that he could not refuse, end your father having what in his mind was cause for beating you and making you fight, and allow you and your parents to be moved close to the palace that we may easily and without intervention invite you here. This is just the obvious parts of what was created by all of our requests of the oneness and following the energy. The very universe itself conspires to deliver what we request of it. So, it is also your request Bilal that has brought you to us and created you sitting here today."

Bilal is stunned. It is so plain and obvious yet baffles the mind that this could be possible and knowable – and he could in no way deny the truth of it. So much of what he had been asking for his entire life was coming to fruition in these few short days with the unfolding of these events.

"As I am sure Ra has said to you, it is not a question of how, it is that we can. We never have to figure out how, we get the adventure of finding out the magical ways the oneness will deliver our requests. We can always trust that it will eventually, in a way far greater than we could come up with on our own. Every element of creation is by our side supporting us if we will but ask. And reality is far more changeable and shapeable than most imagine. I wonder what you might imagine and request Bilal?"

"This is so much more than I have ever considered. I dare say, I am sure I do not have an answer for you!" says Bilal wide-eyed and rapt with attention to every word Angyet has said.

They all laugh.

"Well, I am sure we will all enjoy finding out as you continue to explore this new world of possibility opening up to you Bilal," Pharaoh says contentedly. "Truly this is just the beginning of your introduction. And there is much more to reveal of our current situation."

It is now Mila that continues, "It is my mother," she says with a bit of sadness. "She is working to make sure I never become Pharaoh and will try to take the place of father if she can. She thinks we do not know, but even I can tell and I am only five. She is not very bright and she thinks she is very sneaky. She plots against us with The Movers."

"Oh," says Bilal in surprise. "Tell me about the Movers. I have seen them in the quarry as they make their way to the pyramid with the stones. How do they do that with making the stones float in the air and move like a boat on the water? Surely they are very powerful."

"Well they certainly think they are," replies Angyet with a smile. "The Movers are like a newborn baby in terms of their capacities with connecting with the oneness. They think this one capacity of moving objects without touching them is the penultimate in power and ability. They seriously lack in imagination. To move objects without touching them is impressive to see, yet is only one small thing. You have noticed the ceremony and how they always have six of the Movers to transport the stones? I can do what they do by myself, Bilal."

"Somewhere in days past a man sold enough people on the idea of the greatness of this one aspect of connecting with the oneness to create a following. He turned this simple act of connection and request into complex ritual, form and structure. He did this to make sure what he taught would be difficult to achieve and require his tutelage and approval. He created a structure for having power over people by making him and his teachings the source of this possibility. His name was 'Runihura' and his legacy lives on past his days. His name means 'the destroyer' and he certainly has reached far in creating destruction of people's awareness of what is true of the oneness. You will find the universe has a perverse sense of humor and the truth is always revealed in ways one would never expect. As this man's name reveals so much of what he is about and created."

Pharaoh-Ra continues, "My wife has whole-heartedly bought into the glamorous powers of the Movers and she thinks they will give her the powers she seeks to take and keep the seat of Pharaoh. They also work to usurp the purposes and function of the pyramid itself and they believe because of their position in placing the stones they will be able to accomplish this. They know Angyet is a Builder and in theory can single handedly replace them. The advantage we have is they have not ever seen Angyet do what they do, so they have convinced themselves she is not as powerful as they are. We keep them in the dark with as much as we are able to so they may remain blinded in their delusions of grandeur and power."

"My wife would have to kill me and my daughter to take over and she is willing to do so. At this point we are fairly sure she waits only for the completion of construction of the pyramid, if that. We have no doubts of her intent and what she works towards, it is only a matter of the pieces falling into place that she feels secure enough to make her move. So as you see the most imminent threat is within our very walls," says Pharaoh-Ra with a sigh.

"I see," says Bilal, very surprised. "This may be a little blunt, but why have you not arrested her already, or put her to death if both your and Mila's life is threatened? If you know of what she plots, why not stop her now?"

Pharaoh-Ra replies, "Well, as ill intent as she has, it is my hope that there is still a chance for a different possibility. I have no reason to hope this, but I cannot help but provide every opportunity for her to take a different direction. I still care about her, it is because of that caring that I am not so hasty to move against her. We always have choice, no trajectory is set. A point will come where all the doors of possibility close, until that day I will be patient."

Angyet continues, "Our willingness to know this and be completely aware in every moment is what keeps us safe. We see Ra-Maharet for who she is. We are all far more than a hundred steps in front of her, however we cannot always arm ourselves against every stupidity. Your willingness to contribute to the safety of Mila exponentialize all of our capacities and awareness. The connection we are willing to have with each other as the oneness makes us a thousand times stronger and more aware to the degree we are all willing to have that connection. This is why you are here Bilal."

"Not only do you help keep me safe, we all get to play with the oneness! It is the most fun thing ever! You'll see. My mother does not like to play. She is very serious and likes to be the most significant person in the room. She would demand the sun to shine on her all day if she could command it," says Mila rolling her eyes. "We have all tried to show her the sun really would shine on her if she was willing to request it, receive it and have the connection that would allow all she requests to show up. She does not understand that request is far more powerful than demanding obedience to her will."

Pharaoh-Ra goes on, "She believes request is for the weak and lowly. She sees her position as a place to command from, she wishes to rule over all. This goes against everything that I aim for and is true for me as Pharaoh of this Land. I look to empower each person to be greater than they think they can be. I invite everyone to be connected to the oneness and bring forth that which would bring them joy of living. I know this is a radical departure from the past and what all have known and expect a Pharaoh to be. It is not what a Pharaoh is according to anything they know. Many reject the very idea of such independence and freedom. They look to me to rule over them and run their lives. I can do that. I have been trained my entire life to do so. I seek something else and I welcome and embrace those who would contribute to this endeavor. I see you as such a person Bilal. Am I mistaken?"

"No Lord Pharaoh, you are not. You continue to put words to my lifelong heart's desire. You speak of a world I would like to live in and a life I would like to have. And you have already shown me it is something I can have, it is mine for the asking. I know how much you have given me that opens me to that of which you speak. I have no words for the depth of gratitude I have for your invitation," replies Bilal. "You have plucked me from the depths of a miserable existence and given me a sense of ease of being that has been difficult to achieve in the life I have known. Or course your generosity of home and fine clothes, good food and beautiful environment sure makes it a lot easier too!"

He smiles. "It has been a miracle of transformation for both me and my parents. Every day we celebrate and give thanks for the generosity you have shown us. We savor and soak in the elegance and decadence of the ease you have bestowed upon us. I would like to show you my thanks, not just speak it in words. I will be by Mila's side as long as she will have me there."

Mila goes to Bilal hugging him, she now rests her head on his large shoulder. "Thank you Bilal. Can I show you my guards now?"

Pharaoh-Ra replies, "Yes, this is good for now. It is much to take in and we can continue this conversation later. How about a meal this evening, we can continue then. Please return to my chambers at that time."

Plans for increasing the oneness are now moving as rapidly forward as the plans for taking over the pyramid and turning it into a source of power over rather than the empowerment of all that it is meant for.

Chapter 21

The sun is high and finally Eka-ar arrives in Ra-Maharet chambers. He is elated with the latest plans with the pyramid's construction. The Movers have discovered how to ensure the secret chamber in the center of the Pyramid is created as they would like.

Angyet shares construction plans only as needed with the Movers as they require for proper placement of each stone. The base has had enough stones placed that it is revealing the simple inner layout of the pyramid. They have worked diligently to take over and alter the construction plans sufficiently to their needs. Eka-ar and Arphiro have been piecing it together and now have the information they were missing. Angyet was never there when they placed the stones, so they assumed she trusted them totally to place them as she asked and instructed.

The plans show no entrance, no way to get into the center chamber. The Movers think it is supposed to be representational and not a functional space. The true powers of the Builder are inconceivable to them. That Angyet could transport herself there by request they cannot and do not imagine or consider possible.

They have figured out how to create an entrance without the Builder Angyet knowing. They assume no one will ever actually go into this space since there is no entrance, except by the secret way they have devised and will now begin to construct. Gaining access will give them control of the powers of the pyramid by entering the center and holding their ceremonies there. The most magnificent gathering of energies the world has ever known. They have deducted that this will amplify their powers beyond what they can imagine giving them everything they require to seize what they already consider rightfully theirs; the seat of Pharaoh.

Ra-Maharet commands everyone to leave her rooms as Eka-ar lays out the papyrus papers with the altered construction plans drawn out. When the room has cleared he says with exaltation, "Come look. We did it! We did it!" Eka-ar points out the alterations and explains the simple movement of stone required to reveal the access from the outside. It will be invisible except to the very few who know. It is perfect.

Ra-Maharet looks down her nose in triumph, a devious smile and sparkle in her eyes. Their plans are coming to fruition. "Let us drink to our success Eka-ar! Our day is coming, and not a thing is suspected! You are brilliant, brilliant my friend!" They toast to their success and sit back reveling in their own brilliance, congratulating themselves.

Eka-ar has left Ra-Maharet's chambers. As she passes by, her guard is returning from escorting Eka-ar to the door. He comments, "I do not like how he looks at you!"

She raises an eyebrow, "Oh really?" Biting her lip she leans in and grabs hold of his crotch saying, "Just because you have had this between my legs you think you have the right?"

She squeezes his crotch more firmly. "You have no right to be jealous unless I tell you to be." Leaning into him, she whispers his name, "Re-iyk."

She lets go and saunters off, being sure to exaggerate the sway of her hips, taunting him, as is one of her favorite pastimes.

It is late in the night when the palace is quiet. Only in the dark and quiet of night it is that Re-iyk may go to her. He moves silently and stands waiting for her to acknowledge him. She keeps her back to him knowing he waits, finally she turns beckoning him to her bed. She slips the strings of her dress off the shoulders leaving her bare to the waist as she climbs on the bed.

He strips his clothes as he heads to her. Pulling him to her with a deep kiss, she turns his body pushing him down, she straddles him. Pinning his shoulders she kisses him briefly. A flicker of the tongue on his ear lobe, her bare breasts graze his chest. Running her tongue lightly across his lower lip, pulling back as he moves toward her; she will not allow another full kiss. Pushing him down again she reaches for scarves tucked in the bedding and ties his hands to the bed. He yearns to touch her and is both frustrated and aroused by his incapacities of being tied.

Teasing him, taunting with fleeting kisses, the touch of his body always a little less than satisfying; she rides him to the familiar moans indicating he is at the brink of release then stops. She whispers as she releases his bonds, "I am done with you."

Rising from his lust filled body and leaving the bed, she once again sways the curves of her hips, letting the light catch her body's contours. He punches the pillow next to him in the frustration of denial of completion. It is a rare moment that she allows him all he desires, only often enough to keep him reaching for more.

Ra-Maharet only smiles to herself as she walks away, running her finger along the table as she had been touching his body only moments ago. Oh how she loves to torture this man.

He grabs his clothes and storms off looking for some cold water to dowse himself with.

So many get pleasure and joy from the sense of jealousy, wanting and lack they can create in others. Women such as Ra-Maharet thrive in their malice and sense of power over others. Yet there are a few who live their life happy for no particular reason, generous with everyone in their joy of living.

Chapter 22

Maafah had been a beggar on the streets of the palace city for as long as anyone could recall. He was old, a man of skin and bone and deep sun drenched wrinkles. No one knows anything about him except that he is old, yet somehow never dies. For no particular reason he had always been happy. Anyone looking at him could see no good reason for his joyful kindness, yet no matter what life brought his way this was his bent in life. He could find the humor in anything.

When the Movers announced they were recruiting new disciples he knew immediately this was something he desired to be. Maafah had mostly kept it to himself that he already has some skill with moving objects. He would sometimes use it to make money by entertaining people with his skill. Mostly he would move things without touching them for his own amusement while alone in his shack. He loves the spinning lightness of energy that rushed through him when he did. It always left him with a sense of well being and he would sleep peacefully in its wake.

From all realms recruits were vying for position as a Mover. Those chosen would have the honor of moving and placing the stones of the pyramid. It would be their skill that would erect this great monument; a spectacular achievement to be part of.

Today was the day for the testing to begin. The Keeper of the House of Movers was known as Eka-ar. A very serious man, he stood before the gathering crowd and when satisfied with enough initiates having gathered he described how the testing would work.

Upon meeting Eka-ar, Maafah thought to himself with a giggle, *"What an angry uptight man, surely he must have constipation."*

The testing for consideration was simple. Five stones set in a row arranged by size. The smallest would fit in the palm of a child's hand and the largest was roughly the size of a person's head. The test was to move any of them as high off the ground as one was able to. Nothing else was specified.

It had been several hours and few had done more than wiggle a few of the smaller stones. One younger girl had lifted a medium size stone just briefly. Another man lifted the largest stone swiftly hurtling it a good twenty feet in the air to the applaud of the onlookers. He smugly took a bow and greeted Eka-ar as someone entitled to be accepted by the Keeper of the Movers.

Maafah noticed he just let the stone drop to the ground, it was not controlled on the descent. It made for a good spectacle, but lacked finesse of any kind.

Just a few more people and it was Maafah's turn. He sat a few feet from the stones, clapped his hands together rubbing them as though to warm up and reached out relaxed. Sometimes he liked to use his hands movement to encourage the motion of the objects he would be moving without touch. Instantly all five stones rise into the air smoothly and simultaneously stopping at a height of four feet. The crowd begins to cheer. Then with a slight rotation of his finger in the air the second largest stone begins to circle around the largest. Then the next smaller begins to circle around the one larger than it. Maafah spreads the stones out in the air making room for the next smaller to be circled by the one smaller than that. By the time Maafah had all the stones spinning around each other the crowd had gone silent again and began pressing closer to get a better look. They were in utter awe of the spectacle. Just as simply Maafah then lowered the stones in place gently and arranging them in the opposite order that had been originally presented.

The crowd exploded in an uproarious cheer. Maafah looked to Eka-ar and the previous man trying out, who was scowling. Maafah bowed to Eka-ar and gave the angry man next to him a wink. Bursting into laughter himself he welcomed the celebration of his skill from the crowd. Recovering the stunned look on his face, Eka-ar approached Maafah reaching out to shake his hand. "Well done, well done. Welcome to the House of Movers."

That was two years ago. The first five recruits from that day years ago were initiated into the House of Movers. Twenty others had been invited to undergo rigorous training to see if they could develop the skills needed for moving the massive stones that would construct the pyramid. Maafah had become a teacher beside Eka-ar, as his refined skill, patience and kindness created quicker and more lasting results than Eka-ar's heavy handed demand.

Only fifteen of the initiates continued on as they began to improve in their skill with the endless practice and indoctrination into the complex beliefs Eka-ar insisted were fundamental to the skill of being a Mover. He was very strict and anyone not willing to fall in line with what he demanded where relieved of their participation. He followed his teacher Runihura's tradition and style of instruction to the letter.

With Maafah's easy going nature it was a wonder he remained. Personally, he knew that not much of what Eka-ar taught as a belief system had anything to do with the ability of Moving. It was more often his touch of the student's shoulder while practicing, the words of encouragement and the student's trust in themselves that they could do it that created the ability. He kept this to himself however, as he loved both working with the students and the grand and important task of moving and setting the pyramid stones. He never put much stock in other people anyway, so it was easy for him to appear to go along with what Eka-ar demanded and yet choose to live by what he knows to be true. He knew he was making a difference with the students and contributing to the development of more Movers.

When a beggar can become an inspiring teacher, surely a child can know what she desires to create as her future. The child Pharaoh-to-be, Ra-Milania has the privilege to make it so at her request and by following the energies of oneness.

Chapter 23

Ra-Milania had asked her father if she could create her own guard. Men she could pick out herself and that would train on their own, separate from the others. She said he could have the final say, and this would be in addition to his guards, not in replacement of; at least yet. Pharaoh thought it an odd request for a five-year-old, but it had been her day of birth celebration and he was quite used to both unusual requests from her, as well as granting anything she asked for.

He asked her why she would ask for such a thing and her reply is that it was practice for when she would be Pharaoh. She desired to practice her knowing with regard to people, among the other skills she put to practice.

It has been almost a year and she still is not very satisfied with her results so far, all except Kylar.

Kylar is her best guard. She has made him leader of her guards in training as he is one of the few who truly appreciates her capacities and embraces the vision she has for them all. He knows his task of recruitment and training that Mila has given him and he works diligently to fulfill her request for a competent team of guards.

He is wonder struck with her request and awareness of what she both requires and desires. Who knew a child could have such clarity and knowing. It makes him proud to serve such a one as her. Whatever her future held he wanted to be there to see it and be part of it, he would contribute all he was capable to achieve her request.

Kylar's family has been Keepers of Arms for fifty-eight generations. They have supplied all weaponry, armor and metallurgy for the House of Pharaoh. Many of their family members have also been guards in the House of Pharaoh, though Kylar is the first in a long time to have a true appreciation and interest in the oneness. Something he has kept to himself until knowing Ra-Milania.

Mila sits on Bilal's shoulder which is her new favorite thing to do ever since their first meeting. As they arrive at her personal guard's training grounds and building she asks Bilal to set her down at the seating area, which was created presumably for her to be able to easily watch her guard train. "Please wait here Bilal. I would like a moment to speak with my Keeper." She walks towards the building entrance that is across from the seating area. Before she reaches the door a young man steps out and kneels before Mila. Bilal notices his hair is unusually lighter than most for someone with such dark skin. Most with the tight curls of someone having heritage of the south of Pharaoh's Land have black hair.

They speak intently and after just a few minutes she beckons Bilal to join them.

"Bilal I would like you to meet someone. This is Kylar, he is Keeper of my guard. He has just been telling me of some new recruits filled with possibility. Kylar, this is Bilal, my new personal guardian." Mila is bursting with obvious joy for them meeting.

Kylar stands saying; "It is a pleasure. Your reputation precedes you. I am happy to be working with you. You have many skills we could use training on." He says with a wink and extending to shake his hand. Bilal is a little hesitant, no one had every reached to shake his hand before and this man seems to know him somehow though he does not recall having ever met.

Taking his hand, Bilal looks him in the eyes and he is taken aback. He does not let it show on his face, but he is truly surprised to see such green eyes. There is only one other person he has ever seen with green eyes. This was most unexpected. He only utters, "The pleasure is mine."

"Please show us what you've got," says Mila. They head to the side of the mini arena where the elevated seats are arranged for shade and ease of viewing. Kylar returns in a few minutes with twelve new faces whom he has stand in formation. They will be performing a series of drills to start.

As Bilal and Mila take their seats, Mila begins to explain what she is up to. "I am looking for particular skills and personality. I am looking for those who do not fear the oneness."

"How will you know?" Asks Bilal.

"You'll see, watch this." Mila says with a devious look in her eyes.

The men and what appear to be not much older than boys line up in two rows of six and begin their drills. They first turn to the left and march in unison for fifteen feet, then about face coming back to where they started.

Mila whispers to Bilal, "See that guard walking in the rear of the group, watch this." With the slight wave of her finger towards the ground the young man suddenly stops. As he was taking the next step forward his back leg will not lift from the ground. The young man looks around confused, he starts pulling on his leg trying to move it.

Mila begins to giggle. Energetically she has pinned his foot to the ground. Seeing that he is starting to get distressed and pulling on his leg harder, she lets his foot loose and he stumbles.

The other men training with him hear his confusion at suddenly being unable to move. They rush over to him asking if he is okay and what happened. He has no idea, but Kylar does. This one obviously won't do, he tells one of the trainees that looked most bothered to take him back inside in the shade for some water. The rest he called back into formation.

The two head inside and mumble amongst themselves, the older of the two in training explaining the little he knows of the powers of the Pharaoh-to-be. It is alarming and keeps many of the guards in wonder and fear; never knowing what she might do or what she is really capable of.

The few guards who have become sort of used to it usually find it humorous, though it does disturb most of them.

How is it possible that such a little girl could have so much power and ability to control men's bodies that they can't move? It utterly baffles the mind. Some of them feel lucky to be in the presence of such greatness. Others tremble in fear and would rather be doing anything else, be anyplace else in the palace than in the presence of the Pharaoh's daughter Ra-Milania.

This is how Ra-Milania weeds out the ones that she will keep. She messes with their mind using her abilities with the oneness to see who has the courage to stay. She is only interested in the ones who respect her and are open to the magical possibilities of the oneness. Those who fear the oneness she will leave to other people to serve and protect.

Now back to reviewing the possible recruits. They have now been instructed to do different formations with sword in hand. Wooden practice swords drawn, they begin. Mila puts her attention on one of the younger of the lot. This time she stops his arm from swinging, the boy looks wide-eyed then giggles. She lets his arm go, and on the next movement stops his arm in mid motion again. He giggles again. This continues for another minute each time Mila stops him and then releases him again he laughs more until he just can't stop himself from outright laughter. All stop now looking at him quizzically, except Kylar who looks to Mila who is also giggling with an ear-to-ear grin.

"We have a possibility with this one," thinks Kylar. Mila motions to Kylar to bring the boy to her. Composing himself

he approached with Kylar. Smiling Mila says, "What's your name?"

The boy drops to one knee still grinning. "I am called Zek," he replies.

"How old are you Zek?" Asks Mila.

"I am twelve," says Zek with pride.

"You are a little young for a guard aren't you? What makes you think you can be my guard?"

"Well," he says a little hesitantly.

"Don't be shy Zek, tell me," says Mila.

"Well, you are also young and when you grow up you will need someone big like me, older I mean. And by the time you need me I can be ready. And was that really you who made it so I could not move my arm? Can you do it again? That was so funny!" exclaims Zek. He suddenly catches himself being so informal and straightens up, becoming silent but still smiling ear-to-ear, head bowed.

"Yes we can do that again, but not today. I like that you are thinking of both my future and your own. Kylar continue with your exercises, Bilal and I will be going now. Zek, you must work very hard to make sure you are ready, and I will be happy to have you as one of my guards. Listen to everything Kylar teaches you."

"Really?" Zek jumps up in the air with excitement. "Thank you. I will not disappoint you."

With that Kylar gets back to work with the young men and Bilal and Mila head out. They will return to Mila's rooms to have a meal and talk more about her guards. They step just outside the arena and Mila looks around to see that there are no people. Taking Bilal's hand and pulling him to the side she says, "Here Bilal. It's another set of pillars, do you see it?" He notices some of the rocks of the wall are a different pattern than the rest of the wall, looking wider he sees the outline of a door. "Ah very sneaky, yes I see the outline of a door in the rock wall," he says with a smile and they step forward and out into Mila's rooms.

The world of possibilities for something greater is so much more vast and inclusive than Bilal had ever considered. He never thought it could be so practical as well.

Chapter 24

"We still have awhile before meeting father and Angyet, but I'm hungry now. Let's eat something!" says Mila with a sigh and plopping down on her day bed. "Piloma, please bring something to eat."

Bilal sits next to her on the day bed again, as he did the day before. "So what is the plan with Kylar and these guards of yours Mila?"

"I wanted to see how good I could do at finding guards who would be willing to be connected to the oneness. I will be Pharaoh one day and I like what my father is doing. I wish to continue what he is aiming for, but I am not going to wait for him to be gone before I start. Besides, all of us working together makes it easier to achieve. The more people there are to play with and create our future, the faster that future can show up," says Mila matter-of-fact.

"I like that. Can you tell me about Kylar? How did you meet him? What made you pick him Mila?" inquires Bilal.

Mila replies, "Oh yes! His family has a very long history of being guardians for my family and providing swords and armor. Longer than anyone remembers his family has served my family. His father is always here at the palace, so Kylar has been here many times. Whenever there is an occasion for family to be here he would come. He was always friendly to me, not like other older kids who would pretend to be interested or nice because of who I am. He was different. He actually would talk with me like a grown up person instead of treating me like a stupid and annoying child. He was already in my father's guard so I asked him if he would help me."

"I see," says Bilal. "And how did you know he was interested in what you are asking for?"

"It started with the way he would speak to me and that he always has questions and was genuinely interested in what I have to say. Then, there was one time when I was being dismissed by someone because they are an adult and I am a child. They had neither the rank or position to speak to me in such a way and Kylar put them in their place. Most people would have ignored it. He made them bow to me in a public spectacle that honored who I am and who I will be. He showed me his support when he did not have to." Mila smiles recalling the moment.

"He was the first person I asked to join my guard. Then I got to spend more time with him and I learned of his interest in the oneness. He had kept it hidden from his family as they respect and fear the capacities of oneness but have no interest in it. They think it a kind of mystery thing, not something that can be used to make every day easier and more wonderful," replies Mila.

"He has proven to be good at finding those who would be loyal and who have a possibility of connection with the oneness and he is good with people. Most people like him and he has a way of making it easier for people to enjoy themselves. He actually recommended you, you know."

With a look of surprise Bilal says, "What, really? I have never met him before today, how can that be? I did notice he seemed to think he knows me."

"He knows all about you. He said he has been to almost every fight you have ever had. He said you can do things that people should not be able to do at your age. He said you always win."

"This is true. I do always win." Bilal says this without pride.

"He says you can teach him how to fight better than anyone. He says you would be the best to make guardians that are greater than anyone has ever seen before. He is very impressed with your skills." Mila beams with admiration of Bilal as she is discovering the kind of man she has plucked from the Laborer's Realm.

"I see." Bilal gets quiet contemplating the idea of reputation. He never considered people talking about him. His life was made up of laboring daily in the quarry and often fighting at night. Fist fights were almost once a week and a death match was about once a month. His daily life rarely altered from these two things. The time in between was spent healing and resting. He noticed people always would say hello to him, but he did not get this was not normal for everyone else. That a young man from the Keeper's realm followed his fighting and came to almost every one of the matches was eye-opening. He had no choice in it and did not relish the accomplishment of it, so the idea of having a fan had never occurred to him.

He did not really notice the crowds when he was fighting as he was always focused on getting a fight over with. He was used to people looking at him since he was one of only three people with hair the color of wheat and eyes the color of the sky, besides being larger than anyone else. It had also never occurred to him that people would notice him for anything else.

"Have I upset you Bilal?" asks Mila quietly.

"No Mila, you have not. It just never occurred to me that I would be admired for fighting. It was never my choice Mila, and if I did have choice in the matter it is something I would never do. I do not enjoy it as sport like so many people do."

"Oh, I see," says Mila. "I did not think of that. Would you fight for me if you had to? I mean to protect me? I will never ask you to fight for sport if you do not wish to."

Bilal replies without hesitation, "Yes, I will protect you always, no matter what I must do. It is okay Mila, I can fight. You have given me the choice to do so and that is what means most to me. It is true I am good at fighting and I know how to take a life with my bare hands. I cannot undo what I know, at least now I can put it to a use that I believe in and support. You are removing the ugliness and shame of it Mila, your request of me is a purpose I can live with and do so gladly. Thank you for asking, you do not know how much that means to me little Mila." Humbled, he chokes back tears once again with the knowledge of how this girl honors him with choice.

"I will be very glad to share whatever I know with Kylar and train him as best I can," says Bilal earnestly.

With that arrives the food Piloma has brought to them. She also lays down a new garment next to Bilal. "This is for you young man," she says with a wink. "Rimmel has made you a shift befitting your new station. He says it will do until he has time to properly outfit you."

Instantly Bilal runs his hands across the fabric, it looks sturdy but is one of the softest fabrics he has ever touched. It is a bright cream color, the bottom edges are embroidered with gold thread in a simple pattern and the neck and arms are wrapped in a supple light tan leather trim, also the softest he has ever touched before. It was the standard shift for the palace guard and far more luxurious than anything Bilal had ever owned.

Mila jumps up excited, "Try it on! Try it on!"

He takes off his belt and removes the new but very simple rough brown shift he has on and slides the new one on over his head. He takes a deep breath and exhales. "Ah" he says, "I have never felt anything so wonderful. I did not know fabric could feel like this!" He makes sure it is arranged properly, and putting his belt back on, moves his arms testing the fit and lay of the garment. "Please tell Rimmel it fits perfectly, it is wonderful! Thank you." Bilal smiles ear-to-ear, luxuriating in every movement and the pleasure of such fine fabric caressing his body.

Mila sits back with a look of satisfaction, enjoying watching

Bilal's pleasure in the sensations and beauty of his new shift.

Who knew joy, pleasure, satisfaction, caring and kindness could be not only desirable by a Pharaoh and his family, but something they strive to encourage and develop in others. It seemed magical for Bilal.

Chapter 25

As the sun goes down the Builder Angyet, the Pharaoh-to-be Ra-Milania and her personal guardian Bilal reconvene in the private chambers of Pharaoh-Ra. He is waiting for them, a smile and calmness masking the child like excitement flowing through him.

He has arranged a round table about four feet across with chairs for each of them surrounding it. Several items are on it; a fire bowl that is unlit, a glass of water, a piece of cord string and three gold coins. A small round leather ball and what looked like wood chips of different colors and shapes are also on the table.

Upon seeing what is on the table Mila gets a big smile and claps her hands with excitement, but does not say anything. They all sit, and Bilal looks to each in anticipation, but also does not speak. He waits to see what everyone is up to as he perceives the excitement they all exude.

Looking to Pharaoh-Ra and Mila, then Bilal, Angyet begins. "You have seen the power of the Movers as they lift and transport the stones of the pyramid from the quarry to the pyramid itself and put them in place?"

As she speaks of this the small leather ball suddenly lifts from the table where it rests near Pharaoh-Ra, and moves a few inches above the table and towards Bilal just as a pyramid stone glides when the Movers walk in procession. Then the ball suddenly changes direction, now moving in a small circle growing concentrically larger as it rises up above their heads.

"We would like to show you that you can do this too, among many other things. We will practice tonight and demonstrate only the beginning of what you are capable of Bilal. Would you enjoy this?" asks Angyet.

"Yes!" exclaims Bilal enthusiastically as he looks up at the ball floating in the air and circling like a bird on a string above. With that Angyet lets it drop to the table with a small thud.

Bilal looks to her with a huge smile. "What else can you show me?"

With that Pharaoh-Ra looks at Bilal while he waves his fingers over the fire bowl and a flame bursts into existence.

"Wow!" says Bilal.

Mila is next. "Look at the wood pieces." With that the little pieces of colored wood begin to tremble and slide around arranging themselves into a pattern in front of Bilal. They take shape as an intricate flower design of wood inlay pieces perfectly fitted together. Mila has done this without moving a muscle as far as Bilal can see.

Angyet hands him the glass of water. "Please, take a sip so you can see it is simply water then set it down." He takes a sip and it is water. He sets down the glass in front of him and Angyet waves her finders in a wavelike motion pointed towards the glass of water. Suddenly a soft rose color begins to swirl in the clear water and the color gets deeper and richer as it swirls through the liquid in the glass. When she is satisfied, she stops. "Now taste it again." Angyet opens her hand palm up, indicating he may proceed in tasting the contents again.

Bilal lifts the glass, looking at the dark red color of the contents and sips, his eyes grow wide and he almost chokes. "It is wine!" he says flabbergasted. "How did you do that?" He sips again allowing his mind to begin catching up with the reality of his taste buds. "It really is full-bodied wine, no hint of water taste at all. You can do that? Oh, wow. That is incredible!"

"It is very likely you can do this too Bilal. We shall see. Each person's capacities with the oneness are a little different. What one person finds very easy, another person may not. It is up to each person to play with their capacities to both discover what those capacities are and develop their potency with it. If you can conceive of it, often you are capable of doing it. If you totally reject the possibility of your ability to do it, then you absolutely will not be able to. It is a matter of question, curiosity and your willingness to play."

"And if you can do it, you can undo it" says Pharaoh-Ra as he waves his hand over the flame extinguishing it.

At the same time Angyet waves her finger at the glass and in moments the liquid in the glass is again clear water.

Bilal laughs in glee with the marvel of what he beholds. "Okay, what shall I try first?"

Mila asks him, "What would be the most fun for you Bilal?"

"The ball, let me try moving the ball. How would I even begin?" He asks as he looks to each, his eyes twinkling with excitement.

Angyet replies, "First let us connect with the oneness more. Take a moment and feel your feet on the floor, also feel the floor on your feet. Do you notice you can sense both? Notice that you are able to sense the floor as it touches your feet? Now extend that sense to everything in the room. Sense the objects on the table, and the table as it is touching each object. Do you notice the subtle differences in energies? Those subtle differences are the energies that create the molecular structure of each of those objects."

"Notice the energy of the leather ball, its vibration if you will. Now, by your request you can be that same energy of the ball. Right now, just ask yourself to be that energy, that same vibration. Good, notice how you 'feel' like the energy of the ball. Now this part you will have to play with, I will describe what I do and be and we'll see how it works for you. Do what I am talking about as I describe it with your energies."

"Notice again the energies of the ball, ask to be that energy and notice as your body is beginning to vibrate and hum just like the energies of the ball. Now reach your energies out so they are surrounding and flowing through the ball, so your energy is filling the space between the molecules making up the ball. Reach out like you reach into the space when you are standing on the cliffs edge. Occupy that space in and around the ball and imagine and request that it lift now..."

The ball quivers and lifts off the table like a wind that effortlessly lifts a feather, the ball floats up into the air.

"Ha! I am doing it! Look, look, ahahaha!" Bilal is thrilled, and with that the ball drops to the table with a thud. "Oh, drat! Okay, let me do it again." He leans forward focusing intently on the ball, he begins to squint his eyes with focus, nothing happens.

"You are trying too hard Bilal, it is not about focus and effort. It is your request, your connection with the oneness. Take a breath, relax, expand out. Walk yourself through it again. Sense the ball on the table and the table touching the ball. Expand your senses as you notice the energies of the ball that are different than the other objects and the table itself. Become that energy...fill the space around the ball and between the molecules of the ball itself so there is no separation between you and it. Yes, like that. Now ask with all of your being for the ball to lift, rising up...Ah, yes, there like that...Very good," says Angyet.

Mila claps and squeals with delight.

Once again the ball is rising up above the table slowly floating upwards. It begins to sway to one side, then slowly change direction, swinging the other way, it turns again swinging back, this time taking flight and dropping four feet away. "Oops," says Bilal. "I was trying to get it to go in a circle like you were before."

"Well," Angyet says with a smile. "What you just did flinging it over to the side there is actually more difficult than making it float in a circle! You are doing wonderfully Bilal!"

The four of them sit around the table for another few hours playing with moving the objects, letting Bilal practice, talking him through it. He manages to not only lift the string, but is able to tie it in a knot and undo the knot again. It is done loosely, but none the less tied. All of them delight in the practice of it and Bilal's glee in playing with them and his new found capacities.

"What about the flame, or the wine?" Bilal looks at the fire bowl and glass of water each, then to Pharaoh-Ra and Angyet wide-eyed with excited anticipation.

"Let us leave that for another day dear Bilal. Your accomplishment with moving items is greater than you know! It took me several months to do what you have done in minutes, and I'm still not that adept at it," says Pharaoh-Ra with a big smile of satisfaction. He is pleased with Bilal skill.

"You did so well Bilal! Isn't it fun? We all play with this stuff all day like this, practicing," says Mila.

"This is the fun stuff, there is more practical use of it all, this is your introduction and a place to start." Angyet speaks a little more somberly, but still with a large smile.

The sun has gone down but the night is still young and Bilal is totally energized by the practice and play with his three new friends. "I have so much energy! What do you do with yourself? I feel like I could run for hours!" exclaims Bilal.

"Yes. That is the oneness flowing through you. It is the very energies of living and vitality. The more you practice, you will no longer get sickness, you will sleep less, you may likely eat less. You see, the oneness does not ever deplete you, it only gifts to you. There may be times of rest, but you will notice it is a deep sense of relaxation, not the kind of tiredness or exhaustion you have known in the past. You may very well desire to run for the sheer joy of it, Bilal," says Angyet with a laugh.

Mila says, "I would like you to stay here tonight Bilal. We have prepared a room for you attached to my rooms. On one side you can enter the hallway, the other side enters my chambers. Piloma is also in the room next to you. As you recall we said you would have a place here, in the guard's quarters and in your home with your parents in the Artisan Realm. The more quickly you can become familiar and make this place your own, the better for us all."

"It is one of the few disadvantages at the moment Bilal, that you do not know the palace as we do. However with the secret pillars, this can make up for some of it," says Pharaoh-Ra with a wink. "Now let us say goodnight for the evening and we shall see you again in the morning."

With that Mila takes Bilal with her to her rooms by way of the secret pillars in her father's chambers, she will show him to his sleeping area adjoining her chambers.

Having been situated and saying goodnight to Mila and tucking her in, Bilal leaves Mila's rooms with Piloma. He has never left either Pharaoh's chambers or Mila's except by the hidden pillars of The Pathway. Overflowing with energy from practice with moving objects, he is going to walk the gardens and go by way of walking there through the palace. Piloma is showing him which way to go. They exit Mila's rooms and Piloma points to the right. "Down the hall there goes to Pharaoh's chambers. Straight ahead and to the second left you will come to wife of Pharaoh's private chambers."

"The first left will take you to the great stairway that enters into the public hall and out into the garden's as you likely know. Don't be gone too long. I will be here but it is also your duty to be close by." Says Piloma sternly. With a pat on the arm and a smile she leaves Bilal and returns to Mila's main room.

Bilal looks around at the few guards stationed at intervals down the halls on every direction. He strolls toward the great stairway and each guard nods at him as he passes. They have all been informed of him and his station, though none have met yet. His fighting prowess is legendary - the slave fighter who has never lost a match in five years. From the unbelievably young age of thirteen until now at eighteen he is undefeated.

Though they nod, none speak to him. They will be properly introduced soon enough.

Bilal sees the top of the stairway and to the right a walkway extends that overlooks the stairs. He sees a woman coming towards him, he would know her anywhere...it is his precious Lili.

Chapter 26

"Bilal?" says Lili with joyful surprise.

"Lili, is that really you?" exclaims Bilal as he goes to her.

He wraps her in his arms lifting her as he steps into the side of the hallway in a nook. She has one arm around his neck as the other is filled with the contents of her errand. They are kissing before he sets her down. They had not seen each other in almost a year and did not know when they ever would.

"Bilal, what are you doing here?" asks Lili.

"I am now the personal guardian of Pharaoh's daughter he says proudly. Lili I am a Freeman now. My parents too! There is so much to tell you, so much has changed since I have seen you. I thought I may never see you again Lili. Wherever have you been?"

"It is a long story for me as well. Oh Bilal, I can't believe you are here," says Lili with a sigh and savoring the sight of him.

"How is it you are here?" asks Bilal.

"Master Iberak gave me to the wife-of-Pharaoh a few months ago. He hopes to gain favor and you know Master Iberak, he has me report things to him as well. It seems I will never escape that foul man;" she says as she wrinkles her nose. "The Pharaoh's wife is not a nice woman, but at least I get to be in the palace. And now you are here, oh Bilal I thought I might never see you again!"

They kiss again. "I must go, I cannot leave Ra-Maharet waiting or there will be pain to pay."

Regrettably she pulls away from his warm embrace saying; "Now I know I will see you again my love." With that she departs continuing on her errand. Bilal is elated, how did he get so lucky, he wonders?

Bilal and Lili have known each other well. She was eleven and he was thirteen when they first met officially. She had tended to him after his first fight. Since then it was Lili who most often tended his wounds after any fight. Her soft and gentle hands cleansed his body and applied salves so he would not get infection. She was the first to show him kindness other than his mother and she was his only true friend. They could always talk about anything.

She was born of a woman from the brothel whose name was Khepri. Lili had the most amazing green eyes, unlike any he had ever seen until meeting Kylar. He had never seen that color before her.

She was a rare beauty and Master Iberak found her to be profitable, putting her to work from age twelve. Her green eyes got her top payment. It was no surprise what would be expected of her being born to a whore and raised in a brothel. And she was more beautiful than most, so Master Iberak was more selective with how she was treated and who he would allow bed her. She had been trained and prepared.

He was so protective, though she mostly received patrons at Master Iberak's brothel in the Keeper's Realm, he would bring her back to the Laborer's Realm so that she was not so easily available. Master Iberak would control every transaction that involved her. It was she that would attend to Bilal after his fights, as Master Iberak's way of easing Bilal's pain and injury and rewarding him with her comforting touch and beautiful to look at company.

And it was Bilal who was always there for her when things were difficult, as she had been there for him. They found solace and friendship with each other in their lives as slaves, where their life was not their own to choose. A comrade in what comfort they could be for each other in the ugliness of the world they lived. They both new they had at least one person in their life there for them no matter what happened. It made it all a little more bearable.

What they had was precious to them both and they know many would and could use it against them, especially Master Iberak. Nothing was allowed without his permission. Both Bilal and Lili were two he kept an especially tight grip on as they were of his most valuable assets. They would reveal as little as possible to keep what was precious to them, just for them, guarding their tenderness to keep it in tact.

Lili was there for him when he needed her most. Thinking back Bilal recalls when he was fifteen. His father and Master Iberak had just delivered the news. It was to be a death match. The blood drained from Bilal's face, "A what? A death match?" Bilal stammers.

"Yes," Drekkar says enthusiastically. "You are ready, your next match will be a fight to the death. You are undefeated, you will do it," it was both a threat and a willing of his capacity for winning.

Master Iberak continues; "You have won every fight for two years now, you will win this too. No weapons. Bare hands only as usual."

Bilal thought he would be sick. Standing silently, he was screaming inside. Knocking someone out was one thing, killing them outright something totally different. He didn't think he could do it. He recoiled at the thought. He could fight, he had always fought, his father and Master Iberak made sure of that. He had seen death his whole life too, it just had never been at his hand. As violent as his life had been, he was not a violent person if he had any choice about it. He would not choose it if avoidable, and he often kept the peace between other slaves when he could. His huge imposing stature made it fairly easy to dissuade people from fighting him, and it also stopped other people from fighting when he stepped in.

It was usually a new slave that was likely to test him, but that never lasted long. Be it his presence and obvious ability, his reputation preceding him, or pure distraction by his unusual looks, he kept people in line just by being him.

It was the night of the first death match fight and he had won...

He wanted to block out the look of the man's face, the sound and feel of the man's neck breaking. "Please," he thought, "Let me black out with drink."

Master Iberak and Drekkar were ecstatic, they jumped up and down hugging each other, celebrating the victory of Bilal and the large amount of money they had just made in wager. Winded and bloody, Bilal leaned against the wall, barely able to stand. He was reeling with the frenzy of the crowd. The sound of the man's neck breaking was ringing in his ears. He wished he could black out and wipe away the vividness of the death on his hands.

Drekkar and Master Iberak were grabbing him, steering him towards the familiar celebration at Iberak's tavern and brothel adjacent to the fighting area.

Master Iberak was saying; "You made me rich Bilal, you will have women tonight!"

Iberak knew he would win and he had planned for it. All his best women were to service Bilal that night. As Bilal was known by all, and was a prized beauty, the women had different plans; all of them were going to have him this night.

Master Iberak was feeling generous in his triumph and gave free drink all night long. A rare occasion he would be so generous, the place was packed all night in a drunken, sweaty sea of debauchery and mild mayhem of celebration.

He and Lili had been innocent in their affections. He often fell asleep with his head in her lap, silent tears would fall as she stroked his hair comforting his battered and bruised body and pain stricken mind until he fell asleep. At fifteen Bilal had never laid with a woman, he had only had a few stolen kisses with some of the prostitutes. They have almost all been friendly with him, but he didn't get it. He didn't know he was attractive, only that he stood out because he did not look like anyone else. Tonight he would learn different. Master Iberak had instructed three of his women to "Take care of him all night," and so they did.

Inana ushered Bilal to the back away from the noise of the tavern ruckus, and led him to the first event of the evening, which would be starting with a bath they had hot and already waiting for him. Inana and three other women stripped him of his clothes. As the life of a slave being naked in front of others was common and Bilal did not shy from it. The difference of this night was that rather than the utilitarian stripping of his body that would follow in the vein of review and examination of fitness, or to prepare for being whipped or beaten; this stripping down was done with care and gentleness of touch.

The women this night were soft and caressing. Leading him into the bath, they could see he was disturbed by the night's events. They had all seen him before when a fight was done. This was different. It was his first death match, and it was as though the light had gone out of his eyes. They all liked him if they would admit it or not, and it was easy for them to show him a kindness he had never known they possessed. Their kindness of touch was juxtaposed against the brutality of the night's death match. It cracked open the hardness he was bracing against. The tears flowed silently from Bilal and he let them. The gentle presence of these women scrubbing clean his body, the heat of the bath water; it all nurtured him in letting go of the nights brutality. The women made no significance of his turmoil or tears, but rather, singing softly, washing his long blonde hair, they sweetly and softly began removing the ugliness of the fight along with the dirt and blood.

After feeding him and providing plenty of wine, they turned up the pleasure. As the night progressed the women were thrilled to learn that not only was he beautiful to look at he had stamina as well. Bilal was fifteen, and it was his first time, but that didn't seem to matter. It did not take long for him to function like a very experienced man. Through the night each woman in the brothel found her way into his bed sharing their skill, creativity and appreciation or outright lust for Bilal. To his delight he was now discovering what all those long glances and lingering touch of finger tips was really inviting.

Bilal relished the distraction from the horror of the fight. He let the soft, wet silkiness of these women's bodies wash the ugliness of it all away. These women made it easy to let it all go. Bilal had no idea anything could feel so good. He was enthusiastic and willing to try anything. With no previous experience, he was thoroughly enjoying the exploration of it all and had no inhibitions. He was discovering an entirely new playground that was far greater than his imagination had been. He was very happy to find out the reality of what his imagination lacked.

With such variety of appetite, playfulness and creativity of each woman trying to outdo the previous, it was a celebration of hedonism few get the chance to explore. Bilal had always been kind to these women and these women were showing him a kindness of bodies he drank in like water after too long in the desert.

It was late in the night, the candles continued to blaze and the stream of women coming into and leaving his bed was a sea of flesh and distraction Bilal welcomed. He lost track of the differentiation of his body and all of theirs with so many hands caressing, guiding, teasing and inviting. Hands, lips, tongues; so many hands. Drinking in the sights, smells and touches of all these beautiful bodies; he let them flood his senses that it may erase the brutality of the death match. Every sensation of pleasure he let wash over him, as when he stood on the cliffs edge expanding into the space and lightness of beauty. To have his body immersed is such sensual delight was renewing his sense of desire for living.

In the midst of this sea of pleasure where Bilal was losing track of where his body ended and the several women touching him began; a new hand, cool and soft runs up his hard sweat covered stomach muscles, reaching his chest, lightly circling his nipple and tracing up to his neck. He would know that hand anywhere. His eyes fly open to see the one woman he had been yearning to touch more than any other. It was Lili. The waves of orgasm that were currently washing over him had not yet left his body as he caught his breath in surprise with another wave of orgasm at the site of Lili. Naked and willing, she straddles him looking deep into his eyes. He rises pulling her to him, the awareness of all the other women disappearing as he melts into the total embrace of his being by Lili. Tears of joyous gratitude spring from his eyes. Expanding in an explosion of long awaited lust and the immense caring of the only person who truly knows all of him; Bilal drinks in the presence of his heart's desire that is Lili.

Hours later the sun had risen, and the ruckus partying of the night had just quieted to the volume of an everyday conversation in the tavern. Bilal lay in the middle of a pile of satiated bodies, a dreamy smile on his bruised face. The three women that Master Iberak had assigned to the nights tasks were all that remained of the night of hedonism. More relaxed than he ever knew was possible, every molecule of his body was humming with the lingering sensation of bodies. *"What a night that was!"* Bilal smiled on the corner of his mouth recalling.

In the almost three years since that night he and Lili had little chance to explore the pleasure of each other's bodies. As slaves, their life was not their own and it was difficult to find a moment to themselves. Their friendship was such that any moment they had together was precious to them and it did not matter what form that time together took; a stolen kiss, a grazing of hands as they pass one another, a few moments of conversation or a hug. This last year of not seeing her anywhere, even once, had been agonizing.

No one spoke of her and he had no idea where she was. Master Iberak must have ordered everyone not to tell him. He had feared she might be dead. Lili's mother Khepri was in no position to reveal anything to him without Master Iberak's permission which he did not give. Other than a reassuring look or squeeze of his hand from Khepri, he had no idea where his dear Lili was. To be reunited with Lili at this time that he is now a Freeman is more than he hoped for. Finding her in the palace now after a year of absence was beyond words. His heart is bursting with joy and gratitude for it.

Bilal strolls the gardens soaking in the moonlight and the cool night air. With a smile that does not leave his lips, he is marveling at this day and the gift of finding his dear Lili returning to his life. The joy of this reunion and exuberance of connection with the oneness and the ability to move objects it gives him expands as waves of bubbling happiness.

Sensing the tug to return to Mila's chambers he finds the hidden pillars the Pharaoh had shown him earlier on this extraordinary day and steps into Mila's room and his new place at the palace that he can now also call home. He lays down on his new bed, exhausted but elated with the day's events, he falls asleep without removing his clothes, or even his shoes, passing out on top of the covers.

The little he had of joy in his past was joining him in his new future, adding to the expansiveness he was just discovering and would continue to practice each day.

Chapter 27

B ilal wakens before the sun, he thinks. He is not sure as there is no natural light. He is confused at the moment and he recognizes nothing of his surroundings. Then it all comes back in a flood, this is his new room at the palace in little Mila's chambers. He sits up blinking and smiling as he looks down at his new clothes he had fallen asleep in. He rises and goes out into the main room and sees indeed it is before the sun has risen as the sky is ablaze with pink and purple of before the sun breaking the horizon. He takes a seat and sips some water on the table from the night before. Mila is still asleep in her bed at the far end of the room. It is tucked in a nook that the morning sun light does not hit her directly, she could sleep in with ease if she so desired.

He takes in the mind-blowing extravagance of his

surroundings, the light of the soon-to-be-rising sun sets everything in the room on fire and the gold that is everywhere gets brighter with each moment of increasing light. He wonders if he could ever get used to such beauty, it is so drastic a change from the life he had known until just a few weeks ago. He closes his eyes, sensing the energies of all this room contains. The materials of stone and metal, wood and leather, fine fabrics and tapestry; all are a variety of sensorial pleasure he drinks in. He extends his energies touching each object energetically as if he were a blind person taking in the surroundings by touch. It all has such a different feel to it than he is familiar with. He wonders what it would take to be at ease and familiar with this kind of luxury. He smiles knowing he will have the chance with his invitation to become part of this world at the palace.

"What are you smiling about?" asks Mila in a sleepy voice.

Bilal opens his eyes with a start. So immersed in sensing the objects of the room he did not register the sounds of Mila's covers moving or her soft footsteps on the marble floors as she walked to him.

"Oh, good morning! I was smiling with the joy of sensing all the energies of the beautiful things you have in your room here. I have never been in such beauty of surroundings until you and your father brought me here. It is all so new to me, Mila. The house I grew up in was but a shack with dirt floors and scrap wood we salvaged and put together on our own. It was smaller than the room you have given me, and it was for me and my parents all together. And come, look at this sunrise!" Bilal picks her up gathering her in his lap they watch the rising sun together.

"Show me how you do it Mila, show me how you connect with the oneness?" asks Bilal.

Mila instantly takes a breath, relaxing and snuggling into the warmth of Bilal's chest and extending out with her energies and awareness to meet the rising sun. Bilal closes his eyes again sensing the intensity of presence Mila so easily has, and he follows the sense of expansion, spaciousness and vibration of energies Mila is being. He gets the sense of being like a bird flying above the landscape, feeling his wings strong on the air and the air itself as it rushes over the wings. At the same time, he senses a wave of energies like water extending out from Mila and washing over the side of the palace walls and down to the ground and right into the earth. He can sense the cool dampness of dirt and the roots of the plants below the palace that flow to the water's edge. He can almost smell the foliage as his senses pass over them touching every surface.

He is reeling in the details and nuance of sensations as he now also perceives the water and the currents within the flowing of the river. At the same time, under that, he can sense the river bed and the mud and stones of the bottom. The energies intensify and he can now also sense all the life within it. The dirt crawls with insects, the waters are filled with fish and other bugs, there are birds at the edge of the waters he can also sense. He can feel these creatures and how the elements of their environment feel to them. Just as he sensed the leather ball on the table and the table touching the leather ball the night before. All of this fills his awareness, his body and being and he breaks out in a soft laughter tickled with the sensations of all he perceives. The movements of the morning coming alive, the presence and connection of all things, the joy of living bursting open with the rising sun.

Mila laughs now too. "How was that?" she asks, though she already knows; Bilal's laughter answered her in confirmation.

"Wow, there is so much more richness of senses than I have been able to be aware of until now. Thank you Mila, you have expanded me beyond what I had previously been able to sense. Your awareness of connection is way more fun than I had been willing to have. Do you always get tickled by the bugs as they move? I couldn't quite discern who was tickling who, the bugs as they move on the land, or the land as it touches the bugs! Oh, wow!" exclaims Bilal. "I am beginning to understand why you find this all to be so much fun. Thank you Mila."

"Is it really true most people don't know about connecting with the oneness Bilal? It is hard for me to imagine they would not desire to, or not know about it," says Mila. "You do it. Don't other people you know do it too?"

"No one I know seeks to connect with the planet and the beauty of it, and certainly they would not look to be connected with people this way. I have never known anyone else like me little Mila, not until I met you and your father and Angyet. In the world I know, people don't expect to live long, they expect to suffer, not have enough to eat, to be beaten if they do not do as they are told, and do not do it quickly enough or to the satisfaction of their master. There is little kindness and no joy to speak of. They expect to have power over others, or others to be in control of them and their very life. If anyone seeks to connect with the oneness, they certainly have never let it be known to me."

Tears have come to Mila's eyes, she turns in Bilal's lap to face him, "How very sad. I did not know people live in such misery. They live that way their whole life? How is it that you do not sink into the darkness of that?"

"It is only by connection with the oneness that I found I could bear it. Being able to connect with the planet and all the energies and spaciousness it is allowed me to carry on when I thought I could not. I don't know why or how, somehow it gave me enough sense of living that my hope for something greater did not die. It has always made me feel alive again. It gives me the sense that I would like to go on living and seeking something greater, even when I had no reason to hope that something greater is possible. I just couldn't accept that the misery and darkness all around me was all that was possible, when such beauty is also right here," he says pointing to the breath taking beauty of the sunrise before them. "I guess I have always known beauty is just a choice away."

"You are so brave Bilal. That you choose different than anyone else you know tells me why I knew you must come here to the palace to be with me and my father and Angyet. If you can make that choice to connect with the oneness, I wonder what invitation we can be for others to choose it?" says Mila with some hope sparking in her eyes.

"That you would desire this for the people lets me know why I am here Mila!" He hugs her and asks again, "Show me again how you connect with the oneness, would you please?"

Mila smiles wide. Looking in Bilal's eyes she embraces his very being with a joy and sweetness so that Bilal is filled with a sense of relaxation spreading through his body. She is looking at him but somehow also expanding, including their surroundings energetically. She places her hand on his heart. He can sense the molecules of Mila's body vibrating and the molecules of his body begin to match hers. Then like a swift breeze he is expanded and again his energies spread out into the expanse of the view before them, the light of the risen sun shining on them. Together they sense the joy of the earth as the sunlight spreads across it embracing, inviting, nurturing. The living vibrancy of the plants, animals and all the elements of Earth coming to life. They both begin to giggle, tickled by the senses of the day beginning and everything coming alive with movement. For the next ten minutes they sit giggling and playing with their senses of the earth awakening to the new day.

"Time to get dressed!" announces Mila. With that Mila asks Bilal to set her on the floor and she darts off to get Piloma. She is back in a few minutes.

"Mila, can I go see my parents? I did not get to tell them I was staying the night and it seems I will not see them so much anymore. Though they already know I am your guardian, I would like to tell them myself that I do not know when they might expect me to be there," says Bilal.

"Yes, certainly. Come back to my rooms after you speak with them," says Mila.

"Thank you Mila. I won't be long," says Bilal with smile. He steps into the hidden pillars of Mila's chamber and out into the pillars of the top of the hill of the Artisan Realm. He takes in a deep breath of the fresh morning air and heads to see his parents.

Bilal leaves the palace wondering if his parents would allow for themselves such joyful pleasures of communion with the earth. He desires so much to invite them to more.

Chapter 28

So much has happened in the thirty-six hours since he has seen his parents last, he is looking forward to sharing more of the new life unfolding for him.

He opens the door to the welcome sound of soft laughter. What a joy it is to have this becoming the new normal for him and his parents. He walks into the kitchen to find his parents sitting at the table sipping their morning tea. They are holding hands and chuckling as they look up to see their dear son.

"Bilal!" exclaims Emilia. She stands to embrace her son and welcome him. "Come sit, tell us everything! Let me get you some tea." She ushers him to a chair and goes to fetch another cup of tea.

"Son, good morning," says Drekkar patting Bilal on the shoulder as he takes a seat beside his father. "You look well, look at those new clothes!"

Spontaneously Bilal blurts, "Feel the fabric father, it is amazing!"

Drekkar touches the fabric of the sleeve. "I have never felt such soft fabric. That is quite nice. I see you are being treated well at the palace, son."

With that, Emilia returns with a cup of steaming tea and a bit of bread, cheese, pomegranate and figs for them all. "Oh son, tell us how is the palace, what is the Pharaoh like, and his daughter, are they treating you well, did you get to meet the Pharaoh's wife too?"

Bilal laughs at the enthusiasm of his mother. "I'll tell you about it all. Don't worry I won't leave anything out mother. Let me first say, they are treating me very well and making me right at home. I came this morning to say I don't know how often I will be able to make it back here with you. My position is truly as Ra-Milania's personal guard and they will now be expecting me to be with her day and night."

"She is really quite wonderful and I am enjoying her company very much. Though she is only five years old, I find her very interesting to talk with. She is the most unusual person I have ever met and she is much like the little sister I never had. I am finding my duty easy to fulfill and it is an honor I would have never expected to be bestowed with. Pharaoh-Ra has also been most generous and is personally getting me familiar with my duties and what he expects of me. It has been a surprise to have such a personal introduction, but then they are asking me to be with them at all times."

"Oh, the Pharaoh himself? Wonderful Bilal! No one is

stronger than you, I know you will do a great job," exclaims Emilia. "What is he like?" she asks breathless with excitement.

"He has such elegance about him, I mean how he speaks and moves. It truly is being in the presence of greatness. I cannot explain it. He puts me at ease and gives me confidence with his trust in me. I know I have only just met him, but somehow it seems like I have known him and his daughter my whole life. How fun is that? It is a marvel. And the palace! You both must come to the palace, you have never seen anything so spectacular!"

Emilia looks to Drekkar and he is looking at her already. He smiles, seeing the excitement on her face. They have been living in the shadow of the palace itself, yet had not considered actually going there. Bilal encourages them. "You must come. At least come see the public gardens. Come today! You will be wearing your insignia, no one will look twice. Well, other than the usual gawking we always get with our golden locks!" Bilal flings his long braid back over his shoulder and they all laugh. Being the only three blonds in all of Pharaoh's Land they were used to everyone staring and wanting to touch them and their hair.

"Can we really just walk into the palace?" ask Drekkar incredulously. Though the three of them have been the prized property of Master Abar Iberak, he has never taken any of them to the palace in all the nineteen years in Pharaoh's Land.

"Yes, yes you would be welcome. Both the gardens and the great public hall of the palace are open to anyone during the day from sunrise to sunset. I don't know if I would be able to see you there or not, but please come! Come walk the gardens, it is so beautiful," implores Bilal. "You must, I insist."

"Oh Drekkar, lets!" says Emilia.

Drekkar takes both Emilia and Bilal by the hand, looking at them each with a satisfied smile and says, "Yes, lets."

For the next half hour Bilal talks about the palace and his position, being sure to omit anything about the hidden pillars of The Pathway. He does not know how to talk about the oneness with his parents so he stays away from that topic too. So many new sights, there is plenty to talk about.

Bilal squeezes his dads hand and stands up. "I really must get back, Ra-Milania asked I return to her this morning. There is much to do."

"We are proud of you son, go, do your duty and hopefully we'll see you later today," says Drekkar getting teary eyed and voice cracking some.

Bilal bows his head to them but does not say goodbye, he just smiles. Beaming at them both and spilling over with gratitude for what his family has become, he takes his leave.

Chapter 29

It has been a few hours since Bilal left the house and now Drekkar and Emilia have had breakfast and cleaned up, so as they said they would venture out of the house and head for the palace gardens. They put on their best clothes, newly fitted thanks to Rimmel. Emilia puts on the gold insignia around her neck and Drekkar wears his as a broach on the left side and hanging the chain across his chest and pinned to the other shoulder. They wear them proudly, though still a bit self-consciously.

They have been frequenting the Pharaoh's Market and walked every street of the Artisan Realm discovering all the bakers and huge variety of craftsmen creating beauty, the likes of which they have never seen. Though they live only two streets from the bottom entrance of the palace neither of them dare explore it. Now that Bilal has invited them, they will go to the gardens at least. They walk the few steep streets to the top of the hill and stroll across the causeway that leads to the main entrance to the palace. Continuing past that are the gates to the gardens. Many people walk in every direction and most pay no attention to them, wrapped up in their own errands.

They get to the garden gates which are wide open and enter without anyone giving them a second glance, just as Bilal said they could. Arm in arm they stroll straight in. They have absolutely no idea how big it is or where they are going, so they wander. First they walk all the way across the gardens to the river side, the view of the river and valley below is breathtaking. Unlike the Artisan Realm with rooftops and streets spread out before them, this is an unobstructed view. Lushness and beauty surrounds them, the people in their finery, the plants, the architecture; all of it so beautiful. They follow the path that wraps around the edge of the cliff and discover and entire amphitheater sunk below the height of the walkway.

They circle around, walking away from the palace in a large loop back towards the entry gate. They had seen a pool and they wished to go to it. There looked to be drinking fountains near it. The sun was high and it was getting hot. They noticed there were many places to stop for shade and sit in comfort. They find the fountains for drinking from and take a deep drink using their hands to catch the water as it spills forth from the mouth of a fish. The other fountain is the head of an egret, its long beak making a lower reaching fountain for children or shorter people. It is a brilliant creation, neither of them have seen anything like it and the water is fresh and cool.

The fountains are set on either side of a huge stairway going up several steps and toward the main doors of the palace great hall. Looking up they are both thrilled and surprised at what they see. Walking toward them is Bilal. Their eyes pop as they see he is carrying Ra-Milania on his right shoulder. She sits like a poised bird, regal and missing nothing from the view from above.

They laugh with delight, Emilia bringing her hand to her mouth at the sight of it. Bilal sees them and looks as though he is speaking to Ra-Milania. As they approach Drekkar and Emilia kneel before them.

Bilal quickly descends the steps and stops before them placing Ra-Milania on the ground. He says quietly. "Ra-Milania these are my parents, Emilia and Drekkar."

With a large grin she replies, "It is a pleasure to meet you both. Thank you for allowing your son to come to the palace. It has been a great joy to have him here with me." Without a pause, she continues, "Have you seen the reflecting pool yet? Oh, come you must see!" She takes Bilal by the hand and Drekkar and Emilia rise falling behind them as Ra-Milania leads the way. They smile but remain speechless. They have no idea what to say, yet feel welcome with Ra-Milania's casual and open friendliness.

It is only another twenty feet away where the long pool starts. It has a wide edge that is easy to sit on, or lean on to look over the edge and view the reflection of the sky above. Mila asks Bilal to lift her so she can walk along the wide edge as she explains about the pool.

"This is the reflecting pool. It has been made especially for all the world to see its own beauty. It is a celebration of the glory of creation. For the sun to see the beauty of its own radiance as it passes over head. For the moon when it is out at night, that it might fall in love with its own face. It is for the stars to see themselves and know how they inspire. For those of us who walk this Earth to see the beauty of us reflected back in the depths of our own eyes...at least that is what I was told. Come look, lean over and see yourself!" Little Ra-Milania kneels down on the edge leaning over to see her own reflection looking back at her. She beckons to them all to lean over and look at themselves. Bilal is to her left and Emilia then Drekkar on her right. They all lean over and gasp wide-eyed, they have rarely seen their own reflection in anything. Certainly never so clear, they can see their own eyes reflecting back, each framed by a halo of golden hair. They can see their eyes are bright like the color of the sky. It is one thing to look upon each other, it is something different to see one's self looking back. Emilia touches her own cheek and smiles. She looks at Ra-Milania, exclaiming, "That's me?" She did not know she was beautiful until this moment.

"Yes, look how beautiful you are," Ra-Milania says sweetly and gently touches Emilia's hair. "Look again" She looks at herself approvingly, admiring herself. They all peer over the edge now as Ra-Milania continues, "See the dark bottom of the pool, it is what makes our reflection bright and clear. All the light of you reflects back. Can you see the beauty within yourself looking back at you?"

Tears come to all their eyes with the sweetness and sincerity with which Ra-Milania speaks.

They all peer over the edge in silence now looking at

themselves and each other in the reflections looking back at them. It is only the very wealthy that have metal polished to a high shine that allow them to see their own reflection. Most people rarely get to see their own reflection in their entire lifetime. They depend on each other to make their appearance well put together. This is one of the reasons why the wealthy have people who dress them. A personal dresser with a good eye is a prized person in the house hold for those who value social impression.

"Would you like to see something else beautiful?" Ra-Milania asks them all.

They all nod, smiling and saying, "Yes."

"What else would you show us dear?" asks Drekkar a little shyly.

"My horses!" exclaims Ra-Milania excitedly. "We were on our way to them when we met you. Would you like to come with us? I would love to show them to you, they are spectacular!" she says clapping her hands and beginning to lift onto her tiptoes which she does when she gets excited. "Can I ride on your shoulder Bilal? Let's go!"

"Of course," replies Bilal as he lifts her with one smooth motion onto his right shoulder. She lets her hand rest around his neck as they let her point the way towards the royal stables. She would have taken the secret Pathway pillars just past the end of the pool if they had not met up with Bilal's parents. But, she was pleased to visit with them as they strolled the rest of the way instead.

They arrive at the stables and find Ra-Milania's horse trainer and part of her personal guard; Missrah. He is with

Ra-Milania's two most prized horses.

"Hello Ra-Milania," says Missrah greeting them. "Come, see your beauties."

"Thank you Missrah. This is my new personal guardian Bilal and his parents Drekkar and Emilia."

"Very nice to meet you," says Missrah as he continues brushing the mane of the black beauty standing there.

They all gather round an extra large stall with both Mila's horses. They are the largest horses any of them have seen. One all white and one all black. They nicker softly welcoming Ra-Milania as they see her.

"This white one is Beset 'the protector' and this black one is Sekhet, 'she who is powerful' aren't they beautiful?" Mila looks at them dreamily. She is rubbing both their noses as they have reached down to greet her and check for sweets. She speaks with them softly as she rubs their faces.

"Beset is our leader. He is the head stallion here and as Sekhet is his favorite, we keep them together as much as possible. It makes it easier on all of us!" says Missrah with a laugh. "Aren't they wonderful? Wait until you see them move, you have not seen anything like it I'm sure! Shall we show them Ra-Milania?"

"Oh yes!" exclaims Mila. Mila turns to Sekhet and asks, "Will you take me for a walk around the arena?" and the horse nods her head appearing to understand completely. They all step back as Missrah opens the door of the stall to let her out. Only Sekhet steps forward as Ra-Milania heads out to the arena, no halter, no rope to lead the horse. What a sight, a tiny little girl not much taller than this horse's knee followed by this giant of a horse. Bilal, Emilia and Drekkar stand mouth agape, almost forgetting to follow. They snap to with the sound of the stall door closing and when Ra-Milania and Sekhet are almost ten feet away. They all laugh at themselves and quickly follow out to the arena's edge.

They get there just in time to see Ra-Milania pointing at the ground in a full circle around herself as she turns to the right. Sekhet is following her finger in the circle indicated about seven feet away and stops when Ra-Milania stops. Ra-Milania turns her body to face Sekhet directly, then bows deeply to her. As she does Sekhet begins to bow and lowers herself onto one knee. The other foot outstretched to Ra-Milania. As soon as Ra-Milania sees she is settled she quickly scampers up Sekhet's leg and slides herself effortlessly onto her back as she grabs hold of the main in one smooth motion. As soon as she is astride Sekhet lifts herself smoothly to standing and begins to walk around the edge of the arena. Ra-Milania sits tall and nods her head to the small audience, a look of pride and satisfaction on her face.

Missrah, Emilia, Drekkar and Bilal spontaneously begin clapping and comment among themselves. They certainly have never seen anything as amazing as this! They are thrilled with the spectacle of such a sight.

Bilal ask Missrah, "How did she do that?"

"How wonderful!" exclaims Emilia.

"I have never seen such a well-trained horse!" says Drekkar.

"It is amazing what is possible when a horse loves you and

you request of it, rather than tell it what to do. It is one of the secrets of horses very few seem to know." Missrah replies with a wink.

Bilal says, "She just asked Sekhet?"

"Yes, you saw it in the stall did you not? As mighty and powerful as horses are, they are also gentle and nurturing. They wish to take care of us, especially when we ask them. And, *we can ask them*," replies Missrah putting emphasis on it.

"Wow, I never considered that," says Bilal. "Of course I have not had much experience being around horses either. Especially not any so large, my goodness she is massive!" Bilal looks on with admiration.

They all fall silent watching the graceful movement of Sekhet walking the arena with Ra-Milania seated on her back, as regal and elegant herself. They circle back around and stop in front of Bilal. Ra-Milania reaches out to Bilal to be taken down from Sekhet's back. Bilal steps forward and reaches for her, gently setting her to the ground.

"Thank you Bilal. Let's put Sekhet away and return to my father, shall we?" says Ra-Milania.

They all wait for Ra-Milania to lead Sekhet back to the stall, following not too far behind. Sekhet walks back into the stall herself where Beset waits her return munching on straw. "Thank you Missrah, I will see you later," says Ra-Milania with the look of an unspoken conversation taking place. She turns to the Von Kesslars and says, "It is wonderful to meet you. Would you please come again? There will be a performance at the outdoor theatre on the full moon in three nights, it would be my pleasure if you would come as my guests. Please give your names at the garden entrance and you will be escorted to your seats with me."

"It would be our honor Ra-Milania. Thank you," says Drekkar as he bows deeply.

"It is very nice to meet you Ra-Milania, thank you for showing us your horses! It has been a very special day," says Emilia, also bowing.

Bilal quickly hugs both of his parents, thanks Missrah with a nod and leaves with Ra-Milania to go back to the palace and meet with the Pharaoh and Angyet. Such full days overflowing with new awareness, new possibilities and an entirely new world for Bilal, he can hardly stop smiling with the adventure of it all. They head back the way they came. Mila pauses at a small building outside the stables and looks to Bilal. He is getting to know these looks now. There must be secret Pathway pillars nearby. He begins to look more closely at the architecture. The small building is set with just enough of a walkway behind it to allow two people shoulder to shoulder. Ah, there they are on the back side. Out of sight of enough of the daily traffic to easily go unnoticed as they step into the space between the pillars marked on the wall and out into the private rooms of the Pharaoh.

"I just got to meet Bilal's parents! I invited them to the theatre performance as my guests," exclaims Mila.

"Wonderful," says Pharaoh-Ra.

And now it is time for more practice with moving objects and transforming the elements, such as water into wine. They all gather round the table and spend the rest of the day and into the night playing with the small objects. This practice round Bilal was able to get a few of the gold coins to melt into a puddle, as well as lift the ball into the air again. He was also successful in tying the string into a knot once more, but could not quite accomplish getting the inlay pieces to arrange. He tried without success to light the flame and turn the water into wine...Yet.

Bilal wondered if he would ever get to invite his dear Lili to this magical world of playful possibilities. It had been so long since having time together, he was not sure it would ever become possible. But, still he wondered...

Chapter 30

B ilal and Lili finally meet again.

    The sun is down and the day's tasks are done when most have retired for the night, including the slaves and servants. Bilal has finished practice and put Mila to bed. Lili has been excused for the evening. Bilal and Lili have found time to steal away into the night with each other.

They meet at the marker at the bottom entrance of the palace and walk down to the water's edge where there is an endless path for as long as they wish to go. There will be few people if any, so they need not worry about who might see them. Partly from old habit, partly because they are both new to the palace; meeting in relative secret gives them a sense of ease and privacy rare in their life. They walk side by side. With so much to say they first walk in silence taking in each other's presence and the pure enjoyment of being in each other's company after so long.

Bilal begins, "I have missed you Lili. So much has changed and for so long you have been the only one I could share what is actually true of me. I thought I would see you after you were put into service in the Keeper's Realm. You never came back. What happen to you Lili?"

"Oh, it was horrible Bilal. Master Iberak had sold me to the wife of Keeper of Records for Shipping. She wanted someone more pleasing to look at as I would be accompanying her to the palace while she assisted with her husband's ambitions. She thought I would make her look good or something like that. As time went on her husband took a growing interest in me. He knew I come from Master Iberak's brothel as he had seen me there before. He has much business with Master Iberak and is just as foul a man. He makes more money with black market dealings than his already lucrative business managing accounting for trade. Almost all spices come from the ships he is partial owner of and keeps record for."

"Anyway, he began to pay more attention to me than his wife, even to the point of public display. It was more than his wife could take, she was humiliated and took it out on me. She would beat me, only feed me once a day, lock me up at night and still it did not change her husband's attentions or keep him from me. Finally after almost a year she brought me back to Master Iberak and demanded an exchange of someone not as easy on the eyes and who would be obedient. As though it was my fault!"

"I did not seek his attentions and I could not refuse him either. How could I stop him? I have never felt more stuck or defeated. Having absolutely no choice has got to be one of the worst feelings there is. It was so bad, I was actually glad to be returned to Master Iberak, can you imagine? Oh Bilal, it was only because of you I could endure it. I have seen you suffer worse and I knew you would be there for me if you could be. It kept me going when I thought I could not go on."

Bilal stops walking, taking Lili in his arms and hugging her tenderly. His dear Lili, it was difficult to hear of her suffering. She was always the one there for him to tend his wounds both physically and emotionally. She was his island of nurturance in a sea of misery and pain.

"I am here now," he says softly to her.

She let the suffering of the past year drain from her with Bilal's embrace. She had not realized how much she was still bracing against it all until now. There was a joy in him that had not been there last time she was with him for any amount of time. It radiated out filling her, returning her to her. Tears came to her, but they were tears of release and relief, of letting it all go.

"And you, what of you Bilal? Enough of me," she says as she pulls away and wiping the tears. "I want to hear all about how you have become personal guardian of the Pharaoh-to-be!"

"You will hardly believe it when I tell you!" Bilal begins to recount the events that brought him to the palace and the position of personal guardian to the Pharaoh-to-be. He told of the transformation of his father and the new house in the Artisan Realm. It was only a little more than three weeks now since this incredible turn of events. He was just getting familiar with the palace and this new life. He spoke of the kindness of the Pharaoh and the joy of little Mila. He had actually not met the Pharaoh's wife yet. She seemed to live a separate life and he knew why but he would not speak of it, even to Lili.

He kept the conversation about him personally, and things such as the revelations of his heritage, family and customs of his parent's homeland he kept to himself. He was not sure why he did that, as he has always shared everything with her before. He did share about his parents desire and plans to return north and that he would not leave, as this was his home. He wished to make his own life here as a Freeman and personal guardian to the Pharaoh-to-be. He spoke of the invitation to use his skills with fighting for enhancing the training of the entire royal guard. It was so exciting to find something he could be proud of with use of what he knows.

They sat by the riverbanks for hours and strolled all the rest of the night, making their way back just before the rising sun. Standing on the walkway overlooking the river and seeing the sun rise, they both were bursting with the possibilities of their new life and what lay ahead. Thrilled to be in each other's life again, they relished being reconnected and were already anticipating the next time they could meet.

Were there others who embrace such kindness and caring for others as a natural way to be with one another as he and Lili have come to know? Bilal now knew there were a few, but he wondered, could there be more?

Chapter 31

Mila and Bilal have gone to meet with Kylar so Bilal can begin to get familiar with the living quarters and training grounds for her guards. They will start training as quickly as possible. Bilal is interested to see what they have been doing and what he might be able to add to their training. He has never done such a thing but with everyone's confidence in him he does not feel shy about making the attempt.

When they arrive Kylar is there eagerly awaiting them. He greets them with a large smile and as always instantly goes to Mila and bows, going onto one knee so they can speak eye-to-eye.

"Ra-Milania, good day," he says warmly.

"Greetings Kylar," says Mila as she bows her head slightly. She can't help herself with the excitement she has for today and dropping the formality she hugs him around the neck. Letting go she continues, "So, today I would like you to show Bilal what you have been doing with training the men we have so far. Then we'll see what Bilal has to say about it. First let us show Bilal around, shall we give him the tour?"

"Wonderful Ra-Milania! Let's get started." With that he stands and they go into the building for housing her men. They enter the main room filled with weapons, gear and utility tables for cleaning, mending and maintaining. To the side are doors that go to the sleeping rooms that are set up with bunk beds for six people per room. There is a separate room for Kylar when he needs to stay and they show Bilal to another room that has been set up for him. It is small but arranged comfortably with all he would need.

"This is for you Bilal," says Mila.

"Wonderful Mila, thank you. This will be just fine," replies Bilal with satisfaction as he looks around.

Kylar continues, "We have room to house forty more, though at this time we only have seven that Ra-Milania has approved. We are hoping you can help us increase the numbers. Eventually we would like to have the main team we create be capable of leading the other guards that will be under Ra-Milania's command. The future of Ra-Milania's security she would like to have in her own hands and I am here to help her bring that to fruition. I must confess, I have been following your fights for years Bilal. I have not missed any of them for the last four years. I am a huge admirer of your ability. With your skills and know-how, I feel we can make great strides in accomplishing the future Ra-Milania seeks to create. I can't tell you how excited and grateful I am to have you here."

Kylar is two years older than Bilal. He was at his first death match, hidden in the massive crowd. He had already been attending Bilal's fights before the death match, it was always impressive even though he won every time. He did not tire of watching Bilal's prowess and massive strength. Since he was young, his aim was to be guardian to the royal family so he thought it good training to see how this living legend fought. There were no battles in these times of peace so fist fighting was the closest one would get to real training. The fights in the Laborer's Realm were the only place to see genuine grit. None of the flashy showmanship of the fights in the Keeper's Realm would be seen there. Those fighters would be eaten for noon meal in a place like the Laborer's Realm and Bilal's death matches.

Kylar also liked to wager, something his parents frowned upon. In the Laborer Realm he could wager freely with little fear of being found out. He had made a small fortune betting on Bilal's skills. The first death match was a windfall for him. He had bet everything he had knowing he would do well.

Bilal is a little taken aback, he never considered that we would have a fan in this man Kylar, or anyone for that matter.

"Um, thank you. I don't know what to say," replies Bilal a little shyly.

"No need to say anything, it is my pleasure to have you here," says Kylar with enthusiasm. "Come, let me show you the rest." They continue going through the building pointing out the kitchen, bathing area, running water for drinking. Just as they are finishing the seven men that Mila has chosen arrive.

They had just been on a group run. They have all just sat down in the main room winded and quickly stand again falling in line as they see Mila and Bilal with Kylar entering the room. "Perfect timing," says Kylar. "Men, please meet Bilal, he will be joining us from this day forward. You all know of him and I will expect your best efforts in taking in all he instructs. Let us make Ra-Milania proud."

They all nod standing with backs straight and large smiles. It is an unlikely mix of men of all ages. Kylar walks down the line introducing them one by one. "This is Zek, our newest and youngest whom you met the other day. This is Hemel, he keeps our equipment in top readiness. He comes from my family's metal works. This is Karek, he has been servant and guard of Ra-Milania since he was twelve. He knows everything about everyone at the palace and how to not be noticed. This is Madu, he keeps us from being a mess and has extra awareness of people's intent, if there is trouble nearby he always knows it. This is Anzety, he is in charge of all tactical movements for keeping Ra-Milania secure. This is Guyasi, he is our most accurate marksman with any weapon, especially with both bow and arrow and javelin. He is amazing with how he can move physically and is helping us all gain his physical capacities. And this is Missrah who is our expert with the horses and camels and connection with the earth. We all work together sharing what we are good at, contributing to each other to improve in each area as the oneness. Most of us stay here now. We are a team, and we welcome you Bilal," says Kylar. He nods at the men indicating they may break the line, knowing how excited they all are to meet the infamous Bilal.

With that they all relax and step forward to say an enthusiastic hello. They clap his back and take his hand to shake it, all pouring over each other to say hello first and what a pleasure it is to meet him.

"Pleasure to meet you Bilal."

"You are a huge man, I didn't know you were this big!"

"Thank you for coming. It is a pleasure."

"Welcome. Nice to see you again."

"Hello, nice to meet you."

"Hi Bilal. Great to have you join us!"

"Show us some moves Bilal!"

Smiling Bilal takes it in, nodding, saying hello. He is not so sure how to take all the friendliness, *"This will take some getting used to,"* he thinks to himself. His entire life up to these last few weeks he did nothing without the permission of Master Iberak and it was a rare occasion that Master Iberak was not nearby when Bilal was doing something other than working in the quarry or fighting. To be without his watchful eye Bilal realized was a foreign thing. He found it a little disturbing to notice he was thinking of what Master Iberak would be expecting of him in this moment. That moment passes and Bilal takes in the warm welcome as the men are ushering him outside to the arena. They would like Bilal to show them some fighting moves.

Mila follows and seats herself in the viewing area to watch the boys go into action. She indicates to Kylar to join them instead of sit with her. She knows how excited he is about Bilal.

The men pair up with as even sizes as they can. They all begin sparring with each other, warming up as Bilal stands back to watch for a few minutes. Zek is the youngest and smallest but Bilal chooses him to be paired with to demonstrate some moves. Zek stands besides Bilal looking back and forth trying to see what Bilal is looking at and at the same time to watch what the other men are doing. No one has ever asked Bilal to give fighting tips, but he finds himself falling into a natural ease of observing each person's moves and instantly noticing what each man could do a little different that would improve how they fight. In just five minutes he starts to walk around to each pair adjusting their body position and giving them comments about their movements.

With Zek as his demonstration model, he shows a few other movements for them to try out. Continuing to move around and between the men he is caught up in the joy of sharing something he knows about and is good at.

Mila sat with a determined look on her face as she watches her guards in training. Bilal is showing them some defensive moves now. Mila was trying out her usual tricks with pinning a guards foot in place, or stopping then from being able to swing their arm...this time she was trying to do it to Bilal and it was not working! She was having no effect at all. This had never happened before. She could always do it at least somewhat since she was three years old. She wanted to get upset about it but instead burst out laughing to herself. *"Wow, how wonderful,"* she thought. *"Whatever Bilal is capable of it sure will be fun to find out!"*

"Hey Bilal," Mila calls out. "Did you notice any peculiar

sensations in the last few minutes?"

"No Mila," he replies.

She crosses her arms and with a frown and says, "Are you sure?"

"Yes Mila," Bilal replies again.

"Okay," says Mila with a sigh. "Please continue with what you were doing." She sits back watching the training, a large smile on her lips again. She didn't know Bilal was so good at fist fighting. She had never seen fighting for sport before. She was thrilled to find he had skills she didn't know about and that contributed so well to what she had been asking for. Oh how she loves the oneness and the magnificent capacity for delivering what is greater than we can imagine the oneness naturally embodies. A deep gratitude and satisfaction fills her and she lets it spill out into her sense of connection with all the molecules of creation including the men and boys before her.

She would be forever grateful for the man who showed her the depth of possibility that embodying the oneness creates. Naruub was that gift of a man. Now it was time to introduce Bilal to him.

Chapter 32

The evening practice session is done and Angyet has a surprise for Bilal; a new way to expand his capacities and open up his connection with the oneness.

Angyet escorts Bilal to be introduced to Naruub, Keeper of the House of Pleasure. He is her dear friend and colleague for playing with and expanding the capacities of oneness. She was explaining how Naruub has a special talent and ability with bodies, and that he can provide the healing of both his body and being that will greatly enhance his capacity with the oneness. It will give him a boost to progress more quickly, more quickly than without it.

"This is not about sex Bilal, this is about receiving. This is about undoing the insanity of the violence you have been through. When you cannot understand the abuse of your body and being it locks inside you. There was nothing understandable about what you have lived through. You cannot have what you are truly capable of unless you are also including the body and Naruub is truly magical with his healing touch. He will show you the beauty of nurturing your body and including your body completely. You'll see. It is wonderful," she says with a twinkle in her eyes. "Do you have any questions so far?"

"I am not sure. I am beginning to get how vital including the body is. It shows us the energies very dynamically with all those sensations. I don't get exactly what you mean by healing. I don't have any wounds, only some old scars," replies Bilal with an inquisitive look at Angyet.

"Ah, yes. Let me ask you this; those times when you stood on the cliffs edge, for what reason did you wish to jump, and for what reason did you not jump?" asks Angyet.

Bilal was getting used to her directness, and her openness and lack of judgment made it easy to reply from the depths of what is really true for him. "I wanted to jump not so much from the violence, I have gotten rather used to that and not much really hurts me physically speaking. It is the lack of choice, the constant judgment of wrongness, the smallness and constraint of my life, being surrounded by death, torture and hate. So much ugliness, so much hopelessness, people being ugly with each other; it was more than I could stand... but then the wind, the heat coming off the rocks, the beauty before me...it would renew me. It would open things up so I had space to be me again. The 'me' that is not subject to others, the 'me' that is free and untouched by all the ugliness of my life," says Bilal with a sigh.

"Yes, that. That is what I am talking about. How that

connection is possible with the earth and the elements. What if it was possible to have that kind of connection and sense of being you that includes people? You have begun to taste it with Pharaoh-Ra, Mila and myself. I have seen it. We are an invitation and your connection with us is just the beginning of what will become possible, if you are willing. This is the healing I speak of; the healing of your very being, where you do not need to hide any part of you especially from you. Naruub is an expert like no other at giving you an awareness of this healing I speak of. The healing that comes from body and being in communion with each other; the healing that can include another person when you are both being and receiving. Also the healing that comes with connection with and including the earth."

"Do you mean how it feels when you touch me, I would call it being turned on, but somehow it is not quite that. Or when Mila hugs me and I melt? It is like being alive with all the joy and pleasure of living being turned on in me and my body." His face grows a little flush with the admission, but he knows he can say anything with Angyet, and he knows somehow she already knows all this about him.

"Yes Bilal, this is all part of being connected with one another in oneness. No barriers, so separation, no need to hide who we really are and what is true for us and about us. Where there is nothing judgable about any of us, with ourselves or each other. Where the enjoyment and pleasure of our bodies is included, but does not mean any particular action is either required or denied. All is a choice and every energy is allowed. Oneness is about the ability to be any energy at any moment, simply by the request of self and willingness to be it."

Bilal melts open more as he hears what is true for him, that no one has ever said to him before. It is a deep acknowledgement of his being every time he hears what Angyet has to say. In this moment he realizes that she has never spoken frivolous words. She is always direct and to the point, using the least words for the most effect. He marvels at the elegance of her speech.

Angyet has walked farther than needed to give her and Bilal time to speak on their way to Naruub's chambers at the Temple of the House of Pleasure. The timing is just right as they arrive with the conversation at this moment.

"Here we are. This time is for you Bilal. The healing I speak of will be self-evident when you experience it for yourself. It is not something that can easily be put to words, yet it is unmistakable when you receive it. You'll see." She smiles kindly as she ushers him in the door gently touching his back to direct him. With her touch the familiar wave of spectacular space and sensual liveliness her touch turns on in him spreads throughout his body and being.

They enter a room unlike any Bilal has seen before. Every surface, every object is ornate, an explosion of colors, textures and shapes. It should feel busy and cramped but somehow it is like a warm embrace of all the senses. There is a lushness to everything that is very inviting, it makes him want to touch every surface and explore. Sitting in the middle is a man as serene and beautiful as everything that surrounds him. The most exotic looking person Bilal has ever seen. This man is more beautiful than most women, yet does not come across in any way feminine. He exudes a sentualness that makes Bilal instantly wish to reach out and touch him as well. Everything about him is like this room; impossible to take one's eyes from, beautiful beyond anything seen before and drawing you in. This is Naruub.

Naruub speaks; his voice smooth as silk and warm as the richness of the rest of the room, "Welcome Bilal. Please come sit here and make yourself comfortable. Thank you Angyet, it is my honor." He says no more to her but stands and bows to her deeply. With a hand over her heart she makes a small bow back to him with gratitude in her eyes and leaves silently closing the door behind her.

Chapter 33

Bilal's heart begins to race, he has no idea what is going to happen other than this is about healing in both body and being. There is a softness to this man, but again nothing particularly feminine about him. Bilal is finding him to be un-definable which is perplexing and yet enjoyable. As a few moments pass he begins to relax as he takes in the beauty of the surroundings. He walks to the daybed that Naruub has indicated and sits on the edge feeling very much like a virgin on her wedding night. He wants to laugh at the thought but refrains, only allowing a smile to come to his lips and taking a deep breath.

Naruub has taken a few moments allowing Bilal to look around before he speaks.

"Thank you for coming Bilal. You may remain seated as you are, or you may lay back on the daybed. Your clothes will remain on, however I ask that you open your shirt, if you will," he says with a smile in one corner of his mouth.

Bilal looks into his eyes and senses the honor and regard this man has for him, even though they have never met before. With that he begins to lean back so he is sitting up but leaning on the back rest with his legs stretched out before him. He pauses and asks, "Shall I remove my shoes Naruub?"

"Only if you wish to Bilal. In this place, all choice is yours, I will always honor all that you choose. I will also invite you to that which you may have never chosen before, and still the choice will always be yours to make." The warmth of Naruub's words and the meaning of it is like the warm embrace he has only ever known on the cliffs edge at the quarry. It lowers Bilal's barriers to be touched by the presence of being this man embodies.

With the kindness and sincerity with which Naruub speaks, Bilal would like to cry. He has never been invited with such honesty to that which he holds most dear; his ability to choose and have choice in all things. There is nothing more terrible than living without any choice. Bilal removes his shoes and stretches out his legs while pulling open the top of his shift and getting more comfortable. He takes a deep breath relaxing some.

"I would like you to please close your eyes Bilal. Continue to breath and expand, reaching with your senses. I may speak some, I may not. I will touch your body some, and there may be times I will not. If you notice there is a thrum beginning, a pulsing of energy in your body? Allow yourself to sink into that thrum and extend your senses taking in the touch of the

daybed against your body and your body against the day bed."
With the now familiar exercise of expanding his senses that
all of his new found friends practice he easily relaxes into the
guiding words of Naruub.

He takes in a breath as Naruub places his hand squarely
on his chest, it is warm and somehow with more than just the
heat of his body. He feels a wave of energies flowing into his
body hot and vibrant radiating from his chest out to his limbs.
Naruub's other hand goes low on Bilal's belly expanding the
sense of warmth and relaxation flowing through his body.
Bilal relaxes into the touch of Naruub's hands realizing it has
been a long time since he was touched with such kindness.
Not since his last night with Lili well over a year before. The
energies intensify which melts Bilal into Naruub's touch even
more. Energetically he begins to reach for Naruub and the
kindness and caring of his touch, somehow this takes him
deeper within himself.

Naruub moves his hands running them down the length
of Bilal's body, gentle yet firmly present bringing Bilal's
awareness to his entire body. His hands move all the way to
the top of his feet where Naruub's hands now rest, pausing
for a few moments. Now touching the bottom of Bilal's feet
and the energies intensify and expand again lighting up his
entire body. Bilal draws in a deep breath and relaxes more. It
is like he is breathing for the first time, which unexpectedly
cracks open that vault of darkness he so diligently has kept
locked inside.

At that moment Naruub speaks, "I am here with you Bilal.
I am here with you in all you have locked inside and I see no

wrongness. This is a space for all you are, everything you have ever been through is allowed and will be embraced. This is where you are allowed to let it all out," with that Bilal's very molecules begin to clamor and shake.

As Bilal begins to test out what Naruub is saying he lowers his barriers letting more of all that is ugly begin to come to the surface. As he does he finds an embrace of being unlike anything he has ever known. Naruub is there, totally present, an energy of kindness and caring inviting him to go farther and open up a little bit more; each moment just a little bit more. Naruub is moving his hands again touching Bilal all over. His touch continues to expand and unlock memories, sensations and emotions he did not know where there. Naruub speaks softly talking him through it, assisting him in letting it go, a witness to the brutality of Bilal's now eighteen years of life.

Naruub is silent again, he has now added more sexual energies turning Bilal's body on, his touch grows more gentle, yet the intensity increases; this breaks open a depth of pain and darkness Bilal had been bracing against being aware of and his mind wants to fight it and his body tenses with the intensity of memories. "I am here," whispers Naruub.

And again the energies intensify, a wave of lightness as if the space of the night sky and the heat of the rocks at the end of the day is blowing through his body all at once...these energies begin to melt the harshness of what is surfacing. Bilal trembles to the core of his being. He has only known a man's touch as harsh and belittling with malicious intent. The impossibly gentle touch of Naruub's finger tips as they run across his chest is shattering his reality. His mind screams that he should fight; he should reject and shrink away from such kindness and caring of energies and touch. His body and being say otherwise and melt into the embrace of being he always dreamed of but never dare consider possible, not like this. Tears run down his cheeks with the release of the abuse of being he had learned to live with. The trembling at his core spreads to the surface of his body like an earth quake. He allows the sensations to wash over him, grasping the fabric of the daybed he is sitting upon. He does not know if he would like to scream and cry or laugh, and a strange sound that is both comes out of him.

Naruub smiles gently and again increases the turn on and nurturing. He introduces a new energy of joyfulness that shifts the energies flowing through Bilal's being and body. It is too much, Bilal cannot hold back anymore, he lets go and surrenders to the explosion of being rearranging his entire reality...and the laughter takes over Bilal shaking him from deep within; though little sound escapes his lips. A twinkle of aliveness comes into his world. It is the oneness; the embrace of being that brings pleasure to being alive, having a body and connecting with all the molecules of the universe. He would have never guessed that would include the almost unbearable gentleness of an impossibly beautiful man. He never imagined there was a way through that darkness to a peacefulness of being on the other side.

Naruub explained it plain enough and it made sense, even though it went against everything he had ever known. To become the oneness, we must receive every energy without having a judgment about it being right or wrong, good or bad. Where we would reject and separate is the extent of our limitation. Reject nothing, separate from nothing and we have no limitation.

Naruub explains, "You are a man. As a man you would have a problem with the touch of a man or receiving and connection with a man for what reason? To reject other men would be to reject part of yourself as well. It does not mean you have to do anything with it; it is about be willing to have it and receiving it all. It is not about if you choose to put your body parts together or not. That is just a choice and a different matter altogether."

Naruub continues, "One of your greatest advantages and weapons is your willingness to be and receive what other people will not. Those who will not be and receive what you will, they will always find you intimidating and might even fear you. Those who can receive you will find you very attractive and alluring. You will be inspiring and inviting to them. You can use this to your advantage and to manipulate. If you are going to create something greater for us all, it will take a great deal of manipulation and inviting of people in what they have not yet been willing to choose. Bilal, we all wish you to have everything you are truly capable of at your beck and call."

Naruub has stepped away from Bilal's body now, though the intensity of energies continues.

Bilal is both invigorated and spent. He has never felt better or as raw and uncomfortable as he does reclined on this daybed. The touch of Naruub lingers...it is as though he is still touching him. Bilal finds this both exciting and mysterious. Bilal asks about it.

"It is the oneness," says Naruub. "As the oneness there

is no separation. This intensifies and expands your sensory perception. The body is a sensory organ giving us energetic awareness of all the molecules we are connected to; which is all of them. We can increase our awareness of any energy we choose to. You can choose to continue increasing the energies available to you and your body. Right now, increase the energies of the sensation of my touch on your skin. Ask for it."

Like he is being touched again the sensations increase on not only his chest, but his entire body. Bilal's eyes widen and he takes a swift breath in. It is orgasmic. *"I can have more of this upon request? It is so easy. How can it be so easy?"* Bilal is enthralled. He begins to grasp at the energies, trying to hold onto it and it suddenly diminishes. "What happened?" asks Bilal.

Naruub replies "Don't try and hold onto it. You squelch the energies if you try to hold onto them. You cannot own it or possess it. You can choose to be an energy; you can request of it and expand into it. That is what opens the oneness. The moment you contract into holding onto or trying to possess the oneness, it will escape you. Relax, expand again." Swiftly and easily all the energies of expansion, space of being and relaxation return. With this quick exercise Bilal realizes how much work it is to contract and hold on so tightly to the smallness of defending against the ugliness he had previously braced against.

"There, you have it again. You will never truly be able to go back to the contraction and smallness you were before this night Bilal. This is healing; you having all of you. I can continue to show you how to regain you. Come back tomorrow after your work is done and you have bathed, we can play again. Oh, and there are hidden pillars of The Pathway by the entrance, just to the right of the main doors as you are going out. Behind the pillar, face the wall and you'll see it there."

"What? You would allow me back here? Um, thank you!... Thank you." Bilal says in a whisper, he is flabbergasted. He had not dared even wish he could have more of this. That it was so casually and easily invited took him by surprise. He wanted to hug Naruub but was not sure what would be the honorable thing. He dared to ask, "May I embrace you Naruub? I am so grateful, I don't know how to thank you. I never imagined such healing could be possible. Truly, you are a gift!" says Bilal teary-eyed again.

"Yes, Bilal, please. The honor is mine, that you would allow me to touch you in body and being and invite you home to you. Your receiving of what I gift honors me in more ways than I can say. Not so many are willing to receive as you have been."

With that they embrace tenderly for a minute or two, melting into each other, a celebration of the nurturing of oneness and gratitude for being in each other's presence. The gift of two beings simultaneously gifting and receiving everything they are. Honoring one another; man to man, infinite being to infinite being.

With that Bilal sits again and puts on his shoes. Taking his leave and heading out the door, Bilal is floating in a sense of grace. It is several long hallways to reach the main entrance and the hidden pillars of The Pathway. The tears began to flow again as the cool night air caresses him. Every sense is heightened and embraces him. For the first time Bilal has a true sense of possibility for being washed clean of the darkness of his upbringing. He dare not know how much he had locked inside to deal with the violence he had withstood and was demanded that he deliver in his fights and death matches. He realizes how the intense presence without judgment and the gentleness of touch Naruub has shown him is a deep healing he could never image was possible. The tears flowed more with the flood of gratitude he had for such a gift as this.

He need no longer hide any part of him from himself.

Chapter 34

When plans for building a monumental pyramid were announced, Keeper of the Movers, Eka-ar, had come to Pharaoh with his proposal that the Movers have the honor of moving and placing the stones. For many years Eka-ar had demonstrated his ability with moving objects and Pharaoh-Ra knew he put much effort and significance on developing disciples to follow his strict and highly structured training to become recognized as a Mover of the House of Pharaoh. It was a deep honor as much of the major construction projects used the Movers to make building quicker and easier. With their assistance new possibilities for building were opening up, creating a boom in creativity with architecture and structures not previous dared. With the skill of the Movers to transport massive weight and size, considerably fewer people and less time would be required to accomplish this huge task.

It had been a few years and Eka-ar had developed a talented team. Today Pharaoh-Ra summoned Eka-ar to get an update and status of the Mover's progress with construction.

Eka-ar enters Pharaoh's meeting room to find Pharaoh-Ra sitting, apparently waiting for his arrival. Eka-ar quickly makes his usual overly elaborate greeting, "Your radiance shines brighter than ever, good day Pharaoh-Ra." He bows deeply and continues, "I hope I have not kept you waiting your eminence, forgive my rudeness. What is it I may do for you today, my most gracious Lord?"

"Please take a seat Eka-ar. Tell me, how does it go with construction?"

"Beautifully Lord Pharaoh-Ra! The people have been most enthusiastic with the ceremony of placement. The crowds have been quite large watching our procession as we transport the stones from the quarry to the pyramid. The cheers are an unexpected surprise. I do worry that it will distract the disciples in their tasks. Fear not! I have trained them tirelessly, they shall not falter in their duties!" replies Eka-ar.

That was not what Pharaoh-Ra was actually asking, but it did not surprise him that this was Eka-ar's take on the question. "And the pyramid itself? You are having no difficulty in the accuracy of placement?" asks Pharaoh-Ra.

"Oh, Angyet has been quite clear with her instruction and drawings. And she made it easy with the guidance and absolute precision in the first level placement. The foundation has provided a very clear guide to work from. With Angyet giving us only one step at a time, we can focus with total certainty in getting the placement correct. How could we falter with her superior supervision?"

"Yes, indeed. Thank you Eka-ar, your service has been exceptional. I am very pleased with your work so far. Keep it up. That is all," Pharaoh says with a nod of his head and the wave of his hand as he turns to the papers in front of him.

Eka-ar stands, bows, and takes his leave with no further word. He knows when he has been dismissed and leaves Pharaoh quickly.

He dare not stay long for fear of betraying any hint of treachery. He had no idea the Pharaoh is already aware of it all and has his own plans in motion. Pharaoh-Ra has instructed all who are aware; "Let him think he is getting away with everything, thereby he will hang himself in his own web of deceit."

Pharaoh-Ra sits back after Eka-ar has left the room. His memories return to the moment he discovered Eka-ar and his wife's plans for usurping the seat-of-Pharaoh. It was a series of events in truth, all revealing bit by bit the depth of scheming developing over the previous few years. It began innocent enough in Ra-Maharet meeting Eka-ar at one of the many evenings of lavish dinning at the palace. Eka-ar was demonstrating his skills for wife-of-pharaoh's amusement. She was enthralled, mesmerized by his ability of moving objects without touch. He had even lifted her chair entirely with her upon it, moving and twirling delicately. He moved her as though he was dancing with her while she sat floating in coordinated and rhythmic motion a few feet away from him. From that night on she would spend hours with him asking questions about what he did, how he did it and to be amused by his skill. She showed no inclination of desiring to learn to do it herself, but relished Eka-ar demonstrating it for her.

She began to be interested in the more esoteric and philosophical aspects of what was taught at the House of Movers. The power to move objects at will ignited her own enthusiasm for having power over both people and things. She was always interested in anything that increased her power over as a possibility. As the months and then years passed Pharaoh-Ra watched as Ra-Maharet demonstrated an ever increasing intensity and demand for control, subordination of her subjects and assumed supremacy as wife-of-pharaoh. She loved ruling over people more than anyone Pharaoh-Ra had ever known before. It was disturbing.

Pharaoh-Ra noticed as his wife began to speak of herself and Eka-ar as "We." She did not notice her slip-up, as she was so consumed in her own point of view and fantasies of power. She also did not recognize how much she was revealing in these comments.

It was the day the first base stone was set, she had commented, "What a glorious day! When the Movers so elegantly placed its bulk we could sense the increase in power. What a marvel, isn't it?"

Most people would not notice such a comment but for Pharaoh-Ra is stuck out like a lightning bolt. His wife would never be Pharaoh, she had no real place of power other than her contribution to the continuation of the family line by what heirs she would produce. Since her refusal to lay with the Pharaoh after the birth of Ra-Milania, it became clear this wife had other plans. The awareness of that added to these new comments about the power of the pyramid being hers; Ra-Maharet was beginning to reveal her true intensions. By all indications she was reaching for a power grab.

Chapter 35

Night has returned and Bilal is at the House of Pleasure for his next meeting with Naruub.

Bilal enters the room quietly taking it all in. The extravagance of it is breath-taking. Looking around he does not notice Naruub at first, he is getting absorbed in the sights arranged before him. He smiles a little shyly when he finally sees Naruub silently watching him as he is admiring the room.

"Welcome Bilal," Naruub says softly. "What are you noticing as you enter this room?"

"I was struck by how every object is perfectly placed in relation to what is around it and somehow what is behind it as well. I cannot find a single thing that is messy, awkward or unpleasing to the eye. It is spectacular!" exclaims Bilal in awe.

"Most people never notice that Bilal. It speaks well of your powers of observation. Please come have a seat here at the table. We are going to take a different approach this evening," Naruub gestures for him to take a seat at the lavishly laid-out table.

Just as the room, every item on the table is placed with beautiful aesthetic sensibility; from the details of the dishes to the placement of the food and drink items. Bilal has never seen anything like it and it makes him smile as he takes in the sight of it. Looking at the items on the table so intently he did not notice as he takes a seat and takes in a breath at the same moment...the seat is covered with the softest, most plush animal fur he has ever felt. He sinks in just a bit, wonderfully cushioned. The fur touches the skin of his legs and it is like being caressed by clouds. He stands again, he must look at what is on this chair. "What is this wonderful fur?" asks Bilal as he at the same time touches the fur, melting into the touch of softness.

"It is called 'angora' and is from a creature called a 'rabbit', sublime isn't it? Please do sit, enjoy it," invites Naruub with a twinkle in his eyes. "Tonight is about enhancing and expanding your senses of touch, sight, sound, smell and taste. With all we are going to play with tonight you are likely to find enhanced subtlety with your exercises with Angyet, Mila and Pharaoh-Ra. Moving of objects, transformation of molecules by request; all of it becomes easier with increased awareness of the little things and the subtle complexities of energies. Do you have any questions so far?"

Bilal shakes his head no.

"Then let us begin," says Naruub. "First, relax. Close your

eyes. Expand out as you do when you are reaching for that sense of the space of you. Notice your feet on the floor and the floor as it touches your feet. Take a few deep breathes and reach down into the earth sensing the thrum and pulse of energies and all of its living vitality...Good. Let the energies of the earth fill you. Expand farther now, being the space that fills this entire room, then this entire building, good, and farther to the surrounding buildings. Now all the way to the palace and the Keeper's Realm, the markets and the Artisan Realm, down to the water's edge and the other direction to the Laborer's Realm and beyond to the pyramid. And now as far as your eye can see in every direction and keep going out to the desert sands of the north and the fields of the farmers and wilderness to the south and expanding into the sky and the earth below in as large a space...Ah, wonderful. Now you can open your eyes."

"Now look at the spread before you. Notice the placement, the colors, the textures and choose something to taste. Whatever you choose first, pick it up, feel the surface of it, smell it but do not taste it yet."

Upon opening his eyes, he notices the colors are brighter than they were before. Bilal picks up a plump, ripe fig. As he holds it in his hand he notices the weight of it, he rubs his thumb across the surface feeling the smoothness of it. He smells the ripeness of the fig noticing a complexity of scents he never noticed before. He looks to Naruub for what next.

Naruub continues with a nod to Bilal, "When you take a bite, notice all the flavors, how it lights up your mouth in different areas of your tongue."

Bilal slowly takes a bite and juice drips down his lip and chin, he catches it with the swipe of his hand. He chuckles as he sucks in the explosion of juice and flavor.

Naruub continues; "Do not chew it, but move it around your mouth. How many flavors do you notice? Good. Now chew. Do the flavors change the more you chew it? Do you notice different tastes in different area of your mouth? Do you notice any other area of your body light up with sensation? There is no right or wrong way to do this or in what to notice. It is about the exploration of it all and the question of 'what do you notice?'"

Bilal takes another bite, closing his eyes again to discover the flavor of fig like he never has before.

For the next hour they both sample all the food items and variety of drinks Naruub has set on the table. Taking only a single bite of each item they explore the intensity of senses of texture, taste, smell and touch. Sharing what they each notice that they had never noticed before in the things they eat every day.

Bilal is amazed. "I rarely have noticed how complex in flavor everything really is. Thinking about it now it is only in those moments of eating something absolutely wonderful that I take a moment to savor it; so often it is just that I am hungry and I do not take in the flavors, smells or textures. It makes me wonder how much more of the world I can now be aware of that I missed before?"

"Wonderful Bilal, that is exactly what I was hoping you would come into question about! The world is filled with a richness that many people simply ignore, so wrapped up in their heads, in the difficulties of the day or any number of other things. It is this kind of presence with everything that exponentially increases your awareness. The joy of living that is available is simply astounding. Becoming aware of the subtleties and complexities of energies that are really there will be a contribution beyond what you may have yet imagines is possible! I invite you to see what you notice that is different when you leave here tonight. You can tell me about it next time we converse."

After enjoying each other's company a bit longer, Bilal takes his leave. Tonight he will walk back to his room to test out the exercise and conversation of his evening with Naruub. It is easy to wonder at the richness of beauty inside Naruub's quarters; to Bilal's delight he finds when he steps beyond the door of Naruub's rooms the hallway is alive like it never was before. The light of the torches and bowls of fire seem brighter. The colors painting the walls stand out in more detail than they did before. He takes in a deep breath of air and it is more invigorating and refreshing than he recalls. His long strides bring awareness to his body. He feels good, really good!

As Bilal descends the stairs of the House of Pleasure the cool night air envelops him like an explosion of softness and space. The light and twinkle of the stars above is breath-taking. It is like he has never noticed them before. And the smells, so many scents riding on the air. They are as complex as the tastes of food he was savoring, transforming moment by moment. His senses reeling with vibrancy he stops walking for a moment to listen to the sounds of the night.

He does not hear anything at first but silence. Then he

senses the scurry of a mouse and turns to look and see it before the sound has ever reached his ears. With delight he wonders what else he can sense around him. Closing his eyes and reaching out with his awareness he senses people ahead to the left, he opens his eyes to look and sees two people, shadows silhouetted against the light that is behind them as they pass by, too far away to hear their footsteps, yet obvious by sight and sense of their energetic presence. He looks up now sensing the movement in the air above, it is a night hawk flying over head. Increasing the space of question of what else he can perceive he notices the sensations of all sorts of insects, critters of the night and people in their homes, or walking about.

With a deep sense of satisfaction and awe, Bilal returns to his bed in Mila's rooms of the palace for the night. *"What a wonder living is,"* he marvels, as the peacefulness of sleep takes him.

Chapter 36

The sun is high and Ra-Maharet sits on her balcony taking in her favorite view; the construction progress of the pyramid. As the height of the pyramid increases with every added stone, so do the feelings of grandeur and aspirations of power Ra-Maharet envisions for her future. She feels the strength of the pyramid as her own strength, the growing height as increase in her own potency. She was made for this. She sighs with satisfaction, everything is falling into place.

Eka-ar and the Movers have finally succeeded in seizing control of the pyramid right from under everyone's nose. Her trust in the Movers ability and support was sealed with this accomplishment. She was elated. To have such power at her command feeds her confidence. This was the most important aspect of her takeover and she was confident that the rest would now fall into place with ease. This was the leverage she had been waiting for.

Now she could turn her attentions more fully to Master Iberak. Besides Eka-ar, Keeper of the Movers, Iberak was the most ambitious man she knew and he would do anything to get the job done. His ambitions aligned very well with hers and she planned to use it to the fullest. With the goings on of the Laborer Realm fairly far from the palace it was a little easier to develop their plans. She was working with Master Iberak to amass an armed force. They would need weapons and training, and all without being detected by the Pharaoh. She was not quite sure how that was going to work yet, but she was confident that between her and Master Iberak they would be able to come up with a plan and decisive action.

She had already been filtering off funds for several years in any way she could. There was such abundance in Pharaoh's Land that she was fairly certain of her stealth up to this point. Master Iberak had been growing his number of slaves and influence well on his own. With her added backing he was beginning to expand much more rapidly, and they were just getting started. When the Pharaoh had made Bilal and his parents Freemen, he had compensated Master Iberak well for his loss. This played wonderfully into her plans. She couldn't have come up with a better scenario herself, she mused. That was a stroke of luck she had not anticipated. Now the building of her forces to the north could commence in earnest.

The light shining on the growing pyramid inspires her ambitions as she dreams of the brightness of her future-to-be.

For a thousand generations a single family has been Pharaoh of the land. Succession follows from the Pharaoh to their first born, be they male or female. It is the custom that the spouse of the Pharaoh either kills themselves to remain with the deceased Pharaoh, as spouse in the afterlife, or continue on as advisor to the new Pharaoh; their choice.

The spouse of this Pharaoh has different plans. Ra-Maharet was determined; the seat-of-Pharaoh would become hers one day, no matter what it took.

Chapter 37

It has been three days since Bilal met with his parents in the palace gardens. He has a few hours in the morning to visit with his parents more. He has come home excited about speaking with them. Tonight is the theatre performance and he can't wait to share more about the marvels of this new life of theirs.

Bilal finds his parents at the dining table with hot tea in hand and food on the table. They were deep in conversation when he walks in. Welcoming Bilal they make him a plate and pour him a cup of the exotic tea from the Pharaoh's market.

"Son, we have something to speak with you about. Please have a seat," says Drekkar.

He continues, "You have become a man we are proud of son. You are a Freeman now, and we see how you have elevated yourself and are making yourself useful to the Pharaoh and Ra-Milania."

Emilia goes on, "We both can see the pride and honor you have in your duty with them. We could not have hoped for such greatness here in this life. Now that we are all free of Master Iberak and have the generosity of the Pharaoh, and how Rimmel has made us at home, we have never been happier."

"I have dreamed of a life for you without ever giving you the choice, or even the awareness of what I aimed for. It was wrong of me to keep this all from you, and I cannot expect you to desire what I desire for you. You are royalty yourself, but of a family line and in lands you do not know and have never been to. I see now that this is your home son. But it is not mine, it is not mine or your mother's," says Drekkar earnestly.

"What we are trying to say is that your father and I, we could not be happier for you. And, well, your father and I wish to go home. We wish to go to the land of our birth, we plan to go north. We will not ask you to go with us, son. We do not wish to take you from the bright future opening up here. We would like you to make your life what you would like it to be, and now we know you can. After meeting Ra-Milania, we understand how wonderful your life is becoming and we are so happy for you!"

"What? You are leaving? You are leaving without me?" says Bilal, wide-eyed.

Drekkar looks him in the eyes, "You have been a slave all your life, and now you are free. You are the best fighter I have ever seen. You have the favor of the Pharaoh and his daughter. You can marry Lili if you choose," says Drekkar. "We would like nothing more than for you to come with us, but we will not ask this of you. We will not ask you to give up all that you have gained. Your life is your own to make as you will."

Bilal is dumbfounded, he was not expecting this. "When, when are you going? I don't know what to say. You are right, I have no aspirations to leave. But, I can't imagine the two of you not being here!"

"We know, my son," says Emilia softly. She touches his hand and continues. "We will leave next full moon. Now that we have the means, we are gathering what will make our journey more ease-filled. We will get horses of our own, so we no longer have to walk. This will take several months off the time of our journey. It will still take us over twelve cycles of the moon most likely."

"I am happy for you both, but sad for me. What will I do without you?" ask Bilal, feeling like a small child.

"Oh, we have seen you in this new life of yours, we know you will do well with or without us here. Let us take the time we have left to enjoy each other's company as we can. I will tell all that I can recall of the land of your parents birth, of your heritage and how to get there if one day you choose to travel there yourself. You know, I thought you could take back the life I gave up by coming to our homeland with us. However I will no longer strive to burden you with my own aspirations. Instead we will return there and hope for the embrace of my family as we are. It gives me peace to think of returning there, just as it gives me peace to know the man you have become and the life you are creating here. I could not be more proud of you son." Drekkar clasps his son on the shoulder and the three of them sit silently savoring the moment.

They will celebrate their time together in every way they can, exploring the richness offered by their life granted by the graciousness of Pharaoh-Ra. They have yet to know the extent of the beauty they have been invited to experience, but with tonight's full moon they will find out more.

Chapter 38

Evening has arrived and it is the night of the theatre performance. Emilia and Drekkar have dressed in their finest. They had consulted with Rimmel for what to wear, and he delivered the most amazing clothing either of them has ever worn. Emilia wore a pale blue gown, flowing with such lightness as to be like air draped on her body. She had never worn anything so wonderful feeling or beautiful to look at. It matched her eyes perfectly. Rimmel showed her how to make a double chain with the insignia, so the gold circle lay just above her breast. Wearing her hair up, it showed off wonderfully.

Drekkar got his own gold trimmed shift with the soft fabric like Bilal had. Rimmel had included the most amazing leather belt painted with gold in a simple design that matched the trim of the shift. They felt like royalty themselves in such finery. Drekkar wore his insignia as a long necklace. Adding these to the outfits, they were ready to go.

It was a warm night and the full moon was already above the horizon, but not too far yet. There are several people flowing into the palace gardens. They approach a man who looks to be an extra guard at the side of the gate. He is the man there to escort them to the theatre as Ra-Milania's guests.

The guard is courteous but speaks no extraneous words; he leads them silently to the amphitheatre and shows them to seats directly behind and to the left of the seats for the Pharaoh himself, his wife and Ra-Milania as they face the stage. These seats are two steps up so those sitting in them can see above the seats of the Pharaoh. There are several people already seated, but none of the royalty or Bilal yet. Drekkar and Emilia looks around taking it all in. They are in a bit of an alcove at the very center of the theatre and just a little above stage level. There are other seats to their right and some small tables. The Pharaoh's seating is in the middle and at the forward edge of the alcove. The seats are luxurious and more ornate than anything either Drekkar or Emilia have ever seen before. "And these are theatre seats!" exclaims Emilia in hushed tones.

The stage itself has only a few columns on the back edge that appears to drop off into darkness and air. The moon is so bright it is as though lights are on, and they see its light reflected on the water of the river below. They can see for the longest distance as though it is daytime. The valley stretches out before them in the cool colors of the moon light and makes the back drop for the stage.

A few servants arrive, they move the chairs at the back of the alcove creating a larger gap, and rearranging the small tables to be set just behind each of the chairs of the royal family. They all carry several items and suddenly cups, drink, plates with food and other mysterious items are placed perfectly. In mere moments all is set and each stands in their proper place. One servant next to each of the three tables and four others stand to the far right of the back of the seats and out of the way. They all face the back of the alcove rather than the stage. They seem to make no notice of either Emilia or Drekkar and none of them say hello or speak to them at all. Emilia and Drekkar look around behind themselves wondering where the Pharaoh will come from.

The theatre is filling now quite rapidly and the excitement of the crowd is buzzing. The Von Kesslars marvel at the rainbow of colors and beauty of the audience taking seats all around. Just as it appears the theatre is full, it is a very big surprise when suddenly the servants all come to even greater attention in their stance and the Pharaoh steps forth from the space between the chairs and out of the wall itself!

Ra-Maharet is on his arm. Emilia gasps, she has rarely seen wife-of-Pharaoh and only from a distance. Seeing her from the side now, she soaks in the elegance and beauty of the wife-of-Pharaoh. The crowd stands and cheers at the sight of them, and they wave to the crowd as they take their seats. Angyet and Ra-Milania emerge next, followed by Bilal who smiles at his parents when he spots them. Four more guards follow behind Bilal and they all spread out looking around the arena from the alcove. Angyet sits next to Emilia and introduces herself, "I am Angyet the Builder. It is a pleasure to meet you."

Bilal is attending to Ra-Milania who seems to be whispering

to him about something as she takes her seat to the left of the Pharaoh. For this performance Bilal has been given a seat next to Mila, both for her protection and advantage to view the show from.

Angyet makes conversation with Emilia and Drekkar as she takes a seat next to them, asking if they know about the story of tonight's performance. They do not, so she explains that tonight's story is about the constellation Orion who falls in love with the moon. He captures the moon and wishes to posses and own her. The moon seduces him into letting her go and shows him what it is to honor someone with choice. How choices creates something greater for them both. The story will be told by singing. "You will see, it is unlike anything you have ever heard! Most spectacular!" exclaims Angyet.

Soft music begins to play, though no musicians can be seen.

Emilia whispers to Angyet, "Where is that coming from?"

"There is a ledge just below the back side of the stage for musicians, the performers and everything required to put on the show...You'll see!"

"Oh," replies Emilia without any comprehension. She has never seen anything like this and bubbles with anticipation and excitement. Drekkar sits silently but is holding Emilia's hand extra tight and looks around at everyone with a faint smile on his lips.

Everyone has come to a hush with the first notes of music and gets settled as this seems to be an indication of the show about to start but not quite actually having started yet.

Another minute and an actor takes the stage on one side and towards the audience, and a group of others take opposite and back side of the stage. Behind them are musicians quickly seating themselves, instruments in hand.

All goes silent and still suddenly and what seems like an eternity, until a single note of sound pierces the air. Clear and high the sound fills the theatre and somehow seems to come from everywhere. Emilia looks to the group of people to the left side of the stage and sees a young boy with his mouth open, presumably the sound comes from him. It is the oddest thing, Emilia sees his mouth open, yet the sound is all around her. She is in awe. She looks to Drekkar, whose eyes are popping out in sheer amazement.

More sounds usher forth, each new note coming together to weave a tapestry of sound. There are no words, just the most amazing notes lifting the audience into the space of the night sky, expanding the sense of being. The sound passes right through every person's body and embraces them at the same time. Everyone is transported into the beauty of the stars and the vastness of space.

Then comes Orion's voice, deep and commanding. The undeniable presence of a warrior, he is overbearing, consuming the expansive lightness of space. His voice weaves in and out of the sounds creating the heavens, dancing with and overtaking.

Then comes the moon, she is the object of Orion's obsession...a woman enters the stage, her voice more enchanting and dynamic than the purity of single notes weaving together. She draws the audience in with her embrace of being and warm sweetness.

Over the next hour the singer-actors weave the tale of the warrior constellation Orion who captures the moon because she is so beautiful. As a captive she seduces him into awareness of beauty as something to have and be that is greater than owning and possessing it. There is not a dry eye in the house as the story carries the audience in the transformation from violent possession into honoring of being.

The last note sung, a momentary silence fills the space of the amphitheatre before an uproar of applause takes over. Everyone is on their feet cheering and clapping, unchecked tears flow from everyone in the audience. The singers bow, then the musicians and last, Naruub takes the stage. He stands proudly taking in the celebration and nodding to each area of the theatre. The audience comes to new heights of cheer as Naruub receives it all.

Bilal leans to Mila, "What is Naruub doing there, how is he involved?"

"Oh he is the creative genius behind it all! He came up with the whole thing and was involved in every part of it coming to life. Who better to create something of such beauty than the most expert person on the subject in all of Pharaoh's Land?" says Mila with absolute adoration and pride for her friends accomplishment.

The Von Kesslars had no idea such beauty existed; it was the treat of a lifetime to hear such magical sound. That a story with so few words could convey so much and embrace them in such a dynamic experience was beyond comprehension and they all had ear-to-ear grins. At the same time the tears of release of being swept up in the depth and sense of sheer beauty the performance transported them to was exhilarating.

The audience buzzed with energy and no one wanted to leave. Many lingered for almost an hour basking in the glory of such beauty and glowing in the after warmth. It is such warmth that creates lasting friendship unlike that which Bilal has ever known before, and is now discovering. *"Would his parent's homeland hold such possibility for friendship as he was finding here?"* he wondered.

Chapter 39

Bilal and Kylar were becoming fast friends. They had a camaraderie that came easily. Bilal had wanted to bring Kylar to meet his father. He thought Drekkar would have some worthy advice. They were looking to prepare for how to handle larger numbers with Ra-Milania's guard and Bilal knew his father had great skill with planning ahead and what would be required having overseen managing most of Master Iberak's forty-five thousand slaves.

Kylar was very impressed with Bilal's fighting all these years and he was excited about meeting his father, the man behind coaching such skill. He celebrated the glory of the fight, but had no awareness of the darkness that bred it. Yet, with all that had changed between Bilal and his father in the last days and weeks who knows what might become possible?

Entering the front door of the Von Kesslar's new home in

232

the Artisan Realm, Bilal and Kylar were met with the warmth and cheer of a happy home. The jovial conversation poured out from the kitchen into the front court yard embracing them as they entered. With quick steps the young men reach the dining area greeting Bilal's parents who were just setting the table for the evening meal.

"Father, mother, this is Kylar."

Drekkar stands reaching out his hand and before Bilal can say more, Drekkar blurts; "Kylar Bonderfaust of the family Bonderfaust? I would know those green eyes anywhere!"

With a gasp Kylar stumbles in disbelief, "Ah, um, yes, why yes. How do you know the name Bonderfaust? None of my family has ever spoken this name in public, however could you know this?"

Throwing his arms wide he exclaims, "We are Von Kesslars, dear man. I am from the North, very far North." Shaking Kylar's hand and pulling out the seat for him, he continues; "Come, you are always welcome at our table, our families are brethren, the ruling families of the North. Everyone knows the Bonderfaust family name, the Strudwick family, and of course us, the Von Kesslars. Sit, eat, let us break bread and talk, surely there is much to talk about. In my nineteen years here I have not met a single person from the North, and one bearing the most famous name of the North no less. Oh, don't think I have not heard of the family with green eyes here in Pharaoh's Land, for I have. This is the first I have the pleasure of sharing a table with such an honored guest."

Kylar is flabbergasted with the openness of this conversation. He had been raised his entire life to never speak of such things in public and he really had not heard so much about the other families of the North. He is thrilled to hear stories about his family from someone other than his own. They always have the same boring stories; all about the glory of the homeland none of them had ever been to and the family's past accomplishments. If there were other families of significance he certainly didn't know much about them, he was intrigued.

"It would be my pleasure to speak with you on this, I would love to hear all about it! Bilal and I would also love to get your advice. You have many skills we would like to know about in more depth for the tasks we have been given. Shall we break bread and make an evening of it?" says Kylar warmly and taking a seat.

"Excuse me while I get you a setting Kylar, please make yourself comfortable," replies Emilia as she heads for the kitchen. She returns shortly with another cup and plate for each he and Bilal, along with additional food items to add to the meal already set out. The boys had arrived just before Emilia and Drekkar were staring the evening meal for themselves so it did not take much to comfortably have enough for them all.

"Tell me son, what do you and Kylar wish to know? I am happy to assist you in any way I can."

"Thank you father. Kylar is head of the guard for Ra-Milania. The two of us have been given the long term task of developing her security and we would like to hear about managing large groups. The kind of planning it takes and what to be aware of that creates the ease you appear to have in dealing with large numbers of people. I have seen you in action at the quarry and managing Master Iberak's slaves, but honestly I didn't pay attention to much with our past strain in relationship shall we say." He gives his father a sideways grin. They both know he is being polite in his description and they both appreciate the effort in their new found closeness.

"My family has been here so long, many generations. I considered the stories mostly made up and great exaggeration. I am surprised by your familiarity. I will be most interested to hear your version of things!" exclaims Kylar. "Carrying on the name has been a way for my family to hold onto their past heritage. Every generation's first born son has the right to be named Kylar if he has green eyes. It is a strictly guarded and thoroughly recorded lineage. I was the lucky one to be honored thus in my branch of the family line," he says with some sarcasm.

"We will be pleased to tell of what we know of your family and the stories we have listened to since being small children ourselves," says Drekkar warmly as he takes Emilia's hand. "It is something our son should hear about more as well. As slaves in this land we kept our heritage secret even from him, for his protection. It is only since gaining our freedom that we have revealed any of our own true heritage with Bilal and we would welcome what you might also reveal. Really anything you might wish to share would be most welcome Kylar."

"I would be honored Drekkar. It seems we have more in common than we ever considered Bilal, we could practically be cousins!" says Kylar as he looks sideways at Bilal elbowing him lightly.

The four of them talk late into the night swapping stories and discovering all they have in common in a land very far away. Drekkar is generous with sharing what he knows about managing people, preparing for handling the requirements of several thousand people's daily needs. With Kylar's enthusiasm for Bilal's fighting, they even talk of his prowess, recounting the more impressive rounds from any number of matches.

It was a rich history of physical prowess, conquering and the glory of men as seen in this reality; far different than the history of Pharaoh's Land striving for the creation of oneness and harmony with the rest of the planet and the entire cosmos.

Chapter 40

Bilal stands with Mila, Pharaoh-Ra and Angyet. They are on Pharaoh's balcony looking out at the progress of the Pyramid. The morning light has set the stones ablaze seeming to glow with admiration as the small group gaze upon it. Pharaoh-Ra is telling of his family's history and the purpose behind the pyramid.

It was very early in Pharaoh-Ra's family reign that a Builder came with an extreme of awareness and connection with both the cosmos and the earth. She laid out a plan to keep the family in power by connecting with and utilizing the natural energies of creation. This included the earth and the entire cosmos. Not just for the family, this was for the family of all people on the planet. She and the Pharaoh of that time strove to set in motion what would honor and give rise to awareness of and connection to the oneness that is natural in all things.

The oneness is a symphony of living that everything is included in, and contributes to that which gives joy to being alive and having a body. With a deep connection with the oneness so much becomes possible. It was a bold plan that would take many generations to fulfill.

The first monument to oneness would be a huge Sphinx with the body of a lion and the head in the likeness of the first Builder. It represented the dawning of a new kind of rule for Pharaoh's Land, one that would lead to a different future. The Sphinx was built in exact alignment with facing the rising sun in the East. It allows for the calculation of true North and South, by providing the exact alignment of true East and West with the rising of the sun. Not just any rising sun. The rising of the sun on the exact middle of the twenty-six thousand-year cycle of the solar system; when the entire movement of the constellations is in the middle of its cycle of travel across the skies. This was not only the equinox marking equal day and night of Earth, it is one of the two equinox of the solar system's entire cycle. Drawing a line from the middle of the nose, exactly between the eyes and to the middle of where the tail meets the body provided the first line of alignment that everything else would be calculated on.

The monuments were meant to inspire the future generations and speak to the greatness we are all capable of. These monuments would also be a physical actualization of the energies of oneness, not just representational but literal. The location and structure would energetically feed those willing to function from oneness being able to achieve it with more ease and potency. An amplification of how it shows up. The idea was that anyone could function from all the capacity and greatness possible with oneness, and these monuments would make it easier to achieve; a physical contribution to this actualization of energies.

With the process taking thousands of years to accomplish the target was lost on many. Most people considered the Sphinx nice to look at and a testament to the power of the Pharaoh, but little more.

It would be several lifetimes before the time for the next monument, a gigantic pyramid unlike anything built before. It was this Pharaoh who was honored with the task, and it was a natural fit for his aspirations that were so different than many of the Pharaoh's before who did not truly trust the powers of oneness, or believe they really existed. So many have difficulty with trusting in what they cannot see. Following what they know that can be sensed but not explained, to those who do not know, is more than many are willing to have. Many had dismissed the family heritage and were happy to rule over the people, amassing more wealth and power for the sake of having it.

Not until the current Pharaoh-Ra, his previous Builder Hamadi and his current Builder Angyet reignited the original vision with deep study of the scanty written guidance and more extensive verbal history that had been handed down through the House of Pharaoh Keeper of Records and the resident Builder Hamadi.

This Pharaoh had always held a deep interest and gratitude for his true family heritage and that was strengthened with his dear Builder Hamadi. Hamadi had been his father's Builder and Pharaoh-Ra had been raised by his guidance and gentle kindness. He brought to life the magic of the oneness and showed the practical applications of it for creating a greater world for everyone. From day to day living to the construction of the pyramid that was Pharaoh-Ra's task to fulfill, his Builder inspired the joy of living like no one else Pharaoh-Ra had ever met before, or since. A man of great vision and an excellent teacher with seeming infinite patience, his passing was a great loss and still deeply felt by the Pharaoh-Ra and Angyet. Hamadi's friendship and guidance had fueled them to carry on with continued enthusiasm.

The pyramid was to connect with and amplify the cosmic alignment and Earth energies, enhancing the ease of connecting with the oneness. This was its entire purpose; a catalyst and monument to the possibilities for something greater in us all... the capacity for functioning as an infinite being in communion and oneness with all creation.

"What is an infinite being?" asks Bilal.

Angyet replies, "Infinite being is everything you truly are and are capable of. It is the 'you' that has infinite choices in all moments. It is the 'you' that reaches out to embrace the beauty of the world. It is the 'you' that knows a greater possibility is available, even when no one else knows it. It is the 'you' that has no wrongness of being and finds no wrongness in others. Instead you see who and what is before you, just as it is. The 'you' that can request of the elements of the world around us all and they will move and transform, becoming what you request. These are some of the qualities of infinite being."

The Pharaoh continues, "Every exercise we play with, every choice, every request of the molecules and every question will build your capacity for functioning as an infinite being. It is a muscle you build with practice. It is for this reason that we have invited you to join us in this endeavor, you have a natural capacity with this Bilal. Beyond what the people around you have been able to recognize. We wish to nurture this capacity and also receive what you are able to contribute that is unique unto you."

"Everyone is already connected, it is just that most people use that connection to create and maintain limitation and smallness, rather than contribute that which would expand all into greatness," says Angyet.

Pharaoh continues, "Each of us has a different energy, space and consciousness that is easy for us to be and function as. This uniqueness adds to everyone's capacity and expands it. We can each be a gift to each other. If we choose to allow this kind of connection with one another that is from the space of allowance and creation of something greater, all of our lives will expand into greater than we can imagine. The oneness always creates more than we can imagine and it does it in ways we could not come up with on our own. The oneness supports us and would like to increase itself in all aspects of creation."

Mila pipes in with a giggle, "And we have been tricking people into it for some time now with the pillars of The Pathway! Hamadi was so smart. He created the pillars for every person in Pharaoh's Land to have greater connection with the oneness. It would not work if each person did not already have this connection. The pillars use that connection and make it possible for people to pop from one place to another; that is how easy it really is. People don't think it is because of them that this is possible; they blame it on the pillars, the magic of the Pharaoh and his Builder. We would like to show them that truly it is them already. They are the oneness already and the oneness can contribute to expanding the greatness of them and their lives also. Oneness is not just something for the privileged."

"Many of those already in power and seats of position object to empowering all people in such a way. It is my opinion that though I be the Pharaoh, it is not my place to deny anyone this natural capacity. I am not like other Pharaohs before me. I would like to encourage this natural capacity. I see it as creating a greater future than the world has yet known. Who knows, it might be my undoing. However, it is the future I strive to create regardless of the opinion of others," says Pharaoh quietly determined.

Angyet expands more on this topic, "So many believe in lack, and that when others have more it takes away from them. Some will never become aware of what we speak no matter what we do to show them. Others will be inspired by hearing what is true for them. Those are the people we seek to find and empower, no matter what their status or position."

"So you see Bilal, not only is Ra-Maharet's endeavor to take over personally abhorrent, it is also a target that would destroy this future I seek to create. She has no interest in anything we speak of here. She strives to own everyone and everything, consume it, control it, posses it. Hers' is a reality of destruction. It is a world of limitation bent on creation of more limitation. We will stop her, it is just a question of when and how that will show up."

"Why not do it now? You already know what she seeks," inquires Bilal.

"Now I would like to know who she is involved with, who plots with her, how far this plot goes. I will do whatever it takes to stop her. As I said before I will give her every chance to change, and it is becoming very clear that she has no plans to change direction in what she aims. So until we find out more extensively of her plans she will live a free woman."

"As you wish, Lord Pharaoh," is Bilal's only reply.

They all stand silently now looking at the light of the rising sun shining on the face of the partially built pyramid. Wrapped in their own thoughts and enjoying the company of one another they take a moment to simply be, before the tasks of the coming day.

Such inspired greatness was not in the awareness of those plotting to take over. They worked toward different plans that had no concern for what it would create in other people's lives, only their own.

Chapter 41

It is late in the night and Ra-Maharet meets with Master Iberak at his brothel in the Keeper's Realm. He has created secret entrances and exits allowing for customers to come and go in anonymity and discretion. It is a perfect place to meet Ra-Maharet in comfort and secrecy.

Ra-Milania's guard Karek peers from the shadows as he watches Ra-Maharet enter one of the secret entrances of Master Iberak's brothels in the Keepers Realm. He has been following her on these nights of supposedly secret meetings between the two of them. Having grown up in the palace and living as a servant it is easy enough for him to follow her unnoticed and report back to Pharaoh-Ra.

With the darkness of night to hide her and in a hooded cloak too ornate to be truly discrete Ra-Maharet enters the room where Master Iberak greets her arrival.

"Your majesty, breath-taking as always, I am so joy-filled to see you!" He stands and bows deeply. Flattery always goes a long way with her. Abar smiles inwardly to himself as much as to his honored guest with the thought of it. So ambitious, the wife-of-Pharaoh is easily inspired to take bold action that few others dare. Master Iberak loves that about this woman. So easily pliable; and yet wielding her position like a sharp arrow that always hits its target. He could not help but admire her avaricious ambitions. He has so much to gain and so little to lose with a woman like this. He could not believe his luck when she came to him with her proposal. He was just as confident in his ability to deliver what she requested as she was in achieving her aim.

He takes her hand, kissing it and motioning to a chair made ready for her comfort and what will surely be a long night of conversation.

She flops down with a sigh of exhaustion, "It is so tiring pandering to those lesser than myself. When I am Pharaoh things will be different. My subjects will be scrambling to please me, as well they should." Her thoughts wander a bit.

"Certainly your presence shall make them all tremble in awe. Glory be to your brilliant and deserved endeavors. I have good news for you, but first, please help yourself." He pours her a drink, "My best wine. Saved for a special occasion; surely our plans are worthy of celebration from the beginning!" Abar says with flare. This will be their first conversation for a plan of action taken in earnest.

"Indeed Master Iberak. I like your attitude." She waits for him to hand her a chalice. "Has my husband delivered the funds in entirety?"

"Yes he has. He is most prompt settling his financial affairs with me, which works well for us. I have already put it to work on your behalf. My trusted man Omar is headed north as we speak to purchase all who will be had for hire. He will be making sure to find men of caliber to start training and arming your forces."

"Wonderful! That is very good news. Your willingness to contribute your gold so readily pleases me greatly." She says with a bat of the eye lashes.

Master Iberak nods in acknowledgment and continues, "We have roughly fifteen hundred men so far, now tucked away in our encampment and with this new funding we can increase the numbers by three thousand comfortably, maybe more. Omar is a frugal man and will make the money stretch to give you the most for your investment. Only Drekkar is a better manager, oh how I lament his absence." Abar makes an effort to unclench his fists. Drekkar being taken from him still smarts. He shakes it off, "No matter, we shall prevail without him."

"This 'Omar', you trust his discretion?" inquires Ra-Maharet with some concern.

"Implicitly your radiance, I have done business with him for a long time. He is also ambitious, yet he knows his place and does not overstep where he should not. We can count on him completely," assures Abar.

"Very well then. I also come with news." She lowers her voice and leans forward whispering, "Master Eka-ar has succeeded. He has finally found a way to overtake the Builder's plans and turn them to our own use with the pyramid itself! Ah, at last a true victory that is surely but the first of many." Ra-Maharet leans back gloating in confidence with this admission.

Abar inhales, "Really? Ah, glory be to you! That is the best news yet! However did he do it? My slaves cut the stone, but I still don't really know much about the pyramid. Other than it is making me a very wealthy man," he says with a smile. "Can you tell me more?"

Ra-Maharet looks down her nose, "It is the greatest source of power ever created. It shall make me invincible, ever living and give me power over all of Pharaoh's Land. Not even the Pharaoh himself will be able to stop me with the power that the pyramid will give me. Only Eka-ar has the ability to harness this power and bestow it upon me when the construction is complete. He has gained access to this power by his alteration of plans giving him entrance to the center of the pyramid. Together we shall enter and when we exit I shall be undefeatable." She says with a dream-like look of wonder in her eyes. Focusing once more on Abar she continues in all seriousness, "And my forces you gather in the north shall guarantee my will is carried out throughout all of Pharaoh's Land."

"Really? Such power from a pile of stones? This is most interesting. Even greater than the Movers who glide the stones through the air to build this monument?" asks Abar somewhat incredulously.

"Oh yes," says Ra-Maharet wide-eyed. "Many times greater. Somehow it takes those powers and amplifies them. Whomever controls those powers will be unlike any power the world has known before, and it shall be mine," she says triumphantly.

"My graces will be bestowed on all those who bow to me and obey my command. You think you are wealthy now Abar, just wait until I am in the seat-of-Pharaoh. You shall be my Keeper of all Pharaoh's Land, administering my will upon the people. You will become untouchable."

Abar Iberak sits taller as he hears of his future position and the future that Ra-Maharet envisions. *"This is something I can get behind,"* he thinks to himself. The idea of such action as the overthrow of an undefeated royal lineage is most appealing. It has been longer than his lifetime since anyone has challenged the Pharaoh, and to have it come from within the very walls of the palace was the kind of unexpected opportunity he dare not dream of until this ambitious woman's proposal. It sparked his own ambitions to greater heights than he ever considered before. With this added information about the powers of the pyramid, it made him believe even more that all of this could become possible.

Reeling in the grandness of this endeavor he only says, "You are great indeed and will be far greater still, most wonderful news your eminence. Be assured you can count on me to stand by you every step of the way. It would be my honor to put everything I have into your success. Your graciousness knows no bounds. Let me prove my worthiness, let me build you an armed force like no other seen before." Abar Iberak stands and takes a knee before Ra-Maharet. Taking her by the hand he bows his head and says, "I pledge my life to you and this most blessed and righteous endeavor." With that he kisses her hand.

She places her hand on his shoulder saying, "Rise, my most

trusted friend." Leaning forward she whispers, "Together we cannot fail."

Taking his seat once more, they continue to discuss their plans late into the night.

Would their efforts withstand those who live in joy and are beholden to none?

Chapter 42

The shriek of kids playing echoes through the crowded alleys of Pharaoh's Market. Little ragamuffin children dart through the crowd hardly noticed by the adults other than by their annoyance of being bumped into.

Malik has stolen two bread rolls, so small and quick he is unnoticed by the vendor until he hears the shouts from far away behind him. He and Zazza are already gone, around the corner. They are playing a game, running, tossing the rolls back and forth between the crowds, heading for what they will call home for tonight. They run carefree in the waning light of the ending day.

Malik and Zazza have no parents, they have no home. They only have each other and their wit and sly cunning to hide, to evade and to live any way they can. They are both little and very young, so it is quite easy for them to go unnoticed by most. They play all day. They steal whatever they need to eat or drink. They have several hiding places to sleep undiscovered. Though they have pretty much nothing save the rags they wear, they enjoy a sense of freedom and care free most would never suspect. They are happy.

They have run all the way to the top of the hill at the Artisan Realm and the pillars of The Pathway. They are heading to the Laborer's Realm for the night. Tossing the bread rolls back and forth the entire way, they have gotten good at this and are thrilled with having made it this far without dropping any. They have begun to giggle and laugh so much Malik begins to stumble a bit. Zazza makes a large toss right to the pillars and Malik takes a flying leap snagging the bread roll out of the air as he falls into the space between the pillars disappearing into space.

Zazza jumps in the air excited having seen Malik catch the bread, he steps into the pillars of The Pathway to join Malik in the Laborer's Realm.

Malik lands sliding on his back laughing with eyes closed, triumphantly with the roll of bread raised high in his hand. He suddenly stops laughing noticing it is not dirt he is sprawled on, but rather a marble floor. Looking around wildly to take in his surroundings as quickly as possible he catches his breath in shock as his eyes rest upon the sight of the Pharaoh's daughter Ra-Milania sitting, staring back.

Bilal is beside her, it is their evening meal and discussion of the day. He jumps up with cat like reflex reaching this little boy in rags before the intruder or Mila can react at all. Grabbing this kid by the clothing on his back he lifts him off the ground demanding, "How did you get in here? How did you come through the pillars? Do not lie, I will know it if you do!"

Malik stammers "I, I don't know. Where am I? You, you're Bilal the fighter!" wide-eyed, he can't help starting to smile with excitement even with Bilal holding him by the shirt and him dangling in the air.

A little surprised himself, Bilal has set him on the ground now. Suddenly the little boy drops to the ground at the sight of Ra-Milania and finally registering who she is. "Your royalness! Please do not kill me. I didn't mean it. I don't know how I got here. I swear!"

"What were you doing just before coming through the pillars?" asks Bilal sternly.

"I was with Zazza, we were running on our way um, home and he tossed me the bread and I jumped really high to catch it and instead of coming out at the pillars into the Laborer's Realm I came out here. There are pillars in Ra-Milania's room?"

"I don't know you, you have never been here before, I would know it," says Mila surprised but also curious. She masks her curiosity with a look of stern distain. "Bilal, what do we do with liars?"

Before Bilal can reply the boy pleads, "No! I swear, I have never been here before. I didn't know the pillars can come here. Please, I will do anything, please, I didn't mean it. I'll leave, I won't ever come back. I won't ever tell anyone, I swear I won't." He begins to whimper looking at the ground and manages to shrink even smaller into the floor if that were possible. He reaches his arms out pleading for mercy.

"Come boy," says Bilal lifting him off the floor. Still talking sternly Bilal places the dirty ragged child on a small stool and continues, "Tell us exactly what you were thinking when you entered the pillars of The Pathway. Do not leave anything out."

"I um, I was running and I was looking at the palace in the light of the sun going down, you know how it glows when the sun is going down? And I was thinking how beautiful it is and then, then I was thinking, I was thinking how beautiful Ra-Milania is." He begins to get shy but manages to continue. "I was thinking how I had only seen her once before and she is so pretty and how fun would it be to see her again, and then here I am." He says wide-eyed, with a shrug of the shoulders and look of doom on his face.

Mila and Bilal look to each other in amazement. Could it be this boy has such capacity of oneness he can travel to where he desires even with having never been there? This was worthy of Angyet's attention. Mila could hardly contain her excitement, but again, did not let it show. Continuing to sound stern she tells Bilal to stay put with this 'intruder' until she returns. She walks regally to the hidden pillars the boy had emerged from and steps in.

Mila comes out in Angyet's rooms, hoping she is there. Angyet looks up with a smile. It is rare that Ra-Milania comes to her like this, she is curious why the unexpected visit.

Mila runs to her with obvious excitement, "Angyet! You won't believe it! There is a boy, a boy in my room, he came through the hidden pillars. He came just by thinking of me! It's amazing, have you ever known anyone besides you that can do that? I mean, transport to a place you have never been before? Come, you must meet him!" Mila grabs her hand to be transported back to her room through the hidden pillars.

Angyet is the only person in Pharaoh's Land that can travel without the pillars of The Pathway and travel to places she has never seen or been to. Unlike everyone who has to be touching someone else who has been there before, or already know the location and have a marker and pillars located there. In a blink Mila and Angyet step forth from the hidden pillars back into Mila's room.

Malik has been sitting on the stool Bilal placed him and upon the site of Angyet and Mila returning flings himself to the floor and begins to plead again, "Please your worshipfulness, wife-of-pharaoh I will never come back again, please do not kill me I beg you."

Angyet has to try not to laugh. "Please stand boy. I am not wife-of-pharaoh, I am known as Angyet the Builder. Who are you?"

"I am called Malik."

"And who are your parents?"

"I have none Builder. They died two years ago."

"I see. Well where do you live then, who looks after you?"

Looking confused he replies, "No one. I look after myself. I, I um, I do not have a home or a place to stay. I only have my friend Zazza. We um, we find places to sleep and um, ways to eat. Please, I will go away and never come back, I swear it."

"And Zazza has no family either?"

"We are each other's family now."

"What age are you boy?"

"I am not sure, I think maybe this many," he says holding up his fingers to indicate seven years.

"And Zazza?" asks Angyet.

"He is a little younger I think, he is smaller than me so I guess not as old as me. Please can I go now?" He looks with rather desperate eyes at the ground and from side to side looking for an escape route.

"Look at me dear boy," says Angyet softly. She continues, "We will not harm you Malik. Please tell me again what you have told Bilal and Ra-Milania. This is something very special to be able to do what you have done." She steps forward placing her hand on his shoulder, as her magical soothing touch begins to seep into him and he visibly relaxes. She steers him to the small stool again and makes him sit. "Please sit and tell me again exactly what happened. What you were thinking and feeling, what you were doing and what it is you were desiring as you stepped through the pillars of The Pathway."

Malik recounts what he had said to Bilal and Mila ending with a sigh and look of resignation.

Mila can't help herself and blurts out, "You are amazing! I can't do what you did, yet, oh this is wonderful!" She claps her hands. Her joy is infectious and they all smile including Malik. She continues, "Malik, I am looking for boys and girls like you with magical abilities. Would you like to do what you did more? Would you like to learn what else you might be capable of?"

Malik hesitates, he can't understand the kindness of what is being presented to him. No one before has so quickly and easily shown such generosity and he does not know what to do. Seeing this Mila continues, "I know it might seem strange that I would not be displeased with your accidental visit into my rooms. Would you be willing to sit here with us so we might explain more? Here, you can have food and drink, as much as you like."

Malik hesitates, "What about Zazza? I am sure he is wondering where I am. I cannot leave him, we have never been apart for as long as I can remember. Surely he will be frightened."

Mila and Angyet look to Bilal. "Which pillars of the Laborer's Realm where you planning on going to Malik? I will fetch Zazza. Don't worry I can find him. What can I say to him that he will know you have sent me for him?" Having lived in the Laborer's Realm all his life, he knows of the kinds of thing that create trust in a world where death is close at hand.

Malik is a little surprised Bilal knows to ask such a thing and nonetheless gives the information he requires. This is Bilal after all, the most famous fighter in all of Pharaoh's Land. This in itself will likely make it a little easier for Bilal to convince Zazza to come with him. Bilal steps into the hidden pillars that Malik had emerged from.

In ten minutes Bilal re-emerges with Zazza dangling from his firm grasp kicking and yelling "Let me go!" He goes limp and quiet upon spotting Malik sitting with Angyet and Ra-Milania eating handfuls of food.

Bilal sets Zazza on the ground but does not let him go quite yet. "See, I told you. Will you behave now? You do not need to run away. We have food for you and we would only like to talk. You are not in trouble."

Zazza nods, wide-eyed, he quietly goes to sit next to Malik and begins to inhale food like he has never seen it before. They let the boys eat and drink their fill before continuing the conversation. For the next several hours they talk. As with everyone who speak with Angyet and Ra-Milania, before long the boys open up and talk easily sharing their point of view about things, their desires, what their daily lives are like, things they hope to do when they "grow up."

Angyet suspects Zazza has some abilities as well and is interested to explore what might be possible with these stray boys. By the end of the evening it has been decided that the boys will stay in the barracks as new recruits for Ra-Milania's person guard in training. When they hear that they can learn to fight from Bilal and stay where he stays they are eager to play along.

They had not spoken or even thought of it much until now, but with these boys they have found not one, but two who can seamlessly blend into the Laborer's Realm and be eyes and ears there without being noticed. The boys perk up even more at the idea of being spies for Ra-Milania. They are surprisingly aware of the important people in the Laborer's Realms and many of the Keeper's Realm and Artisan Realm. It appears Zazza is the one with this talent for memory and recognition of faces. They knew who Bilal was and have been to many of his fights. They know who Master Abar Iberak is and the other masters of the Laborer's Realm. They appear to have a knack for being there at events of important or notable nature. They already hear about many things without the people who are speaking knowing they are being overheard.

Mila keeps looking at Angyet with a large grin and those eyes that say, "Wow, it just keeps getting better!"

It is now late into the night. Finally the boys begin to fade with eyes drooping. Bilal takes them to the sleeping quarters; which thanks to the hidden pillars of The Pathway, they can step from Ra-Milania's room to the training arena and in just a few minutes they are tucked in bed at the guard house. Bilal will stay there for the night so the boys can be introduced to the rest of the guards in training when morning arrives.

He hopes he will still find them there in the morning. This will be the first test if they are honest in their enthusiasm and agreement for what is being offered.

Morning comes and Bilal is pleased to find the young boys huddled at the table talking quietly. It is early, before anyone else is up. Bilal greets them and starts water to boiling for something warm until Madu has prepared the morning meal. He is glad to find an easy audience and the boys talk freely with him asking many questions, allowing Bilal to continue getting to know them better.

With the departure of his parents coming soon, Bilal welcomed the growing numbers he might one day call friends. Whatever would he do without his parents here, especially now that all three of them get along so well?

Chapter 43

Drekkar and Emilia would be leaving soon, so Emilia is going to the river where the slave women go to wash clothing. She is going to say goodbye to her friends. Thrilled to have the possibility to say goodbye since she is now a Freeman, it is a luxury she did not imagine she would ever have. Before leaving was a well guarded secret, now she could have a proper goodbye with her friends. It meant a lot to her.

Emilia enters the pillars at the top of the hill above the Artisan Realm. She steps out at the pillars of the edge of the river where the slave women do their washing. She had spent many of her years as "Keeper of House Servants" for Master Iberak, making sure the women who would be sent as staff at the homes of the master Keepers were competent at the tasks they would be required to do. It was possibly the single true kindness Master Iberak had shown her and Drekkar. That he allowed her to work with his slaves for housekeeping rather than make her work at the brothels, that was the more likely choice with her exotic looks. Master Iberak had gained both cooperation and some level of trust from Drekkar and Emilia in this choice.

As Master Iberak's Keeper of domestic service, she was stern and demanding but also easy to encourage the men and women or boys and girls in training. She always had a keen awareness of the natural skills and capacities of the people under her guidance. Her ability to advise for good placement gave Master Iberak an excellent reputation for household staff that worked well. Her consideration of people's happiness, competence and well-being made her respected among her peers and well-liked by most.

It is later in the day and the sun is hot. Many of the women like this time of the day to do laundry in the river as they have an excuse to be in the cool and refreshing water while also accomplishing their task. Emilia knew many of her friends would be there and she walked quickly with excitement. She had not seen any of them since becoming a Freeman and there was so much to tell.

She arrives at the river, and her friends are there just as she knew they would be. Kesha, Yakeri and Padur are all waist-deep in the river, standing in a circle as they always do, to visit. Laughing, joking and teasing, these women were a joy for Emilia with the light heartedness they lived their lives from, even as slaves of Master Iberak. They did not live as slaves in their own mind and would always strive to be uplifting with each other. They all have a kindness that was surprising to find in the world they live. This kindness was their bond. It was going to difficult to leave these women behind.

Padur was the first to spot Emilia coming as she was facing the banks, "Emilia!" shouts Padur. She rushes to the bank, dropping her basket of laundry on the ground to give Emilia a big hug. Kesha and Yakeri are not far behind; they all surround her hugging and kissing her cheeks all at once. They had not seen her since hearing she had become a Freeman, they didn't even know where to find her.

"Emilia! Where have you been?" asks Kesha.

Yakeri says at the same time, "We asked everywhere for you, where have you been?"

Padur continues excited, "We hear you are a Freeman now, is it true?" before Emilia can reply she continues, "Oh, how wonderful!"

"Oh, girls! Yes, it is true! I am a Freeman now. You won't believe what has happened since I have seen you last! It is a blessing beyond what I could ever imagine. I don't even know where to start!"

"Start at the beginning!" exclaims Kesha.

"Yes!" reply both Yakeri and Padur in unison.

"Please tell us everything, don't leave out a bit," says Padur wide-eyed and grinning.

"Come ladies, let us get you back in the water and I'll tell you everything as you continue your washing," says Emilia. Always practical, the ladies laugh with familiarity of their dear friend who never wastes a moment in uselessness. Emilia leads the way into the water as her friends follow picking up their baskets of clothing and bedding.

It is a genius system they have for doing wash, and it was Emilia's idea. They have a wide shallow basket with a cloth strap they can put over their head and opposite shoulder allowing their hands to be free and keeping the basket next to them for ease of handling. They have a place to set soap, sand for scrubbing and setting the clothes down and not worry about it floating away, they are already in the water so they don't have to lean over, and they get to stay cool in the process. Many of the other women have taken up this practice, yet most continue with their old ways sitting on the banks at the water's edge.

Emilia begins to recount the mind-boggling and phenomenal events since becoming a Freeman, starting with Bilal and Drekkar coming home arms around each other and both crying and laughing at the same time. Emilia's friends listened wide-eyed, oh's and ah's pouring forth with each new development, rapt with attention to every detail of the story unfolding.

The hours pass as Emilia shares the details of her new life, the new-found joy of her "boys" actually enjoying each other's company and the life they are all becoming accustom to. She points out the veranda which can be seen from where they are in the river. Emilia speaks proudly of her son's new position with the Pharaoh's daughter and of the kindness she has shown them all. She speaks of the palace gardens and the unreal beauty of the theatre performance.

She is a little hesitant to talk about her homeland, as she has scarcely spoken of it in all her years here in Pharaoh's Land.

With a deep breath, she begins talk about her plans to return to the land of her birth with Drekkar. They would be leaving soon, so she would only be able to visit with them a few more times. Emilia, Padur, Kesha and Yakeri all hug and laugh and cry tears of gratitude and sadness together. Gratitude for all that has transpired and the richness of their friendship along with tears of sadness for their dear friend leaving.

So immersed in the moment they did not see the wavy ripple in the water coming from behind Emilia. Her hands rested on the surface of the water to either side of her body, gently moving back and forth caressing the coolness. Silently the water moccasin approached and simply bites her on the wrist. Emilia screams lifting her hand, grabbing the snake that hangs from her wrist and pulling it free in a single motion. She looks with dread seeing that it is black and small, the worst kind as they unleash all of their venom. They are all screaming now. In shock, Emilia rips the snake's head off and tosses it back into the river at the same time heading for the shore. She knows she only has a few minutes of life in her and she drops to the ground as the water's edge, the effects of venom already spreading through her.

In screams and wails of shock and grief Emilia's friends all hug her to them, yelling for help and knowing there is none. They all kiss her and Kesha speaks coherently first saying, "Emilia, is there anything you would like to tell your boys?"

Emilia grabs her hand and looking in her eyes says softly, "Tell them I have never been more happy or proud and I die a free woman. Tell my men to be good to each other." Emilia's last minute is only the screams and cries of agony as the venom overtakes her heart and lungs and just like that her body goes limp and quiet.

Hugging and rocking her body they wail at the shock of it all but do not hesitate long, now they know where her new house is. They along with other women at the river who have gathered round lift her body and carry her up the hill to the Von Kesslar house in the Artisan Realm.

The sounds of crying carry up the streets and Yakeri runs ahead to see if there is anyone home. She pounds on the door yelling for Drekkar and Bilal. In only moments Drekkar flings open the door recognizing Yakeri's voice. "What is it?" asks Drekkar with a look of dread on his face. He knows Emilia has been with her at the river since she left him earlier that afternoon.

Yakeri flings herself at Drekkar tears streaming down her face, "Emilia, she was bitten. A black moccasin, oh Drekkar!" He pushes her aside rushing out the door. The group of women carrying Emilia's body are already just a few feet away and they continue carrying her into the court yard despite Drekkar grabbing at her body. The women gently lay her down and Drekkar scoops her up, hugging her lifeless body to him moaning and wailing incoherently. Yakeri kneels down hugging him and speaking softly in his ear Emilia's last words. He grows quiet listening. Tears stream down his cheeks but he makes no further sound.

Padur had been searching the house, calling out for Bilal knowing he was likely to be at the palace now. Without looking further she heads out the door to the palace, she must tell Bilal. She does not know of any pillars of The Pathway or where to take them within the palace so she runs to the lower entrance that is only a few streets away. She asks everyone along the way if they know Bilal and where she can find him. It is late in the day and Rimmel has just walked out from the lower entrance and approaches her. He had been on his way to his evening visit to the Von Kesslar's.

He grabs her arms to hold her up as she looks like she might collapse. Looking at her intently he is trying to comprehend what she is saying. Finally it sinks in and he hugs Padur to him, then holds her at arm's length telling her to return to the house and he will fetch Bilal. He lets her know he can go to Bilal directly and bring him to the house. At this time Bilal is with the Pharaoh for the evening session of practice, Rimmel had just left them.

In minutes Bilal is rushing into the courtyard of his home to see Emilia's dead body in the arms of his father. He drops to his knees, tears streaming down his face and embraces both his mother and father. They rock back and forth in shock and grief. The women who brought Emilia's body slowly depart, all but Yakeri, Padur and Kesha. They have made themselves familiar with the house and Rimmel is there to also show them where things are. They have made tea and gotten some small bites to eat, knowing full well it is likely neither Bilal nor Drekkar will touch it.

The women have also found a table on which to lay Emilia's body out and prepare it. They would not consider her being cared for as the royal or wealthy, but they have their own traditions as slaves and as her friends. They will wash her body in herbs and flowers. They will braid her hair and dress her in her finest. They will sing her body back to the earth and they will usher her to the arms of Isis, Keeper of death and dying. That Isis may deliver her to Osiris, Keeper of all the cycles and forms of living.

When they have moved the table out into the courtyard Drekkar and Bilal lift her and gently place her body on the table. They cross her arms on her chest and stretch her legs out. Kesha has also brought two chairs out as they know Bilal and Drekkar are not likely to leave her side. Bilal continues to touch Emilia, resting his hand over hers as it rests on her chest. The tears have stopped for now, but it is a grim silence that has descended.

Rimmel whispers to the women and takes his leave. He is going to the palace to speak with the Pharaoh, Mila and Angyet and tell them what has transpired in more detail.

Chapter 44

Several more hours have passed and it is getting late. The night is quiet and Drekkar and Bilal have not left Emilia's side. They sit staring at her still body, they have nothing to say but exchange grief-stricken looks and the tears start anew. Immersed in their sorrow they do not hear the front doors open. It is Angyet and Ra-Milania coming to give their condolences and see what they might contribute to easing the pain of their loss. They go to Bilal first. Angyet places her hand gently on Bilal's back between the shoulder blades and though it does not slow his tears, her touch begins to lighten his world. He begins to be able to breathe just a little bit deeper and relax the tension he did not realize he held.

Mila stands before him and places her hand on Bilal's knees. They both speak softly with him, letting him know they are there for him. As they speak they expand the space bringing a softness to the air and diminish the intensity of loss. Where the air had been still, a small breeze can now be felt caressing them all. Even Drekkar begins to relax just a little.

Sensing Drekkar opening a little Mila goes to him, also placing her hands on his knees and looking him in the face she gently speaks, "Drekkar, it is with great sorrow I hear of your loss. Emilia is most dear and I am so grateful to have met her, even briefly. Is there anything I can do to ease the heaviness of your heart?"

Her sweetness reaches him like a light of softness soothing him. He is surprised by this and grateful. He did not think he would ever be able to speak again, but he finds words coming easily. He takes Mila's hands in his. He marvels at how small they are. "Sweet little Mila. Can I call you Mila?" Mila nods sincerely. He continues, "I would like to make a request. It would mean very much to me if you and your father would allow me to care for Emilia's body in the tradition of my homeland. In the land of my birth it is tradition to burn the body. We would build a pier of wood and place her on it. Setting it aflame, I will sing her journey to the ancestors where the heat of the fire will burn bright fueling her journey through the cold of death to all of her loved ones."

Without hesitation Mila gives permission, "Yes Drekkar. I will see it arranged myself. We will go to the desert sands, I know just the place. When would you like this done?"

"If it is possible for the day after tomorrow at sunrise, I would be most grateful dear Mila."

"Consider it done," says Mila as she squeezes his hands. She lets go and reaches up to hug this hulk of a man. He lets her and melts into a sense of possibility that somehow, some way he will be able to carry on.

Angyet adds, "Rimmel will get the details from you and convey it to us to fulfill."

Angyet and Mila take their leave, departing as quietly as they came. Their presence has been like a salve to Bilal and Drekkar. The men stand and embrace each other, letting their years of harshness with each other also melt away and allowing the loss of the one they both loved most dear to bring them closer.

Chapter 45

R immel has conveyed the simple details of the tradition to Pharaoh-Ra, Angyet and Mila.

The dunes beyond the pyramid construction provide a wonderful view of the pyramids, the palace city and the river. It gives an excellent sense of expansiveness and the sky is endless. Mila had been there once when the choice for building site was being finalized. This was one of the highest points nearby and she thought both Bilal and Drekkar would be pleased with the location. And it was out of the way of any people, so they would have some privacy. This would allow the Pharaoh himself to attend without all of the fan fair.

The guests included Emilia's three best friends Kesha, Yakeri and Padur. In addition Rimmel was invited along with Lili. She was the only one Bilal truly desired to have with him. Though there were many others they knew and who knew them, there were none they wished to invite.

The only other people would be those required to set up and carry Emilia's body to the location and attend the fire. There were pillars of The Pathway on the outer edge of Laborer's Realm that was the closest walk to the site. Those sent to task for setting this up would make it look like the last time Pharaoh went to this vista location. It would not draw much attention and they were able to set everything up in the one day. There is nothing like the power of numbers to get things done quickly.

The funeral party would arrive before sunrise with Emilia's body, and as the sun comes up Drekkar would sing his love's journey to the ancestors.

As Mila promised all the arrangements were made and Rimmel would escort the small party before the sunrise. Padur, Kesha and Yakeri had dressed Emilia beautifully and done her hair. Pharaoh had given an exquisite funeral table for Emilia's body to be easily carried to the site.

It was a few hours before sunrise and Emilia Von Kesslar's bearers arrived from the palace to find all present and ready to go. The air was cool and it was still quiet, not even the bakers had started their day yet. In the darkness they all arranged themselves to walk in procession. Rimmel would lead as he knew the way, followed by the bearers carrying Emilia then Drekkar and Bilal, followed by Lili, Kesha, Padur and Yakeri. Walking to the top of the hill where the pillars of the Artisan Realm would convey them to the edge of the Laborer's Realm and they would walk out into the desert. They all touch as they step between the pillars.

Not since the incredible turn of events that had changed all of their lives had Drekkar or Bilal been to the Laborer's Realm. It seemed like a distant dream, another lifetime that they had called this home. It had not occurred to Rimmel, but they would actually be walking past the Von Kesslar's old dwelling. He smiled slightly to himself, thinking it rather appropriate homage to be walking by it now. Focused totally on Emilia, it only occurred to Bilal as they approached their old home. He nudges Drekkar pointing with his chin to the shack they all called home only a short time ago. It looked abandoned and forsaken in the darkness of pre-dawn. It was hard to believe they had lived there for such a long time, though it was only Emilia that brought warmth to living there. It pained Drekkar to look upon it and he squeezed Bilal's shoulder and hung his head low in silent apology. He had no pride in his past at this moment.

They walked on in silence and tears. In about thirty more minutes they arrived at the location. A large and open tent was arranged about forty feet from the funeral pier. It was not until standing next to the tent itself that Drekkar and Bilal could see the Pharaoh himself, accompanied by Angyet and little Mila standing there already waiting. Drekkar gasps at the site of them. It was the last thing he was expecting. He quickly walks to Pharaoh-Ra dropping to one knee three feet from him. "Lord Pharaoh, I was not expecting such an honor as your presence. I am humbled by your presence and unlimited generosity. I thank you for allowing me to honor my wife in the tradition of our home land." Bilal follows, also kneeling before Pharaoh to formally thank him.

"Please rise Drekkar Von Kesslar and Bilal Von Kesslar. I

have come to honor you and Emilia. She brought Bilal into this world and both of you into our lives. Please do not let me take from this moment, allow me to contribute my thanks for you coming into *our* lives. I am here for you. Please carry on with honoring your dear wife."

"Thank you, thank you Lord Pharaoh." Wiping tears from his eyes and with no further words he rises. Turning to direct Emilia's bearers, they place her body to be ready for the rising of the sun and her journey to eternal rest.

Time passes quickly and Drekkar takes the torch as the light of dawn is beginning to spread across the horizon to the East. It is time.

Everyone has gathered around Drekkar, who stands at her head which is towards the north. They all stand informally behind him as he faces the mountain of wood with Emilia peacefully laid out on the table on top. They can only faintly make out the outline of her body. Without hesitation Drekkar walks over and lights the wood, walking around to the left and starting flame along the way. It lights quickly and easily and he hands the torch to a slave there to assist with keeping the fire.

Drekkar stands tall facing Emilia and the growing fire, he lifts his arms into the air and begins his song. It is strong and clear and in the language of his homeland. Not even Bilal knows what he is saying, but the sentiment is clear. He has never heard his father sing except in drunken tavern ballads. He is surprised and in awe, he didn't know his father had this in him. His appreciation for learning more of who his father really is grows immensely with the heartfelt singing.

His voice is strong and it conveys well the intent of carrying

Emilia to her ancestors.

Drekkar sings for Emilia in the language of their homeland, ending with perfect timing of the sun fully risen above the horizon's edge. He turns to face everyone tear stained yet standing proud. Looking to each of them he begins to speak now in the language of Pharaoh's Land. Bilal is again surprised as his father had always been a man of such few words.

"I will translate for you this eulogy of song. Emilia Von Kesslar of the House of Dukard. Daughter of Victoria and Lucious Dukard, Earl of Aberdeen. Wife of Drekkar Von Kesslar of the House Von Kesslar. Mother of Bilal Von Kesslar. Hunter of the great white winter's Land. Slave of Master Abar Iberak. Freeman of Lord Pharaoh-Ra. Emilia Von Kesslar is ushered upon our hearts love to the land of eternal rest. Following the flurries of lacey snow flake and the wind that is a thief of the breath of life. Take our blessed Emilia in your embrace. Let the warmth of our care for her melt all that would divert her path to dark ends. Let the fires move her swiftly. Deliver her unto the company of all who care for and love her dearest. May the ancestors welcome her home unto themselves. Let the gratitude we have for our time with her deliver her there more quickly."

The sentiment of this eulogy is moving for them all. Pharaoh is interested to hear who these "ancestors" are. "*Are ancestors the gods of the north?*" His sense of it is different, returning to one's ancestors upon death sounds like going home to dear family, rather than the journey to an afterlife among the gods. He keeps the musing to himself for now and is moved by the deep caring Drekkar has demonstrated for his dearly departed wife.

Pharaoh-Ra has arranged for them to have food, drink and comfortable surroundings here in the quiet of the desert as they stand witness to the fires and well wishes carrying Emilia to her ancestors.

It is a great honor to be accompanied by the Pharaoh, and Drekkar is at first at a loss of words for receiving such an honor. He summons his courage and approaches Pharaoh-Ra to thank him again. He kneels before Pharaoh to formally thank him as the son of royalty he himself truly is. He reveals who he is in the lands to the far north that he and Emilia came from. He is to the point with his recounting of his family heritage and how he came to be in the Land of Pharaoh.

"May I ask you a question? What is the term 'ancestor'? I have not heard of it before," inquires Pharaoh.

Drekkar looks a little surprised. He is not used to a ruler being openly inquisitive and so casually admitting something he does not know. Somehow it puts him at ease a bit. "The term 'ancestor' refers to all the family who have died throughout the entire lineage of our family. In the land I am from we believe that all of our family goes to a place of eternal rest and welcomes those who have newly died. We entreat our ancestors to welcome them and we contribute what we can for them to arrive swiftly and easily.

"Thank you for giving my family and I freedom. As a Freeman, I know not yet what I will choose. I had intended to return to my homeland with my beloved Emilia and Bilal. Seeing how happy Bilal has become in the service of Pharaoh-to-be Ra-Milania, I will not make such a request of him. I will honor whatever he chooses. If I stay, or if I go I thank you for the joy you have given my family. Our happiest days were the greater gift you bestowed upon us with the status of Freemen you have given. I do not have adequate words for the gratitude in my heart. You have honored our family further with the gift of today. Thank you Lord Pharaoh-Ra," says Drekkar humbly.

Pharaoh-Ra places his hand on Drekkar's shoulder; "It is I who thanks you. Thank you for trusting me with revealing who you truly are. Thank you for empowering your son to choose what he will and for your blessing in it. I know it may seem unusual to you that I and my daughter would embrace your son not only as Ra-Milania's personal guardian, but also as a friend. He embodies many qualities that we have the utmost regard for and seek in many but find in few."

Bilal feels honored by what is father has shared with the royal family and finds himself just as honored and speechless with regard to Pharaoh's reply.

The surprise of how different this Pharaoh is has not abated. It made Bilal think of Angyet, and Bilal turns his gaze to her in wonder. *"What other secrets does she posses? What has she not yet been able to say to me?"*

Chapter 46

In a blink Angyet stands on the pyramid. She is directly in the middle of the surface stones facing out towards the open sands to the north. Today's memorial for Bilal's mother was moving. Angyet could not show it, but she was excited by these turn of events. The oneness was conspiring to keep Bilal in Pharaoh's Land and she was grateful and humbled by the awareness of it. She liked to go to the pyramid and commune with the earth and the cosmos there. The energies were beginning to amplify with the base stones already in place. Each one increased the thrum of energies singing in a glorious celebration of oneness.

Hamadi's education about the pyramid plans was extensive and he was able to impart so much before the passing of his body into oneness. As the Pharaoh's Builder for almost two hundred years, his connection and capacities with oneness were impressive. Angyet felt blessed to have met him and for every moment of every day they had together. What she gained in the two years she had with him would have taken her at least a hundred years to accomplish on her own, maybe longer. And some of his awareness he shared would likely have passed with him into the unknown without her inquisitive nature pestering him until the end.

She laughed thinking of it; her endless questions. He would fain impatience with all those questions sometimes just to tease her. It brought living into his body, all of those questions, curiosity and demand for more awareness, more oneness, always more. Angyet's interest in the oneness was as avid as his own; he had not met anyone like her in all his years. The Pharaoh had asked much over the years, but not with as much depth and ceaseless, untiring thirst as Angyet. She was insatiable. Once introduced they had spent every moment of every day they possibly could, playing, laughing, learning, expanding, honing skills and practicing endlessly.

Pharaoh-Ra was most pleased for Hamadi to find a true pupil to pass on his knowing, what he could of his capacities and have confidence that the construction of the pyramid was being left in capable hands. Now that Hamadi was gone, if anyone could carry out this task it was Angyet. He had every confidence in her and between the two of them he trusted their ability to assist in carrying out his family legacy. He would also honor Hamadi with the accomplishment of building this pyramid for it would not come into existence without his encouragement, knowing and empowering presence. He inspired greatness in all who knew him and had the privilege of being in his presence.

With Hamadi's guidance Angyet had been trained in the awareness of the energies that were asking to be created with this monument. Standing on the pyramid itself gave absolute clarity of her senses with the progression of stone placement and its proper alignment. Though the elements that were being considered and included in this alignment were complex, the awareness of the energy of it was quite clear and straightforward. It made it easy to know if all was correct or not. She could play with the molecules of the stone itself moving it, altering it, shaping it to sing in harmony with every element that was connected to this pyramid.

And it just felt good; the warmth of the rocks as the day's heat emanated out, releasing into the cool night air. The energies of the earth rising in intensity with the rising of the stones gave Angyet the sense of the grandness of this task and the joy of its possibilities for a future of oneness almost forgotten by past generations. To bring this ancient plan back to life and dare to actualize it was an amazing honor. Hamadi's presence was strong here, she could sense him, hear him even. Speaking words of encouragement, praise and the stories of this task echoed through her.

The teachings embodied by the gods Osiris and Isis...

As Keeper of all life and living, the figure Osiris embodied the teachings of the cycles of creation. The elements, the capacity, the actions and the choices for living...this is an infinite being. Osiris, symbol of the living body and the infinite being in harmony with all that is.

Hamadi revealed to Angyet, "As infinite beings we continue on with or without a body. To allow one's body to live and die is but a choice an infinite being makes. As many times as we choose, as often as we choose; we are not bound. How do you think I got to be so old as to live two-hundred and forty-six annual cycles of the sun? This choice, this awareness is also present in all living things, in the plants, the animals and all bodies. There is a harmony to this glorious event of living, where all living contributes to itself creating its own future and possibility for sustaining. Sustaining is not an act of keeping the same, sustainability is an ever moving action of creation. All life naturally embodies this Angyet. Thus with any choice you make that supports and contributes to living; the entire universe is more than happy to gift what it can that would allow that living to show up and continue on."

Hamadi continued, "Death is included in this process. Isis we know as the embodiment of the teachings of this, as she is Keeper of death and dying. Death can also be a contribution to more living. You can see it as the plant dies and its body transforms into rich soil that allows new life to grow. Or as an animal heard is hunted, it is only the weak and sickly that are sorted out and killed that the vital and healthy may continue to flourish. Or with people, that new choices become available for those who remain living now that a person has passed on. Everyone's life always becomes greater for it, not less. The aspect of death is a part of this great cycle movement, action and transformation of embodying the oneness. There is no such thing as lack or loss as oneness, just change. And all change leads to something greater."

Angyet smiled with the memory of dear, sweet Hamadi. She smiled more knowing he would be pleased with how things progressed up to now.

There was an ease in embodying the oneness, as the sense of loss of those now gone is much less in the awareness of them as an infinite being that still lives, only without the same kind of physical body. She wondered how Bilal was doing with the loss of his mother, it seemed not well.

Chapter 47

B ilal is having difficulty moving forward with the passing of his mother. She has been one of the very few in his life with any amount of kindness and caring for him. Her loss is great for him and he cannot hide the sorrow of it well, it surrounds him like a cloud.

Bilal visits Naruub for another healing session.

He takes a seat on the day bed, laying back, he does not know how to start. He realizes how much he is trying to hold it together. In this space of allowance that is Naruub he begins to crack open. Tears begin to come to his eyes, but he cannot find words to speak.

Naruub removes his shoes for him and brings a blanket to cover him. His warmth of being embraces Bilal while he tucks in the blanket around his body. Naruub's hand rests on

Bilal's chest with that familiar beginning of sessions. He is present with Bilal in a way few people ever are, as to say I am here with all of you; the good, the bad and the ugly and it is all okay. He gently breaks open the sense of loss that Bilal is bracing himself against.

Naruub speaks softly, "When you choose to be present with what is, no barriers, no turning away from it, you will find it will not consume you Bilal. With no point of view you can receive the gift your mother has been to you and have more of it. That gift does not go away with the absence of her body. Her presence lives on, Bilal, as the oneness and as the energy she is as an infinite being. Our being never dies, only our body. You might miss being able to hug her, however if you allow yourself, you can be aware of the energies of her new form that are now available to you to have connection with."

Bilal takes a deep breath. He is beginning to relax as he listens to what Naruub is saying and considers it. There is a lightness to what he says that lets him know that what Naruub says is true. He does not get how, yet a peacefulness is entering his world as the moments continue.

"Now relax more, expand out. Recall the sensations, the energy, not just on your chest but throughout your entire being. I am not only touching your body, I am embracing your entire being. I am including all of you with no judgment, no expectation and having no separation from any part of you. You also have complete access to the entirety of my being, all of me Bilal. As you increase your receiving, you increase your being and presence. As you increase your being and presence, you increase your receiving. Either direction you go, you get more of you. When you connect with another person who is also willing to have this and be this, together you are a thousand times more. More of everything becomes possible. You might find you can also have this with your mother now in a different way than was possible before." With that Naruub energetically pulls outward from the edges of Bilal's entire reality, gently expanding, inviting and caressing his willingness to receive more. He includes the energies of Emilia now. Showing Bilal how he can include his mother's energies in his world in a new way.

Naruub continues, "Good. This will apply to everything in your life. And as you increase this intensity of presence and capacity of being; the energies you have available to make request of and have what you are asking for come to fruition are exponentialized. Being present with everything, no matter how uncomfortable, sad, intense or anything else; will add to what is possible, always."

Bilal takes a deep breath and exhales. Naruub has such a different perspective than anyone else he knows, yet what he says is so simple and clear he knows what he says is true even with never hearing of it before.

Naruub speaks again, "As you go through your days Bilal, ask yourself 'what is possible now that I have never considered?' when you feel yourself becoming lonesome or missing her. And allow yourself to miss her if that arises. Do not hide from whatever is up for you, as this will strengthen your capacity of presence. Vulnerability and having no barriers is the most dynamic choice for increasing your awareness that you have available to you. Use it Bilal, use it to your advantage for the awareness that choice will contribute to you."

Bilal is renewed with a sense of ease and spaciousness that is the gift of time spent with Naruub. He marvels at the miracle that awareness is; how even the most dark of moments is filled with the possibilities for more.

When finished with the session, Bilal thanks Naruub for the gift of a different outlook that he always provides. "I always leave here with more of me than I came in the door with. You are a true gift Naruub." Bilal embraces him and heads for the hidden pillars of The Pathway and Ra-Milania's rooms.

Ra-Milania greets him with her usual directness, "How was your session with Naruub? Did he lessen the ache of your loss, Bilal?" Mila asks with such sweetness and caring he cannot be offended by such bluntness.

"Yes little Mila, he did indeed."

She smiles but says nothing, hugging him and returning to her puzzle pieces she has spread out on the table before her.

"Mila, can I ask something of you?" says Bilal a little hesitantly.

"Yes Bilal, what is it?" Replies Mila.

"Can I cut my hair short?"

Mila laughs, "Of course, why are you asking that?"

"Master Iberak has never allowed me to cut my hair shorter than my shoulders. He said it was my best asset to show I am better than everyone else. Since no one else other than my parents have, or had hair the color of wheat and mine is lighter than them both," Bilal says with a pained look on his face.

"Oh I see," says Mila. She walks over to him placing her small hands on his knee and looking him in the eyes continues; "From now on this will always be your choice Bilal. You may be my guardian but you are also a Freeman now. I will never dishonor your choices for you."

"Thank you Mila!" he picks her up and hugs her grateful and still blown away by this little girl with more kindness, presence and awareness than most any other adult he knows.

"Tell Rimmel when you see him next for fittings. He can also cut your hair," says Mila.

This will be one of the very first things in Bilal's life that he has chosen for himself. He thinks of his mother and is standing taller with the thought of this choice. He will honor her memory and his new life with the cutting of his hair.

Bilal was beginning to heal in ways he could never have imagined were possible. His father did not appear to be faring as well. He did not know how to move on and it showed.

Chapter 48

It has been quiet at the Von Kesslar house. Rimmel still visits daily or nightly as he can. Emilia's friends Yakeri, Padur and Kesha also take turns making sure there is food prepared for Drekkar. Bilal is not there often and they are not sure what to do. Emilia was their friend, but none of them knew much of Drekkar or had done more than meet him in passing all these years. He lived intensely and they had mostly only heard of the hardness between him and his son. None of them knew what to say as they found him polite but not willing to engage in conversation. He would not speak of Emilia. Telling stories of her and remembering did not go anywhere other than to cast a shadow of sorrow over his face and he would withdraw more, or simply go to his room in silence.

Rimmel would talk, even if Drekkar said nothing. He would speak of the day's events and of Bilal and how well he was doing in adjusting to this new life and his duties. He was impressive in all he did and brought a sense of ease, joy and possibility to everything the Pharaoh and his daughter wish to accomplish. He was a great contribution. Rimmel wanted Drekkar to know this and thought it would help Drekkar feel better. He was not sure it was doing that.

The visits of Emilia's friends were quickly getting shorter and Drekkar was withdrawing more into silent darkness of loss.

Bilal managed to make it to the house about twice a week, sometimes in the morning for a bit. He would find his father at the dining table sitting silently as though he expected to find Emilia coming from the kitchen at any moment. The other times he came home was late in the evening. Then he would find his father asleep already or out on the veranda in the dark and silence. He would hug his father hello and good-bye. The tentative closeness they have developed in the last few months was on shaky ground. It was really Emilia who had kept them connected in any way. With her now gone, neither of them were sure how to create a relationship. They most often sat in silence. Bilal had not broached the subject of his father leaving. He had very mixed emotions at the idea of it. He didn't know if he would be happy with that choice or not and did not yet have the courage to ask what his father might choose.

This night Drekkar sat at the table sipping tea when Bilal arrived. "Hello, come sit son. I have something to tell you." Always direct, Bilal caught his breath not knowing what to expect. He said nothing but sat silent waiting for his father to speak.

"Master Iberak has been here. He has been visiting all week, every day in fact. He has asked me to become business partners with him," Drekkar says, matter-of-fact.

"What? He has been in our home? How did he find us? How could you let him in? You are not considering it, are you?" Bilal says accusing.

"I have said yes."

"You what?" shouts Bilal standing to his feet and knocking down the chair. He clenches his fists at a loss for words. "Why, why would you ever go back there? What are you going to do with him?" he manages to say between clenched teeth.

"Everything we were doing before; the work in the quarry, the slaves, the brothels, the training for house keepers in the Keeper's Realm. He even has a few new fighters he would like me to work with. Besides, you know firsthand, beating people is what I am good at," says Drekkar. That stung. Freedom and the unknown was too much without Emilia by his side. He did not know what to do with himself other than return to the familiar.

Bilal let that pass. He knew his father was hurting and he wasn't going to provoke him. Picking up the chair and sitting back down he spoke quietly now; "Don't do it father. A few weeks ago you were ready to kill him to go north and now you are going to be business partners?!" exclaims Bilal. "You don't have to of this. You are a Freeman. You can do anything. The palace guard needs help. You are good with equipment, you are good with organization, there are a thousand things you can do - anything but that!"

Bilal was feeling desperate. He would never go back. He

could not comprehend that his father had already but made up his mind to do so.

"Master Iberak is making me an equal partner, we are going to split everything fifty-fifty. He and I are good at it together, I have already built his empire of flesh being by his side, why not profit from it now? I hate the man but we know how to succeed in our business."

"He is already calling it 'our' business," Bilal thinks to himself. "Well it sounds like it is already done father. There is nothing to say." He gets up to walk out, he can't take this. "Mother would be beside herself," he says glaring at his father. He turns to leave before he does something he regrets and heads for the front door.

Drekkar gets up following Bilal towards the door. Drekkar continues desperately; "I will maintain the house here. We can both still call this home. I don't know how I am going to go on without your mother. If I do nothing I will rot away, but I won't let go of this house and the last happiness the three of us had together."

The only reply is the door slamming closed.

Chapter 49

Bilal's feet carry him, yet he does not notice where he is going. Swirling in anger, confusion, frustration, and loss, he does not know what to do with himself. He is surprised to find himself at the steps of the House of Pleasure when he suddenly notices his surroundings. Tears spring forth and he quickens his step to go inside. Reaching the doors he finds Naruub's hand-servant waiting, looking expectant. "Please come in Bilal, Naruub has been expecting you."

"What? Really? How did he...?" He lets it go in the relief of the invitation given. He enters the room and he is shaking all over now. All of his past is clashing with the new life that is emerging. His father's choice to go back to work with Master Iberak is everything he would rather die than choose. The choice seems a deep personal blow that he can't allow into his world.

Naruub speaks, "Sit here, Bilal." He steers him to the daybed he sat on before in past sessions with Bilal. "Please tell me what it is I can do for you this evening?"

Bilal stammers and sputters, he can barely get it out and it comes in a jumble of incoherent sentences. Naruub lets him spill, not trying to understand or clarify what he is talking about. This is a moment for allowing Bilal to release. When he has gotten to a space of quieting and done with the rant, Naruub asks him a question. "Would you like to change this Bilal?"

This surprises Bilal. "What do you mean?"

"Well, first of all, you cannot change your father. I understand this is a total irritation and a great disappointment at the moment, but you have got to understand this. Your father is living his life and choosing what works for him. You cannot change this, just like you would not wish to be changed by your father and his points of view about what you should or should not be choosing. What you can change is what you are choosing; your perspective, your expectations, your judgments. The quickest way to clarity and ease is to recognize what is. The more you focus on how you would like it to be, that is not how it is, the more limitation and lack you are going to get stuck with. What you can change is how you are functioning with regard to this. So, when I ask, 'would you like to change this?' I am asking, would you be willing to change how you are functioning, even if you don't know what that is? Would you allow the oneness to contribute to you in having a greater possibility with your father than you are currently able to be aware of?"

"Yes. Oh yes, please. I certainly cannot remotely imagine how what you say can become possible, however if you say this can become true, lead the way! I would like to have that kind of allowance for my father. I do know all about what it has been to live with his lack of allowance for me, I would like to change that now, whatever it takes," replies Bilal earnestly.

"Please, lay back and let us first change the energies. When you change the energies you are functioning from, then everything else follows and begins to show up different. You know what it feels like energetically to have no choice, to be stuck in the patterns of interacting with your father from that place of no choice, are you not?"

Bilal nods in the affirmative.

"What if you have choice in all those moments you believed you did not? What I will be demonstrating by the energy I am being is how to be the energies of choice in all those areas of your body and being that you bought into the lie that you have no choice and restore choice as a possibility in every moment, as far back as that goes." says Naruub softly.

"I can change the past buy what I choose now? Really?" This is hard for Bilal to comprehend, yet Naruub has not lied to him up to this point. He allows himself to consider the possibility of this even though he has no idea of the how of it.

Bilal removes his shoes and lays back letting the confusion and turmoil release and allowing Naruub to access all those spaces as best he could. As before Naruub touched his body here and there unlocking all that he had hidden from himself, all that he clung to as no choice and opening up a sense of possibility he never imagined could be his to be. So simple, the introduction of energies and the sweet nurturing embrace of the oneness as a thrum through his body and being. Bilal was surprised to find that he wanted to fight it, this increase in choice and ease of being. As Naruub pointed this out in his gentle, non-judgmental presence he found he could let it go.

Amazing how saying what is, identify the choice being made in the moment could unlock and change it. Naruub called it 'the light of awareness' the oneness embodies. In oneness nothing can be hidden from one's own awareness. The good, the bad and the ugly is revealed and the space of infinite possibilities permeates that which was once hidden and denied. "Oneness includes everything and does not judge, ever," says Naruub simply.

The session ends and Bilal lays a moment basking in the afterglow that the oneness embodied to a degree he never has been before engenders. He smiles, relaxed, spent and curious.

Bilal looks at Naruub, he is a little confused. He laughs at himself and shrugs. Thinking *"Here goes"* he says to Naruub, "These sessions of healing, they make me think I love you Naruub, but somehow I know that is not quite it, do you know what I mean?"

Naruub smiles, "Yes Bilal, it is called gratitude. Gratitude is something quite different than love, it is greater."

"Yes! I wake up every day so happy most the time now. It is not like anything I have known before. I wake up wondering how I got to be so lucky and even the ugliness of the past I do not resent so much. I am beginning to notice that my life before has been contributing to what I am now becoming capable of," says Bilal in wonder.

"Gratitude requires no reason and justification for having it, it just is something you be. When you have gratitude it is as you say, you begin to notice how all of your life, everything you have been through and experienced contributed to greater awareness and greater possibilities. That my friend is the glorious beauty of the oneness in action; your living, your aliveness is not separate from the harmony of oneness as it begets oneness. Every moment contributes. Every energy contributes. There is much to be grateful for when you live from that awareness."

"Why doesn't love create oneness like gratitude does?"

"Gratitude has no definition and no conditions, it is something you choose to have and be. Love on the other hand has so many definitions no one really knows what the other person means when they say 'I love you'. Most people assume their definition of love is the same as the other person's love, yet it almost never is. One way you can recognize this is how most have a reason, justification and conditions under which they determine they are in love with you. However the moment you do not fulfill those conditions or do not live up to the reasons or do not meet their justifications; you find out how quickly that love goes away."

"Do you mean it like those girls who say they love me but if I lay with another girl they no longer will speak to me?" Asks Bilal.

"Yes, that is exactly what I am speaking of Bilal. And how is it with your Lili?"

"I see now there are no conditions for either of us, we just care about each other, no matter what we do, no matter what we choose, no matter if we are together or apart or with other people." A new wave of gratitude flows over Bilal and the tears of release flow, as recognizing what is true for him awakens in his awareness.

"Gratitude is a balm to our being and our body. Deep healing occurs from being grateful. It expands the oneness, increasing it and inviting an intensity of living few are willing to have. You have it, that is why we can have this conversation. I cannot speak of such things unless you can ask about it. And you cannot hear what I say about this unless you are already functioning as gratitude and oneness. This brings me great joy Bilal, you are one of the first in a very long time to ask of such things and know of which I speak. I am grateful for you showing up in my life."

Bilal laughs as the tears of gratitude increase.

"May I ask, how do you feel about your father's choice now Bilal?"

He takes a moment to explore. "Oh, wow. I see how he will do anything to contribute to my betterment in life, even if it means he must go to the darkest of places to do so. Wow, I did not get that about my father like I do now. I have so much to be grateful for." With this new awareness Bilal's tears of gratitude flow even more than before. The well of healing Naruub has awakened runs so much deeper than Bilal had considered. He lets it wash over him, taking it all in; the energies, the awareness, the awakening possibilities.

Naruub sits in silence allowing the healing to take root, being the kind and nurturing presence that invites miracles to actualize.

Chapter 50

Drekkar throws himself into work with Master Iberak essentially picking up where he left off. The new life he had and all that had transpired in the few months since becoming a Freeman could have all just been a dream, he so easily slipped back into the world of the Laborer's Realm and Master Iberak. Except each night he would go home to the Artisan Realm making the reality of his freedom and all the choices he truly had available a reality he could not deny.

Bilal and Drekkar's lack of presence at the quarry has been felt by all. Bilal's prowess was inspiring to many of the slaves to do better, try harder and cooperate with each other to create greater accomplishment overall. Drekkar's sense of organization and what needed to be in place to get the job done was one of the greatest things he had to contribute to Master Iberak's success. With both of them gone things had been falling apart.

It was taking more people to accomplish less and morale was low. The slave drivers were becoming harsher, if that were possible. Violence and death had increased markedly.

It was early in the morning just as dawn was breaking and Drekkar found Master Iberak in the usual spot when he was in the mood for making money, sitting in the tavern eating his morning meal. Drekkar came and sat in front of him, no salutation, just the usual nod of hello they had greeted each other with for years. In the past they would often start their day reviewing what they were aiming to accomplish for the day, along with anything needing special attention.

Today Abar starts with reviewing the state of affairs with Drekkar. Number of lives lost, new slaves, the progress of work cutting stones in the quarry and keeping all the materials for housing, feeding, clothing and managing over forty-five thousand slaves and Freeman laborers. It was more of a mess than Drekkar imagined, as he had not been gone that long. Though Drekkar had always been harsh with his son, he was relatively well-liked by most and respected for his clear leadership and surety of action. He always knew what to do in any situation. Though often appearing stoic, he was fair handed in his dealings and surprisingly thoughtful in leveraging things to turn out better for everyone involved.

Drekkar would spend this day meeting with the other people who managed Master Abar Iberak's growing empire of toil. Some were assigned, some naturally fell into place with their personality and inclinations; Drekkar new them all. Everyone was pleased to see him. Drekkar was like a buffer between them and the intensity and chaotic violent moods of

Master Iberak. Master Iberak had become a worse nightmare when the Von Kesslars had been made Freemen. Drekkar quickly learned of the bloody demise of those who were unfortunate enough to be there when Master Iberak arrived at the tavern in a murderous rage.

Drekkar was a hard man, however he had a sense of honor, dignity and fairness that made everything he did absolutely calculated. Constantly he was weighing the pros and cons of every interaction, situation and possible future outcome he could conceive of. He had a reason or logic he could live with for every choice he made. As Drekkar made his rounds, he mostly found a lack of direction and information where messages were not getting passed. Master Iberak had been assuming that things were in place to take care of themselves, he was not aware of all that Drekkar did to make sure things were in order, being planned for, organized and accounted for. It was largely the lack of accountability of those in place to carry out what was requested that created the break down and mess of things.

It was when he met with Omar that he really got an earful. Omar was Master Iberak's most enthusiastic and prolific supplier of new slaves from the north.

"Greetings Omar!" says Drekkar with a slap to Omar's back. "New stock is coming in well. Getting them mostly from the north still? It seems you have been a very busy man since I have been gone. I came to let you know that I am back and now as a Freeman I am also equal partners with Master Iberak, so his business is my business. Tell me, how is it going for you?"

Omar's eyes light up, he steps a little closer and in a conspiratorial whisper says, "Beautifully Drekkar, beautifully! The numbers are almost there. Considering how popular Pharaoh-Ra is, I never thought we'd be able to put together as large a force and so quickly as we have."

Drekkar has no idea what he is talking about but he goes along with it with an approving nod and slight smile, matching the conspiratorial mood.

Omar continues, "I don't know if it is wife-of-Pharaoh's beauty or deep purses that are inspiring the men but we will be well on target in the time frame she has given. Whatever is inspiring them I could give a rat's ass about, it is making me rich though, rich!" He is bursting with glee.

It must be quite a lot of money he has made. Drekkar considers what to say next. "When is the next trip then Omar? I shall wish to make myself available to view it with my own eyes. Master Iberak has been gloating so I thought him grossly exaggerating his success. Could it really be true? In such a short time?"

"Well, half an annual cycle is time enough isn't it?"

"A half annual cycle? Sneaky bastard," thinks Drekkar in shock. Master Iberak has been scheming far longer than Drekkar would have guessed. He was not all that surprised about the plotting. What he was surprised about was that he knew nothing about it. Master Iberak usually confided everything with Drekkar. He is curious why he had not been included in this. Apparently Master Iberak was more ambitious than Drekkar had given him credit for. That he kept this to himself would indicate the largeness of the plan and the

seriousness with which wife-of-Pharaoh was preparing.

He spent another hour or so making small talk and seeing what additional information Omar might reveal as he pretended to already be in on the plans now that he was an "equal partner" with Master Iberak. He wondered if he would bring it up or wait for Master Iberak to broach the subject. He'll have to feel it out as he goes.

Drekkar knew that the Pharaoh and his wife basically lived separate lives and in all the time Bilal spent with Ra-Milania on a daily basis he had never spoken of Ra-Maharet whatsoever. He had found Ra-Milania very endearing when they had met. She was the kind of person he could be proud of as future Pharaoh. His choice was easy.

Having met Ra-Milania himself, it was hard to imagine her mother plotting to take over. This would require violent force and not only killing the Pharaoh, but also either killing Ra-Milania or making her prisoner as her throne is stolen. He would find out with more certainty for himself before he brought this up with Bilal.

Drekkar marveled at how when one door closes another door opens. He wondered what other unexpected ways new possibilities might show up in his life.

Chapter 51

It had been a few more weeks now, and Bilal had not been back since the news of his father going into business with Master Iberak. He was surprised to see Lili's mother Khepri sitting with his father when he arrived at the house. "Khepri, what a pleasant surprise, it has been too long! Do you know I see Lili at the palace sometimes," says Bilal a little shyly.

"Bilal!" how wonderful to see you, "Come hug me. I am so sorry to hear about your dear mother. Emilia was a wonderful woman and it is a great loss to us all."

"Thank you Khepri, it is very kind of you. We are hanging in there," says Bilal as he clasps his father's shoulder and gives it a squeeze. Drekkar's eyes widen at the generosity of his son's words. This was as close to making up as it was going to get. Drekkar would take it. He squeezes his son's hand back in acknowledgment. Khepri knows very well their history and it lifts her to see them being as friendly as all this. She has never seen it before. All these years at Master Iberak's brothel she was there during and after most every fight, she was often there to tend to Bilal's wounds with her daughter Lili.

"I hope you do not mind Bilal. Master Iberak has heard of Emilia's passing and asked that I stay with your father from now on. A gift of camaraderie if you will. He thought I might ease the loss and be able to tend to your father." She actually blushes a bit. She had been referring to things like cooking but realized it sounded like otherwise, coming from a brothel and all.

Bilal knew all that it meant and more. *"Did she know Drekkar and Master Iberak were now in business together? Was she part of the deal, or just something to sweeten it?"* He let the darkness of these thoughts pass along with the hardness in his heart in all that has occurred. Khepri had always been kind to him and this was Lili's mother. He embraced the possibilities of anything that brought Lili further into his life.

Without hesitation he embraces Khepri again saying, "If father has agreed, then you are welcome in our home. You have always been a good friend, Khepri, and it would bring ease to have you here." Tears come to Bilal unexpectedly. Besides Emilia, Khepri and her daughter Lili were the three people he had always had a sense of comfort and nurturing with. Bilal liked the idea of having Khepri living with his father. She would be both a buffer and a sense of bonding between him and his father with Emilia now gone.

He still was not sure he could forgive his father's choice to continue working with Master Iberak, even with the growing gratitude for all his father has been attempting to contribute to his life. Someone familiar in totally unfamiliar ground between him and his father was welcome. In addition this added one more way he and Lili could be in each other's lives if their parents were now to live under the same roof and so close to the palace.

Drekkar visibly relaxed, hearing Bilal's welcome of Khepri. He didn't know where he stood with his son since the news of going back to work with Master Iberak. He thought she would be welcome, but he did not wish to assume anything with his son. "I am happy to hear this son. Khepri would be a welcome comfort indeed, besides, then Lili and you would have more reason to spend time together; here with us!"

Bilal had never spoken with his father about Lili, but his father was not blind. He is touched by his father's invitation and politely indirect gesture of acknowledgment.

"Knowing you are agreeable Bilal, I will help her bring her things tomorrow. I was wondering, would you be willing to allow her your room downstairs and move you to the smaller room off the courtyard? I don't imagine you will be staying here as much with your duties. Would that be all right son?" asks Drekkar.

"Yes father, that would be just fine with me. It makes more sense for her to have it. It is a lovely room Khepri opening right into the garden below. Have you seen it yet?" replies Bilal sincerely.

"No, it was already dark when I arrived. I will see it tomorrow. Thank you Bilal, you are most generous and gracious," says Khepri with a slight bow of her head.

"I can clear out most of my things by morning actually. It will be several days before I can make it back again, so father if you can arrange the space for me and I'll have my personal items packed so you can just place them in the room and I'll arrange it," he raises his eyebrows in question to his father.

"Yes, I will do so," replies Drekkar with a satisfactory nod of his head.

The three of them spend several more hours visiting and catching up on all that has occurred since they have seen each other last. The conversation lightens the air between Bilal and Drekkar, renewing the ease they have had since their new life here in the Artisan Realm. They were a bit surprised to hear how little Khepri knew of everything. Bilal had thought she would have known more since Lili is now in the palace. But then, Lili has not seen her mother much either. Life at the palace really was a world apart. Drekkar and Bilal were interested to hear how things were going at the quarry and the general goings on of the Laborer Realm. They were not surprised to hear about Master Iberak going crazy with rage when they were given freedom by the Pharaoh. Drekkar also shared what he had heard of that night of Master Iberak going berserk with rage. Bilal raises an eyebrow at his father with a look of *I told you so and what are you doing going back with him.* He just as quickly lets it go.

Khepri excuses herself for the evening, "I will take my leave now dear men. Thank you for welcoming me into your home. Apparently retirement has come early for me!" she says with a wink and a laugh.

Both Drekkar and Bilal burst out in laughter with her, she

always did have a great sense of humor and they enjoyed the ease of laughter they both have with her.

"I'll be going to pack my things to be ready for tomorrow myself." With a hug and kiss on the cheek for both of them, she takes her leave.

Bilal sits back with a slight smile and gazes at his father. "This will be good to have her here," he says satisfactorily.

"I am glad you think so. It is not too soon for you after, after your mother passing?" Drekkar says a little choked up in asking.

"No, father. I know mother is the love of your life and she will never be replaced. Khepri has been a good friend to us both, she would be a welcome comfort. And, as you said, then Lili has a reason to come here too." He does not try to hide the twinkle in his eyes at the mention of Lili.

Chapter 52

Ra-Milania is turning six in just a few more cycles of the moon and to celebrate Bilal and the guard are arranging a surprise for Mila, a performance of sorts. They would like to do something special that she will not expect. Bilal and Kylar have asked Angyet if she will give some lesson's to the small group of guards in training and about his plans to honor Mila on her day of birth celebration. The men and boys could also use some direction in how to go further in developing their capacities, and both Kylar and Bilal are at a loss for what to do next. They know Angyet will know what to do to take them all to the next level. She is the only one who really knows how to go forward and take them further than they can imagine.

Angyet arrives at Ra-Milania's guard facility with Kylar and Bilal to start lessons on increasing awareness of energy, their ability to communicate telepathically amongst themselves and how they can become a stronger team by contributing to each other energetically.

They enter the main living area where all are already gathered. They have been waiting, they were not told for what reason, just to be ready for a guest and a special day of training. Upon sight of The Builder, they all quickly line up standing at attention.

She smiles inside seeing this motley group little Mila has assembled and is warmed by the obvious willingness they all exude. It is so different to have a group who is gathered from their willingness and choice, rather than only because of being paid or out of servitude.

"Good day men," says Angyet as she looks at them each in turn. They all stand taller, proudly giving their complete attention to The Builder. Most of them have but glimpsed her and always step aside to make way. It is a very special occasion to actually be addressed by her directly. They waited with bated breath for what they owe the honor. They couldn't imagine what she might say and they all burst with anticipation. Only Bilal and Kylar smiled wide, knowing a bit of the fun in store for them.

Angyet was just as excited but she will not show it. She is curious to get familiar with this group that Mila has gathered. Though Mila has told her all about them, many she does not have any personal experience with. She has been impressed with Bilal and Kylar, inspired even. Her hopes for a greater future were becoming more than just hope, what she had dreamed was actualizing week by week, month by month; especially this last annum. The previous Builder Hamadi was correct, his sense of future possibilities was coming true. If only he were here to celebrate it with her. Well, she would carry on in all he had gifted and contributed to her becoming capable. In recalling this she herself stood taller ready to begin today's exercises.

"I have come to you today on behalf of Ra-Milania that you may fulfill the greatness you are truly capable of in protecting her well being and her future. She has chosen each of you, personally selecting you because of that greatness she sees in you. I will be pleased to discover the gift each of you can be to Pharaoh's Land and our dear Ra-Milania. It is my aim to give you every advantage possible. Especially those things that give you outrageously unfair advantage," she says with a conspiratorial smile and a wink. She has that same ability to embrace them, welcoming, comforting and inspiring just like little Mila. The men like her immediately.

The group begin to smile and look to Bilal and Kylar in curiosity but they are not giving anything away other than the twinkle in their eyes.

Angyet continues, "Today will be the beginning of many lessons and practice sessions. So, let us begin shall we? I would like to jump right into your first exercise and afterward if you have questions, I will answer anything you would like to ask." She nods to Kylar who instructs them all to get a chair or stool which they line up and then take a seat upon. Bilal has retrieved three chairs he sets facing the rest. Angyet sits in the middle and asks Kylar and Bilal to sit on either side of her.

She begins, "One great advantage for Keeper's of the pharaoh-to-be is the ability to have clear communication. The ability to do that without others being able to notice or figure out what is being said is what we will be practicing today. We are going to practice speaking to each other without using any words." The group makes exclamations of disbelief wondering how they would ever be able to do that.

"You will learn to speak mind to mind, silently. It is called telepathic communication. It might not be as difficult as you think. Let me give you some examples of ways you might already be doing this. How many of you know when food is ready even when you have not been told in advance?" The group looks at each other thinking about it. They all recognize, quite often actually.

She looks to the keeper of Mila's horses, "Missrah knows this with the horses, don't you? Just like Ra-Milania, are you not able to speak to Beset and Sekhet with just thinking your request?" He looks a little shyly and nods affirmatively.

She continues, "Did you ever consider you could talk with people the same way? It works exactly the same really. You will have an advantage Missrah because of all the practice you have already exercised with the horses; you will be able to help the others."

Looking to the rest she goes on, "How many of you are able to finish each other's sentences?" A few of them begin to chuckle and elbow each other, then all look at Anzety and Guyasi.

"This is another form that can be the beginning of speaking mind to mind. How many of you get a tug at your chest that gives you a sense of it being time to go to someone? And you arrive at just the right moment for them to be available to you?

They have just finished their task, or you arrive at the very moment they could use a hand with something?" They look to young Zek who is always there at the exact moment that is most helpful and nod approvingly at him.

"These are all part of your awareness, your connection with each other and your sense of energy. Now energy is the thing that makes all of this possible. Truly everything in creation has an energy to it; including words, including actions, including thoughts, people and more. It includes that feeling you get when you go to different places. It is part of the secret of how you can know everything. When you get good at this, you will be able to know what people are going to do before they do it. That is the bigger target here, but let us now play with this, shall we?"

They all nod enthusiastically, wondering how they would practice such a thing.

"Bilal and Kylar, I would like each of you to touch my knee with yours, turn towards me a bit if you need to, there. Now, I am going to ask all of you to close your eyes and I am going to silently ask you each to do something with your hands, then I will ask you to open your eyes and see how many of you were able to get what I was requesting. Kylar and Bilal, I am giving you the further task of both getting what I tell you and sensing what I tell each of the other men here. I ask you to touch my knee because our body is a large part of what makes this sensing and knowing possible. My body will be teaching your bodies these energies, the subtleties and nuances of it." They each nod to her, ready to begin.

"Alright, close your eyes everyone." She puts in their heads to place the right hand on top of the palm of the left hand. Some of them move right away, others furrow their brow in concentration. "This is very quick, what was that very first thing that came to you? That first tug, that first hunch? That was it. That was what I requested." With that, the ones that were doubting themselves move their hand in place. "Good, now open your eyes." They do and all look around at each other, every one of them was the same; right hand on top of the left palm.

"See look at that, each of you got it! Notice how that came to you, notice what that felt like in your body. Notice how quickly you know." They all smile wide as she continues. "Close your eyes again please." She gives them a moment and they all place their hands on their knees. "Now open. Good, you are all correct." She goes through three more, having them touch their nose with their left hand, put their right hand on top of their head and left hand on their belly, and then make a circle with their thumbs and pointer fingers of each hand.

The next one she asks them all to point to the person to their right. They are asked to open their eyes and they all look around at each other. They all furrow their brows a bit.

Angyet smiles, "Notice everyone is pointing to the person to their right but each of you is doing it a different way? Some of you are using your right hand, some your left, some using your thumb, some a finger. That time I did not give you a specific hand position as I have been doing, I asked you a more general question so you can see you all got it correct, and you also all did it your own way. This is how each of you is different. You were all correct in your awareness, and you all express it in a unique way. This is how it is with all awareness. You get it how you get it, and you express it how you express it, and yet they are all what I asked of you. There is no right way to be aware of energy, there is only getting to know how you are aware of it, how it works for you."

They group "oh's" and "ah's" at this revelation and relax hearing that there is no real right way to do it, they can simply be themselves.

Right away they have all been correct with every request. This is better than Angyet had hoped. Now she will mix it up.

"Okay, close...and now open." They look around and all have their fingers crossed, except Zazza who is touching all fingers tip to tip. He blurts out in exclamation, "Aw, rats!"

"No Zazza, you got it, I told you something different than everyone else, all of you are too good at this, I have to make it more challenging," she says with a laugh. The look of joy on his face is priceless, he is beaming. She looks at Kylar and Bilal asking if they noticed the difference in energies with that. She does not wait for a reply as they will all be discussing it later. They again nod, they get the task at hand and what they are supposed to be looking for and noticing.

Angyet continues with the exercise taking turn of who she gives a different hand position to. She starts to add more movements like standing up, leaning over, touching the person next to them on the shoulder. Hours go by without any of them noticing, they are all having such a good time with it. Finally she calls for food and a break. Madu gets up to prepare something and they all dine together, having a great ease and camaraderie with the warmth and friendliness of Angyet. They all talk easily and ask many questions and share how it is they sense what they were asked to do. Laughing about what they thought it would be like compared to how it actually is.

Bilal, Kylar and Angyet share with the group some of the exercises they will be practicing over the coming days. "I am very pleased, you have all been far better at this than I had hoped, so your training will become more advanced much more quickly. Ra-Milania will be very pleased indeed when I tell her how well you did."

Angyet re-emphasizes, "You are noticing how each of you is a little different in how you sense energy, yes? Some of you have no thought involved, you just know and it is instant. Some of you hear it like someone had said it, yet there is no volume, like a thought. Some of you just get a sense as how to move your body, as though it is something you would like to do. There is no one right way to sense energies."

Angyet also speaks with them about how they can contribute to each other increasing what they are capable of. "These exercises are about getting to know how it is you personally sense energies and learning that you can trust your own knowing. The friendship and caring you have with each other makes this easier. That you would like to encourage each other and do the best you are capable of is an energy you gift to each other that will make you truly great. All of you will become able to achieve things you should not be able to because of this."

"This also includes your body. By your body touching another body it gives the awareness of the energies the person is capable of. It also allows you to become capable of things you may have never considered before. It is a way of 'learning' that is really about becoming an energy you did not know you were capable of. If one of you can be an energy, then the rest of you can also be that energy. By touching, you and your body can know more easily and quickly. A simple touch on the shoulder, a hand, your foot, it really does not matter. Then it is just discovering how it works for you. Even though you can be an energy someone else is, how it shows up as an ability will be unique to you. Just like knowing other people's thoughts and communicating silently shows up a little different for each of you. It is all of your tasks to practice this every day with whatever you are doing. But play with it, do this for the fun of it boys!"

To think that playing with all this is what is required, rather than being serious is a huge relief. That they all know they can do!

Angyet continues to expand on how to practice all of this. "If one of you is better than the others at something, share it. If you are able to have the other's touch you while you are doing that thing you are great at, it will pass on easily. It need only be moments. This does not have to be long and drawn out. You have seen how quickly you get what I was telling you telepathically, it is very fast. It can be the same with other kinds of activities. If you are the one who has the ability and you are sharing it, I ask you to notice when the other person you are showing energetically matches your energy. It may be only seconds, it may take longer. You are all so fast, it might be that before you start the person has already begun. Again, play with it. This is not an exact thing, it will just take whatever it takes. Practice men!"

It is dusk by the time Angyet leaves for Mila's rooms with a smile of satisfaction and lightness in her step with the day's accomplishment. With the day going much better than she had dared hope, *"What else might these boys be capable of?"* she wondered with glee.

Chapter 53

Angyet returns the next day to continue training with Ra-Milania's guard.

Greeting them, she apologizes. "I realize in my excitement and joy of yesterday's exercises we did not speak of your desire to surprise Ra-Milania for her day of birth celebration. I would be thrilled to know what you have been thinking of gifting her."

Zek speaks first, a little shyly he begins, "Well, we were thinking we would like to do something with moving together as one and something kind of musical, but that is as far as we have gotten."

"Do any of you play an instrument?"

They all shake their head no, but Zek pipes up again and continues; "We all like to make beats together, just for the fun of it, for our own amusement."

"We are getting pretty good," continues Kylar.

"Listen to this!" says Guyasi and he begins to tap the table where he is sitting. Each of them begin to chime in making rhythm by tapping their own body or the table, or grabbing a spoon or cup to make sound with. They get a beat going and then take turns adding their own flare. They are going pretty well for about five minutes until one of them gets off beat and they all lose it, falling into laughter. With a shrug Guyasi smiles at Angyet, as to say, "Well, what do you think?"

Angyet has not stopped smiling since they began, "It is wonderful, simply wonderful." She realizes they have not all yet been to the palace and may not be familiar with the layout and the space they would have to work with. She has an idea, not too complex and something they should all be able to accomplish by the time of the celebration.

She lays out her idea and they all clap, thrilled with it. The group gets to work immediately playing with the idea and working out what they might do. Since it ties in with their daily practice of drills and accuracy of sharing formation mind to mind, it will not take away from developing their skills in working together as a team. With the added task of being able to communicate telepathically, this was a beautiful marriage of skills to bring together. It does not take them long to work out most of a routine.

Knowing Zazza will have all the moves they come up with put to memory they move on to practicing with wooden weapons. They all pair up and begin.

Angyet leaves them to it happy to see such willingness of

Mila's guard to work so hard for her. That they think of the Pharaoh-to-be and work to please her gives Angyet a sense of future possibilities that contribute to the oneness growing in Pharaoh's Land. Ra-Milania has chosen well.

Bilal speaks to the men, "We are going to practice knowing what the opponent is going to do before they do it. What we have been practicing in hearing the thoughts in each other's head, and being aware of what is required or desired with each other, we are going to apply this to fighting. Good fighters do not think about what move they will do before they do it, they follow their knowing and awareness. Knowing is always faster than thinking. A good fighter observes the movement of the eyes, muscles and steps of their opponent. They are totally present with the other person and move more quickly and unexpectedly than their adversary."

"Most people move in four directions. Forward, back, right or left. One of the secrets to my success is that I have four additional directions I move that most people do not notice or consider. I almost always move diagonally, at forty-five degree angles. Back and to the right, back to the left, forward to the right, forward to the left." He demonstrates in movement as he speaks. "One small step and you can be out of your opponent's reach. Even just leaning in one of the diagonal directions can evade a punch. Do not be shy about moving toward your opponent to miss their fist; there is nothing like moving in closer to surprise your opponent." He lifts an eye-brow in emphasis and the knowing years of practice bring.

"Now, pair up and let us begin sparring. One person will be on the attack, the other defense. The person in defense position, I would like you to move only in diagonals. Notice, even though you opponent knows your tactic of moving diagonally they will not be able to overcome your movement most of the time. Start!"

Those on attack gave it their all, and it was as Bilal said it would be. Their swings did not meet the target most of the time. They switched position, those on attack changed to defense. Again, most diagonal movements were missed by the attacker's swing. They were all amazed at how effective this kind of movement was.

Several hours later they take a break to eat and rest for the heat of the day. They have all been thrilled to have the privilege of the legendary Bilal amongst them and he had been very friendly, yet most of them still did not know much about him or his life and they were curious. Hemel was the oldest so he dared ask something he had been thinking about for a long time.

Hemel speaks tentatively, as he is a quiet man of reserve; "Bilal, I know you as a fighter for a long time, your reputation is great. Though I have not myself seen you fight, I have heard the telling of it countless times. Kylar has retold every fight blow by blow in the time I have been with him. We live in peaceful times and none of us have seen real battle. I can't say any of us have seen death too much either, even with the two-hundred thousand slaves amongst us. You might be the closest to a true warrior any of us have known. Other than any of the hunting skills we might have, as far as I have heard of none of us know what it is to kill a man, save you. Can I ask, would you tell us about it? If we are to server Ra-Milania well,

I feel this is something we must be prepared for."

It is a long pause before Bilal begins to speak, "I was a slave my whole life. It is only recently I have come to know what true choice is and to have the ownership of my own life and future. Yes, I have killed men with my own two hands in the fighting ring. The violence my father and Master Iberak trained me with was preparation in a perverse way. I say 'perverse' because it was an unspeakably difficult thing for me to do. Killing a person for sport, for entertainment value goes against everything that is true for me, everything I value as a being. Though I have been celebrated for my ability, I do not have pride in it. Those are some of my darkest moments. At the same time, because of the person I am, I also could not help but become good at it. With every fight I would refine my ability. No one has ever asked me of this before. I would say being willing to be whatever it takes to kill rather than be killed. When those are the only two choices, to desire living so fiercely you will do anything to keep it, that is what it took for me to be able to do it and do it well. It is good to know you think of these things Hemel. It is difficult to speak of, yet I am glad you asked."

"Thank you Bilal. You honor us with your willingness to share what you know and what you have been through," says Hemel humbly.

Anzety speaks, "I have seen killing on the hunt. My father is an avid hunter and he has taken me with him often, ever since I could ride. We were hunting antelope in the far south, there was a small group of us. We did not know it but there was also a lioness hunting the same antelope. Seeing us on the prowl she turned her attentions to us. Unknown to us, she began to stalk our group and she attacked, killing my father's oldest slave who was also his best hunter. It was a gruesome thing to behold, she was fierce and fast, so fast. We could not stop her from killing our man before we were able to kill her. My father still keeps the fur."

"We have all seen blood spilt; street fights, the butchering of animals to eat, hunting, accidents, slaves beaten to death. It is one thing to see it, it is another to do it with your own hands. I am not sure what could prepare any of you for such an event. We will continue to train, and I will contemplate what else we might do to prepare each of you."

"Shall we get back to it men?" says Karek. They all nod, ready to practice some more. Bilal excuses himself to go meet with Pharaoh-Ra and Ra-Milania. He leaves the men to continue on their own. He needs some air, it is always such mixed emotions for him; the fighting. The conflict of his abhorrence of death matches and at the same time being really good at it. That, combined with not having a choice about it as a slave. This new life as a Freeman was still undoing that inner conflict.

To unveil what is true for him and be invited to embody it, with all the gifts and capacities he doesn't yet know he has; the gratitude Bilal has for this new life makes the ugliness of his past less of a burden. He celebrates that not only does he get to travel this path, but each person little Mila has chosen as part of her guard are also invited to know what is great and what is different about themselves. Bilal has yet to find a limit in the creative ways she, Angyet and Pharaoh-Ra invite them all to play in the infinite possibilities and functioning as oneness.

Chapter 54

Today Zazza has been given new clothes and the task of increasing who he knows by spending the day as servant to Pharaoh-Ra and Mila, as they meet and greet people in the great hall. Zazza will stand behind them, pour drinks and filling plates of food when necessary and whisper to them the names and position of those he knows. And maybe surprise Pharaoh-Ra and Mila himself with people he knows that they do not. He and Mila have made it a game to see which of them knows the most people. They have also added talking by telepathy to the list of the days tasks, much to Pharaoh's amusement and delight. The three of them are making a day of it.

Zazza is still a little shy around Pharaoh, he has never met an adult who appears so serious, yet is just as playful as his daughter Ra-Milania, the Pharaoh-to-be. It is disconcerting and he really is not quite sure what to make of it. All the adults that have come into his life are so different than any he had known before; he still pinches himself sometimes just to make sure he is really awake and not dreaming it all. He can hardly believe he and Malik's good fortune, that such a magical life has become their own. In one happy accident they have gained an entire family of friends; odd though they are of all ages, backgrounds and rank. More than just shelter, food, clothing and company, it was a life beyond imagination at the beginning of infinite possibility.

In her usual way Mila is quickly making Zazza comfortable in these surroundings. She is telling him by thought how to pour drinks, where to set things, how to arrange it correctly. He has never been a servant before, living on the street he could do what he please and behave any way he choose to without consequence. The palace was still an intimidating place. His biggest concern at the moment was that he not drop something and break it, or accidently spill something on Pharaoh, or Ra-Milania. He may be very young, but he did not live this long on his own by being stupid about his surroundings or whose company he was in. Lucky for him, it was Pharaoh himself and Pharaoh-to-be that are his friends here. He knew others in the palace were not like them and frankly distained his presence. They considered him as taking position from them by being asked to attend to Pharaoh, and many would in no way be forgiving of any errors made by him.

It was still early, so there were not many visitors yet, though the hall was now beginning to fill quite quickly. This was a day for Pharaoh to take requests, hear about complaints, disputes and grievances. As well as receive gifts, get news, make deals and be introduced to any number of people. One day every cycle of the moon a person of any rank or position my approach Pharaoh and speak with him directly. A line would be formed and it was first come first served, no matter who you were. The palace would provide food and drink as people waited to have audience. It was quite a production and took many people to coordinate and keep it from being total mayhem.

"This is surprisingly quiet and orderly for so large a crowd," thought Zazza. He had seen this kind of thing in the quarry with slaves being organized, he didn't think it would be possible with people from the Keeper's Realm. He had considered they would be different somehow, free as they are. *"I guess I am not the only one intimidated by Pharaoh,"* he thought. He hears Pharaoh chuckle to himself, and giggles quietly himself realizing that Pharaoh can hear what he is thinking. This delights him rather than being embarrassing and he relaxes more in the recognition he does not have to hide anything of who he is with Pharaoh-Ra.

Zazza whispers to them through the hours as people approach to implore the Pharaoh, bring him news, make offerings and the like. He tells of who they are, what they do, where they live or interesting details about them and things that Pharaoh and Mila might not know.

Much of the day's conversation between the three of them was silent, they would speak out loud some to confirm if what they got telepathically was correct. Asking questions that expanded on what was said silently they all were acknowledging the accuracy of awareness each of them demonstrated. It was a beautiful confirmation of knowing and capacity that left them buzzing with excitement. Where both

Pharaoh and Mila were often exhausted by the end of these long days of holding court, today they were energized.

Both Mila and Pharaoh are immensely impressed with Zazza's capacity for knowing who people are and details about their life. He knows more of who people are than both Pharaoh and Mila and there is no Realm he does not have extensive awareness of. What a marvel this capacity is. They realize how Zazza does it from the joy of it, it is playing for him. Apparently it has been a great gift for Zazza to have no parents, free to roam Pharaoh's Land as he will. He has taken liberty to roam freely in every Realm, exploring as he like. Insatiable curiosity is what he has lived by, that combined with an infallible memory and awareness of people he was a valuable asset to add to the team.

These skills are unique and will be explored for the joy of it, just as the rest of the men and boys at the guards quarters explore in their own way.

Chapter 55

Zek sits quietly at the dining table of the guard's quarters, he is starting to giggle to himself. Missrah looks at him from the corner of his eye wondering what he is giggling about. He notices Zek looking at his forearm that he has set on the table in front of him. His eyes grow wide as he notices Zek has four flies lined up in a perfect line on his arm. They do not move or fly away.

Missrah asks, "What are you doing Zek? That is amazing! How are you doing that?"

Continuing to giggle he replies, "Bilal and Angyet said to practice having no separation with anyone or anything, and to request what we would like. So I thought I would play with it and ask the flies if they would land on my arm in a straight line and not move, and they are! Look, there are four so far." As if on cue another fly comes and lands adding to the line, all of whom are facing the same direction towards Zek's hand. Zek can hardly contain his laughter but expands the space he is being to not disrupt the flies who have gathered at his request.

It is getting close to morning meal and the rest of the guards are coming into the room, all of them had sensed the joy emanating from Zek that calls them like a tug. They gather round to see what the giggling is about. They all look wide-eyed and smiling at what Zek is able to do. Bilal comes in last from the palace to hear Karek ask, "Do any of them have a name?"

Zek gets a quizzical look for a moment then says, "George, they are all named George." With that Zek burst out laughing. To all their surprise none of the flies move, even with all the noise.

"What kind of name is that? I never heard of it before, what does it mean I wonder?" asks Hemel.

Zek replies, "It means child of George." And he clenches his teeth to stop from total outburst of laughter. The rest do not try to contain themselves, laughing deeply. Zek manages to say, "Expand, expand!" as he continues to laugh silently, his whole body shaking.

Bilal replies now, "I have heard of that name before, it is from my parent's home land in the north. I think I have a cousin or some relation named George." With that they all laugh harder than before, beginning to tear and hold their sides.

Even with all the laughter they keep expanding the space they are being and three more flies come to land on Zek's arm bringing the number to eight, all in a tidy row. They all hush in awe of the spectacle of it. Watching more intently they all look at the flies, who are not even rubbing their front feet like they normally do. Zek whispers, "They are named George also." A moment more and one more fly comes buzzing in a circle seeming to contemplate if it will join in the line or not. The group is silent in their request of the fly to land, they practically hold their breath, watching in anticipation. A few more circles and it finally lands, also straight in line behind the rest. They all make sounds of awe and admiration of Zek's request and the flies' willingness to show up in this way.

In all seriousness Zek quietly says, "This one is called Gertrude." With that they all lose it completely bursting out in gales of laughter. Zek laughs hard but manages to keep from moving his arm and the flies remain still. After recovering the rest go about finishing preparations and serving food. Missrah puts a plate together for Zek and they start their morning meal. They all take turns glancing at Zek's arm to see when the flies will take off, to everyone's amazement they stay through the meal, only rubbing their front feet occasionally. None move position otherwise. When the meal is done Zek closes his eyes and silently thanks the flies for showing him their willingness to be present with him, and the entire group. That they would show up as he requested was a powerful moment of communion that he was grateful for.

"Who knew oneness could include flies landing in a row and not moving like this? Who knew oneness with flies could create such joy?" mused Zek to himself. With the acknowledgement and gratitude Zek emanates and thanking the flies each one by one; at completion all the flies take off in a group.

Zek's inspirational request gets all of the guard thinking

about the things they could ask for that they never considered before. They go forth into their day with a greater sense of expansion and possibility in the adventure of asking for what they have never considered asking.

Chapter 56

The sun has gone down and yet the pyramid still radiates warmth from the heat of the day. Angyet likes to stand on the pyramid, sensing the energies as they increase with the rising of the stones placement. It is here she finds Hamadi's teachings come to life; giving her an energetic experience of what he spoke of while he still lived, by it actualizing as the stone beneath her feet. He left her an energetic trail to follow. By his practice with her she became aware of the energy that was the target to be achieved with the building of this pyramid. Stone by stone she could sense the energies become a match to what Hamadi had revealed to her. She was bringing it into existence along with all the people who participated in the pyramid's construction.

All of the people and events up to now were contributing to the oneness actualizing in a new way. As she stood on the partially constructed pyramid she allowed herself to receive all that she had contributed to getting this far. Expanding out her senses to include the stone beneath her feet and out into the land stretching in all directions she embraces the entire Earth. Extending farther out into space she allows her senses to caress the moon and out to the other planets, and continuing on to the sun resting on the other side of the earth. Reaching out more she continues to expand touching the stars themselves in a feather touch lightness of joy. The spaciousness of her is so expanded it is a coolness that leaves her with a sense of floating and at the same time totally present with every molecule in creation. The space between the molecules is filled with the presence of her as she touches and blends with the presence of the consciousness that is embodied in all things.

Angyet cocks her head to the side and lifts her hand motioning to come forward.

Malik comes forward from the starlit darkness behind her and speaks, "How did you know I was there, I did not make a sound!"

"I do not need to see, nor hear, nor smell you to know you are there little one," replies Angyet.

Malik sniffs his own arm, checking if indeed he does smell that much.

"Your skills of transmigration are improving well, I see you were able to get here without Zazza's added energy. Very good Malik." Angyet chuckles, "Don't worry, you do not smell. I know you are there by awareness of your energetic presence. You have a particular energy to you, just as each person has. Have you noticed when you think of someone and then you transport yourself to them, it is the energy of that person that you are sensing and going to? As you have just come to me, was it not your sense of the energy of me tugging that let you know I was here waiting for you?"

Malik grows a little wide-eyed, it still surprises him just how much Angyet knows without him saying anything. It is wondrous to him; he is always excited to get to speak with her and listen to what she has to say. No adult before her spoke to him directly, and especially not with anything interesting to say! Unless he was in trouble, getting caught or being ordered around, no adults ever spoke to him. He did not know there were adults like her in the world, let alone an entire group of them. He could hardly believe his luck with what he had found in the Pharaoh, Ra-Milania, Bilal, along with the other guard and the Builder Angyet.

"So you know I am there without hearing me, seeing me or having told me out loud to meet you here? I mean, I know you summoned me, I could sense the tug to come to you. That is what that is; awareness of the energy? The energy of you?" asks Malik.

"Yes."

"So, does everything have energy? I mean, can I know everyone and everything by my sense of the energy of it?" ask Malik.

"You tell me," replies Angyet.

Malik thinks on this a moment realizing that it is true, every person has a different feel to them. Someone like Master Iberak has a creepy, dark and intense feel to him. Danger exudes from him. Ra-Milania is like the sunshine dancing joyously, radiant, bright, warm and inviting. He contemplates each person in his life and the sense he gets when he is with them or thinking about them.

"Good," says Angyet. "You are seeing that what I say is true? You know this from your own life. Now you can extend that to locations. Notice what your sense of the Laborer's Realm is? Now notice the palace in the great hall. Now the gardens. Now the Keeper's Realm. Good. Now the Artisan Realm. Very good."

"You know when I am sensing each one?"

"Yes. You think quite loudly Malik. Also, when you sense each location, it is like an opening to those energies. Those energies are more present and available as you reach to perceive them, you become those energies somewhat and I in turn perceive that in you." says Angyet.

He laughs a little, becoming a bit shy. His curiosity wins out and he asks, "What about things, like objects or animals?"

"Of course. Everything has an energy to it and you can develop your awareness of the nuances of energies that is different in each thing. Take this pyramid for instance. Notice it, the edges of the stones, the mass of them, their presence; notice how there is an intensity to it, a hum or buzz if you will. Now notice the sand itself below us and all around, notice the spaciousness and lightness to it. Now go down deeper into the earth, notice when it changes from sand to rock. Notice how you can sense the edges, the change from the sand and all the spaces between the grains of it, to the bedrock and its solidness." Angyet takes him on an energetic journey, intensifying his sense of the elements of pyramid stones, sand

and rock.

"Wow, that is amazing. I never thought of doing that before," says Malik.

"How about you make a game of it and over the next several days see what you can notice only with your awareness of the energy of a thing. Notice if you can sense the mice at the guard house before you see them, or the flies. Notice if you can recognize the person coming before they enter the room. As you notice when you get it correct, acknowledge it. If you are not correct, notice what it is you are doing that is different than when you have it correct. This is how I played with developing this ability. I did it for the fun of it to see what I could notice and how often I could get it correct," replies Angyet.

"Okay, that sounds like fun, I can do that!" says Malik with delight. He likes it when Angyet suggests an exercise to play with. It is so much more fun than being lectured at or told what to do. The invitation to find out things for himself has been an endearing quality of these most unusual adults that have come into his life. "I do notice the pyramid stones do not feel like anything else that I have ever sensed before. It sure is loud energy, it makes me tickle all over. Especially standing here right on it, why is that?"

"I am glad you asked Malik. That is why we are here tonight. I would like to tell you about this pyramid and why the Pharaoh has asked that it be built. Come next to me. Let's lay down on the warmth of the stone so we can look up at the stars and I will tell you all about it." She sets down two shawls folded into small pillows, one for each of them. Once they are laying down she tosses her cloak over them both that they may view the stars in comfort.

Once they are settled she begins.

"This pyramid is part of a great plan to invite more oneness into the world, into the people of the world. Many lifetimes ago, there lived the first Builder of Pharaoh's Land. Her name was Satari. She would devise a map to build structures that would enhance the energies and capacity for oneness, making it more easily available to all people. Not just in Pharaoh's Land, but across the entire planet. These monuments would connect with the natural energies of not only the entire planet, but the entire cosmos including all those stars up there in the night sky.

She was so sensitive to energies she could sense the very movements of this planet, the moon, the sun, other planets that are invisible to our eyes and all the stars in the sky. There was a movement of the stars that was so large and took so long that no one before her knew of it. She became aware of how everything moves in circles. Spinning circles within circles within circles. The greatest circle she could sense was the one in which the entire night sky moved. This circle took twenty-six thousand cycles of the sun to complete. She also observed that there were certain stars that marked this path of travel and that these stars could be used to navigate and lay out structures here on Earth." With this Angyet pointed out the three sister stars that line up almost in a straight line, with only a slight arch to them.

"Those three stars there are the ones from which we are measuring the direction to build the pyramid. It started with the Sphinx. The Sphinx was built in exact alignment with the moment when it was the rising sun of the middle of the twenty-six thousand cycles of the sun. On that day you could draw a line from what would become the middle of the tip of the nose of the Sphinx to the middle of the base of the tail of the Sphinx. If you continue that line you get to the alignment and direction of one side of the pyramid. That is how we know what line to make the pyramid face. It is all very precise, nothing is random or casual about it."

"The more accurately we can match these alignments the better it all works to amplify the energies of oneness. The buzz you feel now is only the beginning of what the energies will be when the pyramid is completed in its construction. We are taking the natural harmony and oneness inherent of this planet and all the starts in the sky and this cycle of movement and marking it with these monuments. By these structures we are adding to the ability of people to notice and be connected to these energies. Like you said, we are making it so loud with the energy that anyone can notice it and recognize that they can also be in harmony. They can function as the oneness if they so choose."

"All of this has gone into putting these rocks in a pile? Wow. I never knew anyone could think that much about such things," replies Malik in wonder. "I would like to be able to sense the stars moving. I wonder what it would take for me to do that?"

Angyet laughs as she thinks to herself; *"Nothing like a child to take any significance out of a moment."* She is grateful for his lack of significance combined with the curiosity he showed. *"He will make an amazing Builder one day,"* she muses. "Start with the mice and the flies!" is Angyet's reply. "Really. It only takes practice and your curiosity in wondering what it will take for you to one day be able to Malik. This is enough for tonight, shall we go get something warm to drink?"

"Yes!" replies Malik. With that Angyet takes his hand and they disappear in a blink.

Chapter 57

Only moments after Angyet and Malik have returned from the pyramid, Bilal enters Angyet's chambers. Having left Mila to her evening bath and bed, he is free to continue his education with Angyet.

"The last base stone has been cut from the cliffs today. Things are going more quickly now that your father has started working with Master Iberak again," replies Angyet casually. She sees the shadow cross Bilal's face. It still pains him to hear it. "Bilal, your father is a Freeman, free to choose as he likes. This may not all be as terrible as you think."

Bilal is silent with Malik still in the room. Noticing this she excuses Malik wishing him good night and reminding him to play with what they have been speaking of. In another blink Malik is gone, back to the guard's quarters and bed.

As soon as Malik is gone, Bilal blurts, "I just can't understand it. How could he go back?" Bilal was not sure if he would like to break down in tears or punch something, maybe both at once.

"Maybe it truly is his way of moving forward Bilal. Did you ever consider that? The oneness supports us in all things and for some reason I cannot yet grasp there is a lightness to it that tells me he is not wrong." Looking to Bilal she rests her hands on his, "Come with me to the quarry tonight. Let me show you as I smooth the surface of the stone. You can help." Angyet's touch was always deliberate and Bilal relaxed a little allowing the soothing energies that flowed through Angyet seep into his body and being. He takes a deep breath beginning to let the angst go.

"Besides if you keep that look on your face I might just wish to die myself." She says with a laugh. "Come, it is dark now and everyone will be gone from the quarry." He nods and in a blink they are there at the quarry.

As she knew it would be, the quarry was quiet. With the drudgery of the day done and everyone gone it was easy to commune with the stones. They hummed with the energies of the earth, speaking to her of their willingness to be.

This was Bilal's first time back to the quarry since gaining his freedom and he was curious what it would be like now for him. He stood at the quarry like so many times before and surveyed the familiar surroundings. Even in the darkness of night he could sense where everything was. His eyes had already adjusted and the starlight was enough to give a faint outline to everything. He took in a deep breath and to his surprise found a sense of home here in the dust and rubble. He had been here almost daily for his entire life. It was a place he was celebrated albeit with threat of beatings and death always looming. But then death too was familiar and often welcome friend in a place like this.

He flexed his arms, stretching his chest wide with the recollection of wielding sledge hammer to stone. The one gratifying part of his life until the Pharaoh plucked him and his family from this place.

Angyet watched Bilal in curiosity, taking in how he responded to being in the quarry. She could sense the memories and energies that made up his life before. It was interesting, he was one of the few slaves she had ever met who was in no way defeated. She marveled, thinking to herself, "*Imagine your whole life a slave yet somehow managing to not buy it.*" He had a sense of himself as man few posses. It had not yet ceased to impress her.

Bilal looked to Angyet, "Shall we shape some stone then?"

Angyet laughs softly, "Yes Bilal, let's get to it." They walk in silence over to the cliff face where the last of the base stones had been cut loose.

Angyet runs her hands across the surface letting her senses spread through the entire stone. She looks to Bilal, "You can either place your hand on my shoulder to sense the energies as I request of the stone, or you can place your hands upon the surface of the stone yourself. What would you like to choose?"

"Hmmm, I think I will touch the stone. But would you talk me through what you are asking of the stone? I like the combination of my own sense of energies and the insight and inspiration of you describing what you are doing and being," says Bilal.

"Okay. I will touch you to start so you can get a more dynamic sense of the space you must be to accomplish this." She lightly places a hand on his chest and a warm rush like the wind blowing through him permeates the space between the molecules of his body and being. In an instant his senses increase in intensity. He is suddenly aware of the warm winds of early night as they blow across the sands to the north east, the ruffle of tall dry grasses to the south west, the endless sky above and the warm smells of wet dirt deep down and stone below his feet. He breathes in deeply expanding as the air fills his lungs and spreads through his body. He can sense the exuberant joy of the air as it caresses everything it touches. At the same moment he is aware of the stone his hand is resting on and the structure of the minerals. He becomes both the space between the minerals and the minerals themselves.

"Now we may begin," says Angyet softly. "Notice the space around all the elements of this stone. Notice the difference of the physical elements making up the stone and the space around those elements. Sense the edges of this stone. Notice where it touches the earth on the bottom. Notice the air on all the other sides. Notice the ripples and divots on the surface. Now include in your awareness the pyramid structure as it is, the energy of it, the vibration. Notice the difference. The pyramid energy is the energy we are asking this stone to become compatible with, to be in harmony with. We are asking this stone under our hands to be a contribution and expansion of what the pyramid already is. We are asking what it can be to make it greater. Notice the molecules of the stone beginning to vibrate and hum. Now add to it, increasing the intensity. We are asking the stone to become smooth and be a precision of shape that touches the stones it will sit next to seamlessly.

Suddenly a tremble washes through Bilal and the entire stone and he senses a ripple of smoothness move across the stone's surface. Bilal's eyes opened wide, it was as though the very earth trembled, yet looking around it was only the energies that shook. In a moment the massive stone was smooth on every side, he could sense it even on the bottom side touching the ground. Not only that, it now hummed with the same vibrations as the rest of the pyramid. He knew exactly where the stone would be placed and how once there, would increase and expand the overall energies of the pyramid. Bilal was astonished. He was wide-eyed and speechless. Angyet simply laughed softly, delighting in his wonderment.

"And that is how you ask a stone to change its shape. Everything on earth lives in harmony with everything around it already. There is nothing discordant. The fun of it is there are infinite possibilities for what form that harmony and oneness can take. By asking the stone what it can be and knows about, by increasing and expanding what it already naturally is, you will find total willingness by the stone to fulfill your request. I was not telling it how to do this, I was asking for what it already knows about this and at the same time unleashing its creativity and capacity to become. Gifting the stone whatever energies would make it easier to become what I request. That is one of the secrets of oneness; when you request of a stone for example, to become something that will continue to be harmonious with everything else in existence it is more than willing to do so. Oneness begets oneness and will always easily go towards that which increases oneness and harmony of everything in creation. No matter what form something takes, if it expands possibilities of oneness it will be supported."

"That was so easy! It surprised me that something so massively huge could change in a blink like that. And the earth trembling, did you feel that? I know the earth didn't actually move, it was the energy, but I was sure the earth itself was shaking!" laughs Bilal. "Is it always like that with the stone?"

"Yes," replies Angyet. "It is the shift in reality of the stone and the entire world with it that you were sensing. The building of this pyramid is a life altering, world altering undertaking. At no time before have humans built a structure whose entire purpose is to be in oneness with the entire universe. A structure built to contribute to and increase the oneness and harmony available on the planet has been done before, but not the entire universe, not like this. It is only people who choose to not be in harmony with everything else in creation. It is only people that forsake the oneness that is available to them. This pyramid is to both inspire the choice to function as oneness and making it easier to accomplish. To make it desirable and easier for people to function as oneness, that is the target.

"Come, let us return to my chambers to continue this conversation, I could use a drink." Angyet holds out her hand which Bilal takes and in a blink they are in the stifling warmth of Angyet's rooms. Getting a cup of wine and walking to the balcony ledge in hopes of a bit of breeze Angyet says, "Is there more you wish to ask?"

Bilal inquires, "What is a molecule again, can you explain that to me one more time?"

"Only once?" laughs Angyet. "Yes, of course. Molecules are the smallest element of physical matter. As I have said the oneness consists of energy, space and consciousness. Molecules are the physical manifestation of energy, space and consciousness. Change any or all of the energy, space and consciousness of a thing and you change how the molecule shows up. You as a being are this oneness and as such you can request of the physical world. Most people believe in the solidness and realness of the physical world. They believe that much of the world is unchangeable, rather than having the awareness of how malleable and changing even physical things are. It is this awareness of the true nature or reality that allows me to place my hand on the stones of the pyramid and smooth them simply by my request of it to become so. By the energy, space and consciousness I am both willing to be and willing to become that would contribute to this change I am asking for."

"How is it possible?" wonders Bilal.

"Let me see if I can explain this in a bit of a different way to give you more awareness of this." Angyet reaches for a single piece of sand resting on the ledge of the balcony. "This single speck of sand is basically a small stone, correct? Many of them together make these walls strong, solid and lasting for a very long time. What if though the walls appear solid and real they are actually mostly space? Notice the size of this grain of sand compared to the space of this entire room. What if there is also that much space inside the grain of sand?

Imagine there is another smaller grain inside this one, surrounded with the amount of space in this room, again all inside this tiny, tiny grain. That is an example of how much space there is between every molecule."

Bilal considers this.

Angyet continues, "Here, let me demonstrate what I am talking about." She takes the thin pottery mug she had set on the balcony ledge and gently taps it on the ledge making a clink sound. She then taps it against her forearm. "Notice, it is solid and hard both against the balcony wall and my arm. What if it is also mostly space?" with that she moves to tap it against the balcony again, yet this time it passes through the wall as though the wall is air."

"What? Whoa!" exclaims Bilal.

Next Angyet does the same thing with her arm. Instead of the cup hitting against her arm, it passes right through it. Lifting an eye brow, she now does it the other way around. Holding the cup she passes her arm over the top of it allowing her arm to go through the cup, rather than the cup move through her arm.

Bilal's eyes are bugging out, he is amazed and very excited, "How do you do that? Can I do that? Can you show me?"

For dramatic effect she then drops the mug allowing it to shatter on the ground.

"Yes, certainly. All of the guards should learn to do this if they can. It will make it possible for the blade of a sword to pass through you and not cut for example. This would be a huge advantage if faced with real combat. Think of the surprise of your opponents if you and the guard are able to accomplish this ability!"

Bilal laughs in glee with the idea of it. "That would be incredible! Do you really think we can do it? It is so unbelievable, I just watched that with my own eyes and I still don't believe it!"

"You have all impressed me so far, I see no reason any of you would be unable to become capable of it. We'll see, shall we? I can do a demonstration for the men and we'll see if they are willing to try. It will be fun!"

The joy of exploring one's skills and outdoing oneself is a joy not found with most of the Movers. Instead, the Movers believe in hard work, pain, and the struggle of long and arduous practice. Playing with one's capacities for the joy of it does not occur to those in charge, only to a few who keep quiet about it.

Chapter 58

"Get out of my way, before I break you, Maafah," barks Arphiro.

"Yes of course you are right, your sneeze could probably break me you are such a brute of a man," says Maafah with an expression of mock fear. He chuckles to himself at his own sense of humor.

Arphiro glares at him, if Eka-ar did not value him so much he would have broken the skinny little man a long time ago. *"He is like a pestering flea,"* thinks Arphiro.

It is an important day. Progress is being made with construction of the pyramid. More importantly the alterations of building plans have now become clear. This is a triumphant accomplishment in Ra-Maharet's plans for taking over Pharaoh's Land. Arphiro wishes to make sure everything was ready for today's ceremony of transporting the last base stone and placing it.

"He never takes this seriously," thinks Arphiro to himself about Maafah. He is perplexed how such a man has come this far in life; always laughing, joking and making light of everything. It angers him to no end.

Arphiro is a man who has fought his way through life using intimidation, force of will and brute strength to accomplish. It had gotten him here, the esteemed position of "Mover of the House of Pharaoh". To be equal in position to such a man as Maafah was insulting. He took every opportunity to make sure Eka-ar knew as much. Angering him further was that Eka-ar paid no heed to it. Arphiro did not understand.

He had considered himself to have earned his arrogance and demand of others. He relished his command of those below him. He barked his orders to the initiates who were to observe today's procession. They scurried to line up and listen.

"Today, watch closely. It is a momentous day. The final base stone will be placed, taking us to the next phase of building. Notice how your superiors carry themselves today. Notice the special care taken with incantation as we move from the quarry to the pyramid. Notice the pace, the height of the stone, every detail, so that one day it may be you who joins us in this sacred duty. It is one hour until we leave for the quarry, do not be tardy. That is all."

Arphiro goes next to the meditation hall where those who are participating in the ceremony are gathered in silent preparation for the task of transporting the massive stone by levitation. They sit in a circle. Maafah has now joined in the circle and Arphiro takes his place next to Eka-ar. They quiet themselves in body and being; linking their energies as Eka-ar has instructed and becoming one mind, one body; a unity of purpose. They would sit in silence, cross legged and building their energies and connection with one another until they rise to walk to the quarry.

The time has come; as they approach the pillars of The Pathway near the entrance of the House of the Movers the incantation begins. To those uninitiated the sounds of the Movers is unintelligible, as it was designed. Eka-ar had created his own language designed to invoke and strengthen the capacity of transporting the stone by levitation. It was a repetitious string of sounds, deep and guttural. Once they start the incantation it does not end until the stone is perfectly placed and Eka-ar has given the signal. By ending the continuous sound with the end of the movement of stone as it takes its final resting place on the pyramid, it makes for a dramatic ending to their task. A resounding silence after such a display fills them all with pride, to have the crowds burst into applause afterward is unlike anything else. They all relish the praise and public notoriety of it.

It is only Maafah who is humbled by participating in such an act. He is often left in tears of gratitude by the end of this ceremony. He senses the dynamic increase in the hum and thrum of the oneness when each stone is placed. Like the volume of the harmony of the earth itself getting turned up. He marvels at the mind who conceived of such a plan. He knows it is not Angyet who came up with the plans for construction, however she is the one bringing it to actualization. She is the leader for this task and he hopes to one day get to speak with her. Eka-ar forbids approaching her with any questions, or for anything at all except for formal greeting. He had not the courage to breach this rule, but his curiosity keeps him awake at night sometimes. And now more than ever he struggles with the rule of silence Eka-ar enforces.

Standing tall, the Movers take their positions around the massive base stone. At Eka-ar's signal the stone silently rises, hovering a hand-length off the ground. Seamlessly they all move in unison, step by step walking from the quarry to the pyramid; the impossibly large stone floating between them as they all move it toward its resting place.

The crowd is the largest yet. It bolsters their pride to have an audience for this endeavor. The energy of the crowd feeds their body and the energies that are available to accomplish this task. Their wonder, enthusiasm and excitement is like added fuel. The Movers let it contribute to their forward motion and it is all accomplished with more ease.

Only Maafah notices this increase of ease that the crowd has contributed toward the successful transport and placement of the stone. In his many years he has noticed that oneness begets oneness. He is again humbled by the awareness of how all of creation, including the people of Pharaoh's Land have added their energies to the day's accomplishment; and how that has added to the thrum of energies of oneness that the pyramid itself exudes. It makes him smile that no one else seems to notice. He wonders what Angyet knows about all this.

Chapter 59

"Yeah, that is Omar for sure," says Zazza in a whisper to Malik. They begin to speculate about the conversation Omar is having with Master Iberak since they are too far away to hear much. So engrossed, they do not notice the man approaching behind them until he has a firm grip on one of each of their ears. They yelp but do not try to pull away, instead they slowly turn around to face their captor. Upon sight of him they both take a breath in and say in unison "Drekkar!" in quiet awe.

Drekkar is very taken aback that these two ragged boys know him. He almost lets loose of them, but instead tightens his grip. "How do you know who I am?" he asks with a glare at them.

"You are Drekkar, everyone knows who you are!" replies Malik. Seeing this does not satisfy Zazza quickly adds "Bilal is our keeper! We only speak with Bilal."

Drekkar's eyes grow wider still, however he lets go of the boys. "I see," he says tentatively. For some reason he believes them. Though he can't recall ever seeing them before that they would use Bilal as reference and say he is their Keeper is not something anyone he knows would claim. It is the boldness of this remark that he trusts. "What are you doing here? Why are you spying on Master Omar and Iberak?"

Malik and Zazza look back and forth to each other and back at Drekkar. They are not sure what to reply. Before they speak Drekkar continues, "They are rotten men, surely up to no good. You say you speak only to Bilal? And you are familiar with the Laborer's Realm?"

The boys nod affirmatively.

"Would you give Bilal a message for me?"

They nod again.

"Tell him there is a rumor that Master Iberak is creating a secret armed force in the north for Ra-Maharet. Like the rumor that you have never lost a fight in five years. Will you tell Bilal exactly the words I have spoken?"

Zazza and Malik nod affirmatively in unison.

Drekkar continues, "I will be substantiating this rumor as quickly as I can. Tell Bilal I am completely willing to report to him with all I discover. Boys if you would take messages back and forth I would be most honored. If Bilal is agreeable, he will reply with the name of my older brother, that I may know you boys are who you say you are. Speak to me only out of sight of Master Iberak and Omar. Agreed boys?"

They both say in unison "Yes" with another nod of their head and like a dart they both leave with large grins on their face. With his back to the boys he does not notice them join hands and disappear into thin air just a few paces away.

Looking at Omar and Master Iberak deep in conversation Drekkar stands tall and heads to the table they are sitting at. The air is blowing towards him as he approaches and it carries a few of the words between the men. They speak of numbers growing satisfactorily. He greets them from several strides away so he is sure to interrupt their conversation and not appear to be listening in on the conversation in any way.

"Drekkar, greetings my friend, it is a fine morning is it not?" says Master Iberak loudly. "Come, sit, eat, drink. We are just going over numbers of workers and new bodies coming in. There is much to discuss now that you are on board, boy do we need your help. You were always so much better at managing large groups than I." Master Iberak shoves a pint of cool beer towards Drekkar as he takes a seat at the dusty work table set to be in the shade of the few remaining trees.

The acknowledgement surprised Drekkar. *"Would this be the moment for Master Iberak to reveal what he is really up to?"* wondered Drekkar. He was going to have to play it cool, not too inquisitive. "Tell me about it," he says casually.

"Well, you know we have been increasing our numbers to keep up with the demand to get this pyramid done but there is more," Master Iberak says in a conspiratorial tone as he leans forward and lowers his voice. "We have a windfall of opportunity that has landed in our lap Drekkar, you won't believe it! And I can't do it without you. You have come back at just the right moment!"

Drekkar just gives a grunt with a half smile. He leans back knowing full well Master Iberak is about to spill it all, his silence always drew out Iberak's desire to lead the show. His leaning back and settling in gave Iberak all the prompting he needed to know Drekkar was on board.

Omar was silent, eyes bulging a bit waiting for disaster, for in these few seconds he realized he had made a grievous error and revealed secrets to Drekkar before Master Iberak had. Something Iberak would consider unforgivable and surely kill him for on the spot. Not knowing Drekkar very well, except by reputation and the business dealings they have had for a few years, he really did not know what to expect of him. He began to slowly breathe again as he watched Drekkar keep this indiscretion to himself. He acted like he was hearing it all for the first time and did not give anything away in the least. *"Wow,"* thought Omar, *"this is a man who can keep a secret unlike any I have known before. I owe him for this."* He didn't mind owing him on this count. Drekkar earned his further respect and a large measure of loyalty in just moments with this simple generosity.

Master Iberak had been bursting to tell Drekkar, it had been an agonizing six cycles of the moon to keep it to himself but he wanted to make sure of his position with Ra-Maharet and in this last month that Drekkar really had come back to work with him. The loss of Emilia was great and though Drekkar never spoke of it, Iberak knew well the toll of it and he was hesitant to push, especially now that Drekkar was a Freeman with the favor of the Pharaoh. He needed to make sure Drekkar was still the man he could trust as he had come to in these previous nineteen years. This last week had given him enough to know Drekkar was back.

Invigorated as though he was a young man again, Iberak revealed the depth of plot he was involved with to get Ra-Maharet on the throne. Omar and Drekkar were his most trusted men and he had ambitions to take them with him to the top of this lofty endeavor. Ra-Maharet had promised much to him and he planned to deliver on his end of the bargain and achieve this future position. Money and power were all it took to entice Master Iberak and this was a quick road to that goal, or so he thought. The opportunity of a lifetime that he reveled in and grew in confidence knowing Drekkar and Omar were with him.

Drekkar had a sense of redemption washing over him as he listened to Iberak's plot. That he could share this with his son, who then could share this with the Pharaoh himself mended something inside him. He would be happy to do anything that brought this man's life to an end. That it would bring stronger amends between himself and his son just added to his gratitude for finding himself in the position he is in.

Chapter 60

Malik and Zazza ran straight from their encounter with Drekkar to tell Bilal all about this rumor of Ra-Maharet's plot to create a secret armed force in the north. Bilal is a little surprised at his father, and gratified knowing his father is the man he now knows him to be. He had not really ever considered that his father would be loyal to him like this, it had not occurred to him with how it had been growing up. It warms his heart to have this message from the boys. This was a big break to have an inside man sort of speak and it not only was the kind of advantage they had been seeking, it was providing some clarity about what Ra-Maharet was really up to. With the added discretion of Zazza and Malik relaying messages between Bilal and Drekkar, they would now be able to devise a plan for defeating Ra-Maharet based on more thorough and accurate information. Now they would be able to know how far she really had gotten in her endeavors.

"Tell Drekkar he does not have an older brother, he has two. Hilm is the eldest and then Brock. Boys, be sure to stay out of sight of Master Iberak and anyone he works with. You can do that easily enough can't you?"

They both reply "Yes" and "Of course" and giggle, looking at each other.

"What is it?" asks Bilal.

"Your father said the same thing to us," says Malik. "Don't worry, we know how to hide and we also know we never would like to be caught by Master Iberak. He would cut our throats just for the fun of it. We have seen how he is."

"Good," says Bilal. "Do not ever underestimate the viciousness that man is capable of. He is dangerous and it is our task to outwit and out maneuver him, and use every advantage we have over him. Tell my father he can provide information through you Zazza and that you will remember every word of it exactly. And Malik, tell him of your ability to show up anywhere he is by request in his mind. Make arrangement for you to practice with him a bit."

"Are you sure Bilal?" asks Malik a little incredulously.

"Oh yes. He can be trusted. Would you like to have some fun with it?" The boys nod in unison. "You are going to scare the wits out of him with your ability. Will you tell me the look on his face when you return from seeing him next? See if you can give my father a reply today, otherwise as soon as you are able, boys." The boys giggle, nodding again they take off like rockets and grabbing hands disappear into thin air. Off to more lesson's with Angyet. They will find Drekkar again later when they sense he is alone.

Bilal looks at the space they were at just a second ago, amazed at how quickly they were developing in their capacity. No one else of the group has yet been able to travel to pillars they have never been through on their own, let alone travel with no pillars at all. It was a marvel to behold. When they had learnt of Angyet's ability to do so they were not so surprised, they could imagine that of The Builder. But, a street orphan? Malik was incredible. And Zazza was willing to contribute energetically and go on the ride himself, so the development of this capacity had been exponentialized for Malik.

These were thrilling days of magic and possibilities beyond what any of them had ever considered and the joy they all shared in it permeated their lives.

Bilal left the guard training facility and headed straight for Pharaoh, he must know of these new developments immediately. He sends the thoughts to Pharaoh with the energy of urgency, he is coming with important news. Bilal emerges from the pillars placed outside but nearby Pharaoh's private chambers and waits for someone to come out and let him know he may enter. He trusts his growing capacity of telepathic communication and knows both that Pharaoh received the energy of the message, and also that he will ask for Bilal the moment he is available. That Bilal should wait to be invited in for audience with him. There is an air of formality with regard to whomever is with Pharaoh now. It is becoming more familiar, that energy and Bilal will get confirmation of who that energy is soon enough when the person emerges from Pharaoh's chambers.

Sure enough it is Ra-Maharet who is in Pharaoh's company. She walks out pretending not to notice Bilal, the usual sour and disdainful expression he has seen on her face as she leaves the presence of Pharaoh. Graceful like a wind storm looking to devour all in its path, wife-of-Pharaoh disappears down the hall toward her own chambers on the other end of the palace.

It is Rimmel who emerges next to summon Bilal inside, a welcome sight indeed. "What a pleasant surprise, come, come in." He ushers Bilal into Pharaoh's rooms where Ra sits, a tired look on his face. He lights up seeing Bilal. "What news do you have for me Bilal?"

"Are we alone?" asks Bilal in a hushed and serious tone. With such news he would like to make sure that no other servants are expected who might over hear this conversation. He knows Rimmel can be trusted, however he would like to make sure Pharaoh has the choice to dismiss him as well if he should choose.

"Ah, I see. Rimmel, thank you, can you please see to my wife's request? Mila's day of birth celebration arrives soon enough, there is much to prepare with the grand event Ra-Maharet is planning." He sighs in exhaustion just thinking about it again.

"Of course," replies Rimmel with a bow. As he departs he says to Bilal, "I will see your father tonight Bilal, would you like me to give him a message?"

"Why yes, tell him I will come home tonight and to please wait up for me. I will try not to be too late. Thank you Rimmel, you are a good friend." With that Rimmel nods again and departs.

When Rimmel's footsteps are gone, Bilal gives it a few more moments then begins to recount this new turn of events as Pharaoh pours wine for the two of them.

"Malik and Zazza were caught by my father today trying to overhear a conversation with Master Iberak and Omar. Drekkar spoke with them and said there is a rumor that Master Iberak is working with Ra-Maharet to secretly create an armed force in the north. Drekkar said it is a rumor, like the rumor that I have never lost a fight in the last five years. Which of course is to say it is not a rumor at all. He will report what he knows to me. Malik and Zazza will also relay messages for us. I'm not sure if you heard, my father has gone back to work with Master Iberak as his business partner. I was furious at first, but I see now it is a huge advantage and we are likely to find out everything Ra-Maharet has been up to with Master Iberak. My father has been Master Iberak's confidant for all of my life, he is likely to tell my father everything. He is also paranoid, so I am not sure if he has yet brought my father in on his scheming. I will find out tonight."

Pharaoh-Ra leans back relaxing into his seat, "Ah well, there it is." He shakes his head and yet is smiling with the revelation of this news. "At last, now I know where all that money has been going! Ra-Maharet is purchasing her forces to overtake Pharaoh's Land. Thank you Bilal, this is the kind of break we have been asking for. And you are sure your father is on our side? We can trust him?"

"Yes, he already had plans to kill Maser Iberak. Even with

my mother now gone, I know he would never side with Master Iberak. My father is an honorable man and he will do what he says. We can count on him," replies Bilal. He furrows his brow as he looks at Pharaoh. "I am confused Pharaoh, you do not seem upset about any of this. How can you not be angry with this news? I do not understand."

Pharaoh-Ra looks at Bilal for a long moment before her replies, "There are three types of anger. Rage, hate and fury is one kind of anger. This type of anger is destructive and takes a lot of energy to maintain. It also cuts off your awareness. The second kind of anger is when there is a lie, spoken or unspoken. A lie will always anger you, however when you spot what the lie is all the anger goes away in the light of the awareness of what is actually true. Then there is anger that is actually potency. As the energies of potency that feel just like anger, you become alert, present, intense, willing to be whatever it takes to accomplish your target. Consider it, when you had your death matches, were you ever truly angry, or was there a potency and intensity of presence that let you get the job done?"

Bilal replies easily with the clarity in which Pharaoh has framed this information. "Yes, putting it as you have, it is very easy to speak to what it has been for me. It was potency of presence that I was being while fighting. I never had rage, fury or hate. Those who did always died the most quickly. Their temporary surge of strength they would get from it and their frantic efforts could never overcome the calm, cool, collected and calculating that potency gives. So what is it for you with this news of Ra-Maharet?"

"The anger I have had with her is mostly in the realm of the lies she speaks and all the energy she puts into hiding," replies Pharaoh. "The news you have brought is bringing the clarity I have been seeking. It has allowed me to spot many of the lies, which brings me a sense of peace, ease, relaxation and clarity upon hearing it. So you see, this is good, this is very good." Pharaoh grows silent now and seems to be a bit distant in contemplation.

"Is there anything else Pharaoh?"

Pharaoh takes another moment more before he replies, "Yes Bilal. My wife is making extensive plans for Mila's day of birth celebration. She is asking for six days of celebration with many entertainments and would like money to make some of the arrangements herself. She is also asking for more time with Mila, she would like to take her to the markets for some new jewelry and such. I don't like it. She has not asked to have Mila accompany her for such things in a very long time. It makes me uncomfortable, but I also do not wish to say no to her at this time. She must not suspect that we are onto her in any way. My wife will not say it to me, but she is likely to say you are not required for these outings. That her own guard will suffice. Allow her to have this if she asks, but do not let Mila out of your sight. Wear a cloak if you must, whatever it takes, do not stay more than fifteen paces from her at any time."

"Of course Pharaoh, I will stay close by. I will have her guard assist me in this endeavor, they will have no problem being unnoticed. Shall I give Angyet the news of today's events?" ask Bilal.

"No my friend, I will be seeing her later, thank you though.

Please, visit your father and discover what you can. Though I suspect I will not enjoy anything Drekkar has to say, I must say it has brought me a sense of ease to hear all of this. There is always a spaciousness that opens up when hearing what is true, even if it is something ugly and one would wish is not true. What is true always gives a sense of lightness, while a lie always creates heaviness and contraction. The lies of secrecy Ra-Maharet lives with have been weighing on me, so hearing these details is like a weight lifting off my shoulders. Get every detail you are able to Bilal."

"My father is a very thorough man, he will be able to provide great detail I am sure. I will let you know soon enough. Good night Pharaoh." Bilal bows and withdraws to leave Pharaoh with his own thoughts and concerns.

Bilal will head to his father's house immediately.

Chapter 61

Bilal enters the family home interested to hear what his father might say. It still makes his head spin that his father might actually be fighting for him, rather than against him as he had seen it for his entire life. Of course, his expression of it continued to be a source of consternation. Bilal has yet to be able to totally trust that his father's choices really are from caring for him, with their ideas of what caring are being so different from one another. No matter what it was going to take, Bilal was grateful for the changes showing up that both he and his father were choosing.

It was rather late in the evening, and Drekkar had the table prepared with food and drink as he waited for Bilal's arrival.

"Hello father."

"Ah, Bilal. Thank you for coming. Here sit, I have set out food and drink for us," says Drekkar as he pulls out a chair for his son.

"Wonderful, I am starving!" he says clapping his dad on the back and taking the seat. "So, what is going on?" he asks casually.

Drekkar is always direct and gets straight to it. "Ra-Maharet is plotting to take the seat-of-Pharaoh. She is amassing an armed force in the North with the help of Master Iberak and Master Omar. The Movers are part of it too, but I don't know that much about them. I can give you extensive details about the forces in the North. Master Iberak is expecting me to be full partners in this endeavor as well as the rest of his business. He has given me the tasks of making sure these forces in the North are fully prepared in terms of equipment, and the means for traveling here remaining well fed and such. I would like you to know I will do anything the Pharaoh asks of me."

"Thank you father. I am glad to hear it, and so will Pharaoh. We already know about Ra-Maharet's plot, we have just been missing information on how far she has already gone towards this endeavor. Pharaoh has heard whispers of the forces in the North too, and we are grateful not only for your confirmation but also the details you can provide. We know about the Movers and Ra-Maharet, again we don't have many details yet, but we will. Her days are numbered. The only thing Pharaoh has been waiting for is more clarity about all those who plot with her. The information you are providing is very helpful, father."

"Master Iberak would like me to go North to see things for myself. I will be leaving in a few days."

"Good. Your firsthand account will be most welcome.

And I will say again, you can trust Malik and Zazza with any information. They will be able to find you anywhere you are so information can get to me and the Pharaoh very quickly, in just moments."

Drekkar looks at him rather perplexed, "Really? What do you mean? How is that possible?"

"You'll see," says Bilal with a smile. He will say no more about it.

They talk for a few more hours going over numbers and more details of what Ra-Maharet and Master Iberak have put together so far. Drekkar had discovered from his conversation with Master Omar that they already had fifteen hundred men in a secret encampment a moon's cycle time of walking north of the palace city. With the morning meeting with Master Iberak and Omar, Drekkar learned that Master Iberak had been paid by Pharaoh for he, Emilia and Bilal and Iberak would use the funds to hire about three thousand more. "Who knew we were worth so much to the Pharaoh? Did you know that Pharaoh had paid Master Iberak for us?"

"No, I had no idea father!" Bilal is rather speechless upon the hearing of this and it is hard for him to keep back the tears in this acknowledgement.

"I don't understand, but I am grateful," replies Drekkar in wonder.

It is at this time the Bilal now shares more of the true purpose of the pyramid, what Pharaoh-Ra, Ra-Milania and Angyet strive for, and how they had invited Bilal to explore and develop these capacities of oneness with them; all for the safe guarding of the future they strive to create, for the entirety of Pharaoh's Land and all of its people. He talks about the personal guard Ra-Milania is gathering and how Zazza and Malik are part of this guard. Bilal demonstrates moving a few of the objects on the table for his father as he talks about the training he has been practicing. Drekkar is speechless, listening intently to every word his son is saying. Revealing for the first time the depth of his being to his father and the meaning of his placement as Ra-Milania's personal guardian, Bilal does not hold back.

Drekkar's eyes fill with tears of gratitude. He is moved beyond words for the great honor of it all. It is beyond what Drekkar has ever imagined or considered possible and now he truly understands for what reason Bilal would prefer to stay in Pharaoh's Land. That he himself could contribute to such an honorable and grand future possibility is a greatness he never imagined he would have the chance to strive for and participate in. He does not understand it all completely, but it has moved him deeply.

The tentative bond that had developed between father and son since being granted freedom by Pharaoh-Ra was strong now. Each new development added to this closeness and trust of character that each of them were coming to know of each other.

Zazza and Malik would only add to this trust and all of their ability to thwart this plot.

Chapter 62

It is early in the morning and Malik and Zazza sense the tug to go find Drekkar and relay Bilal's reply to demonstrate they are truthful in who they say they are. They go to Drekkar easily, sensing he is alone and in a place they will be able to talk with ease. They show up around the corner from where Drekkar is walking and it is still early enough in the morning, there are not many people around. They approach Drekkar directly and step to the side of a building, the three of them together.

Malik speaks first, "You have two older brothers," he says with a smile.

Zazza continues, "The oldest brother's name is Hilm and the younger is named Brock. See, we are truthful."

Drekkar nods with approval. "Very good, boys. Does Bilal have any other message for me?" Drekkar continues before they reply, "Soon I will be traveling north to view with my own eyes all that has been gathered. Bilal said somehow you will be able to meet me along the way and also once I am there to relay messages?"

"Oh yes, we most certainly will. Just make sure you are alone and think of us in your mind, call to us like you are wishing us to be with you and we will be there in an instant," replies Malik with a smile.

"You are joking, right?" says Drekkar with skepticism.

"Oh no, we mean that most truly. Look!" With that Malik takes a quick look around to see that no one is watching them and seeing there is no one touches both Zazza and Drekkar on the arm. In a blink they stand by themselves on the sand dunes with the partial pyramid rising from the golden sand. Close to where the funeral for Emilia was held.

Drekkar's eyes bulge in shock and awe, "What?" he whispers breathless. "You can do that? How did you do that? There were no pillars, how is that possible?"

Before anyone says another word Malik touches them both again and they are back in the spot they started. Drekkar steps back leaning against the wall, holding his arm to himself so Malik does not touch him again. "I take it that was what Bilal was grinning about when he said you can find me anywhere?"

The boys giggle, nodding their head in unison.

"Incredible!" Drekkar whispers as he looks back and forth between Zazza and Malik. Gathering his wits again Drekkar continues, "Okay boys, you sure will make my job easier. The woman doesn't stand a chance. This is very good. I will call to you when I get a decent look at the men that have been gathered."

"Just remember to be in a spot where you will be out of sight of others, or where we can be out of sight. Night time is easiest, but daytime will be okay too if it is a good spot."

"How will you know where to appear, and exactly when to appear?" asks Drekkar.

"The oneness will tell us. We'll know," say Zazza with a smile of confidence. With that Malik and Zazza join hands and are gone in a blink.

Drekkar is rubbing his eyes, shaking his head. Did he really just see that? Did he really just get whisked to the dunes and back again? The extra sand at his feet was the only evidence of it that he could notice. And such little children! The wonder of it did not cease to amaze him as he walked to meet Master Iberak with a slight stagger in his step as though he was a little drunk. A few strides and he managed to pull himself together and walk with sure steps again.

He will be leaving tomorrow before sunrise for the North, there is much to prepare for the journey that will take one cycle of the moon. Omar will be traveling with him.

Malik and Zazza find Bilal to tell him how it went with Drekkar.

"Oh that was such a good one Bilal! You should have seen his face," Zazza imitates Drekkar's eyes bulging as he was taken to the sand dunes by Malik and he. Both Malik and Zazza are holding their sides with laughter as they recount the demonstration they had given Bilal's father.

Bilal quietly chuckles to himself in amusement. It is not often in his life he has been able to pull something over on his father or catch him off guard with such a surprise. He is liking these surprises and is practically bursting with the surprise he and the men have in store for Ra-Milania's day of birth celebration that starts this evening.

Chapter 63

Ra-Milania is gathered in her room with her personal guard. They are all there, having entered through the hidden pillars into her private chambers. Each had been given a new outfit for tonight's celebration. Scrubbed clean, haircuts and beaming, Ra-Milania's personal guard have arrived. It is the first evening celebration where the greater public will come to honor the Pharaoh-to-be for her celebration of living now six annual cycles of the sun.

They gather around her all kneeling upon one knee with ear-to-ear grins. They are bursting with excitement and the celebration of Ra-Milania, Pharaoh-to-be whom they all cherish most dearly.

She looks at them each in turn, proudly. Herself beaming with an ear-to-ear grin she says, "Each of you, my personal guard, give me great joy. Having you in my life is the greatest gift of today's celebration. I am so lucky to have you here with me and I am grateful for all you have done to train yourselves diligently and protect me. You are greater than you know. Just by being you, you are contributing to creating the future I seek to come into existence. I could not be happier!" She goes around the half circle hugging them each in turn. She clasps her hands, "Shall we go celebrate now?"

They all bow their head and stand. Bilal asks, "Mila, may I carry you on my shoulder?"

Clapping her hands and lifting onto her toes as she does when very excited, she says "Yes" and reaches up to him. Taking her hand and in the smooth singular motion they have achieved with the previous six months of practice, she sets upon his right shoulder. Resting her hand around his neck, they are headed out the doors and to the staircase.

The sound of the great pubic meeting hall filled with people and lively conversation spill to the upper halls. Her guards fall in line behind her and Bilal by height, from tallest to shortest ready to descend the stairway to make a grand entrance. Upon Bilal's first step a loud 'Clack' sound is heard. Mila spins her head around to see all her guard with decorated sticks in hand. They hit them together again in unison making another 'Clack' sound. Mila giggles with delight and turns to face the crowd, sitting tall on the shoulder of her dear Bilal.

As they descend the stairs her guards make a simple 'Clack' in time with each of Bilal's steps. The sound overtakes the crowd and they become silent watching the procession come down the stairs. Upon reaching the bottom they all stop and move in turn from behind Bilal to in front of him. They kneel creating a stairway of knees upon which Ra-Milania may step down from Bilal's shoulder.

Hemel lends his hand for Mila to take in hers. Kylar is shorter and stands giving his hand for her to step upon as the first step is a bit too far. Kylar lowers her a bit so she reaches Hemel's knee with ease. With the next step is Missrah, then Madu and Anzety, next Guyasi and Karek, followed by Madu, Zek, Malik and little Zazza. She takes two steps on the smooth marble floors and the 'Click-clack' of the sticks continues again. As she walks to her seat of honor between her mother and father the rhythm of the sticks grows in complexity.

'Click-clack, click-click-clack, clickitty-clack-clack-click, click, click-clack'; and so it continues. The guards begin to move, no longer just hitting their own sticks, but now using each other's in a dance of sorts. They move in formation, creating sound with each movement and each new step of the formation. As they continue in complexity and speed it riles the crowd in wonder of this unique sound they have never heard before. Thrilled with this surprise spectacle, Mila is standing on her seat in excitement of her men's performance. It ends with a singular strike to the floor with all her men again in unison kneeling on one knee, heads bowed and arranged by height facing her from shortest to tallest.

Seconds of awed silence pass until Ra-Milania bursts into clapping and cheers. The crowd explodes into cheer. This was unlike anything else any of them had seen before and it has stunned them all. Little Mila beamed with even more pride for the wonderful performance of her guard. What a surprise! She had no idea they could do such a thing and she could hardly wait to talk with them and hear all about it later.

The evening commences with a stream of guest bearing gifts for the Pharaoh-to-be. Those with title are announced, others come forward with more humble gifts, some only words of kindness and well wishes. Mila receives them gratefully, acknowledging their honoring of her.

The crowd hushes as the announcer says, "Leader of the Tuareg, people of the Blue Desert and Sea of Sand, Blue Men of the East, Pharek Mobar Mohadi." Everyone turns to look at the rarely seen and often spoken of infamous leader. Known as "The Blue Men" for their indigo robes, it has been many years since he or anyone of his tribe has been seen. Everyone cranes their neck to get a look at him. The crowd parts like a knife cutting through to clear the way to the seats of the royal family. Silence fills the hall as every person strains to hear what he might say.

A tall and rugged looking man approaches the family, he bows his head offering more grace and genuine honor in this simple gesture than all the previous guests elaborate well wishes. He has command of the entire room by his very presence. His voice fills the room, warm and embracing so that even those farthest away can easily hear as though they are up close. "Ra-Milania, Pharaoh-to-be, I am Pharek Mobar Mohadi, leader of the Tuareg people. It is my privilege to honor the day of your birth. You have grown up bright and beautiful since I have laid eyes upon you last. May your future greatness shine upon us all as the sun that nurtures living, vibrant and abundant possibilities. I come with a gift of our people, would you hold out your hand to me dear one?"

He steps forward, taking one knee so that he may be eye-to-eye with Mila who eagerly holds out a hand to him. With a flourish of his apparently closed hand over hers, Pharek places a blue butterfly in her hands. Her eyes light up and become as wide as her smile. She giggles, looking with glee at each of her parents.

"Now close your hands over it and open them again."

She does and upon opening her hands the butterfly has become a huge sapphire, as big as her palm. The crowd gasps in awe. Ra-Maharet leans forward, mouth dropping open as she gets sight of the largest most beautiful sapphire she has ever seen. She begins to reach for it and realizing it stops herself and touches her chest saying, "My, such an extravagant gift for one so young! You must be very...powerful Pharek Mohar Mohadi." Quickly regaining her composure, she closes her mouth but remains leaning forward to see what might happen next.

Pharek motions to the man behind him to come forward. Kneeling and bowing, the man holds out a finely carved wooden box, opening the lid in a singular motion to reveal six more sapphires, just as brilliant and progressively smaller in paired sizes. Perfect for a magnificent necklace or crown.

"For when you become Pharaoh, to create what you will at your pleasure. For safe keeping, please lay the stone in its nest here." He gestures to the box where Mila places the huge sapphire. Dramatically Pharek closes the lid, and opens it again and now all the sapphires have become dozens of butterflies and fill the air as they take flight to Mila's delight.

With total joy Ra-Milania leans forward and kisses Pharek on the cheek. "Thank you Pharek Mohar Mohadi, they are wonderful! I thank you for such an honor and I shall make something very special with them. Can you show me how to do that, make sapphires into butterflies and butterflies into sapphires?"

Pharek laughs a great booming laugh, "My secrets shall be yours, dear one," he says with a wink. Closing the lid once more, Pharek rises and hands the box to Bilal who stands between and behind Mila and Pharaoh-Ra. Pharek takes Bilal in approvingly wondering who this giant of a man is, he will look forward to finding out.

"Thank you my dear friend, I am very pleased to see you, come sit with us when it is time for dining. Until then, Naruub will take you to refresh yourself as you have traveled far to get here," says Pharaoh warmly.

Without further word Pharek nods again stepping to Naruub. They embrace briefly as Pharek says quietly, "Grandfather, it is good to see you." Bilal jerks his head around, did he just hear that correctly, did Pharek just call Naruub 'Grandfather'? He barely manages to stop himself from blurting out his disbelief. Silently he hears Mila, Angyet and Naruub reply by thought in unison, "*Yes.*"

"*Oh, wow, I can't wait to hear about this!*" Bilal's mind is reeling, how can this be? Naruub does not look any older than thirty cycles of the sun. Pharek looks old enough to easily be his father, yet Naruub is Pharek's grandfather? Bilal is shaking his head trying to take it in and wondering how this could be possible. Almost every day he is introduced to the impossible being real in ways he could never imagine. He is coming to appreciate the adventure of discovering all that is beyond his current imagination and has much delight in his mind being blown on a regular basis. *"Living is so much more magical than most will allow"* he marvels, thinking to himself.

In the privacy of Pharaoh's chambers, he can't wait to hear about whatever else might be revealed that he does not yet know about. He has yet to find bounds to the mystery of these people whose lives he has been brought into the middle of.

Chapter 64

It is late in the evening, Ra-Milania, Pharaoh-Ra and Ra-Maharet have finished receiving gifts and greeting guest, feasted and the dancing and festivities have started in earnest. Pharaoh-Ra and Pharek retire to Pharaoh's private chambers. Arms over each other's shoulders they sing their way up the stairs, drinks in hand appearing to have had a little too much, they sway as they walk. They enter Pharaoh's chambers, patting each other on the back they both stand up straighter, suddenly looking altogether sober. Making sure the doors are closed and everyone is cleared of Pharaoh's rooms they both sit heavy on Pharaoh's reclining couches.

"Jordan, boy you have got yourself a hand full of trouble my friend!"

"You have come just in time, I could really use both your council and a kind ear old friend. Thank you for heeding the tug to be here now," says Pharaoh with a sigh.

"Of course, I would never deny my best and oldest friend in a time of great peril. Please, tell me the details. The room was filled with the energies of intrigue, danger, betrayal, greed, you know, the usual palace crowd!" he laughs, though without much humor. "I sense your greatest danger is held closest to you, your wife?"

"Yes, as always you see with much clarity. My wife plots to overthrow me. I have not wanted to believe it, yet I can no longer deny the reality that she is willing to kill both me and my daughter and is planning to do so. Her scheme is quite grand. She has been filtering money for some time, and there were rumors of her secretly hiring men to the North and arming them that have now been confirmed. She works with the largest slave owner Master Abar Iberak to buy men to do her will and overtake Pharaoh's Land."

Pharaoh-Ra continues in the relief of unburdening all that is transpiring with someone he knows he can count on to have his back. "Keeper of the Movers is also working with her but it has not yet been revealed exactly in what way they are working together. Our sense is that she believes the Movers to be far more powerful than they really are and that aligning with the Keeper of the Movers will help guarantee her position. None of them have awareness of the destruction they strive to create for all our futures with their blind ambition. They cannot see past their own selfish desires. Not only do they have no awareness of what the pyramid is truly being created for, even if they did, it holds no value or interest for them. They see it purely as a symbol of their own power and means for control over Pharaoh's Land."

"The sun does revolve around her in her own eyes, that much was obvious. And her covetous look at my gift to Mila gave me much insight of her absolute drive to own and take what she has determined should be hers by right. She has no qualms about what she strives for and how she will get there, does she?" Pharek rubs his chin, contemplating.

"I fear not. My sense is she truly will do anything to get what she wants. Though there has been little outright action, she works secretly in many directions. It is the safety of my daughter that is of utmost concern. You have seen her new personal guard Bilal, hard to miss him, huh? Without any other heirs, her death would open the door to the larger population embracing Ra-Maharet as Pharaoh more easily."

"My daughter and I have been preparing ourselves to be resilient to all sort of poison and my daughter has taken it upon herself to develop her own personal guard that she and my Builder train separate from all other guard. You would be quite impressed my friend! She has gathered a small group of warriors in training, that though a somewhat motley assortment are impressively diverse in capability and completely devoted to her. You will meet them if you are here for a few days. Can you stay?"

"At such a young age? Very interesting. Yes, I can stay seven nights, I would be most pleased to see what your daughter has created."

Pharek and Ra speak of Ra-Maharet's coveting the sapphires. Pharek says, "Don't worry I have made them invisible to her or anyone who would steal them. They can only be seen by those who know what generosity is. Obviously that is not going to be any time soon with your wife." He says without humor. "Let tomorrow reveal more."

Chapter 65

It is the morning after Ra-Milania's celebration of birth. Bilal lay in bed looking into the dark of his room enjoying the quiet of early dawn. He awaits the sounds of little Mila stirring and the now familiar sounds of Piloma arranging clothes and morning food and drink. He smiles at the sound of pattering feet and closes his eyes to pretend to still be asleep as he anticipates the impending leap onto his chest. He chuckles to himself then rearranges his face to feign sleep.

Mila takes a flying leap landing on Bilal's chest with a giggle and hug. Bilal grabs her with a laugh, "Ha!" Mila lets out a shriek of laughter. "Good day little one! How does it feel to be six?"

She looks at him funny. "Just like it did when I was five." She rests her head on Bilal's chest with a sigh of contentment. "Pharaoh would like us to come to his chambers this morning."

"Yes, I sensed his tug to be there. I was waiting for you to rise little one. Shall you get ready now?"

"Yes, but you are so warm and snugly. Thank you for a wonderful day of birth celebration Bilal."

"It is my pleasure Pharaoh-to-be," he says with a hug. A bit reluctantly she drops to the floor and scampers off to get dressed for the day.

He rises to rinse his face and put on fresh clothes. He is curious about this morning and what might be revealed about this wonderful and mysterious Pharek and about Naruub. *"Grandfather?"* He couldn't wrap his head around the discrepancy of the words with Naruub's youthful appearance. He was intrigued. He shook his head with a laugh, how incredible was the world? Beyond anything he thought he knew he mused with gratitude. His world had been so dark and small before, what a liberating revelation the expansiveness and greatness that is really possible. *"Thank the stars,"* he thinks to himself.

Mila gives a shout, "Ready!"

Bilal enters her chambers expecting to head out the door. "No, father said by the secret pillars today. He does not wish anyone to see who is gathered."

Bilal takes Mila by the hand following her through the familiar ripple of the pillars of The Pathway. They step out into the great room of Pharaoh-Ra to find Angyet, Kylar, Pharek and Naruub already there, sitting drinking tea.

"Perfect timing Bilal, come sit," gestures Pharaoh. Reaching his arms out to Mila he says, "Good day my daughter, did you sleep after such excitement?" Ra-Milania takes her usual exuberant flying leap into her father's arms. "Why yes, I think I did not move at all. The covers were undisturbed except where my body lay! Wasn't that the most wonderful celebration? The best one yet! Did you like the party Pharek?"

"I did indeed. Seeing you was the best part." He replies with a wink.

She smiles with the look of, you know that is not true and says, "Actually Bilal and my guards were the best part, but you missed it. They gave me the most grand entrance I have ever seen! They were amazing! But enough of that, let's talk about why we are all *really* here shall we?" With that she takes a seat with the air of authority of an adulthood that would not be appropriate for many years to come.

They all laugh with the astonishment of her maturity and directness at so young and age.

Bilal speaks before anyone else can. "Would it be rude if I first ask; how is it that you Naruub are Pharek's grandfather? How is that even remotely possible? I can hardly stand the anticipation of finding out!" Bilal asks with an ear-to-ear grin. He would really like to hear this one!

Pharaoh, Mila, Pharek, Angyet and Naruub all laugh. Kylar is silent as he is also curious, not knowing.

"Oh, it is better than that, I am actually his great, great grandfather. I am two-hundred and fifty-six annual cycles of the sun." Naruub says with a large smile, he pauses for it to sink in.

"What? No way, really?" Bilal and Kylar look to each other

in awe. Bilal knows that Naruub does not lie to him and yet he cannot remotely comprehend how this is possible. "But you don't look more than thirty cycles of the sun. What is your secret? Can you tell me? Really?" he is giving a quizzical look trying to take it in.

"You have been learning of the oneness, and of my capacities for healing of both body and being, yes? You have noticed that you are eating less, sleeping less and yet have more energy to accomplish than you ever did before? What if there is no limit to the generative capacities of your body? I have found that living and your body is not a natural process of deterioration unless you create it as so. The thing that kills your body the most is judgment and having fixed points of view. If you truly have no judgment and everything is truly just an interesting point of view; this gives you access to what I know as 'indefinite living'," says Naruub serenely.

"What is 'indefinite living'?" asks Bilal.

"You know how everyone has the point of view that we must certainly die? That it is an absolute. Well, what if it is not an absolute, what if it is a choice? Indefinite living is that you have complete choice as to when you die or to keep on living. Indefinite living is embodying the oneness so much that your choices contribute to your body having everything it requires to keep living. All the energies that give your body vitality, youthfulness, agility, ability to heal and change are available upon request. Or, you can just as easily choose to allow your body to die; quickly and easily, even without pain and suffering."

Bilal considers this. He has known how easy it is to

choose to die and recognizes that simple truth. Living on the other hand, living as an ongoing vitality and not a process of deterioration; that is a totally new idea for him. He likes it. The healing sessions he has had with Naruub have shown him how the aches and pains of physical labor can go away, as well as the invisible wounds of one's own inner world. He is intrigued. Bilal suddenly remembers everyone else in the room and ask, "What age are the rest of you? You aren't all hundreds of years old are you?" He is wide-eyed and breathless waiting for their reply.

Pharaoh-Ra speaks first with a laugh; "I am eighty-two."

"You don't look a day older than forty. That is from your communion as oneness?"

"Yes, and the help of Naruub's touch, and Mila's joy and the excitement for Angyet's capacity for bringing into existence that which has never existed before, and Pharek's friendship and your enthusiasm! There are so many things that contribute to my body and me having youthfulness." Pharaoh says with a warm smile.

Ra-Milania is next, she says, "I am six...huuunnndddrrreeed! Noooo, not really. That would be so fun though! I wonder what I would be capable of then?" She taps her fingers together in contemplation and laughs at herself, leaning back in her chair once again.

They all laugh at her humor and wit.

Bilal turns to Angyet who is next, with a mischievous smile she says, "Thirty-one."

"But you have such magical capacities, how could you be

so powerful and so young?"

"Age has nothing to do with it. Only desire and willingness, along with what you were born with and strive to become as the infinite being you truly are."

"Ah, yeah. Okay," says Bilal nodding his head affirmatively. Continuing around the room Kylar is next. "Twenty-three," he says with a nod.

Pharek is next, he says, "Eighty."

"You are younger than Pharaoh, yet you look older than him, why is that?" asks Bilal curiously.

"Here in the palace city it is to Pharaoh's advantage to have a youthful and vigorous appearance. Beauty and youth, combined with power is hard to ignore. It inspires, shows superiority and all of the qualities most consider to be greatness embodied in a place such as this. Especially now that he has been Pharaoh for so many years, that he does not age in front of them adds to the prowess of Pharaoh. For me on the other hand, it is to my advantage to look older as that is what is valued by my people. Experience, wisdom, having lived life and having that show in one's appearance is respected and honored. So, some grey hair, some wrinkles. They work to my benefit, much more than a youthful appearance would," says Pharek matter of fact. "I may look older, but my body is vigorous and youthful in ability."

"Interesting." Bilal's head spins with the awareness of both appearance and age being a creation of one's choices. The lack of definition of one's body had most definitely never occurred to him before. He looked forward to exploring the possibilities of this more in the future.

Pharaoh begins, "Pharek and I have spoken through much of the night. He has been apprised of the situation, however I would like to go over all of it again with each of you adding to what you know. Your opinions and advice are also welcome."

"Shall I begin, Pharaoh?" asks Bilal.

"Yes, speak of what you have learned from your father and of Mila's guards."

"Yes Lord Pharaoh." He says with a slight nod of the head. "My father has recently become business partners with a man named Master Abar Iberak. He is the largest slave owner of the Land. Until recently I along with my mother and father were his prized possession. I was born under his ownership. Thanks to Pharaoh granting my family and I freedom, I have now become Ra-Milania's personal guard. I will get to our progress with that in a moment. My father has just been let in on the secret of the personal armed forces of wife-of-Pharaoh. She has effectively purchased a force of almost four-thousand, five-hundred and is arming and supplying them as we speak. My father is on his way to verify all of this with his own eyes. Two of Mila's guard will be relaying information from when my father gets there until his return. Master Iberak knows my father can make sure this army is prepared and what is missing before they can move south for attack. It is what my father did before as Iberak's slave, he oversaw the management of forty-five thousand slaves. This is what I know so far."

They are all grim in silence, considering this information.

Angyet speaks next. "The Movers have plans to alter the construction design of the pyramid. I do not yet know what exactly it is they are changing, yet I can sense it coming like a slight irritation that does not subside. Their energies move towards disharmony with the entire project. This confirms my suspicions of them working with Ra-Maharet. Their lack of training in the oneness and emphasis on the singular capacity for moving objects has clouded their awareness. They do not know what their actions are truly creating."

Kylar speaks to Pharek next, "I am Keeper of Mila's guard. We are a small group, yet mighty in our capacities and we grow stronger day by day. But I wonder Pharaoh, do we have enough able bodied to protect the palace and both of you and Mila's well being with the guard we have? I would like to increase our recruiting efforts, not only for Mila personally, but for the entire royal guard. I would like to double the numbers we have as soon as possible. With your blessing Pharaoh, I will begin."

"Yes, I have been thinking the same thing Kylar. Whatever you require, you have my permission. If I must come up with a story for Ra-Maharet of what reason I am increasing the guard I will say that I am considering an exploration party to the Far East, farther than anyone from Pharaoh's Land has ever traveled. I will send them for new resources and meeting people we do not know of; that I will first make sure of their loyalty and training as my guard here," says Pharaoh.

They all nod in agreement.

"Let us reconvene tonight again after this nights celebrations and bring me your ideas or more insight into this plot. So let us enjoy our day as we can and call on the oneness to guide us in changing and undoing this future Ra-Maharet seeks to create," says Pharaoh-Ra.

THE PHARAOH'S BUILDERS

Chapter 66

Ra-Maharet goes to Mila's room pretending a casual visit, she is there to find the box of sapphires. She looks everywhere in the room, but it is invisible to her. She asks Mila about them, "Are you hiding them in a secret spot?" she asks with a causal laugh.

"What do you mean, they are right here mother." She walks to the dressing table and as soon as she touches the box Ra-Maharet can see it. Mila opens the lid to reveal the sapphires and gently closes the lid again. Walking away and back to her mother, she doesn't notice the covetous look on her mother's face. The box is invisible to her again as soon as Mila has walked away. The irritation and rising anger passes over her face as she quickly masks it again. Turning her attentions to her daughter in mock interest of what she is saying, her mind reels with how she can acquire those sapphires. "What was that dear?"

"Did you see Beset's long strides? And Sekhet, she is almost dancing with me now. Will you come watch me ride my horse later?" asks Mila. She knows her mother will not, but she asks anyway.

"I would love to watch you ride but you know how the smell of the stables bothers my nose. I don't know how you stand the stench there. I will watch your performance from the stands with your father tomorrow, but not your practicing today. Come, let me plate your hair. I have brought you new charms for your adornment. They will look wonderful for your performance." She sits and beckons her hand maid Lili to bring the strand of gold with little discs that dangle and catch the light. She picks up Mila and sits her next to herself on the bench in front of the polished metal plate mirror, that she might add the gold strands to her hair while her daughter watches.

One thing Ra-Milania admired is her mother's talent for adornment. She was always impeccably dressed. It is one of the few skills of her mother's that she sees any use for. She will learn what she can while she has these rare moments with her mother. In these times alone Ra-Maharet would speak of the advantages of being a woman and how to use your natural assets to the greatest effect. She gave her daughter dancing lessons. Though Mila was young and would not necessarily require the skills of seduction for some time; her mother began with dancing lessons for the grace of movement that can be developed at any age and applied in every area of living. For Ra-Maharet every moment with her body was an opportunity for seduction, inviting admiration, lust and envy or intimidation. Whatever it took to have all eyes on her was the target, and she never failed to hit her mark.

She would speak of how it contributed to her getting everything she wanted and how it could serve Mila to develop her own capacities for seduction. As the Pharaoh-to-be, Mila would already have the power to get her way; with the powers of seduction she would be able to get people to think they desire to do anything she asks of them. They would become more willing and pliable according to her mother's revelations on the topic.

"Of course you already charm everyone you meet my little Mila," she says with a soft pinch to the cheek. "Now that you are six cycles of the sun we shall get you entirely new clothing to celebrate. Come to the markets with me, we will pick out fabrics together. And allowing the people to see their Pharaoh-to-be will inspire. You must always consider the impression you are making to your subjects, that they always love you. Or you can simply chop off their head if it please you!" Ra-Maharet laughs with just a little too much glee with the comment. "I will come for you later, after our mid day meal."

Ra-Maharet did not wait for Mila's reply, she simply got up and left as was her usual manner when she was done.

All week Ra-Maharet has been sharing more with her daughter than ever before. Speaking to her about all sorts of things she never has. Ra-Milania wanted to believe her mother was growing fonder of her, but she new better. Everything her mother did was calculated. There was something off about it all, she knew it, yet couldn't quite grasp what niggled at her awareness. She both wondered and couldn't help but be worried a bit about finding out what that niggling energy was.

Chapter 67

B ilal and Pharek walk the gardens together.

"We live in such a beautiful and magical world, how is it so few people notice it? Even in my darkest moments it was the beauty of things that would keep me going. I could always find something beautiful. I would think to myself, world show me something beautiful; and it would," wonders Bilal out loud.

Pharek laughs, looking at him sidelong. "You really don't get how different you are, do you dear Bilal. Considering you were born into slavery, that you would even look for beauty in anything or ask to see it sets you apart. That you would seek it Bilal, that is the difference."

Bilal raises his eyebrows, he had not considered that. For

him it was normal.

"What I have observed is that most people do not notice because they are too busy trying to get others to see them. But they will not see themselves, thus no one else can. Ironic, however until a person will see themselves, which is really to say *be themselves* they are not likely to notice much. They are not able to. Their eyes look inward and do not see anything of the world or of other people. Except to how that other person might fit or deliver what they seek from that person. Nothing else exists for them." Replies Pharek.

He continues, "You can use that to your advantage in several ways. One is to make yourself invisible to people. With so much attention most put inward, they are often not very observant of the world around them. Making yourself invisible is easy in such a world as this where people are so unaware. Just be space and they will not notice you whatsoever. Practice in a crowded street and you will see what I mean, people are likely to walk right into you. You will have to move fast to not be run into."

"How do I be space?" ask Bilal.

"You do it already don't you? How often do you approach a person and they do not notice you until you are right up next to them?"

"Often" says Bilal.

"That is from being so much space that the person has no solidity to knock them out of their distractions going on in their own head. They don't 'feel you coming' when you don't have much solidity in your world. Your head is often quiet is it not?"

"Yes, except when my father would beat me. Then it would be like a hornet's nest, sometimes for hours if I let it," replied Bilal.

"Right. That is when you are contracting you and making you smaller than the space you really are. When you are being you...silence and complete presence with what is in front of you, yes?"

"Yes, exactly." Bilal had never heard these things put into words. Once again he was surprised and grateful for the clarity these insights gave him as Pharek put words to things he knew but no one had ever spoken with him about. He knew that what Pharek spoke of was true by the lightness it ushered into his world.

"Tell me again, what do I do to become invisible in a crowd?" ask Bilal.

"Expand the space you are being. What are the moments that you feel the most care free, the most spacious and at ease and also totally present with your body and every nuance of your senses? Be that and see what happens. Come, we'll go to the markets and try it out."

It is only about ten minutes walk to the crowded and narrow market alleys of the section of the Keeper's Realm known as Pharaoh's Market. It is bustling as usual. As they enter Pharek speaks of expanding the space he is being and does it energetically also. He contributes to Bilal also expanding his energies as Angyet, Naruub, Mila and the Pharaoh have all done with him in their own way. Bilal notices as people begin to not look up at them, or turn the other way. Considering how often Bilal usually draws the looks of every person he passes this is most surprising.

"Watch this," Pharek steps to a vendor with no other customers and attempts to get his attention. The man is fiddling with his produce, arranging, sorting, doing anything but notice Pharek standing right in front of him. Other people come to the vendor and the man greets and assists them immediately. Pharek beckons Bilal to stand next to him and they test if either of them can get the vendors attention. They cannot.

Bilal bursts out laughing, thinking to himself, "Could this really be?" With the sudden outburst the vendor finally notices them along with the rest of the customers who all turn to look at who is laughing. Pharek and Bilal walk away chucking to themselves. "Wow, that was way more literal than I ever expected was possible. Not only could they not see us, they couldn't hear us or anything. We really were invisible to them. I'm going to play with that one! Thank you Pharek, that was most valuable."

"Certainly Bilal. We are having a good time here, however your task of protecting Mila's life is quite serious. I will gladly contribute anything I can to give you advantage in that task. Without her living to take the throne when her day comes, I fear this land will suffer greatly. I have not seen one with so little awareness be so close to taking such power as Ra-Maharet. This cannot be. We cannot allow it."

"I thank you Pharek. You are most generous in your wisdom and skill. I am grateful," says Bilal earnestly.

"I must be honest with you, I also fear that our dear Pharaoh has possibly waited too long to take action. Whatever you need of me, just ask. Are you familiar with the tug Bilal? That sensation of pulling on you when someone is in need of you?" inquires Pharek.

"Yes," says Bilal. "All of Mila's guard and I have increased our use of that in gathering together for meals and for practicing. I can't say that we have used it for much else!" laughs Bilal.

"Yes, young men certainly have an appetite! Consider using it with less obvious tasks like meeting in different locations you don't usually meet and make it unplanned. As you develop your skill with speaking mind to mind, the tug can add clarity to the request," says Pharek.

"Thank you, I'll have my men play with that. Shall we head back to the palace now? Speaking of the tug, I get the sense of it being time to return before Mila comes here to the Pharaoh's Market with her mother."

"Ah, there it is, you have what I am speaking of already at your disposal!"

Continuing to enjoy each other's company they return to the palace together.

Chapter 68

It was just as Pharaoh new it would be, Ra-Maharet dismisses Bilal saying her guard Re-iyk can take care of them as they go to the markets. "Besides," she says, "We will have six other guards with us as well. You are not needed."

Bilal thinks to Mila, *"I will go to your father to tell him now. Don't worry, I will never be more than a few paces from you dear one."* With that he goes down the hallway to Pharaoh's rooms.

Pharaoh is waiting for him when he enters, "Is it as I said it would be?"

"Yes Pharaoh. Ra-Maharet also does not have her usually gaggle of women in tow this time, it is to be just her and Mila and her guard."

Darkness washes over the Pharaoh's face, "Take the pillars

of The Pathway here in my room. There is a secret one near the palace side of the market. You know the first building on the right, between that and the next is where the hidden pillars are. Think of the clay urns the second shop has, as they are usually placed by the back corner, stacked two high. That is the marker you can use. Go now. You will have plenty of time to get there before my wife. Be aware, have all of your senses on, something feels off about it all, more than usual today. You are observant Bilal, use both your powers of observation to notice the people and your senses to perceive the energies. I trust you with my daughter's life."

Pharaoh embraces him and stands looking him in the eye with his trust and confidence, "Go."

Bilal steps into the pillars of Pharaoh's chambers and out into the darkness of the alleyway between the first and second buildings of the markets. Just as Pharaoh has said, there were the clay urns stacked two high at the back corner of the second shop as he steps out of the hidden pillars to see that in front of him. He takes a quick look around to get his bearings, see if anyone noticed him suddenly appear and if Ra-Maharet and Ra-Milania have made it to the market yet.

The way was clear. No one had noticed him appear and Ra-Maharet was not yet in sight with her guard and Ra-Milania. He still had the nagging sensations of danger that were increasing moment by moment. Much like his death matches, it had a similar quality of energy to it; he could sense the impending life-threatening situation.

The shopping party was now in sight of the market, making their way from the palace. The crowd gathered more than usual with this being an entire week of celebrations for the day of birth of Ra-Milania, this was only the second day of celebration. Tonight there would be more spectacle in the palace itself and many were out buying new jewelry or clothing for tonight's festivities of music and dance.

Bilal summoned all his will to call on his guard to come to the Pharaoh's Market *now*. Calling to them in his mind and using the tug to pull energetically that they may come as quickly as possible. He sent images in his mind of which street of the market the wife-of-Pharaoh was headed down.

Ra-Maharet was leading the way and had gone further into the more narrow section of the Pharaoh's Market where the merchants with particularly fine cloth are located. It had been the usual kind of "time together" Mila had grown familiar with, which at the markets often consisted of Ra-Maharet looking to dress Mila in her own image. Finding jewelry and clothing that she would like for herself and often choosing the slightly lesser version for her daughter.

Ra-Maharet had no interest in Mila's opinion so Mila often followed quietly, unless she was in the mood to have everything be about her mother being right and wonderful. If she was showing interest in her mother's point of view they could have endless conversation and appearance of closeness. Ra-Milania would play along today; it was for her day of birth celebration after all, there was plenty to talk about.

They had been chitchatting all along however Mila was beginning to notice her mother move farther ahead of her, it seemed odd and stood out to her. She expanded her senses out farther realizing her mother was having that familiar effect of making the world appear to only include her. Her mother was so self-centered she was like a wind storm that instead of blowing outward, would suck in everyone around her. This always lessoned Mila's awareness and she was slightly annoyed with herself at getting sucked into it. Something was off, really off.

Bilal has been following behind the crowd of Ra-Maharet's small entourage of guard staying out of sight yet close enough to keep Mila within five or six strides. He was using the new exercise that Pharek and he had been practicing earlier that day for becoming invisible. He could expand so much as to make himself infinite, being so much space that people around him do not notice him in the least. He is noticing he had to literally dodge people so as to not be run into. It was amazing to be in a large crowd with the hustle and bustle of the markets and have no one notice him. He was so used to being noticed this would be pure delight if it were not for the sense of something being wrong.

Being so expanded in his senses he began to suddenly prickle with a sense of danger in a wave of intensity. He reached out searching for the source of this energy and was flooded with information. Every detail of what was about to unfold came in a barrage of knowing. In that very instant he went into action, no thought, just total presence with all that is. Everything went into slow motion while also heightening in intensity of color, sound, sight and knowing exactly what to do with the screaming demand of all of the molecules that this is changing...

Expanding out he energetically grabs hold of Mila freezing

her as she reaches for a gold embroidered fabric on the table before her. She grew wide-eyed as she found herself unable to move, she had a split second of panic until she got the flood of information from Bilal. At the next moment a dart punctures the pile of fabric just an inch from her hand. The hold on her releases and she drops to the ground as two more darts strike where her back had just been. She heard them hitting hard with a thump into the wood of the table under the fabric. As she drops down she turns to look at her mother as she is curling into a ball on the ground.

She sees her mother looking at her with glaring intensity as she is also dropping to the ground and suddenly screaming Mila's name and reaching out to her with a look of distress and yet at the same time making no movement towards her what so ever. Ra-Maharet's personal guard's highest duty is to protect the Pharaoh, and second the Pharaoh-to-be, Ra-Milania; yet he was moving to protect her mother with his body, not her.

Ra-Milania noticed the timing was off as it was only after her scream that several men step forward from the crowd, swords drawn and beginning to clash with the guard of Ra-Maharet.

The next moment she hears Bilal speaking in her head *"Two more steps"* and he will be at her side. She feels Bilal's strong and sure hand reach around her waist and lifting her to him while the shouting increases. She clings to his neck, holding on tight so if he has to let go of her, she will not drop.

His drawn short sword clashes with the attacking men for only a moment as Mila goes into action freezing the swing of the attacker's arm. Bilal is moving quickly, his size easily pushing aside people in the way. Reaching a cross alley that comes from the direction of the stables; the thundering sound of horse hooves on stone echoes through the market, coming closer. It is Sekhet.

The crowd is scrambling to get out of Sekhet's way as she is running toward Bilal and Ra-Milania. In the next motion Bilal is holstering his sword, taking Mila in both hands and flipping her into the air. She spreads her arms like a bird as she comes over backward spotting Sekhet she sees that she can land squarely on her back. In the oneness they both functions from, Sekhet maneuvers under Mila's small body scooping her up. As Sekhet feels Mila land squarely and grasp on her mane she takes off into a greater speed down the alley way that heads out into the open causeway in a few hundred more feet.

Mila again goes into action herself, stopping people from moving forward into their path and shoves people aside energetically who are not noticing the eleven hundred pounds of muscle hurtling through the alley way towards them. In a new barrage of images Missrah lets both Mila and Sekhet know he is just up ahead and will drop down from above onto Sekhet's back landing behind Mila.

Just a bit farther up ahead of that is Malik, he stands only slightly to the side holding out his hand. He begins to run forward towards them. Missrah reaches down using their momentum of opposite directions so that Malik can swing up behind him. Now three of them astride Sekhet, Malik lets them all know he is going to transport them into the great hall of the palace.

Sekhet is slowing down as quickly as she can without her

riders toppling over her head. They all disappear into thin air and re-appear in a sliding halt on the marble floors of the palace great hall. Though wide-eyed, Sekhet remains calm even though she is sliding across the slick marble floors to a quiet stop near the bottom of the stairway.

At that very moment Pharaoh-Ra and Pharek are descending the stairway to them. Missrah slides off Sekhet's back speaking to her softly, calming her and reassuring. Pharek grabs hold of Malik's hand that Malik may transport him atop Sekhet.

Reaching out and grabbing Mila's hand Pharaoh says, "Go with Pharek, he will protect you until it is safe for you to return. Malik, take them to the bend in the river that is the last that can be seen from Mila's rooms. You know the one?" Malik nods. "Wait for Angyet to come to you."

Pharaoh-Ra and his only child Ra-Milania lean their foreheads together, she places her small hands on his cheeks in a moment of warm embrace of being, all their hopes of a future exploding into possibility down a path yet unknown. Pharaoh speaks softly but sternly, "Now go, go!"

Another blink and they are gone.

THE END

the PHARAOH'S MOVERS

Book Two of the Pharaoh's Land Series

Look for it at the beginning of 2017!

For Sneak peeks, Giveaways, Meet the Author Events, Book Trailers and all things *The Pharaoh's Builders* visit the official website at www.thepharaohsbuilders.com